NO
SECOND
CHANCES

KIM
CARTER

STREET CHRONICLES

NO
SECOND
CHANCES

To Vera —

Enjoy!

Kim Carter

Dedication

To the true loves of my life…
My husband Julius, my sons Austin and Hayden,
and my daughter Emily.

Acknowledgements

No book could ever be written without the expertise, and knowledge of those that are unselfish enough to share it. This book is no exception. My thanks go out to:

John Cross, deputy director of the Fulton County medical examiner's office (Atlanta, Ga), who never once refused my calls in his busy schedule. Many times he looked up information and got back to me immediately. This book would never have been written without him.

Warden Fred Head and Terry Duffy from the Georgia Bureau of Prisons, who were kind enough to answer my questions about executions and other aspects of prison life.

Hubert Ricks, who has spent his entire career working in the Federal Correctional System. You taught me so much about prisons and even more about life itself. You will never know how much respect I have for you. You've been a fabulous mentor.

Charles V. Harrelson, who became a helpful and insightful pen pal. His poignant viewpoint from beyond the wall was always astute.

Doctor Prince, who told me every time I saw him, "Write, Write, Write."

My sister and biggest fan, Pamela Carter Youngblood, who read and re-read until the pages were worn thin to help me get this right. I love you.

Most of all, I want to thank my husband Julius. None of this could have ever happened without your love and support. You believed in me when I couldn't believe in myself. Fairy tales really do come true!

PART ONE
The Murder

CHAPTER 1

A siren wasn't an unusual sound to hear at the small hospital, though it wasn't a very frequent one. Dr. Charlie Evans had seen a little of everything during his tenure, ranging from ear infections to small lacerations, but he didn't work in a trauma center and wasn't accustomed to anything life threatening; those cases were usually transported directly to Cedar Sinai.

Charlie listened intently, struggling to hear the garbled words of the medics over the radio as their ambulance sped through the few intersections that made up the tiny town. The blaring siren sounded almost as frantic as the men delivering their injured patient. The doctor knew all the men and women who wheeled his patients in; if not by name, he at least recognized their faces. He also knew they lost their cool only on rare occasions.

The doctor watched in horror as the three paramedics ran in, pushing a young boy on a gurney. It was obvious from the sheets and the floor that the bleeding was profuse. A police officer was running beside the rolling contraption, carrying something wrapped in a blood-saturated towel, leaving a dark red trail behind him. The officer's face was ashen, and he made no effort to wipe the tears that rolled continuously down his young, chubby face.

The boy couldn't have been any older than ten, but he appeared calm and sedated. His face was pale, and sweat was beading heavily on his forehead, drenching his short red hair. The medics had done their best to prevent shock by wrapping the victim in blankets and elevating his lower extremities.

Dr. Evans ran toward them carefully, so as not to slip on the blood. "What have we got here, men? Quickly!" he spouted. For what seemed an eternity, no one spoke, and Dr. Evans had to scream again to jerk them out of their stunned fear.

The cop spoke first, his voice heaving and cracking like the timid answer of a young child who'd been sternly reprimanded. "He was playin' on the train tracks with his friends, trying to jump between the cars. They…they… The trains were going slow, trying to connect to some other cars, the boys thought they could make it, but…" The cop's body shook as he handed the sodden towel to Dr. Evans. "We found this. It's… God, it's the boy's leg, what was left of it. Took it off right below the knee," he said, looking as if he might pass out.

"Sweet Jesus." Dr. Evans turned to the nurses and ordered, "Get this on ice immediately." He handed the bloody parcel to the closest nurse.

"Yes, Doctor," she said and bravely took the lower leg and dangling foot and scurried off.

The doctor turned to his head nurse. "Tell the parents to meet him at Cedar Sinai. Explain how important it is for them to remain calm, for the child's sake."

She didn't give a reply but left immediately to speak with the family.

"What's your name, son?" the doctor leaned down to ask.

"Richey," he answered. "I'm sorry, but I'm really scared. Are my friends all right?"

"They're fine, Richey," Dr. Evans answered kindly. "They are just fine." Dr. Evans wasn't sure if the boy knew the extent of his injuries, but he knew it wasn't the time or place to tell him. He knew all too well that shock could be lethal. "Listen, do you feel up to a helicopter ride? My best friend works at another hospital, and they'll fix ya right up over there. Besides, the pilot's a pretty cute chick, if ya like blondes," he said with a wink. If the circumstances had been different, Charlie would have laughed at himself; it had been years since he had said "chick."

"Yes, sir. I…guess so," Richey said, weakening and growing paler by the second, indicating that there wasn't much time.

The helicopter had already landed. While the whirring of the blades would have been a welcomed sound for a soldier being pulled from a battlefield to safety, at the medical facility, it was a sickening sound that never meant good news.

Richey was loaded up, and off they went, the swish of the blades becoming fainter by the second.

Charlie watched until the chopper was out of sight, and then he hung his head low, resting his chin on his chest. He had wanted to be a doctor for as long as he could remember, but he still found it heart-wrenchingly difficult to deal with children in pain. He briskly walked back into the building to page his friend and former college roommate, Dr. Phil Sawyer. Phil was the best orthopedic surgeon Charlie had ever met, and he knew that if there was any chance of saving the boy's leg, Dr. Sawyer was the man for the job.

Dr. Sawyer answered the page within a couple minutes. "Hear you got a little guy headed my way. How does it look?"

"Pretty bad. I hate to be pessimistic, but it's gonna take a miracle if you can save that leg. I've seen you perform a few in your lifetime, Phil, and I hope this kid'll be another one of them." "We'll do our best, Charlie. I'll give you a follow-up call, but it'll be a few hours. Kiss Janet for me, would ya? We've gotta get together soon."

"Yeah, I know. Hey, don't forget to call…and take care," Charlie said, ending their phone call on a mournful note. He held the phone to his ear for a few seconds before laying it back on its cradle. So many memories flooded back into his mind whenever he heard Phil's voice. He was about to take a trip down Memory Lane when thoughts of poor little Richey jolted him back to the present. *What a tough break, especially for someone so young.*

"Dr. Evans," Nurse Jenkins said, interrupting his thoughts, "we've got quite a backup out there. Do you want me to call Dr. Harper in to help catch us up?"

Charlie contemplated the question fully before he answered. He alternated with Dr. Harper and hated bringing him in on his off days. He also had to consider the residents of Jasper. Many of them couldn't afford treatment and waited until they just couldn't stand the pain anymore. By the time they actually came to the hospital, they were in no condition to wait for hours. "God knows I hate to do it," the doctor finally said, "but page him. It's frustrating for all of us to be this far behind, but let's not forget to keep our prayers going up for that little boy who's landing at Cedar Sinai right about now."

As Nurse Jenkins turned to page Dr. Harper, she pondered what a good man Dr. Evans was. She wasn't alone in the knowledge that he could be successful in his own private practice or a much larger hospital, but she also understood why he chose to stay in Jasper. Charlie was one of a dying breed, a man of great character. The staff gave him the benefit of thinking he was fooling them when he gave free care or medication to families in need. Sometimes he still made house-calls, even drove to their homes in the middle of the night if they needed help and didn't have transportation.

The nurse smiled at the thought and dialed the number, then turned to sort the stack of medical charts according to severity. Unfortunately, the hospital had become a doctor's office as well. Dr. Harper phoned right back and agreed to come in. The nurse wasn't surprised that he was willing to comply, but she was relatively certain he was cursing under his breath, and she surely wasn't looking forward to dealing with his attitude for the remainder of the night.

The ER eventually eased out of such urgency and backlog and into a steady routine and some semblance of normalcy. The worst they had seen throughout the night was a broken wrist from a car accident. Dr. Harper agreed to stay on through his next shift, and Charlie gratefully gathered his thin windbreaker and walked stoically to his fifteen-year-old Volvo.

The old car was still as faithful to him as the day he'd signed the loan to drive her off the lot. Realistically, he knew she only had a few good years left in her, but he intended to cling to her until the end. He had never been a materialistic guy, so it had felt a bit awkward driving a Volvo at first. It just seemed like the doctor thing to do, and he did feel a bit of a high the first few times he drove her through town; behind the wheel of that showroom-new beauty, he had felt important, almost majestic. Now, he was just thankful his wheels still got him around.

Charlie patted her dashboard as she easily cranked over. "Ol' Bessie," he said aloud, "you've been a faithful friend."

It was a quick ride home, as he conveniently resided less than four miles from the hospital. He turned down the gravel road that led to his dirt driveway, then coasted into the carport.

It was a brisk but sunny day for southern California, and Janet was out planting pansies in the back yard. She heard the groans of the car and stood slowly, stretching her short, pudgy body. "Back here, sweetheart!" she yelled.

Charlie met her just as she was taking off her gardening gloves and dirt-smeared apron. He smiled to himself, knowing he could never love another woman. He had to admit that it wasn't a case of love at first sight, because Janet wasn't exceptionally attractive. In fact, he often cringed at the remembrance of his mother saying, "Why, she's as plain as an old brown shoe." Nevertheless, it hadn't taken his mother long to fall in love with her too. Janet was warm and kind, funny and energetic, and the good doctor knew he would never tire of her.

They met in town, during her first year of teaching in Jasper. They shared a few mutual friends, and after some little get-togethers, the rest was history. She brought out the best in him, and their marriage fit like a glove. Janet had never longed to live beyond their means, like the wives of some doctors did; the artwork, furniture, and possessions that adorned their household were all handpicked for sentimental reasons rather than clout or monetary value. They loved refinishing flea market finds and sitting on the back porch with domestic bottled beer, for the imported stuff was an expense they saw no need to incur. Truly, both of them enjoyed the simple things in life, and they also enjoyed each other.

Even as Charlie climbed the ladder of success in the medical field and his salary increased, Janet still insisted on teaching. "I need something to do with my time," she always said, and he knew she could never give it up. It was as much her calling as medicine was to him.

For years, they'd tried to start a family, but that hadn't happened yet. It was important to both of them, but they refused to go through the rigorous and expensive fertility tests and procedures. They opted instead to rely on hope, to enjoy trying, and to leave the rest up to Mother Nature and God. "If it's meant to be, it'll happen," Janet always firmly said.

"Guess who I talked to today?" Charlie asked, taking a cold beer from his wife and plopping his weary body down in one of the refurbished oversized rocking chairs.

"Couldn't tell ya," she said playfully.

"Phil Sawyer. In fact, I'm surprised I haven't heard back from him." His brow furrowed as he recounted the story of the young boy's unfortunate accident

"I'm sure he'll call as soon as he knows something, hon'. Those surgeries can go on forever, you know."

"He said we should get together."

Janet said nothing, but the look on her face spoke volumes. Charlie could feel the tension in her silence, and he knew she was fighting hard to resist the chance to slam Lara Sawyer.

"Go ahead, honey." Charlie laughed. "Let it fly." He loved to tease her. She cared as much about Phil as he did, but Lara was another story. She was, in Janet's frequent summations, "a trophy wife," and that assessment was undeniable.

"God, Charlie." Janet sighed dramatically. "You know I adore Phil, but please put that little social call off as long as you can. Why don't you and Phil meet for lunch or have a boy's weekend out in Vail or something? Just please, please keep that woman away from me."

"C'mon, Janet." Charlie laughed. "What's one dinner? Anyone can make it through that."

"I would laugh, but it's so terrible I can't even fake it. I'll have to take the tour of the house, from the latest fine artworks to the sculptures to the overpriced oil paintings. Then there will be the latest jewelry, the additions to the gym, and, oh, don't let me forget…her body fat count." Janet hesitated only for a moment, just long enough for Charlie to open his mouth but not long enough to allow him to speak. "Then she'll go on her spiel about all the charities she's donated to lately and ask if I'm still involved in that 'dreadful childcare thing.' I almost took the time to explain to her once that it's all about education, but then I thought, *What the hell's the point?*"

"Okay, okay. I get it. We haven't nailed down a date yet anyway. Just consider it…free entertainment," Charlie laughed.

"Entertainment? Yeah, well, about as entertaining as a car accident."

He grinned and sat back in the rocking chair and studied his wife. It was relatively easy to see why Janet might be jealous of Lara Sawyer. By most people's standards, it would appear that Lara had everything going for her: wealth, beauty, a well-known and respected husband, and a new Mercedes every other year, always in a different color. Charlie knew Janet wasn't jealous though. She wouldn't trade her life for Lara's for anything. She detested fake, shallow people, and the two women had nothing in common, not even enough to get through one night of conversation.

"I've gotta admit," Charlie said, shaking his head from side to side, "I'll never understand what Phil sees in her."

"Not in her, dear. More like *on* her. I can think of two oversized things that probably drew his attention, and they're about as real as the rest of her." Janet laughed. "Now let's eat."

The aroma of hearty beef stew, wafting out of the crock-pot in the kitchen, made Charlie realize how hungry he really was. He reached in the fridge and grabbed two more beers just as the phone rang. "Hello?" he said, answering it quickly so he could eat.

"Hey, man. Sorry it took me so long to get back with you."

"Not a problem, Phil. It did take a little longer than I expected, but I understand these things take time. Just give me some good news, would ya? How's the kid?"

"Not a lot to give on this end, my friend. We worked for hours, but there was too much damage. We couldn't save the leg." Phil paused long enough for Charlie to let it sink in. He knew Charlie had a big heart, and it would be quite a blow to him, even if he didn't know the boy personally. "The good news is that the amputation was below the knee, so there's a much better chance for a workable prosthetic. He'll stay here a while, then undergo physical therapy."

"Damn. I hate to hear that. Seemed like such a good kid."

"Charlie," Phil interjected, "he isn't dead. He'll lead a fairly normal life. He's young and resilient. He'll adjust."

"Yeah, I guess you're right," Charlie answered.

Phil took it as his opportunity to change the subject. "Listen, Lara and I would love for you and Janet to come out next Friday night, say, 7 o'clock?"

"Sure," Charlie answered, still unable to mask his disappointment about Richey. "We'll bring the wine, but can we bring anything else?" Charlie could see Janet mouthing vulgar curse words at him, and he had to struggle to restrain his laughter.

"Oh, wine will be fine. Look forward to seeing you, Charlie…really."

Charlie hung up the phone, knowing that Phil meant what he said. They hadn't talked much, but he'd chalked that up to their busy schedules. With great caution, he turned to face the enemy.

"You just said yes right away," Janet snapped. "What if I had plans?"

"Did you?"

"No, but that's not the point," she said. "You owe me, buddy, and I mean big…silver, gold, diamonds, a purebred horse or something."

Charlie knew she was kidding, and it only took a moment for her to laugh at her own comment.

As Charlie went to bed that night, he thought of young Richey's small foot and calf, lying in wait in a clear plastic bag, in a refrigerator at the morgue, waiting to be incinerated. He struggled with why such a horrendous thing would happen to someone so young, but deep inside, he was a God-fearing man and knew nothing happened without a reason. As a doctor, though, he often found himself questioning what those reasons could possibly be, and leaving a ten-year-old boy without a leg begged a lot of questions for which Charlie had no answers.

CHAPTER 2

Phil Sawyer was a terribly handsome man and a genius in the art of orthopedic surgery. He knew it all too well, but he never let it go to his head. It was a job, no doubt his calling, but a job all the same. He hung his lab coat in the small closet in his office and grabbed his car keys. It had been a long day, and he was anxious to leave the chaos of the hospital behind. It had taken years, but he was now finally able to do that, to just walk away and not look back until the following morning.

That was the difference between him and Charlie Evans. As far back as medical school, Phil had always known it would be that way. Charlie was a good man and, without a doubt, Phil's closest friend. *Strange*, he thought. *Charlie's really the only friend I have.* Sure, there were coworkers and acquaintances who invited him to cocktail parties now and then, but they weren't people with whom he shared any personal thoughts or a close personal bond. He still kept in touch with a few other college buddies, albeit not on a regular basis. Charlie was the only one who'd really stuck around as a permanent fixture in his life.

As he drove down the freeway, busy even at 2:00 in the morning, he knew Charlie would still be thinking of the young red-headed boy. Phil would think of him, too, and check up on him from time to time, but he knew the kid would ultimately be all right. Besides, there would be another Richey the next day, along with a few happy endings to take the edge off the sad ones. Those were the ones he lived for.

Phil pulled into the driveway of the massive house and swore aloud when he saw the lights on. That meant Lara was still up, and he would have to listen to her shit before he could go to bed. For eight years, he'd dealt with their empty, shallow marriage, but he had never found the time or energy to end it and put them both out of its misery. The bottom line was that med school and his internship had almost killed him. By the time he made it all the way to Cedar Sinai, he was ready for the Mercedes, the gaudy, ostentatious house, and the trophy wife. In some way, giving any of it up would feel like defeat.

They had met at a cocktail party, where Phil was instantly attracted to her. Lara caught his eye the moment she entered the room. Maybe it was the black Vera Wang dress that fit like a second skin over her perfectly taut, tan body. Maybe it was the flowing blonde hair or the crystal blue eyes. More than likely, it was a combination of it all. It took him two hours to build up the nerve to make his way over to her, and for the first time in probably twenty years, Phil was rendered completely speechless when Lara turned to him, holding a glass of chardonnay in her hand with all the ease of a model walking down the runway. By the end of the night, he had asked her to dinner, and the rest was a whirlwind of history, poor decisions made in terrible haste, smacking them together in a marriage that never should have happened.

Lara had a degree in the arts from Yale, and it only took one about ten minutes to wonder how in the hell she had gotten it. *Probably the same way she reeled me in*, Phil often thought. Her conversations never varied from anything other than the latest Versace dresses to redecorating some portion of the house to who had the unfortunate luck of recently putting on at least five pounds.

Fortunately for Phil, he found plenty of intelligent conversation at work, and he had God to thank that when he got home, his mind was far too exhausted to pay her drivel much attention. Two glasses of scotch would help him pretend to listen before he marched off to bed, likely alone.

For the first two years of their relationship, their sex life was brilliant—good enough, in fact, to entirely mask the shallowness of the marriage. But, as with everything else, Lara soon tired of it, and what little lovemaking they now shared was just routine and poorly acted out. Phil was not naïve enough to think his wife was faithful, but he frankly didn't give a damn. In that particular month, the pool guy had come by to "clean the pool" four times a week. Phil had seen him once. He was several years younger than Lara, with a muscled body, bleached teeth, and a deep tan. That was really all she required. Phil had recently started using a condom when they slept together because he couldn't keep up with her flavor of the month, and he had no intention of sharing in any of the recent diseases.

Once again, it was the usual. Lara was unhappy with the maid—not because of her performance but because her accent was too difficult to decipher.

Phil poured his scotch straight and sat back on the plush, oversized sofa. He listened to the vehement complaints for a few minutes, then got up to pour another drink. *Tonight it might take three.* "I talked to Charlie Evans today," he said, knowing she didn't give a damn. When Lara said nothing, he continued, "I invited him and Janet over for drinks and dinner Friday night."

"What!?" she asked, shocked.

"I said they're coming for dinner Friday."

"Shit, Phil. You're always planning things without telling me until the last minute. God, we just have so little in common with them. She's just dreadful, with her boring conversation and lack of fashion and flair."

Phil couldn't help but laugh until tears rolled down his cheeks. "You can't possibly be serious. 'Lack of fashion and flair'? Wow. That's a new one. What do *we* have in common with each other, Lara? When was the last time we discussed anything other than your new clothes or your hired help or your latest hairstylist? Have you ever even heard of politics? Do you know who the vice president is?

The secretary of state? It won't kill you to spend one evening with someone who doesn't give a damn about your trivial little bullshit." His face was red and filled with disgust. "Have someone cater it, or else we'll pay Rosa extra to prepare the meal, but it needs to be ready by 7:00...and you better be pleasant!"

Lara just sat there, stunned. Her anger was so immense that she couldn't think of how to react until Phil had left the room for bed. She was pissed, and she would make sure he heard about it in time, but she was smart enough to know that he meant every word he said.

* * * * *

Five a.m. came early, but after years of such a schedule, Phil was used to it. Rounds started at 6:00, and surgeries were usually set up around 8:30, unless some emergency took precedence. His first stop was to see Richey, who was still fairly sedated but managed a weak smile. There were seven other patients to check on before he could grab a doughnut and coffee in the cafeteria and prepare for surgery. On this particular morning, he'd be tasked with setting the arm of an elderly woman who'd taken a fall in her tub. Phil wondered who would help her with her daily activities when she was dismissed, and as he washed down a glazed with coffee, he made a mental note to speak with a social worker on her behalf.

Around 2 o'clock, he texted Charlie to update him on Richey's condition and to confirm their dinner get-together for Friday night. "I'll try to get Lara to act civilized," Phil said. "Tell Janet how much I appreciate her patience. God knows, that woman of mine can drive any sane person mad."

Charlie tried to mask his laughter, although it was a fruitless effort. He felt sorry for his friend. Phil had so much, yet so little. "When are you gonna move on, Phil? You need more than your work. There's someone out there who's perfect for you, just waiting to be found."

"One of these days, my friend, when I can find the time."

Charlie wanted to say more, but he didn't want to cross the line. "Well, we're looking forward to Friday. See ya then."

CHAPTER 3

The week was rather routine for Charlie, with the exception of a few late nights at the hospital. Otherwise, he was home early enough to help Janet in the gardens that were coming along nicely, just as they did each season. She had put on her garden apron and changed into jeans, but she was still wearing her Halloween sweater from school. Charlie smiled to himself, just as he always did when he thought of her. Janet had a sweater or outfit for every season, just to bring a little excitement and life into her classroom. She even had a denim dress with a cornucopia full of vegetables for Thanksgiving and a green one with shamrocks for St. Patrick's Day.

He watched as she hummed some children's song and dug holes for her latest mums. Charlie wished deeply that Phil could feel the joy he did, the desire and need to come home at night for more than scotch and a little sleep. He secretly dreaded their dinner invitation as much as Janet did, but he wouldn't betray his friend by saying so.

"Did you bring home some rubber gloves like I asked, the ones without powder?"

"Sure did. Dare I ask why?"

"Tomorrow is our class Halloween party. We're going to use candy corn for fingernails, fill the gloves with popcorn, and top them off with a plastic spider ring for just the right effect. By the way, I hope you don't have any plans for tonight. We have to pop about four grocery bags of popcorn on the stove. That microwave crap has too much salt and butter."

"Oh, for heaven's sakes," Charlie joked. "Little minds need too much butter, salt, and candy. Otherwise, what is the point in living?"

"I love you, Charlie." Janet laughed. "I really do."

He walked over and kissed her lightly on the forehead. "I can think of nothing I'd love more than spending my night popping corn with you. I imagine that's what every other doctor is doing tonight too."

"Smartass. You are not above this, you know. Oh, I almost forgot. I spent a whopping $250 on a dress, hose, new shoes, and a gold-plated broach today. I am determined not to feel inferior to that gold-digger tomorrow night."

Charlie laughed, a good, hearty chuckle that came straight from his gut. "That's so unlike you, Janet...but I gotta admit that spunk kinda turns me on," he said suggestively.

"Don't get too turned on. We've got corn to pop. I ordered dinner. It should be here any minute."

Charlie was surprised that she'd made a special shopping trip just for the dinner. Janet usually took it with a grain of salt. He never realized that maybe she did feel a bit intimidated by Lara's appearance. He thought about himself and Phil and what a contradiction they were. Charlie was on the shorter side, slightly balding, and even though he hated to admit it, he had put on a few extra pounds through the years. He was quick to laugh, he enjoyed a good joke—even distasteful ones at times—and he loved the simple things in life, like planting pansies, picking out the biggest pumpkin, and carving it "just right." He loved stringing cranberries for the Christmas tree and riding the trolley in San Francisco.

Phil, on the other hand, was the more serious type. In fact, Charlie couldn't imagine anyone at the hospital sharing a joke with him. He was brilliant and good-looking, dedicated and efficient. Charlie reached back into his memory to med school and recalled a few pranks Phil had been involved with, a few frat parties when he had a little—or a great deal—too much beer, and a few road trips they'd somehow eked out on a college student's budget. In spite of those, though, on the whole, Phil was always a serious student, and Charlie couldn't think of anyone he respected more or anyone he considered a better friend.

When the doorbell rang, Janet yelled, "I left the money and tip on the counter, hon'!"

Charlie opened the door and, to his surprise, found someone other than a delivery boy standing there.

"Hi," Phil said, wearing a look of deep embarrassment on his face. "I just thought I'd stop by for a few minutes. Sorry I didn't call first."

Charlie tried to conceal his surprise as he hugged his friend and motioned him inside. "No need to be sorry," he said, quite genuinely. "It's damn good to see you man."

Janet walked in and, with a look of surprise on her face, wrapped her arms tightly around him and smiled. "You have to be the best-looking pizza guy this town has ever seen!"

As was the case every time Phil visited their home, he felt instantly comfortable, and a look of relief washed over his face.

"How about a beer?" Charlie offered, pulling three from the fridge.

"I've never turned down a cold one."

For a while, the two doctors sat and discussed a few cases, munching on the pizza after it finally arrived.

"Sorry to break up the party, guys, but there's work to be done," Janet said, motioning them both toward the kitchen. She handed each of them a bag of popcorn kernels and pointed at the two large pots with oil already heating in the bottom. "Four grocery bags full, and you two guys are off the hook."

"Some class project," Charlie said, rolling his eyes playfully at Phil. "You picked a great time to stop by. Look what I get for being the teacher's pet."

The two poured popcorn into their stockpots and, ever so often, shook them back and forth.

"Damn, Janet!" Phil suddenly yelled across the room. "Mine is overflowing and still popping like hell."

She pulled out a roll of white craft paper and spread it across the table. "Pour some on here and keep popping," she instructed.

He did so, with beads of sweat forming on his forehead.

"Take it easy, Phil." Charlie laughed. "This isn't brain surgery."

After several small mounds of popcorn filled the tabletop, Janet decided it was time to relieve the men from their duties. "Okay you two," she said, shooing them away with both her hands, "off to the den. I have papers to grade and popcorn to bag."

Like her students, the two men instantly obeyed her commands and walked into the den.

Phil looked around at the clean but cluttered room as Charlie added a couple logs to the fire. The warmth of the crackling fire wasn't really necessary, but it certainly added a soothing touch to the ambiance. Phil knew Lara would never be able to tolerate the untidiness of such a room. *That uppity bitch would probably come up with some lame excuse to leave, then ramble on all the way home about how appalling the place is.* Phil, though, loved the room and found it inviting. It was furnished with an old but comfortable sofa and two mismatched, overstuffed chairs. It was hardly what one would picture in a doctor's home, but it was delightful just the same. He sat down on the couch, beer in hand, and began looking around on the end table for a place to set it down.

Charlie smiled to himself. "You can just set it on the table," he said. "We're not too fancy around here."

"Really?" Phil laughed. "If you knew how much I've spent on coasters over the years, you'd have a damn heart attack."

Charlie took his shoes off and crossed his feet on the coffee table. "Is everything okay, my friend? You look a little…tired. Aren't you due a vacation soon?"

"Yeah, that'd be great, but with Medusa herself? I think I'd rather spend a day in Hell." His thin lips made a small effort to smile, but his troubled, sad eyes told another story. The flames from the fireplace made the tears forming in his eyes glisten. As they rolled down his cheeks, Phil used the back of his hand to try to inconspicuously wipe them away, hoping Charlie did not see him; Charlie, of course, was kind enough to pretend he didn't.

Before they could say anything more, the phone rang.

"Charlie, Susan Hendrix's next-door neighbor's on the phone," Janet said. "Susan's phone is disconnected again, and the baby's been running a fever. She says it's pretty high, but she doesn't have a thermometer." Janet walked into the den and, in a hushed tone, told Charlie, "That worthless boyfriend of hers took the car again, and he's been gone for days."

"C'mon, Phil," Charlie said, putting his shoes back on. "Make a quick run with me."

Janet told the neighbor that Charlie would be there shortly, then kissed both the doctors as they walked out the door.

* * * * *

"What are we doing?" Phil asked, already knowing what his friend was up to.

"Sad story. It's a young girl in town, lives in poverty, with two children and no education. Maybe tonight we can make things a little easier for her."

"You amaze me, Charlie. You really do."

"Hey, don't make me out to be some superhero now. I'm just following the calling I believe God gave me."

They pulled into the dirt front yard, devoid of any type of defined driveway. Camping lanterns lit the tiny but neat living room of the small, dilapidated old house.

"Damn. Electricity's been cut off again," Charlie whispered to Phil before Susan opened the door. The baby, about a year old, was crying and burning up with fever. Using an ear thermometer, Charlie measured a 102-degree temp. He looked down the baby's throat and did a general exam before looking into both ears. "Another ear infection," Charlie reported.

Susan's chin and lips began to quiver.

"Now, now, Susan. We've been through this before. It's nothing medicine can't cure." He reached into his bag and pulled out a small bottle of penicillin. "Do you still have the dropper I gave you?"

"Yes," she answered meekly.

"Use that to give the medicine to her. It seems to work best. It'll take about ten days to clear up entirely. Even if she seems better, keep giving her the medicine till it's all gone." Charlie reached for the young mother's forearms. "Remember that, or the infection could come back." He wrote the dosage down for her and placed it behind a magnet on the old refrigerator that had turned warm from lack of electricity. "Oh. Forgive me," Charlie said. "This is my best friend, Phil. He was visiting, and I couldn't very well take a chance of leaving him there alone with my wife."

Susan forced a grin.

Suddenly, the sound of little feet came running into the room. "Dr. Charlie, Dr. Charlie!" Sam said, grabbing his leg. He was about five, and although his pajamas were too small and a little threadbare, they were clean, and his hair was combed neatly to the side.

"Okay," Charlie said playfully. "You get one guess."

"Left pocket," the little boy said, his eyes shining.

"It must be your lucky day!" Charlie said. "Why don't you reach in there and check?"

Sam reached slowly and carefully into Charlie's coat pocket and pulled out a pack of sugar-free gum and a trial-sized tube of children's toothpaste. He seemed pleased with his presents and hugged Charlie hard around his legs.

"Okay now. Go on back to your room and get in bed. Sally's sick, and your mama is tired."

Sam did as he was told, smiling broadly the whole way.

"If you need anything else, you know how to get in touch with me," Charlie said kindly to the young, thin girl.

Susan looked so pitiful. She had never had much of anything, but she still had her dignity. She looked down at the floor and quietly thanked Charlie.

He patted her shoulder thoughtfully and walked out onto the front porch. "Take care…and remember to give her that medicine for all ten days."

She gave a solemn wave and closed the old door that didn't quite meet the frame surrounding it.

In the car, several minutes passed before Phil said anything. "It's been so long since I've seen such poverty, Charlie," he finally spoke. "I mean, that was real poverty, not like when we scraped up quarters for pizza in college."

"Yeah, there are a lotta sad stories around here. We just do what we can and accept what we can't. It'll swallow you whole if you start thinkin' you can change the world."

When they got back to the house, Phil hugged his friend in a playful but hard hug. "I gotta hit the road," he said. "Thanks again for tonight, Charlie. It really opened my eyes to many things—real life, for starters, one I haven't been living. See ya tomorrow night."

"Drive carefully," Charlie said, concealing the concern he felt for his friend.

CHAPTER 4

When Phil finally returned home, to his surprise, Lara had already gone to bed. It was a relief he deserved and rarely got the pleasure of enjoying. His mind had been reeling since leaving the Evans place. He thought of the popcorn spilling off the table and onto the floor. He thought of how quickly Janet had demanded that two doctors cook popcorn over a stove instead discussing patient cases. Phil loved her. He truly loved so much about her. He guessed it was because she was everything Lara wasn't, everything she could and would never be. Janet was the closest thing to a sister he had ever known, and she got something from him he rarely gave away: respect.

Phil's mind then drifted to Charlie and how big his heart was. He thought of how generic his own patients had become to him, and he vowed to take a closer interest in all of them in the future. Phil could admit that he was a good doctor, yet somewhere along the line, he had forgotten how to care, at least in the way he should have.

He ascended the spiral staircase as quietly as he could, so as not to wake Lara, then eased silently into the bedroom they shared. He laid his clothes across the wingback chair and slid into bed in his underwear. She never heard him or felt his slow, methodical movement as he rolled over with his back to her.

* * * * *

It seemed as though Phil had just closed his eyes when the alarm went off. He hit the snooze button twice, something he rarely did. Lara rolled over and, without saying a word, went right back to sleep.

He showered, shaved, dressed, and walked down to the kitchen. Rosa wouldn't be in for another couple hours, so he ate two pieces of dry toast and half a cantaloupe. He filled his small silver thermos with black coffee, then cranked his silver jaguar, giving it time to wake up as well.

Phil's first stop was to see Richey, who lay still and quiet in a painless sleep. He rubbed the little boy's bright red hair with his fingers. One of the nurses walked by and looked at him as if he'd changed bodies with someone else, and Phil laughed to himself; it was really quite out of character for him to do something as simple as to brush a child's hair away from his face.

He finished his rounds and discovered there were only two surgeries scheduled for him for the day: a broken leg from a basketball injury and two arms and a leg from a motorcycle accident. *When in the hell will people learn to stay off those death machines anyway?* He was glad that at least this particular young man was smart enough to ride with a full-face helmet.

Phil hung his lab coat up at 5:00 and actually said goodbye to the nurses, who stood at the station filling out the mounds of paperwork their jobs required. They looked up in surprise, and only two were able to stammer a reciprocal goodbye. *Damn, I must have been some kinda hard ass through the years*, he thought, catching their shocked glimpses in reaction to his common courtesy.

Lara wasn't home, but Phil knew she would make an appearance just in time for the dinner. Rosa was busy in the kitchen, singing a Hispanic song softly to herself. He slowly looked around the corner and startled the housekeeper into a scream that was quickly followed by a blushing giggle. Her salt-and-pepper hair was always pulled back into a bun and covered with a clear hairnet. She was at least forty pounds overweight, but as well as she cooked, he could understand why. Rosa had been their cook since the onset of their marriage, and Phil adored her.

"Can I just grab a sample?" he asked playfully.

She pretended to slap his hand before handing him a piece of mozzarella cheese.

As expected, Lara whooshed through the door with her hair styled high and her makeup done to perfection. She was carrying a plastic garment bag in one hand, a new dress, and a large shopping bag in the other, overflowing with the day's purchases. With twenty minutes left before her guests were to arrive, she downed a full glass of merlot and walked unsteadily up the main staircase.

Phil refused to waste time speaking to her. Instead, he poured himself a scotch, retreated into the library, and sat behind his desk. It was a refuge for him, with heavy sliding doors that locked from the inside. When he walked into that safe haven, everyone knew to leave him alone. This time, he didn't bother to shut the doors, because he knew Charlie and Janet would arrive on time, yet another admirable trait in a long line of those he respected about the two.

When a long, deep, cathedral-like chime sounded from the doorbell, Phil rose to answer it before the housekeeper could. "Good to see you guys," he said, hugging them both with a vigor even stronger than the night before. "Come on in and taste some of Rosa's snacks. They're delicious, as usual."

"That would be hors d'oeuvres, darling," Lara corrected snidely as she made her way down the stairway with great fanfare, as if the paparazzi themselves were looking on. "You'll have to forgive my husband's...lack of civility," she sniped, obviously appalled by his casual appearance and attitude.

"Oh, it's okay, dear," Janet said, purposely plopping down on the sofa. "We call them snacks too."

Oh God, Charlie thought. *Let the games begin.*

Phil did not dare to smile at her response, but his eyes danced with humor he wouldn't be able to contain much longer.

Rosa brought out platters filled with marinated mushrooms, prosciutto, provolone cheese, hard salami, ripe olives, and marinated artichoke hearts.

"Rosa," Charlie exclaimed, "you've outdone yourself. This is a meal in itself."

"Rosa is compensated well for her work, let me assure you," Lara said with a twinge of jealousy.

Rosa was used to Lara and had no trouble overlooking the rude remark as she thanked Charlie profusely. "I enjoy cooking," she said, laughing as she pointed to her protruding belly, "and tasting!"

"You may be excused," Lara snapped, turning to get another glass of wine.

"You look lovely tonight, Janet," Phil said sincerely.

"Where did you ever find that dress, dear?" Lara asked, mindful that such a frock could not possibly have come from any of the esteemed fashion houses where she, herself, shopped.

Janet looked at her with all the seriousness she could muster and answered, "There's a quaint little chain store next to the grocery in town. I simply couldn't resist. My Charlie always encourages me to buy nice things."

Phil held his breath, dreading what would come next.

"I know what you mean," Lara said, holding her hand over her mouth, pretending to stifle a laugh. "With dresses costing between $5,000 and $10,000 each now, you'd think I'd wear all of mine at least once, but they do become so humdrum after a while. Are you still doing that sweet little childcare thing?"

"Yes, I am…and I enjoy it quite a bit."

"Darling," Phil interjected, turning to Lara, "Janet is an educator, a teacher. It's not just 'a little childcare thing.'"

"You're right, dear," Lara said coolly. "Our children are our future."

"The curriculum changes yearly," Janet said to Phil. "It is amazing how much we are able to accomplish in such little time."

"Curriculum?" Lara asked, laughing much longer than was appropriate. "No offense, luv, but you make it sound as if they're ready for college after their first year with you."

Phil refused to humor her by scolding her, knowing she loved nothing more than arguing, so he simply laughed the jab off and winked at Janet. "What a tremendously brave woman you are to take on the kids of today."

With that, the two men excused themselves and walked into the library.

"Your Janet will get a star in her crown in Heaven." Phil sighed. "God, Charlie. I've been thinking about what you said. I'm so sick of dealing with that materialistic bitch. There's gotta be more to life than this. I hate to think I've worked this hard just to live a miserable life."

"What more are you looking for?" Charlie asked, with deep concern.

"Well, God knows children are outta the question. Lara wouldn't risk her figure, and I'd be too afraid they might turn out like their mother."

Charlie offered a faint smile, but deep down, he was painfully sorry for his friend.

"Dinner is ready to be served, Madam Sawyer," Rosa said humbly.

Lara went to the library to get the men. As she sashayed to the table, she made sure to tell all of them about the very specific instructions she had given for the night's meal. "We are having *agnoloitti di zucca*," she said haughtily. "Janet, that's basically a butternut squash stuffed with ravioli, just so you know."

"Oh my," Janet answered in a dramatic display. "Why, I've never heard of that kind of squash. Charlie and I only have yellow squash in our garden. I can hardly wait to see a butternut squash!"

Lara looked extremely pleased as she walked into the dining room.

Phil stifled a laugh, and Charlie poked Janet in the side and gave her a glare.

Janet just smirked at him, then raised her shoulders and gave him an innocent face that made Phil laugh out loud.

CHAPTER 5

As Phil entered the bedroom, he heard the shower running. He pictured Lara attempting to wash out all the hairspray that had held every hair in its proper place. He recalled her grand entrance of the evening, as if she was attending some royal gala, and he looked down at his relatively humble and casual corduroys and polo shirt. *So much for compatibility,* Phil thought. As he pondered his wife, he had trouble remembering what she was even wearing that night; it was then that he realized how little attention he even paid to her anymore. He rarely even took a second glance at her or questioned where she would be, in case an emergency required him to contact her.

Phil kicked off his loafers, lay on the bed with his clothes still on, and let his memory carry him back farther, to the beginning of it all. He was young when they met but old enough to be a decent judge of character. He thought of how alluring Lara was that first night, her breasts so firm and tanned. In spite of her youth, she carried herself with the sophistication of an older woman. Phil was hooked almost immediately and, for the first time, intimidated by a woman. That challenged him, and until a few months into the marriage, he was so blinded by it that he was not able to see the forest for the trees, as the old saying went.

The two of them rushed off to Vegas and tied the knot in some nondescript chapel, with an elderly man and his wife presiding over their vows. Phil did recall what she wore that day: a beautiful, generously beaded gown that cost him more than a month's salary. He didn't think twice about it back then, because he wanted to give her the world. It didn't take him long to discover that for Lara, even the world was not enough.

In time, Phil's workload grew, and his reputation grew along with it. He moved from one hospital to the next, until he reached his dream, Cedar Sinai. *Now,* he thought, *my real life can finally begin.* Sadly, all that really began was his career. For the past few years, he'd settled for that, still feeling that he was greatly blessed to have pulled at least that wish out of the sky.

Through it all, Lara had been by his side, if only at the powerhouse parties, where she could show off her beauty and her latest expensive gown. She charmed the men with her looks and never had to bother making conversation with the women, because they all resented her. Thinking back on it, Phil realized that was probably for the best. Lara was brutally critical and despised competition. She flew to Paris twice a year to shop with her family, but beyond purchasing her tickets for those expensive junkets, Phil had never had to deal with any in-laws.

Based on what Lara told him about them, they all came from the same mold, and he had no desire to ever go to Seattle to meet them.

She came out of the bathroom, her hair still partially damp; she never subjected it to the hairdryer for too long, so as not to damage it. Her long locks still shone with blonde beauty as she brushed it continuously, without missing a stroke. She smelled of Chanel No. 5 and her latest brand of body lotion. She was naked, with the body of a goddess, but Phil was not aroused; he knew what lay beneath. Her tan lines were proof that she'd spent a lot of time in the sun, wearing only a skimpy bikini and not a tennis skirt and sleeveless top. That was no surprise. He watched as she sat at her vanity, rubbing night cream on her face and studying her own beauty. As he stared at her admiring herself, Phil felt bile rising in his throat. *How can something so beautiful disgust me so much?*

"Phil, you need to know that tonight was the last time I will waste an evening with the Beverly Hillbillies," she said flatly. "Frankly, it is insulting that I was forced to. I don't understand why you are so determined to rub elbows with the lower echelon."

Phil felt his anger rising to a level it had never reached before. He was speechless. His mouth fell agape, as if to fashion words, but his lips refused to form them. Because he could say nothing, he was forced to listen to her continue.

"You should invite some of the real doctors from the hospital over for cocktails before they start to think you have social issues, darling," she said calmly, with ice in her tone. "You don't owe Charlie or his overweight wife anything just because you shared a small dorm room years ago. Face it, Phil. You made it, and he didn't. For Christ's sake, you don't have to feel guilty and keep trying to make that up to him. It isn't your fault the guy ended up being a loser." Lara continued to alternate between rubbing the cream on her face and brushing her mane.

Phil reached for his heart, for fear that his rage would stop it from beating. He sat in angry silence for a moment, then stood so quickly that Lara cowered. "You little bitch," he said calmly, but then his voice rose to such an octave that it seemed to shake the walls. "You're just…"

Lara, no longer feeling in control, slowly made her way over to the wall to allow it to hold her up. She had never seen him like that, never known him to lose his cool, and she wasn't sure where he was going to go from there.

"You call Charlie a loser and insult his wife, but you're nothing but a cheap whore who got a good ride when you charmed me into marrying you. You will never be half the woman Janet Evans is. Men might act impressed when you prance your beauty around in a crowded room, but they really think nothing of you. They all know you're just a good-looking, dense blonde who had better play her trump cards while she can. Janet has character, real beauty—the kind on the inside. Everyone sees it in her, not just on her, like they do with you. Tell me, Lara, who are your real friends? Do you even have any?" he screamed, so furious that the veins were sticking out on his dark, reddened face. "Funny. For all your talk about how popular you are, I've never seen any of them come around much, especially when you're sick with the flu or even on your birthday or holidays. If one of your checks were to bounce, your overpaid hairstylist wouldn't even admit to knowing you on the street!"

Phil paused for a minute, swaying with anger as he reached up to his face to feel the heat radiating off it. He looked over at Lara as she shivered in her nakedness and, for a very brief moment, he felt pity for her, for her selfishness, for her ignorance, for her inability to love.

If nothing else, Lara was confident in herself, and it only took a moment for her to pull on a silk robe and regain her composure and rein in her own anger. "How dare you, you son-of-a-bitch?" she seethed through her freshly brushed teeth. "Don't try to fool yourself, and you sure as hell aren't fooling me. You love being the envy of every other man in the room. Your precious reputation is just as important to you as saving arms and legs."

Phil laughed a mean, evil chuckle that sounded almost like a noise that would come from an injured animal. "How dare you compare the two? Saving arms and legs? Is that all you think I do, you stupid bitch? I'm not some damn plastic surgeon! I've had it with you, with all of this, Lara. I've had it with this tacky, oversized house that couldn't possibly ever feel like a home to anyone. I've had it with drinking a double-scotch every night just to try and block out your bullshit. It's over, Lara…over! We'll let the judge decide who gets what, and until then, I'll stay in a hotel or get an apartment." Phil wouldn't have taken a million dollars for the look on her face. He felt the best he had in years, and he let her know it with a snide laugh.

Lara turned on him with a vengeance so great that it put ice in his veins. "Oh no you won't! You'll never get away with that. In fact, I'd like to see you try."

What frightened Phil was the calmness in her voice. She sounded evil, with the sincerity of someone who knew she was in jeopardy of losing everything but simply wasn't going to stand by and let it happen.

"You won't leave this house alive, Phil, and don't fool yourself into thinking otherwise. With enough money, that pool cleaner, the gardener, and even your sweet little housekeeper, Rosa, will say I've been abused for years. Anyone can be bought, my dear. You know, with all the stresses you docs are under, it's no wonder you sometimes take your tensions out on your poor little wives. Any jury will rule in my favor, especially with a few snapshots of bruises and lacerations."

"That's just your style, isn't it?" Phil screamed. "You greedy whore."

"Don't ever sleep too soundly, my dear," she said sweetly, then nonchalantly sat back down at the vanity to finish her normal evening ritual.

At that moment, Phil felt something in himself click, something he simply could not control. Without a single thought, he grabbed her silky hair and jerked her roughly to her feet.

Lara, wide-eyed, screamed out in pain as he wheeled her around to face him.

"Never, never in my life have I even imagined despising someone as much as I detest you," he said, not even hearing his own voice as it spoke in smooth, even tones.

Lara looked smugly at him, her eyes now dancing with thoughts of revenge.

Phil grabbed her chin and forced her to look into his eyes. "You will never again be graced by my presence, never again insult my friends, and never again spend a dime of my money."

She laughed as hard as she could with her chin still in his tight, controlling grasp.

Phil never saw it coming. His large, highly skilled hands reached carefully around her thin, smooth neck, and he squeezed. It wasn't so hard at first, perhaps just an attempt to scare her, but the smirk on her face goaded him on. That snide expression dared him, even above her pain, berated him, told him he would never have the courage to go through with it, that he would never have the guts. Emasculated by her silent smugness, Phil squeezed until he felt his neatly manicured nails digging into the soft, freshly moisturized flesh on the back of her neck. He almost lost consciousness as he felt the fractures of the larynx and hyoid bone. He felt her weight collapse as her legs fell beneath her, and Phil immediately pulled his hands away as though they weren't even his own. He didn't bother to soften her fall; she didn't even deserve that. He looked down at his wife in her $400 robe, now wet from urine. Her neck was twisted and distorted, like a poorly drawn cartoon character's, but amazingly, her eyes were still staring up at him, still silently taunting, *"You'll never have the balls."*

Phil went into the bathroom and didn't make it to the toilet before he vomited all over the floor and even the countertop. He lay on the floor in the puddle of his own vomit for some indeterminable amount of time, for minutes stretched into a confused eternity. Finally, he pulled himself up to his knees, then his feet, and got in the shower, still dressed. He washed off the bile, stomach acid, and remnants of butternut squash ravioli, then removed the wet clothing and threw it on the floor. He stood for several minutes, just shivering in his nakedness, before realizing he needed to dress. He threw on a pair of underwear, some jeans, and an undershirt before gazing at his wife again. He halfway expected her to be gone, like all those sick horror movies where the monster never really died, but there would be no sequels for Lara. She was still there, a corpse with her eyes open, and the sight made him shiver again, this time with disgust. Phil was surprised that he felt no remorse, not even for the simple fact that he had taken the life of a human being, no matter how selfish and unkind.

The one emotion that did hit him like a fighter's blow was panic. He knew he had to do something. *Call the police? Call...someone? Charlie!* Phil picked up the phone, his hands shaking so terribly that he dropped it several times before punching in the numbers.

"Hello?" Charlie answered on the second ring, his voice groggy but alert.

"Charlie," Phil said, for the first time breaking into hysterical sobs. "Help me. Come quick!"

"Phil?" Charlie said. "Are you okay? You're not hurt are you?"

"No," he said, sobbing. "I... She's gone, Charlie."

"Who? Who's gone?" Charlie asked. "What's going on?"

"I-I killed her, Charlie. I killed Lara!"

"Uh...I'll be right there," Charlie said, maintaining his cool, as always, so as to make everyone feel comfortable; Charlie had nothing if not the perfect bedside manner.

"Should I call the cops or—"

"No, no, don't call the police yet. Just wait till I get there, and we'll figure it out. Hang in there, buddy. Everything will be all right." With that, Charlie jumped up, threw on his clothes, and simultaneously filled Janet in on what was going on. "I've gotta get over there now," he said.

"Not by yourself, you're not." Janet quickly slid her legs into a pair of sweats.

The two made it to Phil's place in record time, and when they pulled into the drive, they saw him standing at the open front door. He was pale and weak, barely able to stand.

Inside, Janet fixed him a straight scotch, with no ice, and helped him to the sofa. As Phil held the drink in his shaky hands, she rubbed his back in silence.

"Where is she, Phil?" Charlie asked, as gently as he could.

"Upstairs, in the bedroom, on the floor. I didn't even move her to the bed, man, didn't even care enough to do that. What kind of animal am I?"

"Shh," Janet said, trying to console him. "Don't do that to yourself, Phil."

"I'll go have a look," Charlie said. He climbed the stairs and walked into their room. As he leaned down to examine the body, the thought crossed his mind that she might not be dead at all and was merely unconscious, but there was no such luck for his friend. He walked slowly down the winding staircase with his shoulders slumped, trying to think clearly. "We need to contact Arthur Morris first," he said matter-of-factly, trying to remain calm. "The coroner has to pick her up soon, and we've gotta make some plans and arrangements. Do you have a number for her relatives?"

"They should be in her directory in her vanity. I hate to ask, but could you handle that, Janet?"

"Sure, dear. I'll do that and anything else you will need. C'mon, honey," she said and led Charlie back upstairs.

Charlie covered Lara's body with a silk sheet from their bed before he let Janet in the room. While she went through whatever few personal items she could find, Charlie went back downstairs to contact Arthur, their college friend and a damn good attorney.

Phil was sitting on the sofa, nursing his almost-empty glass of scotch and staring off in a trance. Charlie feared he was going to really lose it before he'd have a chance to talk to the attorney or the police. Still, for the sake of everyone, Charlie wouldn't allow himself the indulgence of thinking of the consequences to come. He knew he had to hold it together. "Phil," he said quietly, prying the empty glass from his friend's hand, "where can I find Arthur Morris's number? He needs to be here for you when the police arrive."

Phil pointed blankly toward his office and answered, "In the middle drawer of my desk. There's a brown book of numbers."

Charlie refilled the glass, against his better judgment, handed it back to Phil, and walked into the study. Everything seemed so surreal. Just a few hours earlier, in that very same house, the four were sharing dinner together. He shook his head and rubbed his sleepy eyes. "Keep it together," Charlie kept telling himself, over and over again.

It took Arthur less than fifteen minutes to arrive, briefcase in hand. Dressed in jeans, a Harvard sweatshirt, and canvas boat shoes, he looked anything but the attorney type, but he was, by far, the best one in the city. He was tall, about six-three, and built like a brick shithouse, with biceps that bulged blatantly under anything he wore. His black skin was smooth and dark, and his smile showed off a bright set of perfectly aligned teeth. His hands, which had carried both footballs and basketballs for Harvard, were oversized and thick. People were often intimidated by his good looks, his deep voice, and, most of all, his intelligence, but underneath it all, Arthur was as normal a guy as anyone could find. On this particular night, he was wearing horn-rimmed glasses and a concerned look that reflected both the shock of the event and the concern for a good man who'd always warranted his respect.

Phil rose to shake his hand, but Arthur held out his arms to hug his friend close to his broad chest. He ended the embrace with a couple hard pats on Phil's back, then stepped away. "Where is she?" he asked, as if Lara was still alive.

"Upstairs," Phil answered, his voice vacant of emotion.

"I'll take you up," Charlie offered, "and I'll send Janet back down to be with you," he said, motioning to Phil.

The two men were silent as they climbed the stairs and made their way to the bedroom.

Janet looked exasperated and nervous and held up her hands in surrender as Charlie walked in with Arthur. "I can't really find anything here," she said. "Maybe when the body is moved, I'll feel more comfortable looking around."

Charlie looked down at the floor and the silk sheet covering the small-framed body. "Damn. I'm sorry, Janet." he sighed. "I don't know what I was thinking, leaving you in here. Can you just go sit with Phil down in the living room? I don't think it's good for him to be alone too long."

"Sure," she said as she stood and looked at Arthur. "Hello," she smiled weakly, trying to conceal her worry.

"Oh, I'm sorry, darling," Charlie intervened. "This is Arthur Morris, a friend of Phil's and mine. He's also the best attorney in town. Arthur, this is my wife, Janet."

"Nice to meet you, Janet, though I wish it could have been under better circumstances."

Janet nodded and made her way out of the room.

The two men stood above the body, wondering who would be the first to pull back the sheet. Obviously, neither was eager to do so.

"What time did this happen?" Arthur asked, pulling a small notepad out of his back pocket.

"Let me think," Charlie answered, trying to calculate the time it had taken them to get there. "I don't know how long it happened before he called me. He sounded pretty out of it." Charlie then reached down and slowly pulled the sheet back, revealing the top half of her body.

Arthur took a couple steps back and almost fell over a chair. "Damn, man. Can you close those eyes?" he asked. "I've seen a lotta dead bodies, but those eyes! They still look alive, angry...almost evil."

"I don't wanna touch her very much, or the medical examiner will be mad as hell. You know how he is."

Arthur nodded in agreement. He knew all too well, for he had locked horns with Martin Rudyard enough times to know there was no winning any battles with him. He was a powerful man who took his job as seriously as anyone he had ever met. Arthur had to respect him for that, and he knew Charlie was right. That last thing he needed was to be accused of screwing with a crime scene on a case he was going to be working.

Charlie bent down and looked more closely at Lara. "Let's see. It took us about an hour to get here, and livor mortis is noticeable. I'd say it didn't happen long before we got here, because that presents as early as one hour after death."

"You mean rigor mortis, right?" Arthur asked, moving a little closer to the body.

"No. Livor mortis is the discoloration you see in the body after death. The blood settles with gravity." Charlie pointed at Lara's body and said, "Here. See? This area of skin is sort of a purplish red."

"Yeah, I see what you're talking about."

"If we move her, Martin will be able to tell. Blood won't settle on the hard areas her body is lying on, as they prevent blood flow. There will be pale areas over her scapula and buttocks. If we move her—"

"Okay, okay. I get it. I'm not in the mood to move her either, Charlie."

"The temperature will hold the rigor down, but her jaw looks somewhat stiff already. It's the first thing that goes rigid, followed by the elbow and knee joints. That'll take hours though. My guess is she's been dead about two and a half hours, but I'm no forensics man."

"Coulda fooled me," Arthur said as he bent to pull the sheet back up.

Charlie watched him shiver, as if a cold wind had just blown through. "You all right?" Charlie asked.

"Yeah, man," Arthur answered, "but unfortunately, we've gotta make that call. Do you wanna do it, or should I?"

Tears stung at Charlie's eyes, and his heart rose into his throat making his voice sound like a croak rather than an answer from a grown man. "You know the right people," he answered. "You better do it. I'll be downstairs, with my friend."

Janet was sipping on a scotch herself by the time Charlie descended the stairs, something Charlie had never seen her do in all the years of their marriage.

"Uh…Arthur's gonna call Martin at home, then call the police. It's better to call Martin first. He's a hard ass, but he knows you're a good man, Phil. He'll be fair to you."

Phil looked tired, and his eyes were red and swollen from the crying that had finally ceased. "I just can't believe it," he said. "After all these years of hell, I shoulda just divorced her. I just…lost it. That's all I can say for myself."

"I understand," Charlie said, gently placing his hand on his friend's knee. "We're human, Phil. We are all human."

Arthur descended the stairs slowly and sat across from the three of them. "The police and Martin are on their way. It shouldn't be long. With it being Friday night…er, Saturday morning, it'll be Monday before I can get you out on bond. Hang in there, Phil. It'll be all right."

"Bond?" Phil asked in disbelief. "You'll be able to get me out?"

"It'll cost you," Arthur answered, "but we're going for voluntary manslaughter. You need to get a few things together before they get here. Lara will have to be taken to a mortuary after the autopsy, and plans will need to be made for a funeral. Her family needs to be contacted, etc."

"We'll take care of all that, Phil," Janet assured him. "You just take care of yourself and your state of mind. That's what is most important here."

"I guess I need to sign some checks," Phil said, for the first time rising from his seat. He went into his office and walked back out with his checkbook. He signed several blank checks and handed them to Janet. "Use these for whatever you need—my bond, the funeral, whatever. I won't need money where I'm going."

"You'll just be held in the county jail until Monday," Arthur answered, "and I'll make sure you're treated right. I know several of the captains over there, and they owe me a few favors."

The doorbell rang, its cathedral music blaring like a symphony from Dracula's castle. Martin had beaten the police, and he had a small entourage of photographers in tow, along with a couple young men carrying a stretcher and body bag. "What in the hell's going on here, Doctor?" he asked blatantly, then stood in the middle of the room, silently waiting on a reply.

"I strangled her," Phil blurted out, then started to cry again. "I don't know what happened. I just snapped. I couldn't take it anymore."

"A beautiful woman can do that to a man," Martin answered, showing a little more empathy. "Where is the body?"

"I'll take you up," Arthur said.

A short while later, the police arrived, and they all marched up the stairs to gawk at her before beginning the forensics part of the investigation. Pictures were taken of the entire bedroom, even areas that had nothing to do with the crime, but it was all part of normal procedure and protocol. Several snapshots of the bathroom were also taken, and Phil's wet clothes were placed in a plastic evidence bag. The silk sheet was tagged and bagged as well.

Martin bent down to look at the body. "Rigor beginning in the jaw, though not yet in the other joints," he said into his handheld recorder. "Body appears to have been left where it fell." He then stopped his recorder and said aloud to himself, "Pretty strong strangulation."

His assistants were ordered to bag her hands, and Arthur watched as they handled the thin, soft hands as carefully as they could with plastic gloves. He knew that any attempt to grab at the assailant would have left evidence under the nails. Since she was barefoot, they also bagged her feet.

The two men standing by the stretcher looked her over in a lustful way, which gave Charlie a sickening chill. "Damn," he said. "Can't you just get her outta here already?"

"Let me remind you…Dr. Evans, is it?" Martin said sarcastically.

"Yes."

"Regardless of who the murderer is or why the murder occurred, all investigations are handled thoroughly through our office. We will do things in an orderly fashion, as we see fit."

In a bit of a huff, Charlie turned and walked back down the stairs to find the police talking to Phil, with Arthur by at his side. Very little dialogue was exchanged as they allowed him to get a shirt and his shoes before cuffing him. Phil handed his wallet to Charlie and, with his head hung low, walked beside the policemen and got into the back seat of their car. Before Charlie or Janet could even wave goodbye, the cruiser was zooming down the long, well-lit driveway, en route to the county jail, carrying the best orthopedic surgeon Cedar Sinai had ever known, a brilliant surgeon with his hands in cuffs.

Phil felt the bumping of the police car as it carried him to his fate, and all he could think about was how much he loved the cobblestone driveway, his only contribution to the construction of the house. It reminded him of his undergrad days at Georgetown University, and that warm recollection brought a smile to his face.

CHAPTER 6

"Hope you guys don't have plans," Arthur said after a few brief moments of silence. "We've gotta do some digging, find numbers for the vic's family and friends so the local police can notify them. Then we'll go from there."

"We're here to help," Janet said. "I'm not surprised Lara never mentioned her family. She was too…into herself." As soon as the words left her mouth, Janet looked embarrassed. "I know we're not supposed to speak ill of the dead, but let's be honest. She wasn't exactly well liked."

Arthur shrugged. "I never really talked to her, but I did see her at a few parties. It was impossible not to notice her. She knew how to work a room."

"That's putting it politely," Charlie scoffed.

"I'll have a look in the office," Arthur offered. "If you two don't mind, maybe you can go through her things. I'm a lawyer, for Christ's sake, not a coroner."

Charlie nodded, knowing Janet didn't want to be in the bedroom by herself. "C'mon, honey," he said. "Let's see what we can find."

The quiet in the room was deafening. They began with her vanity, the place where she'd last sat. Janet pulled the drawers all the way out and laid them on the bed. They thumbed through receipts from plush boutiques and dug through several trial-sized bottles of the latest perfumes, but nothing personal was found.

"She's gotta have something—a phonebook, letters… This doesn't make sense. I mean, the woman had a family."

"Maybe she didn't want anybody to know about them," Charlie answered. "Phil said he never met any of them."

"Hmm. In that case, we're probably looking in places too obvious. If she wanted to keep her family hidden from him for some reason, she wouldn't stash anything in the vanity, basically out in the open. What else do you know about the house?"

"Not a lot. We can look around, but you're a woman. Where would you hide something in this place?"

Janet thought long and hard before answering, "My lingerie drawer. Phil clearly wasn't interested in her, and I'm sure their sex life was faltering. She would feel confident that he wouldn't look there." Janet went through several drawers of lingerie before she came upon a sachet. She untied it and found a safety deposit key. "Bingo!" she said, passing it to Charlie.

"Wow. My own personal Matlock," he said, winking at her.

"I prefer Columbo," she said, grinning at him. "I'm not sure which bank this belongs to, but we could find out."

"It'll take a subpoena to get into it, but I'm sure Arthur can arrange it."

"Here's a letter too," Janet said. "It looks like a child wrote it. The return address is in Nebraska." She opened the letter carefully and read it to Charlie: "'Dear Laraleen… I am writing to you because I am at a new foster home. I thought you might want to write to me. I haven't heard from you in a year. I hope you are okay. They say I will be here until I turn eighteen because Daddy won't get out of jail until I am a grownup. It would be nice if you would come and get me. We could get ice cream. Love, Lilly.'"

"Lilly?" Charlie said. "Hmm."

"Don't tell me she has a little sister in foster care and she wouldn't even get her," Janet said. "How horrible."

"I'm sure there's more than meets the eye here," Charlie surmised. "You said the return address is in Nebraska?"

"Yes," Janet answered sadly. "Bedford Group Home, in Norfolk."

"Well, at least it's something of a lead. Let's check with Arthur and see if he turned anything up down there."

When they met Arthur in the study, he announced that he'd found nothing of real pertinent value in Phil's desk. They gave Arthur the letter and the key, hoping it would lead to something.

"Unfortunately, it's Saturday," Arthur said. "There isn't much I can do on the weekend."

The three continued to search until they found both the marriage certificate and Lara's driver's license.

"This should help," Arthur said. "We should all go get a few hours of sleep, as there's nothing more we can do for a while. I've got your number, Charlie. I'll give you a call, hopefully in the next eight hours or so."

"Okay," Charlie answered, his voice dripping with guilt. "I just feel like leaving here is like…leaving Phil."

"You'll have plenty of time to be there for him."

"Should I write one of these checks to you?" Janet asked. "For a retainer?"

"Nah, I'll settle up with Phil later. I know he's good for it. Listen, I appreciate your help. I'm gonna need you two on this."

"No problem," they both answered, tears flowing as they walked out the door and locked it behind them.

CHAPTER 7

The two policemen talked amongst themselves as they drove to the county jail. It wasn't often that they arrested one of the wealthy upper class for murder, but it was all in a day's work. They would drop him off and never see him again, unless he made the morning news. Both officers were in their mid-thirties, and they casually discussed grabbing a beer and a sandwich at the end of their shift and grilling out together the next afternoon.

Meanwhile, Phil felt as though he was somehow outside his own body. There they were, discussing a Sunday afternoon barbecue, and he had just squeezed the life out of Lara and left her lying there for everyone to see, yellow urine staining her ivory robe, with nothing underneath to cover her nude body. Phil searched the depths of his memory to try to determine what had really happened, when he'd actually given in to the urge to murder her. It was almost like an automobile accident; at times, it seemed to play over in his head in slow motion, but at other times, he had no recollection of it at all. He did remember that there was no remorse, no regrets, and as he searched his soul, he still couldn't find any.

Phil knew Lara was not worth it. Because of her, he'd lost everything he'd worked so hard for. Gone were the dreams that had taken so long to reach, along with the opportunity to help people. *Funny. I guess none of that really matters now.* He pictured his stark white lab coat, with "Dr. Phil Sawyer" embroidered in royal blue. He wondered how long it would hang there and who would finally gather the nerve to remove it and do away with it. Most of all, though, he was relieved. He felt a release, and he was tired, as if he'd been through a bitter battle and was glad it was finally over.

The horn sounded twice, and the garage door of the jail creaked and moaned as it made its way up for them to enter. The police got out of the car and spoke to the correctional officers, then went inside for a few moments. They returned with some steaming coffee before coming back and opening the back door of the car.

By then, Phil had lost all concept of time, and he felt the nakedness on his wrist where his presidential Rolex had been; Charlie had the foresight to put it in the safe before he left.

One of the men laid his hand on the top of Phil's head to keep him from bumping it on the roof of the car. The other grabbed his elbow leading him inside. They talked amongst themselves as they went through the motions of processing him. Like a puppet's, Phil's body simply went in whatever direction they pulled him. He was grateful they didn't interrogate him or rough him up, both of which he expected.

One of the taller jailers walked up and told him to spread his arms and legs, then quickly frisked him. "Any weapons, sir? Any needles or anything that may injure me as I search you?"

"No," Phil answered, his mouth so dry he was barely able to open it and separate his tongue from the roof. "None of that."

"Step out of your shoes, sir," the jailer said, firm and detached, as though he was talking to a wall.

Phil did as he was told and became openly aware of his fear as his body shivered against his efforts to remain steady.

The tall jailer, whose nametag read "Johnson," barely glanced into his shoes before running his hands down his outstretched arms and legs, as if he was already sure he would find no weapons or contraband.

A quick glance out the window afforded Phil the chance to see his two police escorts backing slowly out of the garage. For a minute, he truly envied them, their opportunity for a beer, a sandwich, and a night's sleep in their own beds. His head swirled, and he realized that Officer Johnson was literally holding him up as they made their way to the fingerprinting room.

"You all right, man?" Johnson asked. "You gonna fall out on me?"

"I-I don't know. I feel sick."

Johnson led him to a chair and pulled over a filthy green garbage can that had obviously been used for similar circumstances. As if reading his thoughts, Johnson said, "A lotta drunks come in here. Just aim in here if you've gotta puke."

As hard as Phil tried not to, he threw up again and again, only to be repulsed and humiliated by his own vomit, pooling in the chunky ooze of countless drunks at the bottom of a garbage can. He laid his head back against the wall and gasped for air as his stomach muscles began to spasm. He had already let go of everything on his own bathroom floor, so now only thick, bitter, yellow bile drooled from his mouth as he heaved over and over again.

Johnson handed him a cone-shaped cup of water and a rough paper towel. "Here, pal," he said, as if it was nothing new to see a grown man vomiting all over the place.

"Thanks," Phil muttered, then tried to drink from the cup before the water started to seep through the thin paper.

"Can you stand now?" Johnson asked. "We need to get these prints and photos taken as soon as possible. You're not the only customer we've got tonight."

Phil stood shakily but was able to do so by himself. He had been fingerprinted before, for his medical license, and he knew to let his hands go limp and allow Johnson to rotate his fingers and wrists as necessary. As the jailer quickly worked his hands, Phil took a look at him. He was tall, maybe six-one or six-two, with chiseled features, blond hair, and blue eyes. Phil estimated him to be in his late thirties, and he wondered what had brought the man there, lured him into such a career, for Johnson looked as out of place in that police station as Phil did. Officer Johnson was professional and good-looking and likely could have been a model; he was anything but the average jailer. An old adage came to Phil's mind: *Can't judge a book by its cover. You sure as hell can't,* he thought again as he stood silently for his mugshots.

There was a bright flash, and then he felt Johnson turning him sideways, as though he were only a mannequin. Another flash followed before he was allowed to sit again.

Officer Johnson picked up an old black phone and punched in three numbers. "Evening Scott," he said, the monotone returning to his voice. "I've got Mr. Sawyer here if Cap's ready." After a couple seconds of silence, he said, "All right. We'll be right over." He turned to Phil and said, "Follow me, Mr. Sawyer," then led him down a long hallway with dirty, olive-drab walls. "You must have some pull around here. Captain Bateman wants to see you personally. Being a VIP always helps in a dive like this."

Phil didn't answer, as he was sure the officer couldn't possibly expect him to make any conversation at such a moment.

At the end of the corridor was an old, gray door, with thick metal blinds covering the glass. It reminded Phil of a janitor's closet, but the stick-on letters on the door read, "Captain Bud Bateman"; the letters in about as good a condition as the rest of the door.

Officer Johnson lightly tapped on the door twice.

"Enter!" a voice said from the other side.

"What's up, Kirk?" asked a young guard when they walked through the door.

"Not much," Johnson answered. "Just got a drop-off for Cap."

"I'll take it from here," he said, rising from the desk and waving Phil forward. "He's waiting on you, Mr. Sawyer," the guard continued. He knocked hard on the captain's door, then opened it without waiting for an answer or an invite.

A small-framed man with a voice much softer than Phil would have expected from a police captain stood from behind his desk and reached out his hand. It took what seemed all of Phil's energy to meet it with his own.

"I'm Captain Bateman," he said, motioning for the guard to excuse himself. "Sounds like you've got yourself in one helluva mess, Doctor. You've got the best lawyer in town, though, and that should help." He paused for a minute and lit an unfiltered Pall Mall. He took two puffs and held the pack out toward Phil.

Phil said nothing and could only shake his head from side to side. He had never been a smoker anyway, and as dry as his mouth was at that moment, he almost gagged at the thought of it.

"Cola maybe?"

"Please," Phil answered. "Thank you."

Captain Bateman pulled a Coke from a small fridge, just like the one Phil had kept in his dorm room years earlier. He popped it open and handed it to Phil, then allowed him to take several swigs from it before continuing, "I've known Arthur about fifteen years. He's a damn good man and a fine attorney," the captain said, drawing in a deep drag of nicotine. "If he says you're good people, I've got no reason to question it. Just seems like you took a long walk off a short pier, so to speak," he said calmly.

Phil couldn't do anything but nod his head in agreement. His shoulders slumped, and his mind swirled with so many confused thoughts that he couldn't pinpoint just one to come up with a reasonable, sensible answer.

"My guess is you'll spend the next couple days with us, till you can get before a judge for your bond hearing. It's not the Hilton, but I'll try to make your stay as safe and pleasant as possible, considering the circumstances."

Phil lifted his tired, aching head to study the small man in front of him. The captain was probably in his late forties, a small man with small hands, light brown hair, and a kind face. *He doesn't belong in this hellhole either,* Phil thought. "What would draw someone to this profession anyway?" Phil thought, unfortunately aloud.

"Well, I s'pose one could ask the same of a man who operates on limbs that are hanging on by a thread," the captain answered, wearing a weak smile.

"I-I'm sorry," Phil stuttered. "This whole thing… It's just too much, a real shock. I…" The tears began to fall again, and his composure was lost. He felt the pain surge through his knuckles as he tightly gripped the arms of the metal chair, trying desperately not to pass out.

* * * * *

When he opened his eyes again, an older black woman was holding a cold washcloth against his forehead and fanning him with the daily newspaper. "Mr. Sawyer," she said calmly, in a deep, Southern accent, "don't try to sit up yet. You're still weak." She placed a small, airline-type pillow under his head and looked down at him with the sympathetic eyes of a grandmother.

Phil's mind began to clear, and he rested on his elbows before lifting himself back into the chair. "Thank you," he said to the woman who was dressed in a nurse's uniform, complete with an old-style, folded cap.

She smiled at him. "Just doin' what they pay me for, at least for the next six months. Then I'll be retired." She looked pleased with that thought as she grinned over at Captain Bateman. "I'll be on my way. Almost time to pass out the meds. Let me know if this one falls out again. Jail can be quite a shock, 'specially to those who don't seem to belong here." She then sashayed out of the room like a teenager.

"Won't ever find a replacement for that one," Bateman said to himself as he thumped a pencil on his desk. He rose from his chair and motioned toward the door. "You'll have a cell all to yourself for the weekend, but that's about the best I can do. Nothing luxurious about this place. You've just gotta take any little breaks you get and learn to appreciate them."

Phil knew he was talking about later on, when he was confined to a real prison, but he nodded in appreciation. He couldn't talk anymore, for he had said all that his body would allow.

"I'll send you with my assistant, Scott. You don't wanna be seen entering the pod with me, as the others don't like anybody who comes in here with some kinda clout. You won't have to deal with any of them though. I'll have your tray sent to the cell. They'll just think you're a dangerous criminal, and that's not a bad reputation in a place like this," he said, forcing a laugh to soften the blow of the situation.

Scott led Phil into a storage room and told him to stand at the counter. "Any personal effects other than your clothes?" he asked bluntly.

"No," Phil answered.

Scott looked him up and down. "You're pretty tall. We'll get you a large jumpsuit. We don't do alterations around here, so it'll be a little baggy and won't fit like an Armani. Shoe size?"

"Twelve and a half."

"No half-sizes. Here's a thirteen," he said, with all the compassion of a bowling alley shoe rental clerk. Scott handed over a pair of stained orange coveralls and some plastic flip-flops that had seen better days.

Phil cringed when he saw the crudely stenciled black letters on the back of the jumpsuit: "DOC."

As if reading his thoughts, Scott clarified, "Department of Corrections." He then picked up a paper grocery sack and stuffed some items in it: a small bar of generic soap, a roll of toilet paper, a disposable toothbrush, a trial-sized tube of toothpaste, two thin gray sheets that had once been white, and an itchy wool blanket with several nickel-sized holes in it. "You can keep your own underwear and socks, but that's it," he said. "Go ahead and strip down. If they leave you here more than two days, I'll let you shower and give you a disposable razor. Don't think you will though. We'll hafta play it by ear."

Phil went through the motions of changing clothes. As he slipped his left leg into the ugly, well-worn jumpsuit, he suddenly and completely realized the seriousness of his situation. His life was forever changed as he stepped out of his own clothes and old life and into the official attire of one owned by the Department of Corrections.

"You'll be in B Pod, Cell 31," Scott said, as though Phil knew what the hell that meant.

They walked through two sally ports and down a maze of hallways, until he pulled out a key big enough to unlock the Bastille. The metal door led to a large room with televisions on each end and tables with affixed benches. The lights were dim, and there was no sign of movement, since it was around 5:00 in the morning.

Scott made no attempt to silence his footsteps on the metal stairs as he led Phil up two flights, to an orange door with "31" stenciled on it. He motioned toward a glassed-in control room, and the door buzzed, giving them access. "Welcome home," Scott said as he handed over the brown sack.

Phil stepped inside his cell, grateful to finally be alone. He looked around at the steel toilet, the small steel desk with an attached stool, and the metal-framed twin bunk, with a mattress no thicker than a grilled cheese sandwich. He put the two ill-fitting flat sheets on the mattress but decided against the blanket; it looked horribly unsanitary and uncomfortable, and he wasn't that desperate yet. Grateful that they allowed him to keep his own socks, he slipped out of the rubber shower shoes and lay on his back on the bottom bunk.

The skinny, tall window was pelted with rain that was coming down in sheets. As the downpour tried to lullaby him to sleep, Phil wondered about Janet and Charlie. He knew they were frantic and were doing everything they could for him. Unfortunately, all he could do for himself was lay there and wait on a steel bed, held prisoner by bars and his own troubled thoughts.

CHAPTER 8

Charlie twisted and turned in his bed, sick with worry.
Janet also lay awake in their bed. Finally she said, "Honey, we have to get some sleep. We'll be of no help to Phil if we're exhausted."

"I know," Charlie answered. "My body and head just won't let me."

Janet got up and grabbed two glasses of water and a bottle of Tylenol PM. She turned the bathroom light on and read the label, then poured out the regular dose plus one extra tablet for each of them. It was rare for either of them to even take an aspirin, but this situation demanded attention. Thanks to the medication and the slight overdose, they got three hours of hard sleep before the phone rang.

"We have to get busy," Arthur said on the other end, his voice as weary as theirs. "Can you meet me at the diner on Juniper and Fifth in about forty-five minutes?"

"Not a problem," Charlie answered, still drunk with sleepiness. "We'll be there."

* * * * *

The three stared at menus for what seemed like hours, until the waitress returned. They ordered the morning special, then sat silently, as if they were waiting on someone else to show up and tell them all what to do.

"They'll perform the autopsy today at the medical examiner's office," Arthur said. "Just a formality, so they don't get caught with their pants down in court. They've been screwed too many times, and they know better. Janet, have you found any of her relatives yet? We'll have to release the body to a funeral home today."

"It's odd, but I've found nothing except the letter from the little sister, and I don't even know if Lara bothered to answer it. I figure we can let Central Time catch up with us and call in a couple hours. That's about our only lead right now."

"Okay. I'm headed over to the police station to see what they can run up on her," Arthur answered. "Here's my number," he said, handing her a card with his cell on it, just as the waitress returned with their food.

"Can we visit Phil?" Charlie asked, feeling as though his friend would feel betrayed if he didn't.

"Yeah, probably," Arthur answered, "but he really needs you working on the outside. I'll see him later today. You two just find some family and a funeral home."

"Okay. Sounds good."

After they quickly devoured their breakfast, Arthur reached for the bill and lightly tugged it from Charlie's grasp. "Allow me," he answered. "I have a feeling we'll be having many more meals together."

CHAPTER 9

"**B**edford Group Home. Helga Schmidt speaking," the woman said, with a strong German accent. Janet immediately pictured her as a short, chubby, older woman with a checkered apron around her waist and a forceful but kind demeanor. "Can I help you?"

"Good morning Ms. Schmidt," Janet said as politely as possible, wondering how she should begin such an awkward conversation. "Um, my name is Janet Evans, and I live in Los Angeles. Unfortunately, I have some bad news for one of the young girls who lives in your home."

"Oh dear," Helga said with concern. "Do tell me, which of my girls is it?"

"Lilly," Janet answered, realizing for the first time that she didn't even know her last name.

"Oh? Go on."

"Actually, I'm afraid I'm calling to let you know her sister has died. I found a letter from Lilly, with the home's return address, so I thought we should give you a call. I only knew Lilly's sister and not the family, but I'm sure this will come as a blow for the girl. My husband and I are willing to purchase a plane ticket for her to fly out for the funeral, and she is even welcome to stay with us for a while. I just really don't know how to handle all this." Janet was then quiet for a minute as she realized the only response was a prolonged silence on the other end of the line. "Ms. Schmidt? Are you still there?"

"Yes," she answered cautiously, "but you must have the wrong girl."

"Are you sure? I read a letter with your return address. Do you have a Lilly at your home?"

"Yes, but Lilly doesn't have a sister."

"She doesn't?"

"I really cannot share much," Ms. Schmidt answered. "Her information is confidential, as per state laws. Surely you understand."

"Yes, ma'am," Janet said, growing increasingly confused. "But the letter was from Lilly at your home. Maybe the deceased was a cousin or an aunt. I only jumped to the conclusion that she was her sister. The letter mentions that the girl's father is in prison."

After another prolonged silence, Helga said, "Yes, he is. Very sad situation, I'm afraid."

Janet's mind raced, as she was desperate to find some relatives. "I realize you don't know me, and I know I'm being rather pushy. It's just that we are desperate to find some relatives of the woman who died. At this point, Lilly is the only name we know. I could fly out today with some photos, if that would be permitted. We need to plan a funeral, and I would hate to bury her without her family even knowing."

"I guess I can understand that," Helga said sadly. She wasn't sure why she even believed the woman on the phone, but she could sense the sincere desperation in her voice. "You can fly into Norfolk Airport. We're about twenty minutes from there, and you have the address. If you can catch a cab to us, I'll have one of the staff members take you back to the airport after your visit."

"Oh my goodness! Thank you, Ms. Schmidt! Thank you so much. I'll call you as soon as I nail down the flight information."

Janet quietly hung up the phone in disbelief that she was going to be flying out to Nebraska that very day, especially without even having consulted Charlie first. She was trying to plot out some sort of strategy of how to discuss it with him when he walked up behind her.

"So you're off to Nebraska, huh?" he asked, obviously having overheard her conversation.

"Oh. Well, yeah. I just—"

He smiled and held a hand up to stop her unnecessary explanation and apology. "Thanks for doing this for Phil. Just when I think there isn't any way I could love you more, you go and do something to prove me wrong."

Janet smiled and melted into her husband's arms, flattered by the compliment. The two then embraced for a long time, not even really aware they were doing so.

* * * * *

It was 9:30 a.m. when Janet arranged a noon flight, unpleasantly amazed by how high the rates were hiked for someone purchasing a ticket at the last moment. "Unbelievable," she grumbled as she hung up. "It's skyway robbery."

Charlie laughed at her pun, then said calmly, "We've got the money, honey. Don't sweat it."

"Oh, I know. It's just appalling."

The departure time gave her just enough time to get back to Phil's to gather up some photos. She and Charlie walked around the house as though they were in a ghost town, a place that would never again see life. Janet found herself almost disappointed that she wouldn't have to tolerate Lara's gloating and her shallow conversations ever again. *At least then we'd still have Phil. Now, we may never even see him as a free man again.*

Charlie's cell phone rang. "Arthur," he said to Janet, then took the call.

"We haven't found out much, unfortunately. The State of Nevada won't release the Social Security number from the marriage license without a court order. I'm workin' on that. Her maiden name, Walden, had to be an alias, because it's not registered anywhere. I'm sure the Social from Nevada is false as well.

I'll get the fingerprints from the autopsy as soon as the prick faxes them over. God, he's a power-hungry bastard. We have determined that her Yale diploma is a forgery—a damn good one but a forgery just the same. Apparently, Little Miss Lara was more than just a self-centered bitch."

"So she was a fake?" Charlie said.

"Imagine that," Janet sarcastically mumbled under her breath. "And she always seemed so genuine and down-to-Earth to me." She rolled her eyes.

"Unbelievable," Charlie said, with a growing fury that Janet was not accustomed to. "Look, my wife's headed out to Nebraska today to meet with that group home about the letter she found. That should help a great deal. After I drop her at the airport and see her off, I'll head back to Phil's. Maybe you can meet me there."

"Good idea. It's no longer taped off as an official crime scene, since the forensics dogs have already done all their sniffing. We can dig around a bit. We're bound to find some more clues. The more we obtain on this gold-digger, the better off Phil will be. I'll stop by the jail after I leave the precinct. I'll see you in about three hours."

CHAPTER 10

Janet packed a small carryon, just in case she had to stay overnight. This whole situation was so unpredictable that she wasn't sure what would happen next. "Charlie," she said, wrinkling her forehead in thought, "we need to call our jobs and take a week off. This is probably gonna get uglier before it gets better. Everyone will just have to make do."

"Yeah, I already thought of that," he answered. "Believe it or not, Dr. Harper is being exceptionally cooperative. You never know how people will act in situations like these. The press is already leaking it."

"Yeah, I saw that," Janet said. "There shouldn't be a problem getting a sub for my class."

With a few snapshots of Lara carefully stored between the pages of a novel, she was ready for the drive to the airport. She placed Lilly's letter in her purse, where it seemed safer. "No need to walk me to security," she said as she kissed Charlie on the cheek. "I'm a big girl now."

Charlie knew she had a distinct fear of flying, but he kept that under his belt. He refused to make his very intelligent, very independent wife feel like a child by walking her through it all.

"I have an e-ticket, so I'll just walk to the gate. I'll call you from the airport when I land. Check around, but I think Lanier Funeral home is the nicest in town."

"I will," Charlie answered sadly. "The medical examiner's office will be ready to move her along. It's pretty quick turnaround on those cold metal tables."

"For heaven's sake, Charlie," Janet said, horrified. "What in the world is the matter with you?"

"I'm sorry. Really," he answered, hanging his head. "I'm just not myself. I feel like I've been living a nightmare for the past twenty-four hours. Hell, do you realize it hasn't even been twenty-four hours yet? Jesus. I'll never make it through this. Poor Phil."

A horn blared behind them, signaling that they were holding up the crowded unloading zone.

Janet took her cue and leaned over to him. "I love you, Charlie Evans. Don't go fallin' apart on us now. We need you, Doc."

"I love you, too, sweetheart. For God's sake, don't go getting in over your head. We can only do so much, and we've gotta leave some of it to the experts."

A second beep of the horn urged Janet to reach for the door handle and slowly get out.

Charlie sat in the car until she was out of sight, then pulled away slowly.

Never in his life had he imagined such a horrible thing might happen. His wife was about to get on a plane to fly to God-only-knew-where, to confront God-only-knew-whom. He turned the radio to an oldies station, keeping the volume low, then drove back to Phil's house. He was not sure what he would accomplish there. All he knew was that if he couldn't be with his friend, Phil's house would be the closest place to him.

*   *   *   *   *

Janet felt the perspiration forming on her forehead as she placed her bag in the overhead compartment. She pulled a Kleenex from her jacket pocket and dabbed lightly at her face, knowing that the moisture would return as quickly as she wiped it away. She found her seat next to the window and cursed herself for not specifically requesting an aisle seat; she detested watching the ground disappear below the plane, and flying through the clouds made her feel as though she was on her way to Heaven far sooner than she was ready to make the trip.

Janet situated herself in the seat and adjusted her seatbelt. It was the time between boarding and taking off that made her the most nervous, and it seemed to last an eternity. In an effort to distract herself, she pulled the letter from her purse and studied it intently. It broke her heart to read that letter in a child's hand, begging to go out for ice cream, as if something so simple would somehow make everything right again. She wiped the tissue across her face again, but this time it was tears she brushed aside.

An extremely overweight businessman wedged his way into the seat next to hers without speaking a word. Janet was glad to sit next to someone who obviously had no desire to make conversation. His face was sweaty from his walk through the airport and his squeeze through the aisle, his worn briefcase bulging at the edges, just as his shirt was. He heaved a big sigh of relief as he squished his large body between the two armrests.

Slowly and carefully, Janet refolded the letter and put it safely in her purse. She picked up a magazine from the seat pocket in front of her and thumbed through it absentmindedly.

A few minutes later, the captain announced their takeoff and confirmed that the weather was clear in both Los Angeles and in Norfolk. Headwinds were also working in their favor, so he was certain their flight would suffer no delays.

Pilots always sound so pleasant and confident. Come to think of it, they're pretty handsome too, Janet thought. *Maybe I should take my cue from them. They've flown much more than I have. Then again, pilots have crashed much more than I have too,* she imagined with a shudder. As they taxied down the runway, she laid her head back and shut her eyes. The engine revved, signaling takeoff.

It was a clear day, and Janet wished her thoughts mirrored the beautiful, calm weather outdoors. She played through her mind the perceived events of the day, knowing in advance that they would not play out that way. She ordered two beers from the flight attendant, fearing that she might not have the opportunity again. Between the day Janet had before her and the flight itself, she felt justified in drinking a little liquid courage, and she could always just buy some mints at the airport on her way out.

The flight arrived on time, as promised. As Janet exited the plane, she felt an insecurity she had never felt before. She had been around children all her life, and she loved them all. She had even dedicated her profession to them, but she was about to show photos to some poor, abandoned child, an abandoned little girl who was about to be abandoned yet again. She wasn't sure she could actually go through with it. She was an educator, not a social worker, and much to many people's dismay, there was quite a difference between the two.

Janet hadn't eaten on the plane because of the growing knot in her stomach, so she stopped at a small restaurant in the airport and had a Philly cheese steak and a soda. She stopped at a newsstand and picked up a roll of peppermint Certs to eliminate the beer and peppers from her breath. Then, hoping to be loved by a child as much as Charlie's bribes allowed him to, she purchased a pack of sugar-free gum and a tan teddy bear with a large red bow around its neck. *Maybe this will soften the blow.*

She was grateful that she'd grabbed a heavier coat than she was used to, as the weather was quite a bit chillier there. She stepped out onto the sidewalk to hail a cab and was pleased that it only took only a couple minutes for one to stop for her. Within a minute, they were on their way to the Bedford Home.

Nebraska, the Cornhusker State, she thought to herself. She watched intently as they passed rolling farmland and grazing cattle. It was so different from Los Angeles, and she wished her students could see the diversity of the United States. The temperature was a frigid twenty-two, as opposed to the eighty-two she had left behind. The palm trees and beaches were missing, but there was a vast array of panoramic landscapes to take their place. It wasn't necessarily better and definitely wasn't worse, but it was different.

As Ms. Schmidt had promised, the ride took around twenty minutes. The driver slowed and finally came to a stop in front of an older gray house that reminded Janet of a tenement. It was desperately in need of repair, but Ms. Schmidt's smile didn't reflect any embarrassment as walked out onto the front porch and flagged Janet to come in.

Janet paid the driver and stepped out into the cold with a shiver, holding her bag in hand.

"Hello there, my dear," Ms. Schmidt said, going for a light hug instead of a handshake. "I'm Helga, and you must be Janet."

"Yes, ma'am," Janet said. "Thank you for seeing me."

"Dear, you must come inside right away. I'm sure your body is not used to this type of weather."

"Actually," Janet said with a smile and then a laugh, "I was thinking the same thing."

Helga was much as she expected. She was probably in her mid-sixties and fairly overweight, just enough to make her fluffy and loveable. Janet liked her immediately.

To Janet's relief, the inside of the house was much better than the outside. A fire was crackling in the fireplace in the large den, which was filled with shelves of children's books and art supplies. There were two large, comfortable-looking couches and an oversized square coffee table that was obviously used for crafts and boardgames.

"Come into the kitchen," Helga invited, taking her hand. "I made a pot of coffee and some pastries for us. Unfortunately, you missed lunch."

"Oh, that smells delicious," Janet answered as Helga politely took her coat.

The two sat and sipped their coffee, and although Janet was still full from her sandwich, she couldn't resist one of the homemade pastries.

"The children are at the library, watching a puppet show. They should be back within the next few minutes. I'm glad I had a chance to meet with you first." Helga wiped her hands on a wash towel and stood up to refill their coffee cups. "Lilly is a beautiful child but also a very sad little girl. She is ten and has been with us for almost eight months now. Her father has been in prison for eight years, almost her whole life. I was told her mother never wanted her and left her with grandparents. The grandfather died, and the grandmother was an alcoholic, so she eventually lost custody of Lilly to the State. She has since died as well. I double-checked our records, and as far as we know, she has no siblings."

"Oh my goodness. How tragic," Janet said. "I can't imagine her recognizing a photo then. How long has she been in State custody?"

"For almost five years now."

The front door opened, and a laughing, excited group shuffled in.

"Throw your mittens and hats in the basket by the door!" Helga instructed in her thick German accent. "Excuse me, Ms. Janet. I'll be right back."

Janet listened as Helga made her way into the living room and asked the children about the puppet show. They all spoke at once, and she listened intently as they told her about it, laughing with them as they tried to imitate the voices of the farm animals.

"I see a good time was had by all," she said with a giggle. "Go on upstairs to rest or read for an hour, and then we'll play some boardgames. I'm sorry, but I feel it necessary for me to be the shoe today in Monopoly."

"Oh, Ms. Helga," one little girl said, "You're always the shoe."

"And I intend to continue that tradition until one of you little ones can beat me," she said, as seriously as she could. "Now shoo, all of you but Lilly. Can you come with me dear? You have a visitor who'd like to see you."

Janet didn't hear Lilly respond, but she did catch the familiar sound of childlike footsteps heading toward the kitchen.

Janet placed her hand over her mouth, so as to prevent her gasp from being heard when the girl walked in. Lilly was a tremendously beautiful child and very tiny for her age. She had blonde hair and huge blue eyes, like a deer's, caught in the headlights; Janet could so clearly see the pain in them that she could hardly open her mouth to speak. She wanted to hold the little girl, to embrace her and make her feel loved, for she could see right away that Lilly was a bruised flower desperately in need of someone to really care for her.

"Have a seat, Lilly," Helga said kindly as she pulled a chair from under the table. "This is Ms. Evans, and she's here to talk to you. Do you mind if I stay with you?"

"No, ma'am," Lilly answered, barely audible.

"Hi, Lilly. You can just call me 'Janet.' You have a nice place here. I live in Los Angeles, and we don't get to use our fireplace very often. I envy you, especially because you get to eat Ms. Helga's good cooking!"

Lilly giggled but never looked up at Janet.

"I have a couple pictures I'd like you to look at, to see if you recognize who it is. Would that be okay?"

She nodded her tiny head and brushed a few runaway wisps of hair behind her ears.

Janet opened the novel, pulled out the photographs, and laid them across the table.

Lilly jumped out of her chair and stood up, drinking in every detail of the pictures. "My Laraleen!" she said excitedly. "Ms. Helga, that's my Laraleen. Is she here? Is she coming to get me?"

Janet felt a lump in her throat, and she could tell the same lump had risen in Helga's. "No, honey. I'm afraid she's not," Janet said. "Is she your friend?"

Lilly looked confused at first, then almost scared. "How do you know my Laraleen, and why did she give you these pictures and not me?"

"I saw her a lot in Los Angeles. I ate supper at her house sometimes," Janet said, carefully considering every word.

"Does she have a big house now, so I can live with her?"

Lilly sounded so hopeful that Janet feared she would lose herself to her own tears before she could finish. "Ms. Helga and I need to know how you know Laraleen first, okay?"

Lilly looked at her suspiciously and began toying nervously with the buttons on her shirt. "It's a big secret. Laraleen will be very angry if I tell you, even if I tell Ms. Helga."

"You can trust us, Lilly," Helga answered. "We would never do anything to hurt you."

Tears quickly filled the little girl's blue eyes and then rolled down her small cheeks and neck before she wiped them away. "So she's really not coming to get me?" she asked, already knowing the answer to her question.

"Is she your cousin or your aunt?" Janet asked.

Lilly wiped both of her hands across her eyes, as if to pull herself together. "No, ma'am, she ain't. She's…my mommy."

The three sat in total silence for only a second; Janet knew she had to speak before the others could hear her heart beating. "Your mommy?" she questioned. "But you call her 'Laraleen'."

"She made me," the girl calmly explained. "She didn't want a daughter, so I have to pretend to be something else to her. Daddy stole lotsa money, and Mommy took it all to Los Angeles. She was gonna make lots more money from it, then let me come and live with her. I found her address in Ms. Helga's files one day." She bit her lip and looked at her caretaker. "I'm sorry I was sneaking around. I'm real sorry about that. I just wanted to write my mommy. She never wrote me back though. I just figured she didn't have a nice enough house yet. She said some bad things about where we lived, but she's gonna be rich." Lilly was calmer now. Her tears had dried, and she looked Janet squarely in the face and bravely asked, "You can tell me, ma'am… I mean, if she ain't comin' back."

"Honey," Helga interjected, "your mommy died last night. I am so very sorry for you."

Lilly looked straight ahead, as if she had known all along that it would eventually end that way.

"Lilly, I came here because I thought you might like to go back with me to the funeral, if Ms. Helga can work it out."

"Can I go read now?" the girl asked.

Helga nodded, and after Lilly slowly walked away, she and Janet sat in silence for what seemed an eternity.

Helga wrung her hands, and tears streamed so forcefully down her cheeks that Janet was afraid she might have a heart attack. "Oh, sweet Jesus," she said, sobbing. "How much can a child bear? God bless her. God bless her poor little soul."

Janet opened her mouth slowly, making sure to choose her words carefully, for her heart ached just as Helga's did. "I-I just can't believe this, Ms. Schmidt. I never dreamt… Gosh, I never dreamt I'd have to say anything that would hurt such a beautiful child."

"No need to apologize. All we can do is the best for her in the here and now."

"I don't know where to go from here," Janet said sadly. "Should we take her to the funeral? Will the State even release her into my temporary custody? My husband is a doctor, and I am a teacher. We can verify all the information."

Helga looked down at her soft, wrinkled hands and folded them, as if in prayer. "I think you should talk to her again. If she truly wants to go, I will make it possible. God blessed me with a sixth sense for good people, and I know you and your husband must be, lest you wouldn't be here at all."

Janet slowly climbed the stairs that led to the girls' bedrooms. She read the crayoned sign that said, "Lilly's Room," and she tapped lightly on the door. When she didn't hear an answer, she cracked it open slightly and whispered quietly, "Can I come in? It will only be for a moment."

"Yes, ma'am," Lilly whispered back, her voice a little deeper from crying.

"I forgot about something I found at the airport. I thought you might like it." Janet pulled the bear out of the bag and watched Lilly's eyes light up.

"Is that for me?" she asked cautiously, as though she was afraid to hope for the best.

"Absolutely. He was sitting there when I bought some mints, and I thought he looked like he needs a mommy. Would you like to take care of him, because I don't think I'll have the time?"

"Yes, ma'am," she said, sadness still reigning in her voice. "I would love that."

"Well, you know, there's one problem," Janet said, looking down at the bed. "This bear doesn't even have a name."

"What about 'Teddy'?" she asked. "Would that be all right?"

"Well, since you're his mom now, I guess you can call him anything you want."

Lilly seemed pleased. She pulled the bear close to her small body, as if he was all she had left in the world; Janet realized that maybe he was.

"I almost forgot," Janet said, reaching in her pocket. "Do you like chewing gum?"

"Sure," she answered, "but I have to check with Ms. Helga first. It gives you cavities, ya know."

"Yes, that's true for most bubblegum and candy," Janet answered seriously, "but that's why I bought sugar-free." She handed it to Lilly. "You'd better check with Ms. Helga anyway."

Lilly looked deep into Janet's eyes, something Janet had never seen a child do before. She then asked, "Did you get to see Laraleen, my mommy, very often?"

"Well, not very much, but sometimes we went to eat at her and her husband's house."

"Huh? She wasn't married," Lilly said firmly.

"She actually was, honey, to a very nice man. He's a doctor."

"Uh-uh. My mommy was married to my father. Grandma said she only married him so he'd give her the money he stole. Then he had to go to jail by himself."

Surely they divorced somewhere along the line, Janet thought, *but... Oh my God! If they didn't, that made Lara a bigamist. Surely that will help Phil in court. Best of all, the marriage* would be a matter of public record, something she could easily verify.

"Do you think you might want to go to the funeral?" Janet asked kindly. "You don't have to if you don't want to."

Lilly held her bear close to her chest and thought for only a moment. "Will you go with me? It might be scary, since I've never been to one before. When my grandmother died, the State said I was too young."

Janet cleared her throat, choking back the tears that threatened so desperately to form. "Yes, Lilly, I'll go with you. I promise you won't be alone. You'll also be with my husband. His name is Charlie, and he's a doctor. You'll like him. He always carries surprises for children. You just have to pick the right pocket."

Lilly seemed pleased. "I ain't never flown either," she said.

"Oh, it's lots of fun," Janet lied. "You can pick any soft drink you want, and they feed you lunch right on the plane. The cars and houses look as small as ants, and you get to fly right through the clouds."

"Do you think we'll see my mom? I mean, now that she's in Heaven and all."

The thought of Lara strolling arrogantly across the golden streets was almost too stomach-turning for Janet to bear, but she said, "We won't go up that far, but you'll feel close to her."

"When can we leave?" the girl blurted out, having made up her mind.

"I'm gonna stay at a hotel in town to give you a little time to pack and get ready to go. I'll pick you up in the morning. And don't forget Teddy. He'll probably be afraid without you now."

Lilly smiled a big, beautiful grin that was so much like her mother's, except that there was nothing fake or pretentious about it.

Thank you, Lord, for keeping this precious child away from that evil woman, Janet prayed silently.

"What else should I bring?" Lilly asked.

"Well, it's pretty warm where we're going, so you won't need a winter coat like here. I'm sure Helga will help you pack. I need to leave now, but I'll see you in the morning."

Lilly wrapped her tiny arms around Janet's neck and hugged her with a force that surprised her.

Helga was occupied in the kitchen, preparing the evening meal for a bunch of hungry little mouths. Her face was stained with tears, and Janet couldn't help but hug her and hold her close.

"So much tragedy in this world, and so much of it impacts our little ones," Helga said, her accent even stronger from the overwhelming emotion.

"She wants to go with me, if you can arrange it. I'm going to stay in town for the night, and I'd like to pick her up in the morning. I'll go ahead and schedule the flights. We'll probably be gone for a couple days, if that will be okay."

"Yes, as long as you leave me with phone numbers where you can be reached."

"I fully understand. Do you have any suggestions as to where I can stay tonight?"

"You are welcome to sleep here, dear."

"I think it's best for Lilly to have some time for all this to sink in. Besides, I have several phone calls to make."

"This isn't Los Angeles," she said, laughing softly, "but there are two motels about five miles away—run-of-the-mill places, clean but not fancy. If you like, you could look for a place closer to the airport, where there are more restaurants and the like."

"I'd like to stay close. I'm not sure we can get a flight out first thing in the morning, so I might snoop around town a bit. I don't get to travel much. Did her mother grow up around here?"

"Yes, though I never knew her. Why are you so interested in her anyway?"

"It's a long story, Helga, and too sad to share right now. Trust me. Do you have Lara's mother's latest address?"

"I guess I can round it up, but this must stay between you and me, ya hear?"

"Understood. Thank you so much."

CHAPTER 11

After finding the address for Janet, Helga asked the maintenance man to drive Janet over to the local hotels. "The first one ain't nothin' fancy," he said, "but they're pretty clean and within walkin' distance of a nice little diner. They got a meatloaf to die for."

"Just drop me off at that one then," Janet said. "Thanks for the lift." She offered him a tip, but he turned it down.

"Ms. Helga'd have my hide!" he said.

"Well, thanks anyway." Janet hopped out, with her purse and carryon. She walked up to the front desk, happy to see a friendly face not marred by all that had happened.

"Can I help you?" the young girl asked. "My name is Sammi." She looked all of sixteen but had a thin gold wedding ring on her left ring finger. Her fingernails were bitten down to the quick, as if she had far more worries than someone her age should have had to deal with.

"Yes, you can." Janet smiled. "I need a single room for one night."

"Okay. That'll be $18 even."

"Eighteen?" Janet asked, shocked. Never in her life had she encountered such affordable overnight lodging. She wasn't sure what she would find, but she was pleasantly surprised. She took her key, rather than a more modern keycard, and headed off to her assigned room.

The room was clean, and it smelled of Pledge, bathroom cleaner, and floral air freshener. The drapes and bedspread were outdated but clean, and the bed was turned back. The phone had a sign taped to it to announce that it would not make long-distance calls, so she was thankful she had her cell phone.

Janet wondered where to find Charlie and decided to try Phil's first. She looked at her watch for the first time of the day and realized that it was 6:00, 7:00 in L.A. "Charlie's probably frantic," she said to herself as she waited for him to pick up.

"Damn, Janet," he said, clearly upset. "I've been worried to death."

It wasn't like him to curse at her, but she knew he wasn't himself. The whole situation had him on edge, just as on edge as Janet was. "I'm really sorry, honey," she said, "but I've had quite an enlightening day."

"Me too," he answered. Before he listened to her update, he hurried out with his own, "That lady—and I use the term loosely—has more clothes in her closet than Neiman Marcus, with the tags still on them. Some of them cost more than a nice used car. Two or three more years of this shopaholic nonsense woulda sent poor Phil to bankruptcy court. Oh, and did I mention the jewelry?"

"No, Charlie, but it doesn't surprise me. Look, I need you to listen. Is Arthur there yet?"

"Yeah. He just walked in from the jail. Why?"

"Put him on the extension, I'm sure he'll wanna hear this too."

A second later, Arthur picked up. "Go ahead. Shoot," he said.

"You'll never believe this," Janet said. "I met Helga, the woman in charge of the group home, and she introduced me to little Lilly. I swear, the child is so beautiful that she took my breath away. She's sweet, too, but she's been through so much pain in her lifetime that my heart aches when I think about it." Arthur's impatient sigh urged Janet to hurry on with the story. "Well, I showed her the pictures of Lara, and—believe it or not—she is…or rather, was Lilly's mother!" Janet could hear their surprise but quickly continued before they had a chance to ask any questions. "She made Lilly promise not to tell anyone because she didn't want a daughter, but she always told her that if she got rich enough, she would return for her. She told the girl to pretend to be just a relative and not her daughter."

"Oh my God." Charlie gasped. "How much crueler can you get?"

"Wait. There's more."

"I don't know that I can take much more," Arthur said.

"Lara married Lilly's father so he would give her a load of cash, obviously dirty, because he's doing time in the state pen. She left Nebraska with the money to, as Lilly put it, 'make lots more with it.' As far as Lilly knows, the marriage is still valid, making Lara a bigamist, among other things. That should be easy to verify, right?"

"Yeah, it should," Arthur answered. "The Yale diploma was a forgery, so there's no telling what other bones are gonna come outta this closet before it's over."

"Well, I'm near where Lara's mother lived. She's deceased now, along with the rest of Lilly's relatives. I'm obviously here for the night, so I'll ask around a little in the morning."

Charlie moaned. "Jesus, Janet. Haven't you found out enough? Just grab the next plane out."

"There's one thing we're forgetting about here," Arthur interjected. "If Lilly's father is in the state penitentiary, that means he's presumably still alive and well. There *is* another living relative."

"Oh hell," Charlie countered. "I didn't think of that. What should we do?"

"Well," Arthur answered, pausing for a moment to think it through, "he'll have to be notified. Depending on the crime and the sentence, some prisoners do allow inmates out to attend funerals. He will certainly have a say in the proceedings."

"Then it looks like I'll have to make a visit to the prison," Janet said, as casually as if she was making plans to go the mall.

"Like hell you will!" Charlie said defiantly, knowing all the while that Janet had her own mind and that it was already made up.

Ignoring him, Janet said, "I'll check on it first thing in the morning. I'm sure they have Sunday visitation, and Helga can help me to get in."

"He must not have cared too much for her," Arthur said, "considering that they didn't have any contact we're aware of. Try to get him to sign a letter to release her remains to us. The prison will have a notary."

"I'll do my best," Janet said, and they both knew she meant it. "Helga, the house mother, said she will give Lilly a pass to come home with me for the funeral."

"What?" Charlie asked, almost screaming into the phone. "Are you sure the kid can emotionally handle that?"

"She wants to come. I think... I feel it's only right."

"That'll be one more worry for the rest of us," Arthur answered.

"You know," Janet screamed into the phone, "you are two of the most insensitive assholes I've ever encountered. That little girl's going to be at her mother's funeral, and, Charlie, you sure as hell better have something special in your coat pockets. I'll let you know when our flight will arrive." With that, Janet hung up. She stifled a laugh as she thought of them standing there, dumbfounded, with their mouths agape and the receivers dangling from their hands. She really didn't care. She was tired and confused, and most of all, she was hungry.

Janet picked up the phone to dial the group home; she didn't want to make the call too late, so she put off dinner for a few more minutes.

Helga answered on the third ring, and Janet could tell by her voice that she was busy with some sort of house-mother chore.

"Hi, Helga. This is Janet Evans. Sorry to bother you, but our attorney just brought a very good point to my attention. Lilly's father is incarcerated, and that makes him a living relative. In order to arrange for the woman's funeral, it is imperative that I see him tomorrow."

"Oh, child," Helga answered, as if Janet was only a teenager. "He's in the state prison. That's no place for a young woman to go."

"I agree, but unfortunately, I am left with no choice. I need your help though. Can you write a letter on the group home letterhead, explaining the situation? Maybe that will help. You can fax it to the hotel."

"Oh my," Helga answered. "I guess I have to do what is necessary, but this situation is getting worse by the minute."

"I know, and I'm terribly sorry, but in order for us to go ahead with the burial, he'll have to legally release the body to us. What is his name?"

"Jeb Palmer. From what I hear, he isn't a very pleasant young man. He's one of those people who's always out for what he can get."

"Well, maybe that will play well for us," Janet answered before she hung up.

As much as Janet hated to, she called Charlie and Arthur back at Phil's house. She was still angry with them, but there was too much to do to remain pissed off.

Charlie answered. "Yes, dear?" he said, somewhat snappily.

"Hey, it's me again," Janet said, trying to contain her anger. "We need a death certificate faxed to the hotel as soon as possible. I'll need it to get into the prison in the morning. Can Arthur get Rudyard to do it on the spur of the moment?"

"There'll be a bit of a fight, but I'm sure he can do it. Listen, I'm sorry about before."

"It's okay. In the last two days, we've been unexpectedly thrown into the lions' den, and we're all bound to be a little testy. Get on that ASAP, and remember, Charlie Evans… I love you."

"I love you, too, and for God's sake, be careful."

CHAPTER 12

Phil Sawyer lay on his bed, looking up at the metal frame that made the top bunk of his cell. Fortunately for him, Captain Bateman had kept his word and left him without a cellmate. His breakfast was delivered via the slot in the cell door, but he'd left it uneaten. He did drink his milk and orange juice, right out of the miniature cartons, as if he was in elementary school. It only stayed down for a few minutes before he heaved it up in a milky-orange puddle in the toilet, leaving him more exhausted than before.

Phil's mind drifted off to Dr. Martin Rudyard and the autopsy. Even though the cause of death and the identification of the body were obvious, Martin would still go the whole nine yards. He shivered as he thought of his dead wife lying on the metal table where so many had been autopsied before: suicides, shooting victims, dirty degenerates from the streets, and HIV-infected drug users. He imagined her there, cold and naked, with her eyelids open, only enough to see a portion of her blue iris and the lower part of her dark pupil. Phil was a doctor, and his mind knew she couldn't feel anything, but the autopsy still seemed so degrading, so impersonal.

Phil had only seen a few autopsies throughout his medical training. Postmortem examination wasn't his field of expertise, but he had to witness them just the same. He found it strange that he was so bothered by the dead. He found them creepy and mysterious, almost as if they were always on the edge of coming to life again. He thought maybe that was why he chose to go into orthopedic surgery; rarely did he have to witness death in his line of work.

His mind flashed back to the autopsies he had witnessed. The procedures were all the same, albeit done on very different people. He couldn't help wondering what their lives had been like and who would be affected by their deaths. For Phil, the finality of death had always made it very hard to focus on just the medical aspect of it.

Phil pictured Lara there, zipped up in that dark, lonely body bag, waiting for her turn to be slaughtered for the sake of evidence. The traditional Y cut would be first. He was always amazed by the sharpness a scalpel could achieve; it cut easily through flesh, as if it were softened butter. They would cut from her clavicles to her sternum, then down to the pubic area. He secretly hoped Dr. Rudyard would place a cloth over her pubic hair and face, but that man had seen too many tragedies to give a damn what someone looked like in death. He would weigh her organs and inspect each one at great length, as though picking out a cantaloupe at the grocery store. It was totally unnecessary under the circumstances, but Rudyard had to cover his ass, especially on this case. He'd probably put them back in the open crevice of her splayed ribcage and sew her up from there. In the long run, it would save money with the cremation company the county contracted out to. He would note the small fingernail marks from Phil's well-manicured hands and photograph them. Phil was sure there wouldn't be any other abrasions, for he could only remember the feel of his nails digging into her neck before he allowed his hands to totally embrace her small fragile neck. He could almost read the autopsy now: *"Strangled with such force as to fracture the larynx, cricoid cartilage, and hyoid bone..."* His body shivered, and he reached for the frayed wool blanket and pulled it close to his chin and around his arms.

Phil's meeting with Arthur went as expected. His bond would most likely be posted on Monday. *Thank God money won't be an issue*, he thought. It had never meant much to him before, but he was grateful for it now.

Arthur wanted to go for a bench trial and take their chances with a judge instead of a jury. "You never know which way a jury will go," Arthur said. "At least a judge will understand being taken advantage of by a woman who's after her man's money."

"I-I don't think I want to know any more right now," Phil answered. "Tell me about Charlie. How is he?"

"Hanging in there but worried like hell about you. He'll make funeral arrangements. Do you have any requests? Is there anything special we need to do, anything she...might have wanted?"

"She loved this one silver, beaded dress—the only one she ever wore more than once. It's gaudy as hell, but she liked it a lot. Maybe they can bury her in that. Her hairstylist is in her address book. I don't know if she'll do it, but it's worth a try. Bright red lipstick and the biggest diamonds you can find. Bury her with them. I sure as hell don't want 'em. Hell, if the mortician steals them...well, good for him. He can consider it a tip."

CHAPTER 13

Charlie inhaled deeply and tugged at the waistband of his pants as he entered the funeral home. A family of grown children and what appeared to be their elderly mother were leaving with tear-stained faces, looking down and shaking their heads. One of the men had his arm around his mother to support her as she made her way to the car. They looked exhausted and were obviously overcome with grief.

Charlie felt odd and somewhat embarrassed to enter the funeral home under such strange circumstances, and he wished Janet was by his side. Unlike him, she always knew how to handle difficult situations in the most tactful manner. He saw a somber-faced man in a dark suit heading his way and thought seriously about turning around and walking out. Unfortunately, he was too late, caught by the salesman before he could get away.

"Good morning," the man said in that voice that clearly had to be practiced and learned from some special school. Not just anyone could pull off the woe-be-unto-you in such hushed, humble tones.

"Good morning," Charlie answered, trying his best to sound sad, to no avail. "I am here to make arrangements for a funeral."

"And the deceased?" the man questioned softly, patting Charlie's shoulder. "Where are they presently?"

"The medical examiner's office," Charlie said. "It's quite an unusual story. It's Lara Sawyer, Dr. Phil Sawyer's wife. I'm sure you have heard about it on the news."

"Ah yes," he answered. "Tragedy, tragedy."

"We are working to find relatives, but we've had little luck, with the exception of a small child in Nebraska, one none of us were even aware of." Charlie deliberately left out Jeb to save Phil from any further embarrassment. "My wife and I would like to take responsibility for the funeral, and the medical examiner has agreed for the body to be released to the funeral home of our choice."

"I see," he said, his brow furrowed as if he had lost someone of his own.

Wow. His psychology teacher really sucked, Charlie thought to himself, realizing that the Lurch-like man would only make the bereaved feel even more depressed.

"What type of funeral do you have in mind? We offer a wide array of services, of course."

"Yes," Charlie said, trying to hide his disdain, "I am sure you do. It's such an odd situation. I don't believe many friends will attend, if any, and as I said, there are really no known relatives. We were thinking a simple graveside service might be appropriate."

"Certainly. We can accommodate that. Do you have a minister to preside?"

"Actually, no. She was not a church-goer."

"I see," he said. "We can line up a minister for you, but you will need to decide on a denomination."

"My wife and I are Baptists. I'm sure no one will have objections to that."

The forlorn man quickly changed his tone and demeanor to business. In fact, the transition was so fast and abrupt that Charlie thought he might suddenly break into laughter. "Do you have clothing in mind? If not, we offer a wide variety of—"

"She had plenty of her own clothes and jewelry."

"Very well. Why don't we start in the casket room?" he suggested, standing and motioning for Charlie to follow him.

They walked into a large showroom filled with caskets of every color, some steel and some wooden. The whole place and his macabre host sent a shiver up Charlie's spine. The man, whom Charlie still didn't know by name, walked him slowly around, pointing out the best features of every coffin, as nonchalantly as if he was selling furniture. *God, I wonder if this guy works on commission,* Charlie wondered.

He deferred his glances as much as he could without looking completely disinterested. Finally, he spotted an oak casket with an ivory lining. He was sure it would be appropriate—not as showy as Lara would have preferred but suitable just the same. Charlie glanced at the price tag dangling down from it. It was rather uncouth, but he was glad he didn't have to ask Mr. Personality about the cost. His eyes almost bugged out at the "$7,800" in front of him, but it was still less expensive than some of the others around.

"That particular casket is in our mid-range price line. We have others around that price point as well, if you'd care to look."

"No, this is the one. It will be just fine."

"I see," the man answered, obviously disappointed that he would not make a more expensive sale. "If you'll just follow me into the office, we can itemize the billing."

Itemize the billing? Great. Here we go, Charlie thought, having heard plenty of horror stories of grieving people being screwed at funeral homes. He sat down at the desk as the mortician began tapping numbers on a calculator.

"Let's see," he said. "There are the basic services of the staff, our arrangement interview, which we just concluded, coordination of service plans, preparation for the remains… You do wish for an embalming, correct?"

"Of course we do, as well as a short viewing for anyone who might show up."

"Very well," he continued. "Embalming, dressing, cosmetizing, and grooming.

There is the use of our facility during visitation, along with available staff, the use of equipment and staff for graveside service, the transfer from the medical examiner's office to our facility and to the graveside, and the casket." He paused for several seconds to review the monstrous list. "Your total will be $19,950, due, of course, on the day we receive the remains. We also offer photography, should you so desire that."

Charlie tried not to choke as he heard the final total. It made him angry to think of all of the elderly widows and widowers who would have to spend their life savings laying their loved ones to rest. "Well, Mr., uh..." Charlie started.

"Landers," he answered. "Mr. Landers."

"Would you like to kiss me first?"

"Pardon me?" the mortician asked.

"Would you like to kiss me before you screw me?" Charlie asked.

"I find that very inappropriate," Landers answered, his jaw stiffening.

Charlie sighed, shook his head, opened his wallet, and took out one of Phil's signed checks, then wrote it out for the full amount. "When will you get the body, and when will she be ready for viewing?"

"Sign this form," he answered coolly, "and she will be picked up today. Have her clothes here no later than 5:00 tomorrow. The viewing will be the following day, from 11:00 a.m. to 1:00 p.m. The graveside service will be held at 2:00."

Charlie signed the form and stood up, refusing to shake Mr. Landers's outstretched hand. He stormed out of the office and passed several more grieving families on the way out.

CHAPTER 14

For the first time in days, Janet enjoyed a good night's sleep. She woke up feeling quite hungry but also that things would work out for the trip home. She called Charlie to check on the arrangements for the funeral and was pleasantly surprised that he had taken care of it. She knew he was uncomfortable with all of it, and that just proved, once again, how loyal he was to his friend Phil.

"Have you heard from Arthur?" she asked.

"Yeah," Charlie answered, sounding tired. "He visited Phil yesterday. Phil told him what dress and jewelry we should put on her. Phil seems to be better, a bit more resigned to all that's happened."

"I don't know if he ever will or should be resigned to it, but I'm glad he's better. Have you eaten since I've been gone?"

"I'm going out to get something now. Maybe it'll dissolve this knot in my stomach."

"Aw. Yes, dear, you must take care of yourself. It'll do no one any good if you whither away. I'm going to make flight plans in a few minutes, and I'll call you back to fill you in. I forgot to even ask Lilly's last name, and I have to know it before I can make the reservation. This whole thing is so weird."

"I know. I'll wait on your call before I go to eat."

Helga was up and busy with breakfast when Janet called, and Janet had to smile at the noise of little girls laughing and playing in the background.

"Good morning," she said. "This is Janet Evans. How is Lilly this morning?"

"She's doing all right. She's very quiet, but that is her normal demeanor. She has spent the morning in her room."

"All right. I'm sure she has a lot on her little mind. I need to make flight arrangements for tomorrow, hopefully early morning or afternoon. Does she use her father's last name, Palmer?"

"Yes. Will you be joining us for lunch tomorrow? It's at noon, sharp."

"I'd love that. Let me tie up these reservations, and I'll get back with you."

The flights out were pretty clear, since not many people were leaving Norfolk, Nebraska for L.A. on a Monday afternoon. Janet called Charlie back and said, "We're flying out at 2:00 tomorrow."

"Great," Charlie answered. "That'll give you enough time to go to the house with me to get Lara's clothes and jewelry. That damn funeral home was eerie enough. I don't wanna go digging through a dead woman's closet. Besides, that asshole can wait one more day."

"Charlie, I'll be bringing a child home with me. I hope you'll watch your language. Also, if you get a chance, please do something to one of the guestrooms to make her feel at home. She must be frightened to death. She's never flown before, and now she's hopping on a plane with a woman she just met yesterday, to see her dead mother in a casket."

"Jeez, when you put it like that... I'll do what I can. Maybe Annabelle can pick up a few things," he said, referring to their neighbor, who had three daughters of her own. "She knows what little girls like."

"Sounds good. I'll take her shopping for a dress when we get there," Janet said. "I'll call you from the airport. Maybe Annabelle can keep Lilly while we take the clothes to the funeral home. Her daughters are all close in age. Alicia is twelve, Allison ten, and Amanda eight. Maybe that will make Lilly feel better."

"I love you, Janet."

"I love you, too, Charlie," Janet said. As soon as she hung up with him, she called Helga to let her know the flight plans. "It'll probably be late Wednesday before I can bring her back," Janet said kindly. "She'll be in good hands though."

"Yes, dear, I am sure of that. What should I pack for her?"

"I'll take her shopping for a dress for the funeral, so just pack the basics. Los Angeles is quite a bit warmer, so she won't need any heavy clothes."

"Okay. I'll see you tomorrow at noon," Janet said, deeply saddened. "This is all so very horrible. That poor girl."

"Oh, honey, I know. It's a sad time for everyone."

CHAPTER 15

"It's me, Charlie," he said, as though his own wife might not recognize his voice. "Arthur talked to Martin Rudyard, and he agreed to fax the death certificate. I think Arthur's gonna owe him his firstborn though."

Janet laughed. "I can't say I blame the guy for being a little aggravated about it. He probably gets sick of people calling him at all hours of the day and night."

"Yeah, well, he's not a pleasure to be around on a good day, but we're getting the certificate outta him, and that's all that matters."

"Great. It's too early to contact the prison, so I'm heading out for a bite to eat. I'll call you as soon as possible, and I'll check for the fax when I get back."

"All right. Be careful."

"Always," Janet said with a smile, then hung up.

She put on a lightweight sweater, which she could have done without, and walked across the street and down a couple blocks to the small diner. She enjoyed walking back in time through rural America, but she would have enjoyed it more if her mind wasn't wrapped up in all that was going on. She ate a hearty breakfast to make up for her lack of dinner the night before, and she felt much better and more ready to deal with the day ahead after two cups of coffee.

After breakfast, she returned to the front desk at the hotel and playfully asked Sammi, "Don't they give you a day off around here?"

"Every now and then," the desk clerk joked. "My husband and I live here in exchange for me running the office. I get a little pay too. The owner's an elderly man who can no longer maintain the facility. He still lives here and watches over us like a hawk. What can I do for you this morning?"

"Well, actually, I'm hoping there are a couple faxes waiting on me."

"You're Mrs. Evans, right?"

"You got it. Please give me some good news."

Sammi shuffled some papers around on her desk. "You've got several pages here actually," she said, handing them across the counter. "Popular lady."

"Sometimes it doesn't pay to be popular," Janet answered. "Listen," she asked the girl, "can you tell me how far the state penitentiary is from here?"

Sammi looked at Janet with a puzzled expression but answered cordially, "About an hour away," she said. "It'd be cheaper to rent a car than to catch a cab. I can arrange it for you if you want."

"Please do. Do you think they'll deliver it here?"

"Yes, ma'am. They'll have it here within an hour. Any preference?"

"Compact is fine. It's just me."

"No offense or anything, but you don't look the type who goes around visiting prisons," she said, trying to sound as if she wasn't trying to pry.

"It's kind of a sad story. I'm really here under rather tragic circumstances."

"Is it anyone from around here?" Sammi asked, blatantly wanting some answers.

"Oh, I'm not sure," Janet answered, suspicious of her curiosity. "Probably not. His wife lived in Los Angeles."

"Hmm. Well, you're probably right then," she answered.

* * * * *

Back in her room, Janet looked up the number of the prison in the tattered telephone book, and she dialed the number at exactly 8:00 a.m.

"Cedar Falls State Prison, Maximum Security. Sergeant Jenkins speaking. How can I help you?"

"Hello, Sergeant," Janet started. "I, uh… Well, I've got quite a dilemma and am wondering if you can help me."

"Continue," he answered, sounding like a man who'd heard about every con in the book and wasn't anxious to hear another.

Janet explained her position in the briefest manner possible and waited on his reply.

He was silent for a few moments, which made her very uncomfortable.

"It's really imperative that I talk with him," she finally said, trying to minimize her desperation.

"You're not on the visitors list, and it is against our standard operating procedure to allow anyone in for a visit if they are not on the list, even if they are a friend or relative. It's especially difficult on a Sunday, on such short notice. However, the warden lives on the property, and due to these…extenuating circumstances, perhaps he will agree to speak with you. Call me back in about thirty minutes, after I have a chance to speak with him." With that, Sergeant Jenkins hung up without a goodbye; Janet didn't consider it rude, because personality was definitely not a requirement for someone in his line of work.

She called Charlie back. "I contacted the prison and I'm waiting to speak with the warden," she said. "Keep your fingers crossed."

"What for? For my wife to go into a prison?"

"Charlie, please. I assume you haven't heard from Arthur this morning."

"Actually, I did. He's hoping for a bond hearing around 9:30 tomorrow morning. He's gonna try to get a subpoena for the marriage license from that other fool who married her, along with several other items."

"Okay. Well, I've got to call the sergeant back. I'll talk to you soon."

The warden agreed to meet with Janet, but the sergeant could offer no promises. *That's better than nothing,* Janet thought as she walked down to the front desk to retrieve the keys to her rental car.

"I'm sorry, Mrs. Evans, but it will be a few more minutes. You're welcome to wait right there in that chair," she said, motioning to a waiting area. "It won't be long." She smiled a sweet, crooked-toothed smile and asked bashfully, "Can I ask you a question?"

"Sure," Janet answered.

"You seem like such a nice lady and all. I'm just wondering why you're going out to the prison? I mean, I know it's none of my business, but—"

"It's really a long, sordid story," Janet said, seeing no real harm in sharing bits and pieces of the terrible tale. "I'm going to visit someone I don't even know. See, his wife was killed in Los Angeles, and I need to let him know. I want to make funeral arrangements for her, but I can't without his permission. I don't think the two have had any contact in years."

"Wow," Sammi said. "That's just—"

Just then, before the girl could ask any further questions, the rental car pulled up.

"There's my ride," Janet said, knowing she didn't have much time to spare.

CHAPTER 16

Arthur had plenty of connections at the courthouse, so he was able to arrange the bond hearing for 9 o'clock. Arthur was seated at the defense table, across from the prosecutor's.

Charlie sat at the back of the courtroom, saying silent prayers with his eyes closed. He gasped when they led Phil out in shackles and cuffs, just a remnant of what his friend used to be, his beard scraggly and unshaven, his hair unkempt, and his eyes hollow.

Phil looked for Charlie and nodded when he spotted him. He took a seat beside Arthur and looked up at the judge.

"We are here for a bond hearing in the case of Phil Sawyer," the judge began. "I will hear statements from both sides. Mr. Morris, you may begin."

Arthur stood and took a few steps forward. His suit was immaculate, his posture straight and confident. "Your Honor, I am here to request bond for Mr. Phil Sawyer. He is one of the most respected surgeons at Cedar Sinai Hospital. He has no prior record, not even a traffic violation. He has a medical degree, a home in the area, and poses neither a threat to flee the area nor a threat to the safety of the general public. Before you is a man who was driven over the edge, someone who simply lost control in the heat of passion. Based on his past behavior and the circumstances, there is no indication that this will ever happen again. There is no record of domestic violence in his home. We request reasonable bond be set so Mr. Sawyer can get his affairs in order before going to trial. Thank you, Your Honor."

"Mr. Morris," the judge answered, "we are all driven to the edge at some point or another, but we don't strangle our wives. There is no justification for that."

"Yes, Your Honor," Arthur countered. "We are not trying to justify the murder in any form or fashion. I am simply stating that Mr. Sawyer has never displayed any type of physical violence before. He is a doctor, and it is simply not in his character."

"Prosecution, you may go ahead."

James Edwards stood, wearing the same look of contempt he wore every time he walked into a courtroom, as if all of his cases were personal. "Your Honor," he started, taking more than enough time to remove his glasses and place them on top of his yellow notepad. "We are dealing with someone who murdered his wife, who violently took another live, and now he is asking us to allow him back into society in as little as two days. Mr. Sawyer may be a good surgeon and a well-educated man, but that does not belittle the fact that he has admitted to murder.

We cannot allow for special cases to receive bond because they lost their cool for a moment. I request that the prisoner be incarcerated until trial. Thank you, Your Honor."

"I will return with my decision in thirty minutes," the judge said, then stepped down from his bench and disappeared through a heavy mahogany door, with his black robe flowing behind him.

* * * * *

"All rise," the voice of the bailiff boomed. "The Honorable Judge Sykes presiding."

It took Arthur's muscled arms to help lift Phil and hold him up as the judge returned from his chambers.

Judge Sykes sat silently for a few seconds before stating, "I have given this great thought. To take a human life is, perhaps, the worst crime one can commit. Whether premeditated or out of anger, in a 'moment of passion,' as you put it, Counselor, human life can never be restored or replaced. We cannot deny that a vicious crime has been committed. Nevertheless, I do believe Mr. Sawyer harbors some remorse for it, and I do not believe he poses a flight risk or a threat to the general population of this state. Surrender your passport and get your business in order, Mr. Sawyer. Bond is set at $500,000. Court is adjourned."

Phil plopped down in the chair, and his shoulders slumped, as if someone had let all the air out of him.

CHAPTER 17

Janet parked her rental car and looked around in awe at the immense size of the marble institution before her; she did not expect such a massive structure. The walls were solid granite and stood at least thirty feet tall.

She followed the signs that led to the entrance steps, and a man in a tower yelled down for her to pick up a phone in a booth to her left. Janet did as she was asked and answered several questions, particularly focused on making sure she wasn't carrying any weapons or in possession of any illegal or prescription drugs. The guard motioned with his hand for her to start up the stairs, and the door opened just as she got to it.

"Morning, ma'am," said a young guard, his tone as kind as his face. "Who are you here to see today?"

"My name is Janet Evans, and I am here to see the warden."

"Yes, ma'am," he answered. "If you'll just have a seat in that room to your right, I'll notify him that you are here. Shouldn't be long."

"Thank you," Janet said as she made her way to the glass-encased room. The tiles on the floors were old and outdated, but they were waxed to perfection—so much so that she looked down at herself and ran her fingers through her hair to fluff it just a little. She put her hands across her stomach to ease the nervousness, then thought of how ridiculous it really was. *How many visitors are actually killed in prison?* she asked herself. *None. Just calm down, Janet.* The room was empty, with the exception of a few black plastic chairs. The minimalistic interior left her mind with nothing to focus on but all that had gone on and all that was yet to come.

"Ms. Evans?" an older gentleman asked, offering his outstretched hand.

"Yes sir? You must be the warden."

"Warden Ricks, but please call me 'Hubert'."

"Thank you very much for seeing me on such short notice. I am in a very awkward predicament."

"So I've heard. Let's go into my office, shall we?"

Janet followed Hubert across the hall, where he pulled out a key and opened the door.

"Have a seat anywhere you'd like," he said.

She took a quick moment to scan the room. It was neatly decorated though nothing too extravagant at the taxpayers' expense. Awards, medals, and plaques adorned the walls, along with framed letters. She chose a leather wingback chair, sat down, and placed her purse beside her.

"I understand you are here to see Jeb Palmer," he said. "It sounds like quite a situation you've been thrown into."

"Oh, you don't know the half of it."

"I went on the Internet after I talked to you and read the L.A. newspapers. Real tough situation. How do you fall into all this?"

"Well, my husband is also a doctor, and he and Phil Sawyer are old college buddies. They've been best friends for many, many years. Phil is a good man and an amazing surgeon, regardless of how the media portrays him. I know it sounds crazy, since he, uh…murdered his wife, but… Well, anyway, in the process of trying to help him get his affairs in order, we discovered that his wife had a daughter who's been living in a group home here in Nebraska. I came here in the hope of finding other relatives. No such luck on that, but I did figure out that she was married to Jeb Palmer, making her a bigamist, among other things."

"Quite a tangled web," the warden said, sitting back in his chair to hear more.

"In order to plan her funeral, we need Mr. Palmer to legally release the body. It is very important that I see him."

"I see," he said, his tone not swaying one way or the other, "Ya know, I've been up for retirement for several years now," he continued. "I just haven't gone through with it. I'm not quite sure if I'm ready. Maybe it's the challenge of rehabilitating these men, at least those who care to be. The wife and I live on the grounds and raised our children here. It's just kind of hard to leave when you're so used to something."

"I guess I can understand that," Janet answered. She wasn't quite sure what any of that had to do with her or Jeb Palmer, but he clearly had something more to tell her. "I am a school teacher, and I can't imagine my life without my job."

Suddenly, Hubert's tone changed and was much more serious. "Mrs. Evans, many of the men incarcerated here are just cons. It's in their blood. Unfortunately, they care nothing about anyone but themselves and will do whatever it takes to survive in this place or out in the streets. To some of them, this is home, and they don't wanna leave it any more than you or I want to be evicted from ours. It becomes a way of life, a security we can't understand." He then opened his top drawer and pulled out a file. "This is Jeb's file. Now, it's strictly against regulations for me to share any of it with you, but I figure you need to know at least some of it."

"Okay. I appreciate that, Hubert," she said, her curiosity piqued.

"Several years ago, he and his wife were like a modern-day Bonnie and Clyde, stealing anything they could get their hands on. Their little town was scared as hell of them, and they got away with it much longer than they should have. Word on the street is that she took the money and ran, abandoning her little girl and leaving him to take the rap. My bet is that Jeb will sign any papers you put in front of him if you're willing to put some money on his books. In max security, they're allowed up to $100 a month. They use it in the canteen for cigarettes, snacks, soda… I don't really condone that sorta thing, paying 'em off, but in your case, it may be your best bet. Get your form signed, I'll have it notarized, and you can be on your way. Oh, and don't leave any way for him to contact you in the future. I wouldn't even give your name or where you're from, unless you wanna be bombarded with further requests for money."

"That seems fair enough," Janet answered. "Sick on his part but fair enough. When can I see him?"

"I'll walk you to the visitation room, and we'll have a guard bring him out." Noticing her apprehension, the warden added, "There's no need to worry, ma'am. They're always angels during visitation. That's one privilege they don't wanna lose, even if it's someone they don't know. For these guys locked up in these cages, contact with the outside world is like gold."

The visitation room had the same waxed floors and several rows of seats partitioned off by small cubicles. Janet was seated on one side of the Plexiglas, staring at the empty chair that was waiting for Jeb on the other side. In less than five minutes, a tall, muscled man sat down. She was confident that if his life had been different, he would have had an opportunity to be very handsome, but the rough life he had lived had erased any chance of that. His strong arms were covered with amateur tattoos of skulls, dragons, and naked women with large breasts and bright pink nipples that seemed to dance as he flexed his forearms. His hair was full and dark brown, and his eyes were as blue as Lilly's and Lara's. His face wore the look of someone who enjoyed intimidation. He sat silently until she spoke first.

"Mr. Palmer?"

"Yeah. Who are you?" he asked, for the first time allowing Janet to see his missing and rotting teeth. He could sense her lingering gaze on his mouth, even though she attempted to divert her eyes. "Lost my dental plan a while back," he said.

"Forgive me. I am an acquaintance of Laraleen. I am here to let you know she died. I'm terribly sorry to have to bring you this news."

"I don't give a rat's ass about that dirty, backstabbing bitch. What happened to her though?" he asked as he snickered.

"Her husband strangled her to death."

"Good for him. Shoulda done it years ago myself. Wait. Did you say her husband did it? Since when can a bitch marry two men?"

"She never told him about you."

"Sneaky bitch."

"Well," Janet said, hesitating before she agreed, "yes, she was."

"Is that the only reason you're here?"

"No. Because you were still married to her, in order for us to bury her, we need you to sign a release form."

Jeb looked at Janet with a glare she feared would cut right through the glass. "I ain't got no damn money, if you're expecting me to pay any part of it. Far as I'm concerned, you can throw her out in the desert for the ants and vultures to eat."

"No," Janet quickly interrupted. "We don't expect that at all. We'll pay for everything. The medical examiner just needs the paperwork so her body can be released to a mortuary."

"Hmm. You seem pretty desperate for my signature, lady. If I sign it so you can get her in the ground before she stinks the place up worse, what's in it for me?"

"I heard you're allowed $100 a month. I'm willing to give you that if you'll sign now."

"You'll bank me a month's worth of money?" Jeb laughed a dirty, foul laugh and motioned for her to send the paper through the slot. He then looked over his shoulder at a guard, who gave him a pen and took it back the second Jeb was finished using it. "Why, ain't it my lucky day?" he said, sliding the signed form back through the slot. "The bitch is gone, and I got a hundred bucks to boot." With that, Jeb Palmer got up and walked away and never once looked back.

* * * * *

Janet left the prison with $100 less in her purse but thrilled to have the proper paperwork in hand. She shivered at the thought of that short glance into a seedy part of the world that she had never dreamt of seeing. "Jesus," she said aloud to herself in the car. "Phil will be with people like that. He'll never survive it." With that on her mind, she cried for the remainder of the ride back to the hotel.

She stopped to drop the keys off at the front desk, but Sammi wasn't there. Instead, there was an older gentleman in the seat. She paid her bill, went to her room to get her things together, and call a cab to pick up Lilly, that poor, precious, fragile little girl.

CHAPTER 18

Phil climbed into Charlie's tattered Volvo, looking like a beaten man. They sat in silence for a few seconds before Charlie started the engine.

"You know," Charlie said, "there are times when a friend just doesn't know what the hell to say."

"Yeah, and there are times when a friend just needs to be there. That's what you've done, and I can't thank you enough for it," Phil answered, looking straight through the windshield.

"You'll feel better after a shower and a good meal."

"You might be right. Listen, I hate to ask this, and I don't wanna cause any problems for you and Janet, but do you think you could stay with me for a while? I don't think I can be there, in that place, by myself."

"Yeah, man. It's not a problem. I'm here for the long haul, and you'd do the same for me."

"I won't ever have to."

"You're right, but I'm not married to Lara."

They both got a good laugh out of that one, a long, healthy chuckle that was greatly needed.

"We're sick, man," Charlie said as he pulled into Phil's driveway, with Arthur behind them. "Always have been, I guess."

Phil refused to look at the house, as if some sinister evil now resided there.

"Take it easy, guy," Charlie said. "Unfortunately, you've gotta be here, at least for a while. There are things that need to be taken care of."

"I know," Phil said. "I've got a lot of loose ends to tie up before I hit the big house."

"Oh God," Charlie said. "Let's put that out of our minds right now."

Arthur got out of the car and waited for Charlie to unlock the door and disarm the security system. "I gotta be honest," he said as they stepped inside. "I didn't expect to get you out this soon. It's a good sign."

Phil walked over to the scotch decanter and poured himself a straight one, without any ice.

"Do you really need that?" Arthur asked. "It's only noon."

"Yes, Arthur. Right now, I need it more than life itself."

"Be my guest then," Arthur retorted.

"Phil," Charlie said, returning to the room, "I put a towel and washcloth in the guest bathroom downstairs. Why don't you take a long, hot shower? I'll bring you some clothes and order us all a big lunch. What the hell. We'll get prime rib.

Everybody needs red meat every now and then."

Phil slugged his drink down and stood up slowly. "You're right. A shower sounds great, and come to think of it, I haven't had a solid meal in a couple days. Make mine medium rare, with basil vinaigrette dressing." With that, he walked off.

"What do you think Arthur?" Charlie asked when the shower came on.

"I don't know, and I'm not one to make guesses. There's no point, as things seldom turn out the way I expect. We'll need to stay with him for a while, day and night. I've seen too many suicides in cases like this, and we can't take any chances. We can take shifts. My other cases can wait a little while. The attorneys in the firm will just have to double up. Let's not pressure him too much today about legal proceedings. Phil just needs a good drunk to take the edge off."

"Right. Well, I'll get him some clothes from upstairs," Charlie answered. "Why don't you phone Remington's Steakhouse for a to-go order?"

"Will do," Arthur said. "I'll pick up some beer too. We don't all need to hit the hard stuff. How's Heineken?"

"Cool with me," Charlie answered, laying a couple hundred dollars on the table. "It's my turn to pick up the check, right? Damn. I shoulda taken the breakfast tab."

They both managed to fake a laugh as Charlie climbed the stairs.

* * * * *

By the time Arthur returned from his food-and-beer run, Phil had finished another drink and seemed to have calmed a bit. They ate their dinner at the coffee table, watching ESPN.

"I hate to bring it up, but I've gotta get the dress and jewelry over to the funeral home by 5:00. Janet will come by and go with me," Charlie said. He wasn't quite ready to tell Phil about Lilly yet, especially since he wouldn't see her anyway. She would be at Annabelle's for the afternoon and Phil wouldn't attend the funeral. Charlie had a few days to play with before he would be forced to break that news to him.

"I can go deliver the dress with you," Phil answered, with a quiver in his voice.

"No, Janet and I will take care of it. We figured a graveside service will be appropriate, since no one will be in attendance except for us. We arranged for a Baptist minister." He swallowed past a lump in his throat and asked, "I know it's an odd question, but do you want to go to the viewing? As strange as it might sound, maybe it will give you some…closure."

"I'll think about it, but I'm pretty sure I'll have plenty of time to find closure during all those years in prison," Phil answered, looking down at his half-empty drink.

"It set you back almost fifteen grand, and that was watching our pennies."

"What the hell? I don't give a shit about the money."

"I know, Phil. I just thought we should add it to the books, that's all."

CHAPTER 19

Janet jumped out of the cab, wrapped in her coat but still shivering. Salty tears stung her eyes as she was smacked again with the realization of what she was about to do. With a bit of hesitation, she rang the doorbell.

Helga answered, wearing a solemn look on her face. She hugged Janet lightly and called for Lilly.

The girl appeared at the bottom of the staircase, holding her new teddy bear close to her chest. Her packed duffel bag sat beside the door.

"Hello, Lilly," Janet said kindly. "Are you ready to go?"

"Yes, ma'am," she said. "Ms. Helga helped me pack."

"I can see that."

"She also made me a bag of goodies to eat on the plane, just in case the sky food is icky. I'll share with you."

"Oh my goodness," Janet said. "I can always use some goodies, especially if Ms. Helga made them."

The comment made Lilly smile, and she moved cautiously toward Janet, then turned and ran to hug Helga.

The long, heartfelt hug from the child made Helga turn her head to keep her tears from dripping on the girl's hair. She swatted Lilly lightly on the bottom. "Shoo, child. That plane won't wait on you. When you come back, I expect you to tell me all about those palm trees, ya hear?"

"Yes. I sure will," Lilly said, for the first time showing a glimmer of excitement. She picked up her duffel bag and refused to allow Janet to help. She walked bravely to the cab and sat in the middle, close to Janet.

The ride wasn't long, and Janet reassured her about their flight and told her all about her Charlie.

"It must be nice to be able to make people well when they are sick," Lilly said.

"It is. He likes his job a lot, and I'm sure you two will be friends. Like I told you, Charlie always has neat surprises in his coat pockets. Just between me and you, there are surprises in both pockets. Don't tell him I told you that, okay?"

"Okay," she answered and giggled.

"When we get to my house, you can put your things away in your room. My neighbor, Annabelle, is going to let you stay with her for a while so I can do a few things. You will like her. She has three daughters about your age. I bet you'll have a great time together."

Lilly looked apprehensive but was willing to do whatever Janet asked of her. "Okay," she said, nodding.

When they finally arrived at the airport, they found Charlie waiting for them at the terminal entrance. He was holding two small bouquets of flowers.

"There he is!" Janet said, motioning toward him, as though they could miss his waving hands.

Lilly smiled as they walked up to meet him.

"You must be Lilly," Charlie said. "My wife said she was bringing a beautiful young lady home with her. I figure every pretty lady deserves flowers," he said, handing one bouquet to each of them.

"Gee, thanks," Lilly said, obviously very pleased. "I never got flowers before."

"Allow me to take your bags, ladies," he said in a butler's stiff voice.

This time, Lilly handed hers over as she proudly inspected her flowers.

"Charlie," Janet said seriously, "Lilly knows you sometimes have things in your coat pockets. What about today?"

"Hmm. I'm not sure," he said as he turned toward Lilly. "Why don't you pick a pocket and see?"

"The left one," she said shyly.

Charlie made a big commotion as he rummaged through his pocket and pulled out a red balloon and a pack of gummy bears.

"Thank you," Lilly said, smiling at Janet as she secretly winked at her.

The ride to the house was quiet, and as they pulled into the driveway, Janet realized just how much she'd missed home. They walked inside, and Charlie showed Lilly to her room. Janet was surprised by how much Annabelle had done, from replacing the old bedspread with a light pink one to placing several stuffed animals and games in the room. Lilly seemed to like it, which pleased them both. After she had a chance to put her bag down, they delivered her to Annabelle's house and headed directly to Phil's. On the way, Janet told Charlie all about her trip, right down to the details about the scary prison visit.

Charlie shook his head, looking over at her. "You're so stubborn," he said.

"And you love me for it," she returned, smiling back at him proudly.

CHAPTER 20

Arthur was still at Phil's house, working on some of his other cases in the library. Phil had fallen asleep on the couch and, judging by the emptiness of the scotch decanter, he needed to sleep off a good buzz. They didn't wake him, but Janet stood over him, almost as though it was Phil she was viewing in the casket.

Arthur came out quietly and, to Janet's surprise, hugged her tightly as she breathed in his expensive cologne. "I know you've been through a lot," he said. "We're making progress. As I told Charlie, somebody needs to stay with him twenty-four/seven for a while. The more sleep he gets, the better. If he wants to drink, we should let him. It won't erase the situation, but it'll let him escape for a while. We also need to keep him well fed. From what I hear from Charlie, you can do that."

Janet laughed and nodded. "I'll do my best."

"C'mon, honey," Charlie said. "Let's go get the gown. That creepy bastard at the funeral home needs it by 5:00. You may need to take it in. I don't think he likes me."

"Charlie, what did you do now?"

"Um, not really important, dear. I'm just…not in my right state of mind."

"That excuse only goes so far, you know," Janet answered.

Charlie smiled and followed her up the dreaded stairs yet again. "And back into the Twilight Zone we go," he said.

"Stop," Janet said. "Really, I've had all I can take right now."

In the bedroom, she opened several closets and was as shocked as Charlie had been by the extravagance in which Lara had lived. It sickened her. Janet flipped quickly through all the designer gowns and found what she was sure was the one. It was heavily beaded with silver, and all the tags had been removed, making it stand out from all the other gaudy, sparkling, overpriced, never-worn garments.

"This has to be it," Janet said, taking it carefully from the closet. She picked out a pair of matching silver pumps, then pulled hose and undergarments from her lingerie drawer. "I don't know if they'll use all this stuff, but I don't wanna make another trip back to the funeral home."

"I can understand that," Charlie said.

She gathered what she could find of Lara's makeup and put it in a satin bag, then pulled a long, white gold chain from the jewelry box. The bauble had a diamond in the center of the pendant, at least four carats. She also chose several bracelets, diamond earrings, and two rings.

"Damn," Charlie said. "We could have just paid the greedy asshole with jewelry."

"Charlie, please," Janet said. "There will be a child in our house for the next two days. You've gotta watch your mouth."

Phil was still out cold when they returned downstairs, and they waved to Arthur, indicating that they were on their way. He followed them outside.

"We're goin' to the funeral home, then heading back home for Lilly."

"No problem. I'll take tonight. I brought some extra clothes, and I can call for takeout. Just buzz me later."

"Will do," Charlie answered.

* * * * *

It was 4:30 when they arrived with the clothing, and the mortician was obviously getting antsy.

"We have a large pool of clientele to attend to, you know," Mr. Landers said abruptly. "I was hoping you would get here sooner."

Charlie, who had refused to sit in the car answered, "Yes, I've heard that people are just dying to get over here." He laughed loudly at his own joke, but Janet only punched him in the arm and apologized profusely on her husband's behalf.

The uptight Mr. Landers huffed and literally snatched the items from Janet's hands. "As promised, the viewing will be from 11:00 to 1:00, the graveside service at 2:00 p.m."

"Thank you again, Mr. Landers," Charlie said. "Your efforts have not gone unnoticed."

The comment only succeeded in pissing the mortician off further, especially since the sarcasm with which it dripped seemed to bring Charlie much pleasure.

"What in the hell is your problem?" Janet asked when they returned to the car.

"Oops," Charlie said. "You're right. We have a child at home."

"Correction. It seems I have two."

* * * * *

Lilly was in the back, playing with Annabelle's girls when they got there to pick her up.

"Thank you so much," Janet said. "I just didn't wanna take her with us to the funeral home or to Phil's."

"I understand," Annabelle said. "She's been fine, and they get along great. I just haven't fed them dinner yet."

"Oh, that's fine," Charlie answered. "We'll take care of that."

"She's so lovely," Annabelle answered, "like an angel."

"As sweet as one too," Janet answered as she called for Lilly.

The girl came right away and appeared happy to see both of them. "Thank you, Ms. Annabelle, for letting me stay with you," she said. "I had a good time."

"Well, maybe we can have you over again before you go back home."

"That would be fun."

"Okay, okay, ladies," Charlie said, trying to sound frustrated. "Enough small talk. It takes a lotta food to keep this belly so nice and round, and I intend to keep it that way," he said, rubbing his midsection up and down like he was Santa Claus.

They all laughed and headed for the car.

Janet looked back to see the pity in Annabelle's eyes. *"Thank you,"* she mouthed.

Charlie cranked the car and rubbed his hand across his chin. "Hmm," he said. "I just can't seem to decide what I want to eat. Let's see. There are hamburgers, tacos, pizzas, and fried chicken… I just can't decide. What about you, Janet?"

"I can't decide either, but I'm starving."

"Looks like you'll have to decide Lilly," Charlie answered. "If you don't, Janet and I will have to argue, and I'm just a little too hungry for that."

Lilly giggled. "Well, at the group home, when we get to go out to eat, we usually just take a vote."

"Well, tonight, it's just you. What's your vote?"

"Pizza," she said happily, "with pepperoni and extra cheese."

Janet and Charlie were surprised that such a little thing had such a big appetite, but they enjoyed every moment of watching her eat.

"Oh, I'm sorry, Lilly," Charlie said, wearing a serious face, "but I have one rule that nobody gets to vote on."

Lilly grinned at him, knowing it would be something good. She could already tell the doctor was a nice man.

"We have to go by the ice cream parlor after we eat pizza, just have to. Janet says it makes me fatter, but it's a rule. Can't break a rule, huh?"

"Nope!" she squealed, jumping up and down in her seat.

The three left and enjoyed ice cream cones as they sat at a small metal table in little parlor chairs.

The ride home was quiet, and neither Charlie nor Janet had the heart to bring up Lara. Besides, Lilly was almost asleep by the time they pulled into the driveway. She rubbed her eyes and got out of the car.

"Would you like to take a shower before you put on your pajamas?" Janet asked, realizing how tired the child had to be.

"Can I wait till tomorrow?" she asked.

"Yes, you may," Charlie answered in some voice he'd stolen from a cartoon. "We don't allow people who are too clean in our house. That's another rule."

Janet looked at Lilly and rolled her eyes, and they both laughed.

"Will you read me a story?" the girl asked Janet.

"I sure will," Janet answered. "Just call me when you have your pj's on."

A few minutes later, Lilly hollered for Janet. "I'm all ready for my story!" she said.

"Let me," Charlie said, rising from his recliner. He went into their bedroom and came out with a box wrapped in white paper, with a white ribbon on top.

Janet smiled to herself, wondering what could possibly be inside.

Charlie tapped lightly on the girl's door before entering. "Do you mind if I read to you tonight?" he asked. "See, Janet and I don't have any children and I've always wanted to read a bedtime story."

"Okay," Lilly said as she sat up in bed and leaned against the pillow. "I brought *Curious George*. I'm probably a little old for him, but he's my favorite."

Janet edged quietly down the hallway and leaned against the wall, just within hearing range.

"Hey, you're never too old for *Curious George*. He's one of my favorites too."

Janet had to strain to hear Lilly as she asked, "Is that present for me?"

Charlie was silent for a moment, then answered, "Yes, Lilly. It's a special present, one I hope you will keep all of your life. Even though you didn't know your mother very well, she was your mother, and having a child is one of the most precious things in the world. I know you were far apart for a long time, but I have a feeling she thought of you every day and hoped you were okay. Life was just different for her. Your mommy had dreams that a lot of people don't understand, but she was your mom. That means she was a part of you and you were part of her."

Janet heard Lilly opening the present, and she waited impatiently.

"Oh!" Lilly gasped. "It's the most beautiful angel I've ever seen. I mean it. It really is."

"Well, you know," Charlie said, "angels are very special. God gives each of us a guardian angel to watch over us and take care of us. We never see them because they are in Heaven making sure our lives go as planned. You won't get to see your mother anymore, Lilly, but she will watch over you. Let this angel be a reminder of that. Whenever you want to talk to her, remember that she's floating just above you."

"I will," she said softly.

"Let's see which book this is," Charlie answered, "because my favorite is the one where he goes to the hospital after swallowing that puzzle piece, the silly monkey."

Lilly laughed and sniffled a little. "It's not that one. It's the one about the zoo. He gets into lots of trouble."

"Yes, I know," Charlie answered, "but the man in the yellow suit likes George anyway, right?"

"Right!" she said.

And with that, Charlie opened the book and read to Lilly until she fell asleep, about five pages later.

CHAPTER 21

Phil lifted his head from the sofa, as if it was a two-ton brick. "Jesus," he said out loud. "What in the hell was I thinking? Did I drink up everything in the house?"

"Well, actually…" Arthur answered from the study. "No, but it was pretty damn close." The chair squeaked as Arthur got up, stretched, and walked into the living room. "Lie back down for a few minutes," he said. "I'll put on some strong coffee."

Phil slowly laid his head back on the pillow, gently, as if it might explode. He closed his aching eyes, and when he did, it all started coming back to him, the nightmare he hadn't dreamt, but was living. He wanted to rub his temples but didn't want to waste the strength it would require to lift his hands.

Arthur returned with two cups of steaming coffee and placed one on the table in front of Phil. "I know it's tough, buddy."

"Did you spend the night?"

"Yep."

"Did you get any sleep?"

"I got a couple hours of shut-eye," Arthur answered, "but in my line of work, sleep deprivation's a given. I'll be fine. For now, we need to get you over this hangover. We've got a lot to do. I'll have a big breakfast sent over, and after we eat and shower, we'll talk."

"Thanks, man," Phil answered as tears started to well in his eyes. "You're a good friend."

"You're welcome, but I'm not here for a damn pity party. Got no time for that. What happened happened, and we can't change it. We've got no choice but to move forward from here."

Arthur brought the coffee pot in and poured Phil some more, then called one of his secretaries and asked her to pick up breakfast for them and deliver it to the house.

"I can be left alone, you know," Phil said sarcastically. "I'm not a child."

"No shit," Arthur answered, "but you've gotten yourself in deep enough. I'm not taking any chances."

It was 9:30 when they finished their breakfast, and it was after 10:00 by the time the two finished showering and dressing. The two BC powders Phil had choked down were beginning to work, and his eyes were coming back into focus.

Arthur sat down across from him and opened an accordion file, then pulled several documents out and laid them across the table. "We have to get through this funeral first, Phil. You're out on bond so we can take care of your financial business, etc., but let's get the funeral behind us before we do anything else. It obviously wouldn't be in your best interest to show up at the gravesite, but you can go to the viewing if you'd like. That's strictly up to you. Some find that it gives them closure, but for others, it's more of a nightmare they'll dream every night for the rest of their lives. It's really a roll of the dice, so the choice is yours."

Phil rolled his head around, as though he was meditating, then answered, "I need to see her. I need to know that I really…" He stopped and shook his head. "I need to see that I really did it, really killed her."

"Phil," Arthur said quietly, "we both know you did. There's really no need to put yourself through anything else if you feel—"

"Just get me in without anyone seeing me, if you can."

"I don't think there will be a crowd. Some media might weasel their way into the graveside service, the sneaky bastards, but there shouldn't be anyone at the funeral home. If you really want to go, I'll make sure you aren't seen."

"Okay."

"There's something else I need to talk to you about," Arthur said. When the phone rang, startling them both, he said, "You stay put. I'll get that." He walked over and picked up the phone, then said, "Sawyer residence. How can I help you?"

Arthur was quiet for quite some time, enough to make Phil curious as hell.

"Thanks for the heads up," he answered, then hung up the phone, with a look of exacerbation on his face. "You aren't gonna believe this shit," Arthur said. "You really won't believe it. That was Martin Rudyard. Lara was…eight weeks pregnant."

"What!?" Phil asked, looking more confused than Arthur. "What does that mean?"

"It means you killed your wife *and* your unborn child. This thickens the plot a bit."

"I know it wasn't my baby," Phil said, his eyes suddenly wide and clear. "We rarely had sex, and it was always protected when we did. I knew she was having affairs, and I wasn't willing to catch anything."

"Rudyard has the fetus, so a DNA match can clear that up. May even sway in your favor. Who knows?"

"Arthur, I really just want to see her to make sure she's dead."

"She is, my friend. She is."

"What were you saying before you answered the phone earlier?"

Arthur rubbed his huge hands across his face, then massaged his own neck. "When Janet was going through Lara's things, she found a letter, written by a child, from a group home in Nebraska. The little girl told Lara where she was and asked if she could come and have ice cream with her."

"Huh? A child? In Nebraska? What the hell are you talking about?"

"Janet checked it out, even flew out to Norfolk. Lara had a daughter, Phil, and she's nine years old. Apparently, Lara told her she didn't want a child, but she promised that if she got a lot of money, maybe she could come and live with her, under an alias, of course, and not as her actual child."

"Jesus Christ. What an evil—"

"There's more," Arthur interrupted, holding his hand up. "Apparently, Lara was married to this little girl's father and never divorced him, rendering your marriage to her null and void. He's in prison on forgery, theft, arson, and aggravated assault charges. It's not his first time, so he'll be calling that hellhole home for quite a while. Her Yale diploma was forged as well. Lara was simple white trash from Nebraska. She just happened to be a looker and used that to her advantage. Clearly, the only beautiful thing about her was on the outside."

Phil began to hyperventilate and stood to try to pull himself together. "Too bad I didn't know about all this eight years ago. She stole my life, that dirty, nasty whore. She stole my whole damn life! Oh God. What's gonna happen to me now, Arthur? Give it to me straight, man, and I mean straight."

"We'll go for voluntary manslaughter. With all that we have right now, you might be out in twelve years, leaving you time to move on and live your life."

Phil's eyes rolled back in his head, and he fainted, giving Arthur just enough time to push him back and let the sofa break his fall.

CHAPTER 22

Janet was up early to prepare flapjacks and sausage. She dreaded the day ahead more than any day of her life. She was pouring glasses of juice and milk when Lilly walked out in her pajamas, still holding her teddy bear. The girl's hair was ruffled and her cheeks pink from sleep, but she was still beautiful.

"Good morning," Janet said. "How are you this morning?"

"I'm okay," Lilly answered, still a little groggy. "I've never slept in a bed that big before. At the group home, the beds are little, for little people like us."

"Well, how did you like it?"

She smiled. "I liked it a lot. So did Teddy."

"Good for both of you then! Are you hungry?"

"Yes, ma'am."

"Just find a seat and sip on your juice while I find Charlie." She walked to the door and found him outside sweeping the carport, even though it didn't need it. "Time to eat, honey."

"Sounds good to me," he said, rubbing his tummy.

"When we finish eating, we have to go to the mall," Janet said. "Would you like to pick out a new dress?"

"Yes, ma'am," Lilly answered, "but it's not time to get new clothes yet."

Janet smiled, realizing that they were probably on a pretty tight shopping schedule and budget back at Bedford. "Well, then let's just break the rules today. How's that?"

"Sounds fun to me!" The girl then smiled, warming Janet's heart more than she would ever know.

* * * * *

Janet and Lilly enjoyed the mall, even though they were in quite a rush. Lilly was easy to please and grateful for anything she was offered. They decided on a burgundy dress with a hat and coat to match, tights, and black, patent leather shoes.

"I'm sorry I don't have any money, Ms. Janet," Lilly said. "I only got to bring $5."

"No worries, dear," Janet said. "This is my treat."

They stopped by the hairdresser Janet used, and Lilly's hair was curled and pulled back into a barrette. They then rushed home to get dressed.

Charlie was already ready to go. As Lilly hurried up the stairs, excited to put on her new dress, he motioned for Janet to join him in the den and asked her to sit down. "Let's wait till noon before we go to the viewing." Charlie paused for a moment, then continued, "Arthur's taking Phil to see her at 11:00. We should give him some time to be alone."

"What?" Janet asked, as if she hadn't heard him right.

"I think Arthur may have encouraged it somewhat, for closure, that type of thing."

"I don't know if it's the right thing to do, if it will be good for him. What if the media is there?"

"They've worked out a plan, so to speak. He'll go in the back way, and that should alleviate him from being seen. The viewing room will be sealed off to the public during that time."

"I hope it's for the best, Charlie. Phil is already tinkering on the edge, and frankly, I'm not even sure if it's the moral thing to do."

"Yeah, I thought of that too. It's kind of morbid, but no one is thinking rationally right now. Let's just stick with him and be as supportive as we can."

"I think we need to talk with Lilly about what she's about to face," Janet said, changing the subject. "She needs us now too."

CHAPTER 23

Phil came down the stairs in a pair of wool slacks and sports jacket, minus a tie; it wasn't that he didn't feel the need to wear one, but his shaky hands couldn't get the knot to do what he expected. *To hell with it,* he thought. *No one's gonna see me anyway, especially not Lara.*

Arthur had showered, shaved, and dressed. His eyes and mannerisms showed no sign of the sleep deprivation Phil had caused. His BMW was out front, and the two men walked out and drove off without speaking a word.

It was about a ten-minute drive to the funeral home, and, as promised, Mr. Landers was waiting around back to quickly rush them inside. There wasn't any media there, which was a relief and a pleasant surprise for Arthur, though Phil didn't seem to care anymore. Mr. Landers guided them through a maze of spooky hallways that led to a back staircase. They walked up the steps slowly, until they reached the top. Mr. Landers paused for a moment, then turned to the left to lead them into the room that held Lara's lifeless remains. Arthur took Phil by the elbow; his career had taught him that it was best to be proactive when it came to overwhelming events.

Phil brushed Arthur's arm aside and walked over to the casket. He looked down at his wife, long and hard, as if performing a military inspection. There was a cheap silver scarf around her neck, tied in an outdated knot, obviously put there by the mortuary. "C'mere, Arthur," Phil said quietly.

Damn. I knew it, Arthur thought to himself. *I don't even know this woman, and I'm gonna have to look in her casket.* He sucked in a deep breath that his body refused to exhale, then made his way over to the coffin. There was no doubt that Lara was a beautiful woman. Even lifeless, she looked like a perfectly formed mannequin, flawless except for the well-hidden bruises under the scarf.

Phil's face was emotionless. There were no signs of sadness, or regret. It almost frightened Arthur and would have had he not known all that he did about the woman.

"You've seen her, man," Arthur said. "Let's get outta here."

Phil dismissed the comment and continued to stare down at her. "I just keep trying to think of some happy times we shared, some reason why I got myself involved with somebody so…cunning and deceitful, so damn scandalous. I'm a fairly intelligent man, Arthur. By God, I just… I don't understand it. I don't understand it one bit." Phil looked at his dead spouse with an odd expression on his face, as if she was some kind of alien who'd been sent to perform some cruel test on the human spirit. He hung his head and whispered to Arthur, "I am just like her, cold as ice. I don't give a rat's ass that she's lying there. I don't have a shred of remorse that, in just a few hours, she'll be buried under six feet of earth, never to see the sun shine again."

"Okay," Arthur said, this time with force. "We're outta here. Mr. Landers. Will you show us to the door please?"

"Yes, sir, I will," Landers answered, as if that type of thing happened routinely in his place of business.

Phil didn't put up any resistance. He just followed them both back to the shiny black BMW, opened the door, and slid into the seat.

The ride back to the house was as quiet as the one to the viewing. No one said a word until they finally pulled into the driveway.

"I can't wait to get rid of this place," Phil said. "It almost feels like prison will be a relief from walking through those doors every day."

Arthur didn't answer, as he didn't feel that Phil expected a response.

Phil used his keys to open the door, but when he reached inside to deactivate the alarm, he noticed that it had been reset. "Hmm. That's odd," he said. "I haven't had any problems with this system since we got it."

They walked in and flung their jackets across the couch.

When Phil noticed that his office doors were ajar, he opened them fully and stood up a little straighter, letting out a gasp. "Arthur," he said faintly, "come here. Quick!"

The office had been ransacked. Papers were everywhere, and every drawer was open. The paintings were ripped off the walls, and the safe was exposed. Fortunately, no one had been able to get into it.

"What the…?" Arthur started. "Why now, after you've lived here so long? Coincidence?" He looked around in shock. "Your bedroom," he said. "I bet they went up there."

They both ran up the staircase, and neither of them were surprised to find it in the same sad state. What was surprising, however, was that very few of Phil's things were disturbed. His closet was as he left it, and only a couple of his drawers had been tampered with. On the other hand, the contents of Lara's closet and drawers were everywhere, even strewn down the hallway. Some of her jewelry was still there, which was somewhat surprising since it was all very valuable.

"This clearly wasn't a robbery," Arthur said, pointing at Lara's expensive baubles. "If it was, you'd have more to deal with than just a mess to clean up. They had to be looking for something more specific, and they must be professionals to disarm your security system like that."

"What could they possibly have been looking for?" Phil asked, more confused than ever.

Arthur shrugged. "With that woman, maybe there's one more skeleton that has yet to surface."

"We're talking about Lara here," Phil said. "I'm thinking there's a lot more than one."

CHAPTER 24

Lilly got bravely out of the car and smoothed her dress like a grown woman would, then slowly brushed her curled hair over one shoulder.

"Are you sure you really want to do this?" Janet asked, feeling the butterflies in her stomach flutter up into her throat.

"Yes, ma'am," she answered, with a firmness that required no more questions.

The three walked up the brick steps and into the quiet building. The classical music playing in the background was so quiet that it was doubtful that it was on at all. It was one of those places, like a library, where everyone automatically spoke in hushed tones.

They signed the memory book, taking note that theirs were the only names in it. An older woman met them this time, and as if she already knew which body they were there to see, she motioned for them to go to the end of the hallway. There weren't any flowers, and Janet wanted to kick herself for not sending an arrangement, at least for Lilly's sake. The casket was to the left of the room, and Charlie reached for Lilly's hand and led her over to it. There was a stepstool already in place for the child to climb up on, and they watched in heartbroken silence as Lilly looked down at Lara, the mother she had never known, which, by all accounts had been a positive thing.

Lilly studied her face for a long time before speaking, as though she was choosing her words very carefully. "She's beautiful, ain't she?" Rather than waiting for an answer, she continued, "She will make the most beautiful angel of all."

"Yes, she will," Janet answered.

"Can I talk to her?" Lilly asked.

"Of course you can," Charlie answered. "Would you like us to leave you alone for a minute?"

"No, that's okay. I mean, I'm not scared to be in here by myself with her, but you can stay if you want," she said confidently.

"Okay," Janet said. "Go on and talk to your mommy then, honey."

Lilly reached to touch her mother's hands, which were folded just below her breasts, but she quickly withdrew her little hand, as if she feared her touch might make her mother disappear. "Mama," she said softly, leaning down to her, "I didn't know you very much, not like Ms. Helga, but I know you were sweet. I'm sorry you left me, 'cause we coulda had fun together, just you and me, like last night, when Charlie and Janet took me to get pizza, and today, when I got my hair curled at a beauty shop and not at home. I know you can see me from Heaven, and I hope you're smiling 'cause I'm wearing this new, pretty dress. I got a coat to match, but it's too warm here to wear it. I understand about you being an angel. Charlie explained it all to me, and he even gave me an angel to hold when I think about you. I'm glad you're an angel. I'm not sad, 'cause I know you can look down from Heaven now and watch me grow up. You woulda missed all that if you were still here. It's pretty here, Mama, like you. I bet you were a movie star, because all beautiful ladies are movie stars and live with the palm trees." Lilly didn't pause at all, and her voice remained the same, without the slightest bit of cracking or hesitation.

Tears streamed down Charlie's face, and Janet motioned for him to go, even as she felt her own throat stinging.

"I still love you, Mama, even though you didn't really want a daughter." She then turned to Janet and said, "Ms. Janet, I'm ready to go now. I told Mommy all I need to, and I'm not sad anymore."

Janet took her by the hand and led her to the car. They had a quick lunch and stopped by a florist for Lilly to pick out some flowers to put on Lara's grave. They decided not to attend the graveside service but to come back later to place the flowers, after she was buried. Lilly seemed to be at peace, and they didn't want to put her through any more pain or trauma than necessary.

The girl lovingly chose nine peach roses. "'Cause I'm nine years old," she said. "Well, almost ten, in another month," she added, "but that doesn't matter."

"You're right. It doesn't," Janet answered as she squeezed her close to her bosom.

CHAPTER 25

The police arrived at Phil's house within forty-five minutes to take a report on the break-in. It was short and sweet, completely by the book. A fingerprint and ID crew came in as well, and they took no longer than twenty minutes.

"No fingerprints," the lieutenant said. "Musta worn gloves and wiped everything clean."

"Apparently," Phil answered sarcastically.

The lieutenant looked at him as though he was about to make a remark but decided against it. He just wanted to leave and get back to his coffee; he wasn't in the mood to argue with some rich dumbass. "Did you notice anything missing?" the cop asked arrogantly.

"Not a thing," Phil answered, then walked away.

"Sorry about that," Arthur said. "He's just having a bad day."

The police officer ignored Arthur's comment and handed him a business card with a case number written on it. "You can pick up a copy of the report within five business days. Call me if you come up with anything else, stolen property or that kind of thing." With that, he turned, walked out of the house, and drove off in his updated police cruiser.

Charlie walked through the door about the same time the police car was pulling out of the driveway. "What's going on here?" he asked, quite aware that nothing could surprise him at that point.

"A break-in," Arthur answered. "Not a robbery though. Someone just ransacked the place, Phil's office and Lara's closet and drawers. Odd, huh?"

"Jeez, at this point, I don't wanna know about anything else the bitch was involved in. It's exhausting. How'd it go at the funeral home with Phil?"

"Eerie as hell," Arthur answered honestly, shivering at the thought. He was almost grateful for the break-in, at least it had taken his mind off the morbid mortuary visit. "How'd the daughter do?"

"Extremely well. She thinks it's better now, since her mother is an angel and can watch her grow up."

"Jesus," Arthur said. "That's enough to break anybody's heart."

"Yeah, well, I can tell ya it broke the hell outta mine. You know what's odd though? Lilly's never asked how her mother died. As long as she doesn't, I guess we won't offer up the information. I sure as hell hate to see the little thing go back to that group home though."

"So why don't you adopt her? I'm sure the State of Nebraska would be glad to have one less mouth to feed."

Before Charlie could answer, Phil walked back into the room. "Hey, man," he said in Charlie's direction. "Quite a day, huh? How'd the girl take it?"

"Surprisingly well actually. She's at the house with Janet. She'll probably fly out tomorrow morning."

"I hate this," Phil said. "I really hate it, especially for her sake."

"Phil," Charlie said, "Lara never even wanted her, had nothing to do with her, chose to abandon her. I guess the little one can't be any worse off than she was. There's one thing I need to talk to you about though. I know you said to leave the jewelry on the body, but Janet had it removed before the burial and put it in our safety deposit box. We figured it might send her little girl to college one day."

"You're always thinking with your heart, Charlie. Maybe that's why I love you so much."

The remark startled Charlie, for Phil had never been one to speak from his heart. Charlie watched as Phil poured himself a scotch then filled a glass for Arthur and him; both men took the drinks grudgingly. Arthur was used to exercising and eating healthy, and Charlie was used to beer, so the hard liquor took its toll on both of them.

"I think it'd be better if you pack up and move in with me for a while," Arthur said. "This isn't a good environment for you right now, Phil, especially after the break-in. You said so yourself, that you can't wait to get rid of the place. Why don't you go pack a few things so we can get outta here?"

"That's a good idea, Phil," Charlie said. "You've never liked this place, and being here now is keeping you from thinking straight."

"I guess you're right," Phil said, laying his face in his hands. "I won't fight you on it. Let me just grab a couple outfits. I'm sure we'll need to make trips back and forth for information."

None of them spoke as they sipped their scotch, so Phil walked upstairs to pack. He shoved everything in a bag at marathon speed and was back down the stairs within minutes. "I'll be a son-of-a-bitch if it doesn't feel like she's still up there, lurking around, waitin' to kill me," he said.

Neither man offered a reply, indicating that they felt the same way.

"Charlie," Arthur said, "I know you've gotta get back to work, man, but could you give us a little time tomorrow? We need to talk about power of attorney and that sort of thing."

"Yeah, sure. I took the week off. I'll come by around noon, after we get Lilly off to the airport. I'll bring lunch, and if we're gonna do the drinkin' thing, I'll grab some light beer." With that, he got up and walked over to pat his friend on his shoulder. "Stay strong. We all care about you. She's in the ground, man, not comin' back, so don't look back. Just look to the future. Whatever price you have to pay, just pay it and move on."

CHAPTER 26

L illy was in the kitchen when Charlie got back home. Her face brightened as soon as he walked in the door, and so did his. "Which pocket?" he asked.

"Right," she said, laughing.

"Hmm," he said. He reached in and pulled out a Milky Way candy bar and a rubber Gumby toy.

"Oh, Charlie," Janet scolded, "not before dinner. What ever happened to sugarless gum and toothbrushes?"

Charlie winked at Lilly and mocked Janet behind her back, and they both burst into laughter. "What smells so good in here?" he asked.

"Spaghetti and meatballs," Lilly quickly answered, "and garlic bread."

"Well," Charlie said in his best John Wayne drawl, "I guess that'll do nicely, ma'am."

Janet popped him on the bottom and told him to set the table, and he grinned and did as he was told.

Lilly talked nonstop throughout the dinner about how warm Los Angeles was, the palms, and all the ladies dressed in expensive dresses, with their hair piled high. She helped to clear the table, then took her bath and walked out in her pajamas. Tears formed in her eyes when she thought about it being her last night with Janet and Charlie Evans. "Ms. Helga will have a cake for my birthday," she said. "Can you come to my party next month?"

Charlie and Janet looked at one another, their faces reflecting the same sadness Lilly felt.

"We will certainly try," Janet answered.

Lilly climbed up in Charlie's lap and fell asleep. He rocked her in the recliner for a long while before carrying her to bed.

Neither of them spoke about her leaving the next day. The plane would take off at noon, and Helga would meet her at the airport. Just that easy, she would be gone. It was amazing how much she had touched their lives in such a short time, how their hearts ached for her already, before she had even gone.

* * * * *

Phil set the security alarm and didn't look back at the house, as if he feared it might follow him to Arthur's place. They drove through some of the ritzier sections of town and pulled up to a security gate before they were waved into the neighborhood.

The two men had been to many of the same parties together, but Phil had never been to Arthur's house. It was oversized, much like his own, a masculine-looking structure that resembled Windsor Castle. They pulled into the garage, and Phil retrieved his bag from the back seat and followed Arthur inside. The home was professionally decorated, Phil was sure, but it was done tastefully. The kitchen was large, although he was sure not many meals were cooked there.

Arthur led him through the vast den and into a guest bedroom. "Hope this suits you," he said. "I'll show you around, and you can make yourself at home. My den is huge because I didn't see the need for a formal living or dining room. I don't entertain often, and when I do, it's just a few of the guys coming over to watch a game or shoot some pool. I can count the times I've eaten at the kitchen table on one hand. I guess it's a bachelor thing."

Phil followed him through six bedrooms and eight baths, a beautifully decorated office with three computers and a wealth of books, then downstairs, to a well-furnished exercise and game room, equipped with pinball machines, pool and ping-pong tables, and even a skee-ball machine. "Whoa. I'm impressed," Phil said, "envious and impressed."

"Don't be," Arthur retorted. "It's just home—probably much too big but home nonetheless. When my family comes to town, there's plenty of space for them to stay over. I guess that's the only reason it's so huge. It's pretty peaceful, something I don't get in my everyday life and my job."

"Why don't you take a load off and plop down in front of the television? I have a few things to work on before Charlie comes tomorrow. There's beer in the fridge, scotch in the crystal decanter in the bar, and snacks in the kitchen. Like I said, make yourself at home."

Phil grabbed a beer and a bag of pretzels and turned on the TV. He flipped through the channels and finally settled on an old Western. Fortunately, he found himself involved in it briefly, and it took his mind off his troubles, if only for a few moments.

Four beers later, Charlie arrived with a bucket of Kentucky Fried Chicken, mashed potatoes and gravy, coleslaw, and baked beans. "More beer in the car," he said as he laid the food down on the kitchen table.

"I'll get it," Phil said. He slipped his shoes on and walked out into the fresh air. He looked skyward and let the bright sunshine warm his face, feeling calmer than he had for the past few days. He looked around the small, perfectly manicured lawn, typical to expensive gated communities, and walked around to enjoy all the flower gardens the gardener had planted. Phil laughed to himself. *Funny I should be taking time to smell the roses now. I guess I'm a day late and a dollar short.*

A few minutes later, Charlie walked outside to check on him. "You okay, man?"

"Yeah. Just got a little sidetracked."

The two men walked slowly to the back yard, around the house, and back to the car.

Charlie huffed as he lifted the case of light beer out of the back seat. "Damn, I need to get in shape."

"Yes, you do," Phil answered.

The three men ate their chicken without any conversation, licking their fingers between bites. It was obvious that Charlie's mind was somewhere other than the kitchen table.

Arthur finally broke the silence, looking Charlie's way, "So? You wanna tell us what's eating at you?"

"Hell, Arthur," Charlie answered, "there are a lotta things eating at me. For starters, my best friend's about to go on trial for murder."

"Yeah," Arthur said, "but there's something else. It's that little girl, isn't it?"

Charlie shifted uncomfortably in his chair and cleared his throat, as though a bit of extra-crispy had gotten caught in it.

"You don't have to feel bad on my account," Phil said. "I'm glad you and Janet were there for her. It doesn't sound like the poor kid's had a very happy life."

"She hasn't," Charlie said. "I feel strange talking about her around you, Phil, but she made a big impact on us. It hurt like hell to see her go."

"I'm telling you, Charlie," Arthur said, "you two should just adopt her. She needs someone, and you and Janet would make excellent parents."

"Let's just change the subject, okay? I'm tired and just need a few beers," Charlie answered.

"Well, if you need my help, I'm here," Arthur said. "Really. I mean it."

"Since when did you start needing beer?" Phil asked, laughing. "I thought I held the market on alcohol addiction these days."

"Yeah, and you need to slow down, man," Arthur said. "We've got some serious business to conduct."

Charlie put the tops on the side dishes and the bucket of chicken and placed them in the fridge. "Right. Let's not prolong the inevitable," he said.

"Well," Arthur began, "the first priority is power of attorney over your funds and other business dealings, Phil. Let's consider the worst-case scenario, you going to prison for a few years. I know you don't wanna hear it, but it has to be addressed, and the sooner, the better. I assume you want to sell the house, or else you could keep it as an investment, which has its pros and cons. You'd have to find a caretaker, somebody to be responsible for the upkeep. There will be insurance and taxes to be paid, along with mortgages, etc."

"No, like I said earlier, I want to get rid of the place as soon as possible," Phil said quickly. "I've got no second thoughts about that. I want it out of my life, along with everything in it, for that matter. The last thing I need are any reminders of that bitch and all she bought on my dime."

"Okay," Arthur continued. "I see that you're adamant about that, so I won't push the issue. It's really in your best interest to sell anyway. Your checking and other accounts will need to be taken care of, and money has to be available for attorney fees, etc. That requires a power of attorney, which I'm assuming you'd be willing to grant to Charlie. Am I right?"

Phil looked at Charlie, long and hard. "You're a good man, Charlie, and the best friend I've ever had, but I hate to put you in this position. After all, you have your life, the hospital, Janet—"

"I also have a best friend who needs a little help right now, a friend who's been there for me and would be there for me if the shoe was on the other foot."

"You know you're the only person, besides Janet and Arthur here, whom I trust."

"The easiest thing to do," Arthur continued, "would be to go to the bank and put Charlie's name on all your accounts. That would ease things up a bit for the power of attorney. Then, of course, we'll have the proper paperwork taken care of. Charlie can sign all legal proceedings and paperwork for you regarding the sale of the residence, etc. I can make an appointment at the bank after hours, so you won't run into your adoring fans and Charlie won't miss any work. I'll look into that today and let you both know."

"Have you decided on a bench trial for sure?" Charlie asked.

"Yeah. I think that would be best," Arthur explained. "We've got enough on her right now to prove she would have driven anyone to the brink, and I hate to take our chances with some feminist jury who might have a heart for the lying bitch. It's a classic case of voluntary manslaughter, and that's what we'll go for."

"What is that in English, Arthur?" Phil asked, instantly looking tired and in deep need of sleep. "I can't handle the legalese right now, man."

"Technically, for someone to be found guilty of voluntary manslaughter, the murder was committed in the heat of passion, due to adequate provocation. That passion has to be provoked by fear, rage, anger, or terror. Provocation, in order to be adequate, must be such that might naturally cause a reasonable person, in the passion of the moment, to lose self-control and act on impulse, without reflection."

"Sounds like you hit the nail on the head with that one," Charlie answered.

"If you men will excuse me," Phil interrupted, "I think I'll go take a nap. I finally feel like I can sleep. I guess everything's catching up with me, and I'm just exhausted."

"Go ahead," Arthur said. "We've done enough for today. Sleep is the best thing for you." After Phil left the room, he turned to Charlie and said, "Listen, I meant what I said about that adoption."

"I know," Charlie answered. "I guess I just don't want to be disappointed.

Janet and I have wanted a child since the beginning of our marriage. I've never considered adoption as an option, and I certainly never thought that little girl would win our hearts like she did. Of all things, the irony of her being Lara's daughter."

"That doesn't seem to affect your feelings for her."

"No. It's just...well, with everything Phil's been through and—"

"I'm sure Phil would understand. You heard him say so himself. He's not a cruel man, and he won't take Lara out on that child. For Christ's sake, give him some credit."

"I know," Charlie answered sadly, "but it's going to be difficult for all of us to put this behind us. I mean, he's selling the house and its contents, Lara is buried, and his trial will be over. I'm sure Phil will want a chance to let it all go and move on, and if that little girl is around... You heard what he said about wanting no reminders."

"That's the biggest crock of shit I've ever heard," Arthur snapped angrily. "You and Janet love the kid, she loves you, and you can offer her a good life, one she otherwise might never have the opportunity to enjoy." "

"How would we get her?" Charlie asked, skeptical that it would even be a possibility. "I mean, aren't there a bunch of rules and legalities? We're not even blood relatives."

"Well, you said she doesn't have any living relatives except her slime of a father, who'll be incarcerated till she's a legal adult. You're upstanding citizens. I mean, my God, Charlie. A doctor and a teacher? Who wouldn't let you adopt her?"

"Doesn't her father have some type of rights? Will he have to sign her over?"

"As cold as it sounds, since her father will not have the opportunity to raise her, she's considered a ward of the State. It can be done, Charlie. Just talk to Janet, think about it, and let me know. If you need help with the legal end, I'm all yours."

CHAPTER 27

With the proper paperwork taken care of at the bank, the house on the market, and everyone praying as hard as they could, Phil entered the courtroom on what would be his last day as a free man for a good, long while. He was dressed in a gray cashmere suit, a starched white shirt, and dark blue tie. His hair was neatly trimmed, he was clean shaven, and he looked like he was stepping into a photo shoot for *GQ* rather than standing before a judge to be sentenced for murder.

Arthur was well prepared, just as they all expected, and he also looked like the picture of masculinity and charm. He sat beside Phil at the large oak table, with an expressionless face and a yellow legal pad in front of him, an expensive gold pen poised in his large hand. The bailiff entered and demanded that everyone rise for Judge Sykes. They all heaved a sigh of relief for a male judge, even though they still did not know which way it would go.

Janet sat in the back with her hands folded beneath her chin and her head bowed in silent prayer, tears streaming down her face. Charlie was in the front row, directly behind Phil, looking unworried and pulled together but feeling his insides churning like hell. All their hopes would be put to the test over the next few days, and Charlie felt himself swaying from side to side to keep from fainting.

Opening statements went as planned, with Arthur presenting the evidence to be shown leading to the voluntary manslaughter plea and the prosecutor arguing that an innocent woman had been murdered.

Phil sat upright and motionless in his chair, having finally come to the grim realization that it had all really happened. He had made peace with it and was ready to move forward, even if it meant spending time in prison.

After only two days of arguments from both sides, Judge Sykes recessed the court and sent everyone home, then assured them he would return with his verdict the next morning. Phil, Arthur, Janet, and Charlie all went back to Arthur's house, with all their nerves on edge.

Phil filled four glasses with expensive wine and raised his for a toast. "Here's to the three people who've made my life worth living, who've kept me sane throughout this insane ordeal. No matter what happens tomorrow in that courtroom, we will not be saddened or angry. I believe in the justice system, and if justice means I am to serve time in prison, so be it. Every day spent there will be a day closer to my freedom, closer to sharing another glass of wine with my friends." Tears streamed down Phil's face, but his voice never faltered. "My life was not a good one before this happened. I denied myself that, and I deprived the people around me of it. Now, I have an opportunity to begin anew, somewhere other than Cedar Sinai, other than Los Angeles. Somewhere out there in that vast world of ours lies my real destiny, my chance for true happiness. Here's to good friends, who've become my family, and to new beginnings!"

They all raised their glasses to clink them, then gulped down the wine. In fact, they all drank from them many times that night, hoping that each glass would deaden the pain just a little more.

CHAPTER 28

Morning came quickly, just as they all expected, but there weren't any signs of the sadness or drunkenness from the night before as Phil stood to be sentenced in front of the courts.

Judge Sykes looked at Arthur and Prosecutor James Edwards, then finally rested his eyes on Phil. "Mr. Sawyer," he started, "I have put a great deal of thought into this, and I am not ashamed to say I have even consulted the Man Upstairs. This case has proven difficult for me. A woman was killed, her life taken far too early, long before one should have departed this Earth, and another person must be held accountable for that crime. I have considered all the evidence as well. For the last eight years, a great deal of your life has been taken from you. Your prestigious career as a respectable surgeon, that great success you worked very hard to achieve, was taken from you and is something that you will not be able to regain. This is a great travesty, not only for you, but also for the patients you might have had the opportunity to help. I feel for you, Mr. Sawyer. I really do. Nevertheless, I sit before you as a representative of the United States justice system, and I have to do what is deemed right by the law, regardless of the circumstances. I hereby sentence you to twenty years at San Quentin. You will serve eight of those years in incarceration and the remainder on probation. May God be with you." With that, the judge stood, turned, and exited out of a large mahogany door that led back to his chambers, his black robe whooshing like a superhero's cape behind him.

The bailiffs were there in an instant to haul Phil off to prison, but they kindly gave him a moment to hug Arthur and Charlie and blow a kiss to Janet.

"I'll be fine," Phil said to Charlie. "Just hold down the fort, buddy. I love you." Then he was gone, the handcuffs glistening behind his back.

Charlie broke down and sobbed on Arthur's broad shoulder, until his suit jacket was wet with tears. Arthur repeatedly cleared his throat, holding back tears of his own. He grabbed Charlie's arm and led him back to Janet. The three embraced, long and hard, until Arthur finally broke down with them.

"I'm sorry, folks, but we're going to have to ask you to clear the courtroom," a bailiff softly said to them.

After pulling themselves together, the heartbroken trio walked out into the sunshine.

"Do you want to go to lunch?" Arthur asked. "My treat."

"No thanks," Charlie answered, finally able to muster a smile. "We have a 3 o'clock flight. We have a birthday party to go to and our little girl to bring home."

PART TWO
San Quentin

CHAPTER 1

Phil found it somewhat difficult to step up onto the bus while shackled to the other prisoners with both handcuffs and leg irons. No one spoke, for they had little to talk about. They were all on the way to prison, and that left nothing pleasant to discuss.

San Quentin. The thought of his destination just kept rolling around in Phil's head. He'd heard all the horror stories, knew about the violence that went down in the big house. He also remembered the one promise he had made to himself that he wouldn't look back because he couldn't change anything anyway.

Phil sat down on a worn, greasy seat and swallowed hard. He looked at the few men around him, trying not to be too obvious about it. Their faces and eyes were blank, masking any fear that was racing through their bodies and minds. The stench on the bus was wretched, a mixture of unwashed armpits and stale cigarette smoke. Phil was still wearing his civilian clothes, so he stood out like a sore thumb and wished he'd have chosen something a little more casual for his trip to prison.

No one had bothered to inform him how long of a ride he was in for on the smelly transport, and it seemed an eternity before they turned onto a dusty dirt road that was full of ruts and crevices. The men bounced in their seats, bumping shoulders with one another, and not in the pleasant way that Phil always enjoyed about the cobblestone. When they saw the gothic building and compound come into sight, a young black kid in the front broke into sobs and began wiping his runny nose on the shoulder of his t-shirt. The rest of the men diverted their eyes from the building. Some hung their heads and closed their eyes, as if they were deep in prayer or were hoping it was just some horrible nightmare they might wake up from.

The old bus creaked to a stop, and the prisoners were greeted by a group of husky, hard-faced men in dark green suits, boasting gold badges that glistened in the sunlight. As the line of inmates walked off the bus, they methodically removed the cuffs from each man, which was a great relief. Phil rubbed his wrists, trying to get the blood flowing back to his cold hands again. As soon as he stepped inside, his name was checked off the list. He was sent to a room where he was stripped of his clothes and belongings and stood naked among the men who were waiting to be searched for any contraband. Phil had heard of cavity searches before, but he had no idea it was far worse than what the movies depicted.

They moved him on and issued yet another orange jumpsuit, the color that indicated he was new to the prison population. The grooming room was next, where hair was cut to the very short standards of the warden and the State. When Phil reached the chair, the barber motioned him through, as he'd just had a haircut; if he wasn't caught in such a shitty situation, he might have laughed at the thought that he'd save forty bucks for his haircuts over the next eight years.

The following week was a blur to him; there were medical exams, skills assessments, and orientations to deal with. He slept on a small cot in a large dorm room, among all his new friends, none of whom spoke for the entire week. They all dreaded their upcoming release into the general population. Phil wasn't sure what awaited him there, but he knew things on the inside were not going to be good.

They were not allowed any phone calls, so he could only wonder how Charlie and Janet were holding up. He hoped they'd be able to go on with their lives. He thought of Arthur, who was probably on to his next case, returning home to his large den with his takeout food. Arthur was such a good guy, and Phil wondered why he hadn't made time for a social life over the years. *I guess he's like me, too busy trying to reach the top of that ladder. If he only knew that it's not all it's cracked up to be,* he thought, shaking his head and trying to doze off to sleep, his only respite from his dire surroundings.

CHAPTER 2

The brutes in green woke the group at 5:00 a.m. and yelled for them to form a single-file line. The inmates walked like school children, until they reached a large room with a counter in the front.

"Today, you'll receive your regular clothing and be assigned a cell number," a large white man yelled, as though he could possibly intimidate them any more than they already were. "You get three pairs of jeans, three blue shirts, three pairs of socks, three pairs of boxers, and a pair of work boots. Your clothes will be laundered once a week, unless your job requires otherwise. Your work assignments are written on a slip in your bag. You will also find a roll of toilet paper, a toothbrush, and other essentials. Should you find that you do not like what we have to offer you, you are welcome to purchase other items at the canteen, at your own expense, of course. You will be permitted to shop once a week." He slapped his hand hard on the countertop and growled out, "Listen up for your name, step forward, get your shit, and go to that door for your cell assignment."

The line moved fairly quickly, and Phil looked down at the small laundry bag that contained all his worldly possessions. He felt like a monk, journeying into the desert with his few pieces of fruit and a loaf of hard bread. He was told he'd be in H Block, "The one where we keep murderers," the officer loudly announced. "You're in Cell 25." Each man then followed a uniformed tour guide who showed them to their quarters.

As Phil walked, a plethora of prison movies began to roll through his mind: *Escape from Alcatraz, Papillon, Cool Hand Luke, Shawshank...* The cellblock seemed to go up for stories, and the noise was unbelievable. Men were banging on the bars like animals, screaming profanities and threats to the new arrivals, and others sat in an open area, men who looked like they wouldn't think twice about taking a life. The men in cells with iron doors shot birds through the small windows. For the first time, Phil felt it in the pit of his stomach: a bitter cocktail of fear, remorse, and the knowledge that he would never survive eight years in there. He swallowed the vomit that filled his throat; he refused to let them see it. He could tell that they thrived on weakness, so he fruitlessly tried to hide behind a stone face, hoping his height might play to his advantage. Phil just wanted to get to his cell, his new home, where he hoped he'd be safe, locked behind the orange door that would encompass his new life. He was glad the cells on his floor were equipped with doors and not just bars; that would make it far easier to hide from the other murderers and keep to himself.

He looked around at his cell and found that it was very similar to the one he'd left behind at the county jail, only smaller, much to his amazement. It was furnished with a steel toilet, a small metal sink, one desk with an attached stool, two metal lockers, and a set of bunk beds. The top bunk was obviously his, as the bottom one was already made, with all the precision a Marine drill sergeant would demand, tucked so tight they could bounce a quarter off it. Phil tried to picture in his mind the men who'd spent most of their lives in that very room, those ghosts of the past who'd struggled through years, even decades, of loneliness and fear, self-doubt and hopelessness. He wondered what had brought them here and how many had died before they were able to savor the taste of freedom again. He closed his eyes and shook his head with a force strong enough to change his thoughts.

When he opened his eyes and looked around the room again, he realized that the cell was really rather clean. There were two pictures taped to the wall beside the bottom bunk: one of a black woman in her forties and another of an older black woman and man. He wondered what his cellmate was like, what type of person he would be stuck with for the years to come. He pictured a large, muscled black man who would attack him the moment he met him.

The metal slot in the door opened loudly, and a tray was impatiently shoved through it. "Breakfast," a deep, angry voice said. "Take it or leave it."

Phil jumped up to retrieve his tray and peeked out the slot, where he saw only the blue blur of a prisoner's uniform. He walked over to the small desk that wouldn't even accommodate the entirety of the hard, plastic tray, and he took a seat on the round stool that barely accommodated his lanky frame. The food didn't look too bad, and he had learned by now that he simply had to force himself to eat whatever they gave him; if he was going to survive in the hellhole, he had to nourish his body. He finished quickly, and when the slot banged open again, he passed the empty tray through it, without any words being exchanged.

Lunch was also passed through the slot, or at least smashed through it. The brown bag contained two peanut butter sandwiches, an orange, and a piece of mushy cake. A milk carton followed, and when Phil took it, his hand brushed the man's on the other side of the metal door. It was his first physical contact with anyone in a long time, and it felt quite odd.

Phil decided to unpack his belongings. He placed his towel, washcloth, shower shoes, and toiletries neatly in the locker. At the bottom of the bag, he found an envelope with his name scrawled on it. He opened it slowly, wondering what occupation he'd been assigned. He pictured himself punching out car tags in a sweaty basement, surrounded by dangerous fugitives who would try his manhood. His hands trembled with apprehension as he opened the note and read it: "Laundry: 7:00 a.m. to 7:00 p.m." He heaved huge breaths, trying to calm himself as he thought about where he'd come from and the fact that his life would now revolve around washing sweaty, filthy clothes worn by the men sentenced to spend their lives in this pit of despair. Most didn't even give a damn that they were there, and now he'd have to wash and fold their soiled socks and underwear.

Time flashed by as he lay on the top bunk. A short while later, he heard a buzz, and the door slid open. In stepped a small black man, probably in his sixties, with graying hair and missing teeth. A strange odor was coming off him; Phil would later learn it was the aroma of the turnip greens he'd prepared for last meal of the day. The man didn't look up or even acknowledge Phil's presence, so Phil decided to take the bull by the horns. "Hello. My name is Phil Sawyer," He said.

The older man finally looked up at him with the same expressionless face that seemed to be common among most of the inmates. "Don't nobody go by a name in here. This ain't no country club, like where you come from. I seen you on the news. We's all did. From now on, your name's 'Doc.' We already settled on that, whether ya like it or not."

Phil sat in silence for a minute, trying to decipher what the man had told him. His cellmate's Southern accent was thick, and his grammar made it clear that he had not gotten very far in his education. "I see," Phil answered. "What does everyone call you?"

"I'm Pops. I ain't had no roommate in a few months, and I ain't too fond of it neither. I hope you ain't a talker. Got no time for that."

"I'll try to remember that," Phil said. He was confused yet relieved; the man looked harmless enough.

"You ain't like the rest of us'ns. You ain't gonna make it here. Just lettin' ya know early."

Phil didn't answer. He couldn't, for his mouth suddenly went dry, and his chest was full of panic. He watched as Pops carefully pulled out a worn bag of Brown Mule tobacco. He took a wad that had obviously already been chewed and placed it in his mouth, then sat down on his bed and pulled a pair of worn boots out from under it. Pops used his washcloth to scrub and clean the boots, until they sparkled like lights on a Macy's Christmas tree. Then he pulled a larger pair out and did the same.

"Must like you more than they like me," Phil said, trying to sound friendly. "I only got one pair of boots."

"Nobody gets more than the next man 'round here, lest you're crooked... which I ain't," he said flatly. "Ten cleanin's gets me a pouch of tobacco. Ain't got no money on the books. I work for mines." He held up his hands, as if to prove his point, both of them gnarled with arthritis. Phil was sure that it was painful, but he could also see that Pops was a proud man, and he respected that.

The doors buzzed open, and an alarm sounded, leaving Phil wondering what the hell he was supposed to do. He sat still on the bed, afraid to ask what it meant.

"Time for chow," Pops explained. "Jus' follow the crowd and try to stay outta trouble...or handle it if it comes yer way. Chow hall and the rec' yard is where folks'll try ya."

Phil got up and followed the others down the stairs and into a huge dining hall. Huge guards stood tall, with their batons out and ready, methodically slapping them against their hands. He picked up his tray and was suddenly jolted back to his first day of junior high, feeling frightened and uncertain about where he should sit. Ultimately, he decided it best to just follow the man in front and sit down next to him. The noise of the place reverberated in his head so loudly that he feared it might burst.

Suddenly, without any warning or provocation, the man across the table from him reached over with his greasy hand, grabbed the fried chicken from Phil's plate, and took a bite before throwing it back on his tray. The table grew quiet, and Phil realized it was a pivotal point, one that would determine how he was going to be treated by the others while he was locked up.

"What ya gonna do, Doc? Gonna kill me like you did yer old lady?"

"Fuck you, man," Phil said, louder than he intended to. "I'm already stuck in this fucking hellhole, and I'll be damned if I'm gonna take any shit from you."

"Oh, Doc's a big talker. What do you know about prison or the streets, motherfucker? You ain't gon' do shit."

Before Phil could even think about it, he reached over and grabbed the hefty man by his shirt and jerked him across the table. "You don't wanna fuck with me, man. Trust me."

Before he could make another move, three guards were breaking them up.

One took a hard swing against the middle of Phil's back, knocking him to the floor. "You aren't starting off too good, are you, man?" the officer asked as he cuffed him and pulled him to his feet. "But it's nothing a few days in the hole won't cure."

* * * * *

Seven days in the hole did cure Phil, but he also didn't regret his behavior. He had done what was expected of him, and he was sure even the correctional officers understood that. They let him out in the afternoon and led him back to his cell.

Pops was there, shining more boots. When he looked up at Phil, his mouth formed a slow, toothless smile. "What were you planning on doin' if the guards wouldn'ta showed up?"

"Hell if I know," Phil answered.

Pops laughed until his thin shoulders shook, and then he shook his gray head. "You done what you had to do, Doc," he said. "Can't never let your guard down 'round here. We ain't on the school playground, ya know. You'll see more violence here than in any hospital. I admit, I didn't think you had it in ya."

The door buzzed, and the alarm sounded again, and Phil felt a knot forming in the pit of his stomach. "Shit, not again."

"Jus' hold ya head up, Doc. Don't let 'em see ya sweat."

Phil heeded that wise advice and sat down in the same place he sat before, praying to himself that God would see him through at least one last meal.

The same beefy creature plopped down in the seat directly across from him. "How'd you like the hole, Doc?"

"I got at least eight years. I guess it doesn't matter which room they throw me in in this shit hole," he answered, trying to sound a little less educated.

The man laughed and threw his roll on Phil's plate. "Don't touch me again… ever. Ya hear?"

"Not a problem," Phil answered, "as long as you don't make me."

The man looked at him for a minute, hard, until his face finally relaxed. "Name's Blaze," he said.

Phil nodded, knowing better than to carry on too much of a conversation. *This isn't exactly a family dinner,* he told himself. He knew it was just Blaze's way of letting him know there wouldn't be any further complications with him.

The noisy chow hall had succeeded in giving Phil another unbearable headache. He dumped his tray and headed back to his cell, but by the time he reached his bunk, he was rubbing his temples with a vengeance.

Pops dug around at the bottom of his locker and produced a small white tablet. "Take this, but don't call me in the mornin', Doc," he joked, handing it to Phil.

Skeptical, Phil looked down at it, then back up at his cellmate. "What is it?"

"Bay'r," he said. "It ain't strong medicine or nothin', but it'll generally kill a headache. You gotta give things a while in here. You'll get used to it."

Phil took the aspirin and smiled with the appreciation it deserved. "Thanks, Pops. It hurts like hell. I don't think I'll ever get used to this."

Pops laughed a soft chuckle through his toothless mouth. "Tell me," he said, sounding a little embarrassed. "Tell me 'bout some of them fancy restaurants you ate at out there. What was they like?"

Phil was surprised by the question and the prospect of sharing a relatively normal, casual conversation with someone who had been so adamantly against having a roommate just the week before. He lay back on his bunk and stared at the ceiling. "It was real nice," he started, trying to stay on the same level of vocabulary that Pops was used to. "Expensive china plates that cost over a hundred bucks a piece, glasses made of crystal, and tablecloths made of fine linen. The steaks were huge, the fish was buttery, and the wine was delicious."

"Ain't never tasted no wine," Pop answered. "Had white lightnin' once. That's moonshine to you fancy folks. The Good Book says we shouldn't take part in any o' that though."

"I guess you're right, Pops," Phil said, "but I've always had a weakness for wine. I've even had a few shots of scotch in my day."

"Ain't you a doctor? Didn't nobody in that fancy medical school ever tell ya that stuff'll hurt ya?"

"Everything in moderation, Pops. That's what it's all about."

They both lay in their bunks in silence for quite a while.

Finally, Phil asked, "Ever been married?"

"Nope. Guess you could say I married San Quentin 'fore I had a chance to find a real lady."

Phil wanted to ask him more, but he didn't dare. He was making progress and didn't want to push it. *Besides, I've got plenty of time to find out more about this guy*, he reasoned. *We've got nothing but time.*

CHAPTER 3

The door buzzed earlier than Phil wanted it to, just when he finally surrendered to his first real night of sleep. He rose up and swung his legs over the side of the bunk, then stretched his arms as far as he could without smacking the ceiling. Pops was already up, brushing what few teeth he still had and getting dressed.

"Damn," Phil said. "What time is it?"

"Five thirty a.m., Doc," he answered. "This ain't no free ride 'round here. We got no snooze buttons."

"So I see," Phil answered, pushing himself off the top bunk and landing with a thud. "My first day at the new job," he said. "Hope I'll make it without a fight."

"Don't count on it," Pops said. "Trust me on that."

"Great," Phil said, rubbing his eyes and preparing himself for his morning headache.

In the chow hall, Phil ate his eggs and overdone toast, drank his milk, and dumped his tray. He asked a guard where he was to report for laundry duty.

The guard impatiently pointed to the left. "Just follow the sound of washers and dryers," he answered dryly, then turned away.

Gee, that shouldn't be a problem, Phil thought. *This place is only as big as a damn ancient castle. I'm sure I'll find it in no time.* He sighed and rolled his eyes at the guard's back, then followed the hallway. He was halfway down the corridor when he reached a staircase and heard the rumblings of the laundry room. He slowly made his way down the steps, holding his breath without even being aware of it.

The room was extremely large, packed with industrial-sized machines and men were already working to load and unload them.

A small guard with thick, outdated glasses marked his name off a roster. "See that man over there," he said, pointing to a large bald man with tattoos covering his bulging arms. "He'll train you."

Phil walked over with the most confident stride he could muster and introduced himself to the brute. "Name's Phil Sawyer," he said. "They said you'll teach me the ropes."

"Yeah, I heard 'bout you. You're a wife-killer, a smartass, and some kinda big shot, an educated doctor. We don't go by birth names here, Doc. We sure as hell ain't family." He waited for a reply from Phil, but when he didn't get one, he continued, "I'm Tiny, and I hope you're a fast learner, 'cause I got lotsa work to do. This ain't a pretty job. We get the wash from the entire institution—the wacko ward, death row, the whole damn works. It's hot, and you gotta handle lotsa shitty stuff—literally sometimes."

"I'll do what I gotta do," Phil answered with a shrug.

"You'll start on the washers. That's always the new man's job." In a quick, efficient, professional manner, Tiny explained how to work the machines and keep the laundry in the right cellblock order. "Detergent ain't no good," he said, "so don't expect to get any spots out or nothin'. Just add what I told ya."

Phil did just that for ten straight hours, stopping only to eat his bagged lunch at the wobbly wooden table that sat among the workstations. No one spoke, but the silence seemed to make the time pass quickly as they all focused on the monotonous task set before them.

When the bell rang, indicating that it was time to go back to their cellblocks, Phil was tired, sweaty, and ready for bed. *To hell with dinner,* he thought.

"Ya didn't do bad for yer first day," Tiny said as they walked out.

For the first time since the cuffs were slapped on him, Phil missed the hospital. He looked down at his soggy clothes and laughed at the contradiction, recalling his crisp, white, starched lab coat. He wondered what everyone at the hospital was saying and thinking, but he ultimately decided that, deep down, he really didn't give a damn. He did, however, wish he had taken the time to compliment the good nurses who always went out of their way to be good to his patients, even if it was just a half-assed pat on the back, like the one Tiny gave him.

Phil walked into the cell, changed his clothes, and desperately wished it was his day for a shower. He would have climbed up on his bunk, but he couldn't muster the strength.

Pops looked at him and gave him a smile that quickly turned to laughter. "Ain't ever worked no menial labor before, have ya, Doc? Builds character. That's what my pa always told me anyway."

Phil rolled his eyes, which only caused the man to laugh more. He washed his face and climbed, slowly and painfully, up to his bunk.

"Last thing you wanna do is fall asleep 'fore ya get a bite," Pops said. "Your body's gonna need tonight's meal. Trust me on that. I started in the laundry. I know."

Just as Phil's head touched the pillow, the doors buzzed open, and he grudgingly rose. "Damn," he said with a groan. "I'm never gonna live through eight years of this Pops."

"Yeah ya will. You'll do what you gotta do."

Phil followed the line to the chow hall, carried his tray to the table, and sat down across from Blaze. They didn't exchange any words, but that was fine with him. He had quickly learned that silence was the best way to avoid conflict.

Just as Phil swallowed his first bite of the roast beef and gravy over rice, he heard a scream that sounded as if it was coming from a wild animal. He turned quickly in his chair and gasped when he saw blood spurting so high in the air that it almost reached the ceiling. "Jesus Christ," he said, racing toward the bleeding man.

The guards didn't seem to be too shocked or in too much of a hurry to handle the situation, but one radioed and reported, "We got a shanking down here in chow hall. Looks like this one will be DOA, so there's no rush."

Phil couldn't believe the callous report as he knelt beside the dying man, who had little energy left to scream. He peeled the man's bloodstained shirt off and pushed down hard on the wound. The stab was right to the jugular, and the guard's diagnosis was unfortunately probably right: He would be DOA before help arrived. Phil looked around at the massive puddle of blood and leaned down, toward the man's face. "It's okay. I've got direct pressure on the wound, and help is on the way."

The man nodded, as if he believed it, but his eyes rolled back as he drew his last breath.

Phil, still holding the man in his arms and covered with blood himself, looked up at the overweight officer and was surprised to see a grin. "Who did this?" Phil demanded. "Aren't you even going to look for the culprit? Maybe somebody should do that instead of gawking at this dead man."

The officer laughed. "That blood ain't comin' outta your clothes, and we ain't issuing you no more. Get used to it. This ain't no hospital. That's an inmate, a damn statistic, and we don't send flowers either." With that, he walked away.

Phil looked around the room in shock, only to find that no one else seemed to care. The other inmates were nonchalantly eating and talking, as if nothing had happened. He felt like screaming, like slapping some sanity into all of them, but he thought better of it.

A couple men in white suits and rubber gloves arrived, obviously in no hurry. They put the young man on a gurney and wheeled him away, with all the prowess of garbage men.

Phil sat on the floor, covered in blood until the last person emptied his tray and left the chow hall.

"Get up and dump your tray," a voice demanded. "Then get to your block."

When Phil walked back into his cell, Pops was taking a used piece of tobacco out of his worn pouch. Neither man said anything. Phil reached for a washcloth, wet it, and tried to get as much of the blood off as he could.

"I respect what you did back there," Pops finally said, "but you ain't gonna make it 'round here if ya pull a stunt like that again. Ain't none of our business, plain and simple."

"I'm a doctor, Pops," Phil answered, tears rolling down his cheeks. "It's in my blood. I can't help it. I can't just let a man die in front of me."

"You better figure out how to help it, or next time, you'll be the one gettin' shanked."

"How do they even have weapons in here?" Phil asked.

"The inmates make knives outta everything. Could be glass, wood, or even them disposable toothbrushes. They got hours to think about nothin' but new ways to kill each other."

"But how do they get them past the guards?"

Pops laughed, as if it was the most naïve remark he'd ever heard. "You really are green, ain't ya? Them inmates is a whole lot smarter than them officers. The guards know it too. That's why they ignore 'em or pretend they can't find 'em. For them, one dead inmate is one less to watch and worry about, no love lost."

"My God. Does it happen often?" Phil asked.

"You're in San Quentin, Doc, the worst of the worst. All you can do is watch yer own back. Don't go playin' doctor in here, or you'll drive yourself crazy and get killed in the process."

Phil rinsed the cloth out one final time, then climbed onto his bunk and laid it across his face. "Damn Lara. Damn her to hell."

Phil was almost asleep when he heard Pops whisper, "It's Welles."

"Huh?" he whispered back.

"Name's Welles, just between me and you."

Phil didn't answer. Instead, he just smiled beneath the wet rag, wondering if it was the old man's first name or last.

CHAPTER 4

The weekends brought a respite from the grind of laundry business, and Phil was grateful for that. He was slowly adapting to the routine, but he knew he'd never fully be okay with the lifestyle at San Quentin.

A letter earlier in the week had let him know that Charlie and Arthur would be up to visit that day, and he had mixed emotions about that. Of course he desperately wanted to see them, but he just hated for them to see him here, in this place, in this condition. Besides that, a glance into the real world would only make him realize what he was missing. He prayed every night that he wouldn't leave this place a changed man, that he wouldn't become an animal like so many around him.

The buzzer signaled that it was breakfast, and he ate heartily, as he had become accustomed to. Work and worry wouldn't allow his body to gain weight, but he needed the nourishment. He was allowed a shower, and he scrubbed his hair and body extra hard, as if he could wash away the stench of the place before he met with his friends. He was also looking forward to canteen privileges. There, he could upgrade the State-issued toiletries and buy his own brands, along with snacks and some soda. Pops always refused any offer to share in his loot, no matter how many times Phil offered.

Phil was also excited to be able to order some books from Barnes and Noble, which the canteen would have mailed directly to the prison. That was another bit of good news, because he was growing tired of reading sleazy romance novels and magazines with missing pages.

Welles was shining boots when the door buzzed.

Phil quickly hopped off his bunk and stepped out of the cell.

"You got a couple visitors, Doc," the young guard said. He had dirty blond hair, and it was clearly a struggle for him to avoid offering a friendly smile. Phil guessed he was in his early twenties, so the place hadn't sucked the life out of him yet. He still had compassion and feelings, and he didn't belong there any more than Phil did.

Phil followed the guard into the visitation area and sat in an old, stained cubicle, next to a black phone that looked like it belonged in a museum. He would not be allowed contact visits for a long time, so he had to settle for looking through the greasy Plexiglas. He glanced across to Arthur and Charlie, their faces mirroring horror as he sat down. He picked up the receiver and motioned for them to do the same. "Hey, you two," Phil said, his voice breaking with emotion. "I'm so damn glad to see you."

They both sat silent for a moment, their faces stuck in the same expression.

Charlie finally broke away from the initial shock and answered, "Good to see you, too, man. You look so…well, thin and tired."

"Hell," Phil answered, trying to put them at ease, "I'm in the big house. What'd you expect?"

Neither of them smiled.

"Hey, if you're just gonna bring me down—"

"No," Arthur said, speaking for the first time, "We're sorry, Phil. It's just hard for us to see you…like this. It's just not right. You don't belong here."

"Well, that is neither here nor there, Arthur. We've just gotta deal with it. It's not so bad. You don't even know how good your faces look right now, but we don't have all day, so let's not get emotional. How's Janet?"

"She's good," Charlie answered. "She just wishes she could be here. She prays for you every night."

"Tell her I appreciate that," Phil said. "I pray for myself every damn night too." He laughed a little at the remark, but Charlie and Arthur didn't even crack a smile. "For Christ's sake," Phil said. "Lighten up."

They both squirmed in their seats and tried to act a little more upbeat.

"How's the lawyer business, Arthur?"

"Busy as hell. I've got some pretty serious cases right now, all of which are depriving me of sleep, sex, and good meals."

"Sounds like this place," Phil answered, a remark that finally drew a small laugh from the two of them. "Tell me about the hospital, Charlie. What about that young girl we visited, the one with the two kids. She's been weighing on my mind, though I don't know why."

"The hospital's busy. Nothing serious, just the usual," Charlie answered, a bit uncomfortable talking medicine to Phil, knowing that he would never practice again. "Susan's doing about the same, still struggling—"

"Listen, I've got a good chunk of money, Charlie, and… Well, I've been thinking. Could you move her into a somewhat decent apartment near town and pay her rent, utilities, and phone for a year? I mean, how much could it be? It won't even make a dent in my pocket. Besides, my money's just sitting there making more."

Charlie looked baffled. "Where's this coming from, Phil?" he asked.

"I've got a lot of time to think here. I mean, a lot, and I keep playing that night over and over in my head. That little one's worn-out pajamas and the tears that stung at their mama's eyes when her daughter was sick. Most of all, all that fear and hopelessness. It may only make a little difference in the world, but I want to do this. Tell her it comes from her Fairy Godmother or Mother Goose or whatever the hell you wanna tell her. Please just do it…for me."

"Okay, man," Charlie answered. "You're a good person, Phil."

"Shit. Cut the crap," Phil said with a laugh. "In case you failed to notice, I'm on the opposite side of the glass, the side the criminals sit on."

"Let's talk about some good news," Arthur said. "The house sold last week. I would have written, but I wanted to tell you in person. You made one hell of a profit, and the buyers bought most of the furniture."

Phil looked down and closed his eyes. "Thank God," he said. "I'm glad it's gone. That evil place is gone."

"What is it you're always drilling into us?" Charlie asked. "Never look back or something like that, right?"

"Yeah. That's right. Now I can really let it go."

"Your Jag sold, but there was a problem with Lara's Mercedes."

"What?"

"It was vandalized, almost like when the house was ransacked, as if someone was looking for something. The seats were slashed, the glovebox torn apart—just everything you could imagine. The insurance settled on it, but you lost a couple thousand in the deal."

"Damn. I wish I could figure out what the hell they're looking for," Phil said into the receiver, his forehead wrinkled in thought.

"Yeah," Arthur answered, "we do too. Charlie's got some more good news though."

Charlie gave him an uncertain look and hesitated.

"Don't tell me," Phil said, holding his hand up and grinning. "You adopted Lilly."

"Yes," Charlie said, sounding surprised. "We did."

"Like I told you, it doesn't bother me any. I'm actually very happy for all three of you. Just because she carries Lara's blood, that doesn't make her Lara. You and Janet have wanted a child for a long time, and now you're all blessed. But tell me… Is fatherhood as difficult as I've heard?"

For the first time, Charlie's face lit up. "I'm so glad to hear that you're okay with it. You don't know how good that makes me feel, and Janet…" His face started to break. "God, she'll be so relieved, Phil. I can't wait to tell her."

"I'll write her myself," Phil answered, smiling broadly. "Tell me more about the kid."

"Well, she's just beautiful, like an angel, and she acts like one too. She's so smart, doing very well in school and adapting to us quickly. She loves to help around the house, and she gets up and ready for school without being told. Just the other day, she—"

"Okay, okay," Phil said playfully. "We've only got two hours. I get the picture."

Charlie smiled wider than Phil had never seen before, and he was so grateful to hear that his friend finally had the family he'd always wanted.

They talked about sports, politics, and everything they could think of, careful not to mention Phil's new life behind bars. It felt good to laugh and reminisce about more pleasant times, but Phil was crushed when he was told that his visit was over. He reached over and touched the glass, and Arthur and Charlie did the same. Tears rolled down all their faces as Phil stood and walked away.

CHAPTER 5

Phil enjoyed his shopping trip to the canteen, and he found most of the items on his shopping list, including several books that he put on special order.

"Takes about two weeks to get 'em here, man," the inmate behind the counter said.

Phil nodded, realizing that in the grand scheme of things, two weeks was as good as tomorrow.

He was thankful Welles wasn't in the cell when he got back, for that gave him time to sneak the new bag of Brown Mule under his pillow, next to the worn, soggy pouch that held the old. For the first time, he noticed Welles had stashed an old, worn Bible there as well. He was just starting to put his new things away in his trunk when Welles returned. "You want one?" he said, offering him a soda yet again.

"I done told ya I don't take no handouts," Welles answered.

"I know," Phil said, "but this isn't one. I just wanna share a drink with a friend. Besides, I'm celebrating."

"Celebrating?" Welles laughed. "What for? Ya didn't get beat up today?"

"No," Phil said, sounding serious. "Two of my best friends stopped by to visit, and I finally put a book order in at the canteen. I need something to occupy my mind, other than that smut they give us to read in here." He passed the soda to Welles. "So drink up, buddy. This is a good day…for once."

Welles shrugged and took the soda. "Guess that is worth celebrating," he answered. His first sip of the drink almost choked him, and his face mirrored that of someone tasting straight scotch for the first time. "Goodness. It's been so long since I've had one of these," he said. He slowed down on his next sip and savored the flavor. "I 'member once, me an' my sister went ta town and paid this white man fifteen cents to go in the general store and get us one of dem Coca-Colas. We split it two ways and drank it so slow that it took us the whole way home to finish 'er off. Wasn't no money for such foolishness, my daddy always said. I reckon he was right, but it sure did taste good that hot summer day."

Phil listened contentedly, surprised that Welles was so willing to share. "Where did you grow up?" he asked, almost afraid to push for anything more.

"Georgia, in the deep South, where the gnats and mosquitoes almost carry you away. My family worked the fields—tobacca, cotton, you name it. I was pickin' in them fields 'fore I could even talk."

"I visited Atlanta once," Phil said, careful not to add that it was as a keynote speaker at a medical conference.

"Hmm. I ain't never been meself, but they say 'lanta's fulla buildings as high as the eye can see, almost reachin' up to Heaven," Welles said.

"What brought you to San Francisco, Welles?"

"Worse thing I ever did," he started, then took a deep breath before continuing. "My cousins from Tennessee came to visit one summer. I was only twenty-one, and they was older than me. They had this car, a real hot rod. It was somethin', better than anything I'd ever seen in my little town. They said they was headed out west, to California, hopin' to see Hollywood, hittin' the big time, ya know? Well, I was rebellious and stupid and wanted away from that farmin' so bad. I left with them and broke my parents' hearts." He stopped for a minute, and Phil feared he might not continue, but he did. "We got 'bout far as Alabama 'fore we started runnin' outta money, but they was determined to keep goin'. They started robbing places, little stores and such. I knew it was wrong, but I drove the getaway car just the same. They didn't identify us 'cause we was black. We got to San Francisco first. My cousin wanted to see Alcatraz, where them big crooks lived. We was outta money again, though, and had to rob another store. I went in with 'em that time. It turned ugly fast, and my cousin shot the man who was workin' the register. They didn't have them fancy things like they do now, those tapes that show who's doin' what. Anyway, long story short, they turned on me, so here I sit. They did ten years, and I got forty-five. Better than the death penalty, I reckon, and I've only got seven more to do."

"Christ, Welles. You'll be sixty-six years old."

"Yep. Don't know nothin' but San Quentin. My mama and daddy are dead now, so I only got my sister Mae. She writes every now and then, and I get somebody to read 'em to me. Sometimes, when I can get somebody to write it for me, I mail her a letter too. She ain't never been to see me. Too expensive." Welles then reached under his pillow for his pouch and felt the slick newness of the one Phil had placed there. He looked at it long and hard, then glanced at Phil. "Said I didn't take no charity."

"I don't know anything about that, Welles. Wasn't me. You're missin' a few chompers. Maybe it was the Tooth Fairy."

Welles looked at Phil, and a gentle smile crossed his face. "Guess neither one of us belongs in here, huh?"

"Is that your family Bible?"

"Sure is," Welles answered, picking it up and rubbing his arthritic hands across its leather cover. "Belonged to my father. When he died, Mama mailed it to me. I hold it in my arms every night when I sleep. Makes me feel God's warmth, and I thank Him for lookin' out for me." He suddenly looked uncomfortable and diverted his gaze from Phil. "Ya know, I thank Him for you sometimes too."

Phil didn't want to make him more uncomfortable by responding, so he didn't.

"I never learned no readin' and writin', but I can look through the Bible and feel the pages my mother read the most, 'cause they're all worn and fragile. She couldn't read much neither, but I figure they must be good scriptures, or she wouldn'ta spent so much time on them pages."

"I could read them to you sometime," Phil offered. "I never spent very much time in church," he admitted. "Guess I didn't have the time, as a doctor. Maybe that's part of why I'm here. I never stopped to take care of the important things."

CHAPTER 6

The laundry room was a tough job, but Phil was slowly adapting to it. He relished the hours when he was busy and the machines were so loud that no one could talk. He hated getting clothes from B Block because they were always soiled with urine and defecation. Tiny informed him that it was a psychiatric unit, and he hated to think of what it was like there.

Phil was pushing his cart of washed and wet clothes down to the next man for drying when he heard a loud commotion in the corner. Several men were gathered, laughing loudly and clapping like rambunctious eighth-graders in a schoolyard. He couldn't help but walk over, even against his better judgment. Several of the inmates had broomsticks and were beating some of the rats that had taken up residence there. They were beating the rodents so severely that blood was splattered all over the walls and the floor, even the ceiling. They pummeled the animals until there was little left, other than a few pieces of matted fur.

As much as Phil hated sharing space with the rats and other pests, he couldn't stand the scene before him. It was vicious and sick, and it caused him to violently vomit all over the floor.

One of the inmates turned around and looked at him. "Well, well. Do we have a pussy in our midst? Can't handle a little blood and brutality, Doc? Hmm. Was it any different with your old lady? Huh? You're a rat-lover and a nigger-lover, but maybe we can let you save a few lives here," he taunted. He then turned to the roaring crowd. "Let the pussy save some of the rats!" He laughed and picked up two animals in each hand, swinging them by their tails.

Four other inmates grabbed Phil and held him down, while others stuffed several rats inside his clothes. They then held his sleeves and pant legs closed, trapping the rodents against his skin. One grabbed a pillowcase and held it over his head, but not before putting three rats inside it too. Phil could feel the rodents gnawing at him, and their squeaks and squeals sickened him as they crawled over his body. It seemed like hours before he finally passed out from the pain.

* * * * *

Phil woke up in the infirmary, still dazed from the events of the day.

A nurse walked over and handed him a pain pill and a small paper cup of water. She had kind eyes, and she looked at him with pity. "They got you pretty good, Mr. Sawyer," she said. "You required a few stitches for some of the bites and scratches, and we're treating the others with antibiotic ointments. You'll start receiving rabies shots in the morning, just in case. I'm going to give you something to eat and some sleeping pills to help you rest. I kept you out as long as they would allow me."

Phil looked at her and tried to sit up but felt searing pain shoot through his whole body.

"Just lie still," she said softly, as if tending to him or showing him any special concern or attention might get her into trouble.

He pulled the sheets back and almost passed out at the sight of his mutilated skin. The wounds were cleaned to the best of the nurse's ability, and he was thankful the stitches had been sewn with fairly neat precision, but the wounds were everywhere. He wanted to see his legs, but he couldn't lift his head far enough to look down at them. The pain in his lower limbs told him that they had not fared any better than the rest of him.

"Ma'am," Phil asked quietly as he motioned for the nurse, "can you let me see my face?"

"Mr. Sawyer," she answered, "you are still sedated. I don't think it would be a good idea. Besides, it always looks worse before it heals," she said, her eyes still full of pity.

"I don't want any food," he said to her. "I'm afraid I'll just vomit again. I imagine it will be that way for quite some time."

She patted his hand lightly, something they both knew she was not allowed to do. "We'll keep you here, in the infirmary, as long as we can. I can't promise much though. You'll have to eat something tomorrow, but I'll let you slide tonight. You should feel pretty sleepy soon anyway. My shift ends in twenty minutes, but I'll be back at 7:00 in the morning. I hope you sleep well."

"Thank you," Phil answered, already feeling the effects of the medication. "What is your name?"

"Nurse Jenny," she answered, then quickly walked away.

* * * * *

When Phil opened his eyes, again it was to the sight of eggs and bacon. Welles was standing at his bedside and placed the tray on the table. Phil could tell his friend was trying to hide his shock, but the act just wasn't working. "How did you get in here?" Phil asked.

"Got special permission from my supervisor. I do a few favors for him every now and then. Sometimes it pays off. I don't got long though."

"Thanks for coming, Welles. I guess I look like hell, huh?"

"Well, you weren't no pretty thing to begin with," Welles said, faking a laugh without revealing his usual toothless grin. "Look, try to keep outta trouble while you're in here. I saw that pretty young nurse, but don't even think about it. I've got some people workin' on a job change for ya, but I can't make no promises."

"Thanks, Welles," Phil answered, touched by the thought and the bond of their quickly growing friendship. They were two totally different people, from the color of their skin to their backgrounds, yet they were really, truly becoming the best of friends, even in such an unlikely place.

Welles turned and walked out without saying anything else, and Phil couldn't blame him; he knew it bothered his friend to see him that way. He'd seen the same expression on the faces of the relatives who visited his patients in the hospital.

Nurse Jenny came by with more pain medication in a small round paper cup, and it reminded him of the hospital. "Do you feel any better today, Mr. Sawyer?" she asked.

"Not quite as sore."

"Well, don't move around too much. We don't want any of those stitches coming out. I'll be back by after you eat to add some more ointment to the wounds."

"Thank you," Phil said, then devoured his breakfast with a hunger he wasn't sure he would ever feel again.

* * * * *

His stay in the infirmary lasted for two weeks, far longer than he would have expected. He was convinced that it was because of Nurse Jenny's insistence. He walked a little every day, and that helped him to feel better. When all the stitches came out, he was happy to see some improvement in his arms, stomach, and legs, but they would not let him see his face or neck; they wanted to prolong the inevitable as long as they could. Before he was sent back to his cellblock, they allowed him to stand in front of a mirror, and the horror that he saw and felt was almost more than he could bear. He looked as though he had survived a chainsaw massacre.

The doctor walked over and placed a gentle hand on Phil's shoulder. "You're a doctor yourself, Mr. Sawyer, one who deals with amputees and serious injuries. You know a great deal of this is superficial. It will heal, and your chances of permanent disfigurement are very slim. As for your arms and legs… Well, those bites and scratches were rather deeply imbedded. Maybe when you get out, you can consider plastic surgery."

Still overwhelmed by shock, by the thought that within a few short minutes in the back of a prison laundry, his body had been changed forever, all Phil could do was nod.

"You'll be off work for at least four weeks, and I'll see you every day for the next two. We can't risk an infection setting in."

Before Phil could answer, an officer was there to transport him back to his cell. Even the officer looked at him with pity, even repulsion, as if he was some kind of freak of nature. Phil walked slowly, with the assistance of a cane, back to his cell, and he was surprised by how happy he was to see it. *Home, sweet home,* he mused as he walked in.

Welles had made his bed with the tight precision with which he made his own, and on the bottom bunk was a small cake with icing. Phil was sure that was also a favor from the supervisor whose boots Welles so meticulously shined. He also noticed that Welles had moved his pictures to the wall beside the top bunk, and he looked at them in confusion.

"Figured you won't be able to make it up there for a while, so I swapped out with ya," Welles said.

"Damn," Phil said, startled, since Welles was usually such a creature of habit. "You didn't need to do all this. I can still climb into the top bunk all right."

"Are ya sayin' I can't? I ain't that much of an old man, ya know," Welles said, sounding hurt. "I been practicin' while you was in the infirmary. Getting pretty good at by now."

Phil felt bad about inadvertently insulting Welles's kind gesture, so he decided to make light of it. "Well, you sure as hell better not fall outta bed. You'll probably break a hip or something at your age."

Welles laughed at the teasing, the old laugh Phil was used to. His shoulders shook, and his gums showed when he smiled.

* * * * *

The four weeks went by quickly, and as the doctor had promised, Phil's face began to heal fairly well. He knew that the wounds would remain red for the first couple of years, then turn dark pink, and eventually fade with time. It really made no difference to him, because he wasn't on the dating market anyway.

He continued to keep Charlie's and Arthur's attempts to visit at bay, but one Sunday, he was called to the visitation room. He was thrilled that he had healed so much by the time he saw them again, but apparently, he didn't look as good as he thought.

Charlie got up and walked away for a few minutes to get some air and to hide his astonishment from his friend.

Meanwhile, Arthur lingered on the other side of the Plexiglas, in a bit of an awkward, precarious situation. He didn't want to ask, but he wasn't sure what else to say, so he blurted out, "Uh…what's up with that?"

"It's really not as bad as it looks," Phil answered, trying to console him. "It'll heal, and it won't be as bad as it is now."

"What in the hell, Phil?"

"I'm in a bad place, Arthur, with some bad people. Things happen."

Charlie finally returned and picked up the black receiver. "Jesus, Phil. Just tell us already."

Phil tried to think up a story, anything that might sound better than what had really occurred, but he knew he'd never pull off lying to his best friends. He told them the whole story, in a calm, even voice, trying not to look either of them in the eye.

"Rats? That's the most appalling shit I've ever heard!" Arthur said. "What in the fuck does the warden have to say about it? I'll have the damn media down here first thing tomorrow morning. This is bullshit. Have you seen yourself? You came in here a handsome man, and now you look like you've been through a meat grinder, for Christ's Sake." He paused for a moment, realizing how cruel the comment was. "Sorry, man. Really. I-I didn't mean to say that."

"I know," Phil said. "But this is prison, not summer camp or Club Med. The two of you have to accept that. Things happen in here, things horror movie makers couldn't even conjure up. The warden doesn't care, so there's no point in bringing it up. Matter fact, that'll probably just make things worse. I'm just another injury report to cross his desk, another inmate who got what he had coming to him. In here, we're all just…numbers."

"My God," Charlie said, his voice weak with emotion. "I'm so sorry."

"Okay, guys," Phil said, "if you can bear to look at me, let's change the subject. How are Janet and Lilly?"

"Fine," Charlie answered, adding nothing more.

"Well, don't tell her about this shit," Phil said. "She doesn't need to know. I'm comin' up on a year in this place. God. Can you believe that? Just seven more to go."

"Stop," Arthur said. "I can't take it, and my ass isn't even the one stuck in this place. Starting tomorrow, we're gonna work on an appeal. They got no business keeping you in here, in a hellhole where rats eat a man and everybody turns a blind eye."

"Time to go, buddy," the guard said, tapping Phil on the shoulder. "The doctor doesn't think it's good for you to be out too long."

Phil smiled at his friends and placed his hands against the Plexiglas again, meeting the place where their hands touched the other side and wishing he could feel their warmth.

CHAPTER 7

Phil was absolutely thrilled with his books: *Walden* by Henry David Thoreau, one of his favorite philosophers; a collection of poems by Emily Dickinson and Robert Frost; and *The Souls of Black Folks* by W.E.B. Du Bois, one he wanted to share with Welles. He was thumbing through them as his roommate came in from working in the kitchen. "I finally got my books," he said, "all of them."

"Good," Welles said. "Think you might could read some of 'em out loud at night, like we do the scriptures?"

"Sure," Phil said. "It'd be a shame if we both can't enjoy them."

It was shower day, something Phil looked forward to with a passion. Ten men at a time were escorted to the showers, and they were granted three minutes to wash their bodies with the lukewarm, weak spray of water. When the cell door buzzed, Phil was all ready to go, with his towel, soap, and shampoo, wearing bright orange plastic shower shoes. The inmates formed a single-file line and followed the young guard with the dirty blond hair and kind, naïve face. There were ten showerheads, with ten naked, soapy men standing beneath them, just like a high school locker room, with one distinctive difference: Things in the prison shower were never, ever predictable.

Three men at the showerheads on the far end called for the young guard to complain that their showerheads had no pressure.

He walked slowly toward them and looked up. "They appear to be working," he said.

Almost before he got the words out, the three jumped him. He tried to scream, but it was to no avail, for they'd knocked the breath out of him instantly. His uniform was roughly ripped from his body, revealing a thin, young physique in all its nakedness. The biggest of the three grabbed him around the waist and began raping him with a vengeance. The young boy's upper body and head just slumped forward, and his screams melted into helpless gurgles as he was passed from horny man to man.

Phil started toward the crowd, but Welles grabbed his arm.

"It ain't none ya business, man. You can't fix it, so jus' keep yer distance."

Phil knew Welles was right, but never in his life, not even during the rat ordeal, had he felt more sickened. His eyes welled with tears that were cleverly disguised by the water from his dripping hair.

When they were through with officer, they dropped his limp body on the wet, hard shower floor and watched as the blood from his rectum mixed with the water and swirled down the drain. Two of the three had the audacity to laugh.

The ten men dried off, grabbed their toiletries, and formed back into their single-file line to walk back to their cells, leaving behind a semiconscious boy who'd never, ever be the same again.

CHAPTER 8

Welles asked Phil to read to him that night, but he couldn't bring himself to do it. He felt bad, considering how much Welles enjoyed it, lying there like a child listening to a bedtime story.

"You gotta let it go, brother," Welles said. "I know it sounds like I ain't got no heart, but that ain't so. Ain't nobody gonna look out for us here, so we gotta do it ourselves. I used to see it in my sleep, but I don't no more. I guess this place has done ate up all my feelin's."

"That's not true," Phil said. "You've just…adapted. It's survival of the fittest in here."

"Yeah, somethin' like that."

Phil reached over and picked up Thoreau's book and gazed at the cover, admiring the serene lake and beautiful trees reflected in the water. "This is my favorite author," he said, almost to himself, though he knew Welles was listening. "He was also a famous poet and philosopher."

"Philosopher? What's that?"

Phil thought for a minute, trying to find the right words to describe it. "Well, I guess it's a thinker, someone who tries to figure out why things are as they are."

"Ain't nothin' to figure out there," Welles said. "Things is the way they is 'cause the good Lord made 'em so."

Phil agreed and laid his head back on his pillow.

"Tell me more about this thinker," Welles said, "and why you think so much of him."

"Hmm. Well, I started reading his work when I was in college. He graduated from the same university I did, back in 1837. I first read some of his quotes and found him fascinating, so I then later read more of his work."

"What all did he say in them quotes?"

"He believed in men living simply. That's what this book is all about. He was also against slavery and politics. He believed every man is an individual and that the government was trying to take that individuality away. He was even thrown in jail once for not paying his poll taxes, an attempt to express opposition to slavery."

"I take it he was a white man?"

"Yes, but like most philosophers and writers back then, he was ahead of his time. Most of his books were published posthumous."

"Post-what?"

Phil smiled but didn't release an audible laugh. "After he died."

"Oh. Sounds kinda odd to me, but I can relate to some of it. Sure you don't wanna read me a bit?"

"I'm sorry, Welles. Tonight, I just want to sleep some memories away."

"Good luck with that, Doc. Ain't never worked for me, and I been sleepin' in this place for decades."

CHAPTER 9

Arthur's angry threats must have had the warden shaken, because Phil was called into his office the next afternoon. When he stepped in, he saw something he hadn't seen in almost a year: color. He saw color in the furniture, the artwork hanging straight on the walls, and the pretty red hair of the lady sitting at the receptionist's desk.

The guard announced that they were there to meet with the warden, and the secretary tapped on his door to let him know. She opened the door and held out her hand to indicate that he was ready for them. "The warden will see you now," she said sweetly.

"Morning, gentlemen," the warden said from the leather chair behind his desk. He slid a folder in front of him and put on his eyeglasses, as if he had some studying to do.

"Good morning, sir," the guard quickly replied.

"Morning," Phil answered, wondering where the conversation was headed.

The warden pretended to read over the information before him, then looked up slowly as he removed his glasses. "Mr. Sawyer, I've reviewed your file, and that is why I called you here. I have been informed that we are…dangerously understaffed in the infirmary. The budget does not allow for us to hire any outside employees at this time, and I feel your medical expertise may be of great benefit to us there, albeit in a limited capacity, of course. Sort of a wet nurse, so to speak. You won't have access to any medications, nor will you perform any procedures on the men there." He paused and waited for the news to sink in.

Phil considered the offer, and he was a bit flattered by it, but he knew where it was really coming from. Clearly, Arthur had backed the warden into a corner, and this was his way of holding Arthur's threats at bay.

"Well, Mr. Sawyer? Would you be interested?"

"Yes, definitely. I'm aware that I'm in no position to make requests, since I'm only an inmate here, but my cellmate is getting old, and working in the kitchen is hard on him. Do you suppose he might be able to deliver the chow to the infirmary and maybe a few other places throughout the prison?"

"My, my, Mr. Sawyer. Quite bold, aren't you?"

"I suppose I am, sir. My apologies."

"You'll start tomorrow, at 6:00 a.m. I'll see what I can do for you cellmate, but I can't make any promises or commitments."

"Thank you, sir. Understood…and I appreciate it."

The warden stood and, trying hard to mask his anger and disgust at being intimidated by a nosy attorney, offered his hand to Phil for a shake. "Pleasure doin' business with you," he said, resisting the urge to frown.

* * * * *

Welles was polishing more boots when Phil got back to the cell. "Why are you still doing that?" Phil asked. "The Tobacco Fairy has been paying you enough visits, hasn't she?"

"Don't matter. I made commitments to the men I work for. If ya ain't a man of your word, what kinda man are ya?"

"I guess you're right."

"Course I am. I'm one of them…ph'los'phers."

Phil smiled. "Hey, you won't believe this," he said, surprised by his own excitement.

"What's that?"

"I got a new job. I start in the infirmary tomorrow. Can't really practice medicine, but I can offer advice and empty bedpans."

Welles looked up at him, wearing a broad smile. "Well now. Ain't we movin' up the ladder fast? Glad to hear it. Least you won't make any enemies there. Them inmates are all gonna be in bed, and that pretty nurse don't look like she could do much damage—least not in a bad way," he said with a coy wink.

"Funny."

"Happy for ya."

"Thanks, Welles. Do you ever think about what you wanna do when you get out of this place?"

"I reckon I allow myself to dream every now and then. I try not to though. It's dangerous, ya know. Too much thinkin' 'bout getting out takes your mind off doin' your time."

"I guess you're right, at least in a sense, but giving up on dreams sucks the life out of a man."

"I think about goin' back to Georgia. I miss the smell of all that fresh-tilled dirt and cut grass. I 'member sitting under them big oaks and feeling the breeze go by. The feel of cotton… It always amazed me that the good Lord could create such things. I wanna taste a real, homemade biscuit, melting in my mouth, with lard, just like Mama used to make. I don't wish for great things, just to be outside and look out over the land, far as the eye can see. I reckon I'm sorta like that Thoreau feller we're about to read about."

Phil was shocked that he remembered the name, and he smiled at the thought.

"What do you dream about, Doc? Goin' back to medicine?"

"Oh no, not that. My license is gone, so I can't. I promised myself I won't regret anything though. No looking back. I'm thinking about moving across the country, making a change, living the slow life. I've got some money set aside for when I get out. I can live off that for a while, till I decide what I want to do."

"Where you planning on settlin'?"

"Maybe Maine. It's such a beautiful state. I'd love to live right on the water, where the big rocks surround the bay. You can see the water licking its way up the rocks, and then it comes crashing back down again. I want a fishing boat—nothing fancy or luxurious, just one I can take out on the water. There are whales out there, you know, big as anything…and lobsters so big you can't even eat a whole one."

"Ain't never even hearda Maine. Sounds like a beautiful place though. I always liked fishin'. I like the quiet, when all ya hear are birds and crickets."

"Oh, Welles, you'd love it there. It's so serene, and in the winter, the snow is whiter than any you've ever seen, like a picture painted by an artist."

"Snow, huh? Well, I don't like cold too much. Ain't never had no heavy coat."

"You'd love just sitting by the fire, drinking hot cocoa. You should come with me. We could fish and see the whales."

"We're different men, Doc. I ain't like your fancy friends. I can't even read."

"To hell with all that. You're as good a man as any of them. We could start a bait business right on the water. The fishermen would love us. We could call it…'Sawyer and Welles.'"

"That'd be 'Manning and Sawyer,'" he said, laughing. "Welles is my first name. Manning's my last."

"Okay. 'Manning and Sawyer Bait and Tackle.' You could stay in Georgia in the winter, during the off season."

"I'm feeling like livin' again, Doc. Ain't healthy, I tell ya. Makes a man yearn for somethin' that's impossible behind these walls."

"Say yes, Welles. You'll get out before me, so you can spend some time in Georgia. Then we can open our business when they finally let me outta this cage."

"Been thinkin' a lot 'bout it, ain't ya?"

"Yes, for a while now. I want a slow, good life this time. I want to see things in a different perspective, to enjoy the little moments that make up a life, the things I took for granted for so long."

"Now you sound like one of them philosophy folks."

"I guess you're right, Welles. Just say you'll do it."

"I'll be there, Doc. I'll be there."

CHAPTER 10

Phil's first day at the infirmary was an eye-opener. He didn't realize exactly how much violence went on in prison, and he wished he'd never had to find out firsthand. He was thankful, though, for a relatively safe occupation on the inside; after what he'd been through at the laundry, that was of some comfort.

There were several sutures to be done, and he was pleased that he was permitted to clean them. Even that simple task gave him life again. He also noticed that his bedside manner had greatly improved after all he'd been through. He watched as Nurse Jenny gently bandaged the wounds and checked vital signs of some of the roughest men in the country. It amazed him, and he wanted to ask her why she was there, but he knew his place.

At noon, there was a light knock on the door, and Welles entered, pushing a metal cart with plates of food on it. "Funny," he said. "I got a cushy job too. Wouldn't know anything about that, would ya, Doc?"

"Let's just say…someone owed me a favor."

Welles laughed that slow, Southern laugh, passed out the meals, and was on his way. It wasn't like him to stop and talk, for he considered that cheating the prison out of an honest day's work.

The clatter of leg irons hitting the floor jolted Phil back to the present, and he looked toward the door in anticipation.

"Drew Isaacs," Jenny said softly. "He's here for his dialysis. He's a death row inmate."

"Oh my God, Jenny," Phil said, then blurted out without thinking, "You shouldn't be here."

"He's of no danger to us," she said, feigning a smile. "They cuff him to the bed."

"Great," Phil muttered.

The door opened, and in walked Isaacs, looking like the picture of health. His face was expressionless, but Phil didn't expect anything different. The three hefty guards cuffed his hands and legs to the gurney with a swiftness that indicated they'd been through the process many times before.

"Good morning, Mr. Isaacs," Jenny said, as kindly as any nurse in a hospital would. "How are you feeling today?"

"Same as usual, ma'am. Nothing's different. They just keepin' me alive long enough ta kill me proper."

"Now, now, Mr. Isaacs," Jenny said firmly. "We'll have none of that kind of talk in here."

Dr. Fletcher walked around and felt up and down Isaacs's arm, until he was confident he could begin the dialysis that would filter the condemned man's blood.

Once the process started, Drew Isaacs just lay there in silence, looking up at the ceiling, waiting for it to end so he could return to his cell. For the duration of the four hours it took, not a word came out of the man's mouth; all Phil could hear were the slow, labored breaths that caused his thick chest to rise and fall. Phil wanted to talk to him, as he was fascinated by one who would never leave the confines of that place, but he held his tongue. If he had learned anything, it was to respect the personal lives of those housed here.

The guards arrived just in time to shackle Isaacs and shuffle him out, and just like that, he was gone.

The doctor looked at Phil and noticed he was deep in thought. "Don't think about it, Sawyer," he said. "That man's just another patient and nothing more. You have to learn to separate yourself from it, especially in here."

"It's always fascinated me, death row," Phil said, his eyes and mind looking as if they'd wandered a million miles away. "I mean, I never woulda pictured myself here, and there are days when I'm not sure I'll live to see freedom. Then I see this guy who knows, unequivocally, that he will die in this hellhole, that he'll never ride in a car again, mow his own lawn, or stand in line at the grocery store with a six-pack and a couple big steaks. It's just eerie, eerie as hell."

"I know what you mean," Dr. Fletcher said, "but you've got to set your mind on getting out of here. The next man has to do the same for himself."

The rest of the day was spent stocking supplies and cleaning the infirmary. Phil didn't mind, for it was a far cry better than the laundry, no matter how menial the tasks. After Nurse Jenny took off, the doctor let Phil leave early as well.

* * * * *

Welles was already back in the cell when Phil got there. "Got me a sweet little deal, thanks to you," he said. "Don't owe me nothin', ya know."

"I know," Phil answered, "but it's nice as hell to see a familiar face in that place."

"Are we gonna read some after dinner?"

"Yep. Wouldn't have it any other way," Phil said.

The door buzzed, and dinner was rather uneventful, a rare occasion that caused Phil to heave a sigh of relief.

Back in the cell, they both brushed their teeth, and Phil crawled back up into the top bunk. He was able to move much easier now, and the climb was good physical therapy for his stiff bones and recovering skin. "So, Mr. Manning," Phil teased, "what's it gonna be tonight? The Bible or *Walden Pond*?"

"I reckon that Thoreau feller."

"Thoreau it is," Phil answered, then opened the book and started to read.

Welles listened intently as Phil read of the man who gave away all his possessions to build a small, one-room shack and live in harmony with nature, to do little more than watch the seasons pass him by.

Night after night they read, long after Phil was ready to go to sleep. Like a small child, Welles was never ready for it to end, and he seemed to soak up every word.

When they finally finished, Phil sensed his friend's deep disappointment. "One day," Phil started, "I went up to the Sleepy Hollow Cemetery in Concorde, Massachusetts to see Henry David Thoreau's gravesite. I guess I was a little curious, but in some strange way, I just felt like… Well, I wanted to pay my respects." He stopped for a moment as he reflected on that day. "I was so shocked, maybe appalled, I guess you could say. The tombstone was about the size of a piece of notebook paper, old and covered in moss. It read simply, 'Henry.' Tree roots were growing across it, and pinecones littered the gravesite. I couldn't believe such a brilliant, well-known man had been buried in a pauper's grave. I laid a small wildflower near the headstone and turned away, unable to look at it."

Welles was silent for so long that Phil began to think he was asleep, until he said, "Doc, did you stop ta think that maybe that was all he wanted? Didn't you listen to yer own self when you was readin' that book to me? He never wished for fancy things. He just wanted to be out in nature. It wouldn'ta been fitting for him to have some big tombstone that cost a whole lotta money. That wouldn't have been his wish at all."

"You know, Welles," Phil said, "you are far smarter than I am. I've never really thought of it that way."

"Well, it'd be about as fittin' as me being buried in some big, fancy place. Not for me, I tell ya. I wanna be buried right next to Mama, deep in that cool, rich dirt I plowed all those years, back, so I can rest eternally in the one place I love more than anything."

Phil was surprised to hear such emotion coming from Welles, but he had grown to appreciate any sort of sentimentality he could get out of the usually rather stoic man. "Ya know, it's funny," Phil said. "I've never really given any thought to where I'd like to be buried. It just gives me a weird feeling, like it's something I'm not ready to face yet."

"Ah. Well, the time'll come when you'll think about it. You jus' ain't lived long enough to find that special place in your heart. It'll come, my friend. It'll come."

"See ya in the morning, Welles."

"You too, Doc, God willin'."

CHAPTER 11

The days seemed to pass easier after Phil secured a new job. Working in the infirmary gave his life more meaning than just doing the laundry. Dr. Fletcher had become accustomed to him and allowed him to do much more than the warden would ever have agreed to.

Drew Isaacs continued to come in three days a week for his dialysis, and he began to open up to Phil. He had been a drug addict for as long as he could remember, but at the age of twenty-seven, his appearance didn't reflect it. His eyes were always clear and bright, hiding the stir of emotions that had to be churning within him. Phil had so many questions he wanted to ask him, but he waited patiently, and as the weeks waned on, Drew began to trust him. Sometimes, when the infirmary was slow, Phil just sat and talked with him. He shared his own story with him, then listened, and Drew eased out more and more information about himself.

"I knew I'd end up here, knew it from the time I was a teenager," Drew said. "You'da thought I'd try to prevent it, but I just didn't give a damn 'bout my life or nobody else's. My mother was a drunk, and my dad never bothered to come around." He paused for a minute, and his normally bright eyes clouded over. "That's no excuse, though, and I ain't never claimed it to be. People come outta the projects every day and make somethin' of themselves. I never had the motivation, never wanted to work for nothin'. Drugs were just too damn easy. I became a user at twelve—beer and marijuana, then the hard stuff. I was seventeen when I first got high on LSD and crack. I went to my grandmama's house for some money. She refused to give me anymore, knowing 'xactly what I was gonna do with it, so I just… I stabbed her to death, man, twenty-eight times, to be exact. Then I took the $20 bill outta the old, tattered purse she carried faithfully to church every Sunday. It got me high for a few hours. My grandmother was the only person who ever cared about me."

By this time, Drew was weeping uncontrollably, attracting the attention of Jenny who walked over to comfort him and to scold Phil for allowing him to get upset during his dialysis. "Am I gonna have to separate you two from now on?" she asked, with a serious look on her face. "Mr. Sawyer, you should know better than to upset the man." "

"I'm sorry, ma'am," Drew said. "Sometimes it just feels healthier to talk 'bout things that ail my heart, claw at my conscience day and night. This is the first time I've talked 'bout my case in the ten years I been here." He turned to Phil, reached for his hand, and squeezed it slightly. "Thanks for listenin', man. I can't share my thoughts on the row. Nobody does. It's just somethin' a man don't do."

"That's okay," Phil answered. "We all need to talk sometime."

Dr. Fletcher disconnected Drew from the dialysis machine, and the guards showed up like clockwork to take him away, back to the world that would hold him until his time came to die. Shivers ran up Phil's spine so severely that both the doctor and Jenny noticed.

"Gotta separate yourself, Sawyer, like I told you before," the doctor said, somewhat harshly, then walked away.

"He's a little on edge today," Jenny said. "There's an execution tomorrow."

"Oh," Phil said grimly. "I didn't know."

"Someone should've told you. You don't have to work tomorrow, unless there's an emergency and we need you. The prison will be on lockdown all day. The execution will be held at midnight."

"Lethal injection?" Phil asked.

"Yes, thank God," Jenny answered. "There isn't any pain. I don't think I could witness it otherwise."

"Jesus," Phil said. "I can't believe they expect you to be in there."

"I'm not just in there. I have to start the IV, and then Dr. Fletcher introduces the drugs."

"Do you have a hard time dealing with it?"

"Let's just say I don't sleep for a few days. I'm all for capital punishment, when justice demands it, but it's… Well, it's different when you have to be in there, that's all. Hearing it on the news is one thing, but talking to a condemned man right before he dies… It's just… I-I can't really explain it." Her face reflected the sorrow she'd witnessed through the years, on the faces of victims' and condemned men's loved ones.

Phil didn't want to tell her so, but he was sure she was just too pure and kind to be exposed to such a thing. Finally, he gathered the nerve to say, "Can I ask you something personal, Jenny?"

"Sure, Mr. Sawyer. Shoot."

"Why are you here, in this place, a horrible place filled with hardened criminals and hopelessness and violence? You're a damn good nurse, a kind one. Isn't there somewhere else you'd rather be working?"

"Many days, yes, but I know my calling is here at San Quentin. I grew up in a wealthy neighborhood, had everything I wanted, all the material possessions I could ever have possibly asked for and all the love my family could give me. I was one of the lucky ones, and I always knew it. My father had pull, so I easily landed several cushy jobs, positions any nurse would be grateful for. Still, it felt like there was something missing, the reason I went into nursing, I guess. The patients in the doctor's offices and hospitals where I worked all had loved ones, people who came to visit them and to sit by their bedsides. I knew that somewhere in the world, there are lots of people who don't have that, people who need a little kindness."

"Don't tell me you're a sucker for these animals," Phil said. "I mean, sure, there are some good people here, but it's dangerous. I know that has to cross your mind sometimes. There are killers and rapists and—"

"Yes, I know. I think about that more often than I care to admit, but something motivates me to come back every morning."

"What does your family think?"

"They're convinced I'm crazy, and they think I just have a guilt complex because I was so blessed with all the better things in life, but it's so much more than that. I had leukemia as a child, and I remember how frightening it was, lying in that hospital bed, never knowing what to expect next. I see that in the eyes of every man here, no matter how cold and calculating he may be."

"Yeah, I guess you're right. I've just never really taken the time to notice." Phil looked at her closely and realized she reminded him a great deal of Janet, in heart rather than appearance. Jenny was pretty, although not beautifully stunning. She wore very little makeup, but she had a natural beauty. Her hair was shiny brown, and although she always pulled it back in a ponytail, so it wouldn't get in the way of her work, he could tell it was thick and healthy. Her eyes were hazel, and little specks of green danced around in them when the fluorescent light hit them just right. She was tiny, and that frightened him; any of the inmates could easily harm her or take advantage of her at any time, and he wondered if she really understood the full impact of that potential risk. Still, she was a grown woman, and it was her choice to make. *After all, I'm just an inmate,* Phil reminded himself. *I've got no right to tell anybody a damn thing.*

* * * * *

The following day, Phil was locked in his cell, just as Jenny had warned him he would be. The guards handed out bagged meals for breakfast, lunch, and dinner. He wrote to Charlie and Janet and then Arthur, for whom he had a special request; he then prayed that Arthur would come through for him.

For most of the day, he read to Welles. Even after Phil tired of it, Welles pleaded with him to read more. They read from Robert Frost, and Welles listened so quietly that Phil was about to close the book and go to sleep. "You awake, Welles?" he whispered.

"Yep," Welles answered in a normal tone of voice. "You ever known me to sleep through your reading?"

"No," Phil laughed, then continued to read. "The next one is called, 'Into My Own'…

'One of my wishes is that those dark trees,
So old and firm they scarcely show the breeze,

Were not, as 'twere, the merest mask of gloom,
But stretched away unto the edge of doom.
I should not be withheld but that someday
Into their vastness I should steal away,
Fearless of ever finding open land,
Or highway where the slow wheel pours the sand.
I do not see why I should e'er turn back,
Or those should not set forth upon my track
To overtake me, who should miss me here
And long to know if still I held them dear.
They would not find me changed from him they knew,
Only more sure of all I thought was true."'

"Read it again, Doc. Matter fact, read it again and again, till it gets stuck in my mind. It's really nice, and I wanna be able to say it to myself when you aren't around to read it."

The request shocked Phil, but he gladly read the poem at least ten more times before closing the book. He then lay there and smiled as he listened to Welles recite "Into My Own," a whisper that somehow brought peace to that dark, stagnant cell.

CHAPTER 12

The execution went relatively smooth, with no complications. Just like that, there was one less ward of the State, one less meal to prepare and deliver, one less cell to be monitored. Everyone was back to their normal routines just a few hours after a man was purposely put to death. Phil was surprised to find that he was still quite spooked by it. As a doctor, he was very aware of the certainty of death, but it still haunted him. This passing was, like every other death, so final, so irreparable—but it was also caused on purpose, with legal permission.

Dr. Fletcher and Jenny arrived on time, their faces masking any feelings from the night before. Phil didn't inquire about it. He was an inmate, and he knew it would be out of line for him to pry. Besides, he really didn't want to know anything about the grim situation anyway.

The day held two cases of strep throat, a bad cut an inmate earned on kitchen duty, and a shattered arm that required transportation to a medical facility for surgery. It all took Phil back to his days at the hospital, and he struggled to get those memories out of his mind.

Phil ate his lunch in the infirmary with the other men, as Jenny and the doctor felt comfortable leaving him there while they ate with the other staff. It made him feel free and trusted for the first time in so long. He was mopping the floor when they returned. Jenny passed out medicine, and the doctor sat down with a slew of paperwork to complete, almost more than the hospital required after a serious surgery.

Suddenly, the door of the infirmary opened with such force that it smacked into the wall. Two large guards, wide-eyed, called for the doctor immediately.

"We got a heart attack on the row," one said. "We need you to come with us, Doc. We think it's too serious to transport him here."

Dr. Fletcher stood quickly, told one of the guards to stay with Jenny, and motioned for Phil to come with him. "I'm gonna need an extra set of hands, somebody who knows what the hell he's doing. Let's go, Sawyer."

Phil was surprised by how fast the doctor could run, even though, at full pace, they were still several yards behind the guard. Still, by the time they arrived, it was already too late: The man was dead.

The guards who worked the unit had performed CPR for twenty minutes, but he'd been without oxygen too long, and his brain wouldn't function properly. The dead man was a young black guy, and to the naked eye, he looked about as healthy as a horse. His biceps and forearms reflected thousands of hours of exercise, and his t-shirt revealed a slim waist and a six-pack of rippled abdominal muscles.

"Doesn't exactly fit the profile, Doc," Phil said, as they walked back to the infirmary. "Did you see those abs? He had to be active, and we're given a pretty low-fat diet. Doesn't always taste so good, but the meals are pretty…balanced."

"Yes, I know. I guess we have to blame this one on genetics, heredity. We see that a lot amongst the niggers, dying before their time because their grandmamas fed 'em lard in their fried chicken and biscuits."

Phil was shocked by the callous, racist remarks, but he wisely kept his disdain to himself. The man had just witnessed an execution after all, played a role in it, so he couldn't exactly blame the man for being so insensitive. Dr. Fletcher, like everyone else, had to accept death the best way he knew how.

* * * * *

Two weeks later, Phil had a visit from Charlie and Arthur. They were obviously pleased with the healing of his scars, and they were openly delighted to see him. For the first time in the past five years, they seemed comfortable to visit him there. Part of that was due to the fact that Phil could now sit with them in the visitation room at a table, rather than behind the Plexiglas, like some animal in a zoo.

Charlie was even relaxed when he talked about Lilly. "Can you believe she's fifteen already? Janet's teaching her to drive. Better her than me, I tell ya," Charlie said with a grin that spread all the way across his face. "Teenagers scare me to death."

The three men shared a laugh and listened as Charlie continued about the daughter he adored so much.

"She's doing really well in school. She hasn't decided on a college yet, but I guess we've got a couple years before we have to figure all that out. Best volleyball player in the school too."

"Charlie," Phil asked, feeling more than a little awkward, "do you have a picture of her? I mean, I feel as though I know her now, and I've never even seen her."

Charlie looked shocked, as though someone was speaking to him in another language, but then his face softened. "Hmm. I guess I've never thought of that, Phil. Are you sure you're okay with it?"

"Yeah, I'm sure. She's my best friend's child, for heaven's sake."

Charlie reached into his back pocket, pulled out his wallet, and handed it to Phil. He opened the worn, overstuffed tri-fold wallet to the pictures.

Phil couldn't hide his emotion as he looked at the beautiful young girl, so full of life, so different from what Lara had been. He flipped through the plastic sleeves and saw Lilly in her volleyball uniform, then her school uniform, and then several more pictures of her with Janet and Charlie. "What a beautiful family you make," Phil said. "I'm so happy for you and Janet. Most of all, though, I'm happy for Lilly."

"Thank you, Phil," Charlie said as he took the wallet and returned it to his back pocket.

"Does she know about me, that I'm responsible for her mother's death?"

Charlie looked embarrassed, and it was obvious he was stalling with his reply. "Yes," he finally said, quite solemnly. "She knows. I'm sorry, Phil, but it just... Well, it eventually came to the point when we had to answer some of her questions. She's a smart girl, and nothing gets past her. It was only fair for us to tell her the truth."

"That's okay, Charlie. I did do it, you know."

"She took it well. We speak of you often, and she knows you are a good friend and a good man. She even includes you in her prayers at night sometimes. At her age now, I think she sees what her mother was really like. Lilly now realizes Lara deserted her for money, that she was selfish and greedy."

"Janet looks great in those pictures. I'd love to see her."

"I know she'd like to see you, too, Phil. I'm just not sure she can handle it, ya know? For that reason, I've dissuaded her from coming, but I can't hold her back much longer. Our house was broken into, and that has her worried, especially with Lilly being there. I just hope no one breaks in while my girls are home. Anyway, she's hesitant about leaving home for any extended length of time anymore."

"Damn. A break-in?" Phil shook his head. "Well, I understand her apprehension then." He then turned his attention to his other friend. "What about you, Mr. Arthur? How is life treating you?"

"Not bad, not bad at all," Arthur said with a smile, revealing that perfect set of shiny white teeth that drove women wild.

"Oh? And why do you say that with such enthusiasm?"

"The man finally has a woman on the brain," Charlie said.

Arthur smiled again, then glanced away in uncharacteristic embarrassment.

"Ah. So you finally decided to put some work aside for a little while, huh?"

"She's an attorney, too, so we have a little trouble getting our schedules to line up, but I gotta admit that I'm pretty taken with her."

"Well, Counselor, tell me more. I don't get any good gossip in this place."

Arthur smiled. "Well, she's tall and thin, with a great mind and a good heart, something I've gotta work on."

"Which part? The great mind or the good heart?" Phil asked, smirking.

"The heart part."

"Well, no shit," Phil said, laughing. "You attorneys are known for being heartless."

"Hey! Watch it," Arthur said. "Last time I checked, I'm still *your* attorney."

"And a damn good one," Phil answered. "Any news on the favor I asked of you?"

"I'm working on it," Arthur replied, his face softening. "Looks like you're growing a heart, too…and in a place like this. Go figure."

"Working in the infirmary is great," Phil said, changing the subject. "I feel like a man again. I don't know what you did, but the warden was scared shitless."

"Well, let's just say I was a heartless, son-of-a-bitch attorney."

They all laughed and hugged each other hard at the end of the visit. Phil waved as they walked away, then yelled for them to write.

CHAPTER 13

Phil had trouble sleeping that night, for the man who'd died of the heart attack was weighing heavily on his mind. He knew nothing about him, and he would have been executed eventually anyway. *But he looked so young, so innocent, so damn healthy...*

Phil climbed out of his bunk and opened a warm soda from his locker. As he walked over to climb back up to his bed, he stopped to look at his sleeping friend. Welles had his worn, arthritic hands, wrinkled with age, wrapped loosely around the family Bible as he slept. It made Phil stop and think about life for a moment, made him realize how lucky he was to have had the opportunity to meet such a man. Welles was so different from him, a man with virtually no education, yet he had taught Phil more than he'd ever learned in the most prestigious colleges in the country. Welles had taught him about faith, about appreciation for the little things, and about being a true friend.

* * * * *

Jenny was on vacation for two weeks, and Phil was surprised to find that he missed her so much. Her absence left him with twice as much work to do, so the days flew by swiftly. Dr. Fletcher was becoming less and less involved with the patients, allowing Phil to take over most of their care, and he loved every minute of it. He was suturing patients, making diagnoses, and dispensing medications, and he felt as if he had some worth again.

Lunchtime rolled around, and Welles came in, pushing the cart and wearing his famous broad, toothless grin. "Got somethin' for ya," he said to Phil. "I been working on it for some time, and I finally finished 'er today on my break." He unfolded a large piece of paper and laid it out smoothly on Dr. Fletcher's desk, then pointed at it. "Had ta get somebody to write out the names, but I did the rest."

Phil was speechless as he gazed down on the plans for Manning and Sawyer's Bait and Tackle Shop. It was as if a professional draftsman had drawn them. The outside of the building was drawn to perfect scale, and Welles had even included the dimensions and rooms for the inside.

"Well? What ya think 'bout it?" Welles prodded.

"Welles," Phil said, pausing for a minute to let it all sink in, "it's wonderful. We haven't talked about it in so long that I thought you had forgotten."

"Gave you my word, didn't I? If I ain't nothin' else, I'm a man of my word. You oughtta know that by now."

"It's perfect. Now it's not just a fantasy. You've made it…real. Manning and Sawyer's Bait and Tackle. I'll be damned," Phil said, smiling for the first time in quite a while.

"The boat's gonna hafta be yer responsibility. Don't know nothin' 'bout no water."

"You got it."

"Anyway, I gots ta get these meals out before they get cold. Folks don't appreciate that too much 'round here." Welles rolled up the paper and tucked it carefully under his arm.

"I can't wait to look at it some more tonight," Phil said, earnestly wanting to hug his friend but knowing it wasn't the place.

"Well, you're in luck." Welles laughed. "We got nothin' but time."

"You're right about that, old man!" Phil said as Welles walked out.

* * * * *

The pace in the infirmary had become a bit hectic, and Phil realized just how much work Jenny did and what a bright light she brought to the place. She seemed happy to be back and anxious to share about her trip to London and Paris. It wasn't really like her to share much about her personal life with Phil, since he was just another inmate to her, but her stories made him feel like he was out in the world again. In a place like this, there was nothing wrong with living a little vicariously through the people who could leave at the end of the day.

"So? What have I missed around here?" Jenny asked.

"Nothing much," Phil answered, "except that Dr. Fletcher's kind of been letting me off my leash a little. It feels great to be needed again."

"I'm glad to hear it," Jenny said. "Just don't work me out of a job."

"Heh. I don't think that'll ever happen. Besides, I've only got three years left, and then I'm on to my other life."

The infirmary was empty when Jenny asked, "What will you do in your next life, if I can be so bold as to ask?"

"I'm starting over, completely over. I don't intend to make the same mistakes again." Phil then excitedly shared his dream of Maine with her, as well as the business he planned to open with Welles. They talked about the fishing boat and the snow in the winter.

"I've only been there once," Jenny said, "but it was lovely."

"I read to Welles every night," Phil said. "We read from all the authors who lived in the Northeast. It must be a pretty inspirational place to produce so many good works."

Jenny's face softened, and her eyes misted over. "You are so kind to him. It makes me feel so good inside."

"He's good to me too. We're friends, and we compliment each other. This place has shown me some horrors beyond belief, but it has also changed me for the better. It has slowed me down from the fast pace I was living—or rather, not really living at all. Now I know there are far greater things than money and prestige. There is friendship, trust, and taking time to read a book I've wanted to read for so long. There are dreams far beyond where my world was taking me…" He stopped, realizing all he had said. Phil felt his face and ears grow warm and red with embarrassment. "Jeez, I'm sorry. I guess I just got carried away. There are bandages to be stocked and Drew's dialysis to set up."

Jenny smiled a kind smile and reached for his hand, which she patted gently. "Phil Sawyer, you've said before that I don't belong here, but you don't either. One day, you'll get out of here, and when you do, you will do great things."

Drew came in, escorted by his normal entourage.

After Dr. Fletcher hooked him up and went back into his office, Phil walked over and sat down. "How are you doing today, buddy?"

"Not bad. I brought somethin' to show you." He reached into his breast pocket and pulled out a picture of his three children. They were smiling brightly as they posed at what appeared to be a Sears photography studio. The two girls were wearing bright pastel dresses, and the little boy was dressed in a light blue suit and bowtie. "It's their Easter picture," Drew said. "Cute little things, ain't they?"

"Indeed they are, Drew." Phil called Jenny over to see the picture.

"They're just angels," she bragged and doted, making Drew's chest swell with pride.

"Are you married?" Phil asked, hating himself the minute that the question left his lips.

"Nope. Never was. I was just a kid when I came to the joint. My girl had the three of them back to back, startin' at fifteen, but she's one helluva mama, 'specially with no one around to help her for most of them years. She brings 'em ta see me once a month. She's married now, lives in a small house not far from here. I'm happy for her though. Her old man seems to treat the kids right, and I can't ask for more than that."

"It's great you get to see them," Phil said, feeling a deep sadness engulf him as he realized that while he would have a chance to make some things right with his life, Drew Isaacs never would.

* * * * *

The week went by in a flurry, with several injuries and one murder. The guards brought a young man in who was covered in a heavy garbage bag, with blood running off the gurney and onto the floor.

"Already dead, Doc Fletcher," one of the guards said. "One too many boyfriends always ends in this shit."

Dr. Fletcher lifted the bag and gasped. "Damn it. What kind of animal…?"

Phil walked over to take a look. In all his years in medical school and working at the hospitals, he'd never seen anything so violent and grotesque. The man's eyes had been stabbed, along with his neck and chest, even his arms. Phil estimated over 200 stab wounds. "Why the plastic garbage bag?" Phil asked the guard.

"Keeps the blood from splattering on the perpetrator," he answered, with little or no emotion. "Pretty smart actually."

"Jesus," Phil said, feeling that familiar knot grow in the pit of his stomach, the one that reminded him again of where he was.

There was nothing they could do but call the State Bureau of Investigation to come and pick up the body. They would do an autopsy and release the corpse to the family, unless they couldn't afford to bury him. In that case, they would lay him to rest in the back of the prison, in a plain pine box fashioned by the inmates.

Jenny didn't come over to look at the body, and Phil was grateful for that. He knew such a sight would linger in his memory forever; it was just one of those things they would all see in their sleep for the remainder of their lives.

CHAPTER 14

In spite of being in prison, Phil still found that the weekends were still a time for much-needed rest and relaxation, and Phil looked forward to them just as he had in the free world. A contracted staff worked the infirmary on the weekends, and he was rarely called in unless they were swamped.

He and Welles spent much of their time fine-tuning the business and thinking about all the little details. Welles knew about bait and tackle, and Phil knew about business and the money aspect. It was fun for both of them to dream.

They also spent a great deal of time reading. Phil had finally adjusted to reading aloud and found that he enjoyed it more than reading silently to himself. "When you're gone, Welles," Phil said, "I guess I'll still be reading out loud in this cell. People are going to think I'm out of my mind."

"Well, they wouldn't be too far off now, would they?"

"Funny, Welles. Real funny."

"You won't be here long after I'm gone, just less than a year. That'll give me just enough time to take care of the homestead before I go off to help you build this big corporation of ours."

Phil laughed, but that chuckle quickly ended when he realized, for the first time, that he would be sharing his cell with someone else. That thought had never occurred to him, and it made him nervous but sad most of all. He was amazed by how easily he'd adapted to living in that small cave, and he had to give the credit for that to Welles. Phil looked around their humble abode and thought of the huge house he had lived in before: the shiny, gold, gaudy wallpaper in the master bathroom, all of the extra rooms that were never used. Now, he found himself in a room half the size of his former closet, yet he actually looked forward to coming home to it at the end of the day. He began to wonder if he would be one of those convicts who'd have trouble acclimating to the outside world when he was released, but then he knew better. "You've come too far, Phil Sawyer," he said to himself.

The door buzzed, and one of the officers tapped on it with his nightstick. "Pops, you've got a visitor."

"T'ain't none o' me," Welles answered. "Ain't never had no visitor. You must have the wrong man."

"She says her name is Mae Manning, says she's your sister."

Welles stood there in silence, and for a minute, Phil thought he might have to hold him up. "Ain't possible, but I'll go check anyhow," he finally said, his voice quivering with emotion.

Welles was gone for over two hours, and Phil appreciated that the prison staff allowed him some extra time with her. He was so grateful that Arthur had succeeded in both finding her and arranging her trip to the prison, a task Phil was sure wasn't easy.

When the door buzzed and Welles walked in, he made no attempt to stop the tears that flowed from his eyes. "Come down here, Doc," he said to Phil, who was resting on the top bunk. When Phil climbed down, Welles just fell into his arms, his shoulders shaking from the sobs that racked his thin body. Welles cried for what seemed like an hour as he hugged Phil as close to him as he could. He was finally able to stop the tears, but he continued to hold Phil in his arms.

"It was Mae, Doc. It was really her, still lookin' as beautiful as the last day I seen her. I know it was you. Sure as I'm standin' here, I know you did this for me, and I can't never thank ya enough. She said some black man told her she won a trip out here, but I don't believe that, not for one minute. She flew out here on a plane. Can you b'lieve that? Said she thinks she saw Heaven and that it was beautiful. Even stayed in one of them fancy hotels last night, and they gave her a shopping bag of brand-spankin' new clothes for her. She had on the prettiest pink dress, with a hat to match. Mae said she's gonna wear that getup to church and make all them other women jealous."

Welles was still holding on to Phil when he suddenly realized what he was doing. He slowly let go and sat down on the edge of his bed, and Phil handed him some toilet paper to wipe his nose and face.

"Mae said the house is still the same," he continued. She ain't never married, and I don't understand that, 'cause she's a fine lady. Prob'ly too late now though. Still, she likes keepin' house, and I told her I'll be home to help her soon. I also told her about my new job in Maine. I scribbled a picture of it on a paper napkin she had in her purse. Mae said she's real proud of me, and I could tell she weren't foolin' by the way she smiled and the way her eyes was shining."

"I'm glad you got to see her. I know she's missed you as much as you have missed her."

"You know, you're right, Doc," Welles said, more tears forming in the corners of his eyes. "I ain't never had no brother, but this must be what it feels like ta have one…you and me, I mean."

"Maybe we've been brothers all along," Phil said, "and we finally found each other."

CHAPTER 15

Monday morning started early, with another heart attack and eventual death. Phil had to hand it to the guards: They did try to perform CPR on the young victim, even if their efforts proved fruitless. Dr. Fletcher used the paddles to shock him, but it was all to no avail. The kid just lay there, the picture of youth and health, with not a beat of pulse in his heart or a breath in his lungs.

Phil and the doctor walked back to the infirmary in silence, but as soon as they stepped inside, Dr. Fletcher said, "Pity. So young. This place houses so many drug abusers. They don't even realize what it's doing to their bodies. Worse yet, most of them don't care."

"Yeah," Phil said, "I guess you're right." Even as he agreed with Dr. Fletcher, his mind was swimming with doubt. The young man showed none of the classic signs of drug abuse. He wasn't thin, wasn't scarred with any needle marks or tracks, and his appearance was anything but unkempt. Truly, it just didn't add up. Phil felt that familiar shiver go up his spine. Something just didn't feel right. He wasn't sure what it was yet, but something odd was taking place.

They got back to the infirmary just in time to start Drew on his dialysis. He looked a little tired, so Phil didn't bother him. Jenny had come in late because of a doctor's appointment, so she was busy playing catch-up on her everyday duties.

Since things had settled down, Phil had a chance to be alone with his thoughts. *These men have to be autopsied,* he reasoned, *so why is everything just coming back as heart failure? Maybe just a coincidence,* he rationalized. He thought about looking through the files when everyone was at lunch, but the doctor always kept them in a locked cabinet. He was curious to see just how many such deaths had occurred and if they were all young black men.

Drew called him over, and Phil sat down quietly beside him.

"You look tired, man," Phil said. "Everything okay?"'

"Yeah. I'm just feelin' a little down. Another execution on the row this week, ya know."

"Yeah, I heard about that."

"He's in the cell next to mine. We play chess through the bars, using a mirror. We never talk much, 'specially 'bout dyin', but I'll be sad to see him go."

"I'm sure you will. I have a hard time dealing with death, even though I was a doctor back in the world."

"I know what you mean. It's hard when you know right when the bell's gonna toll for ya, and my number's comin' up soon. I try not to think about it, but it's always there, in the back of my mind. My kids ain't ever gonna really know their daddy. That hurts the most of all."

Phil didn't know how to respond. He couldn't imagine knowing the exact time of his death or being referred to as "the condemned," a horrible label that no one would want. "I wish I knew what to say, man," he answered.

"Don't worry about it. Ain't really anything ya can say. I did the crime, and now I gotta pay the consequences. It's just… Man, I hate thinkin' 'bout that damn Grim Reaper creeping up my back."

Everyone had left for lunch, so Phil was alone with Drew in the infirmary. He trusted no one in prison but Welles, but he figured he could take a chance with Mr. Isaacs. *After all, he's scheduled to be executed soon. Surely he won't stir up any trouble?* Phil scooted the chair a little closer to him and leaned over so he could talk quietly. "Listen, Drew, I think something funny's happening around here. There've been two heart attacks, both young, healthy black men, just since I've been moved down here to the infirmary. I don't know if it's anything. I just have a gut feeling that something ain't right. Have you heard anything about it?"

"Shit, man. There's so much going on in here that I can't doubt no story you tell me. Inmates are brutal people, and most don't give a damn about killing each other. We're like a pack of wild dogs."

"That's what concerns me," Phil continued. "The dead men didn't show any signs of brutality. They weren't beaten, and there were no track marks on their veins. They just sorta dropped dead, and everyone blames it on heart attacks."

"What are you sayin', Doc? You think it's someone on the inside? The officers, the warden, or who?"

"I don't know yet, but I need to get some statistics about the deaths here. Where would I find something like that?"

"Hell if I know. Don't get involved, man. It can't mean nothin' but trouble."

"All right. Please don't tell anyone I brought this up. I just have to know."

"Did you try Doc Fletcher's files?"

"They're locked up, and he keeps the key with him. If I tamper with the lock, he'll notice."

"Hmm. Maybe I can do somethin' about that…but I ain't gon' lie. This shit's crazy."

"Maybe, maybe not. If I can find the stats, maybe it'll prove you right, that I'm just overreacting. Then again, maybe it will shed some light on something."

"Ya know, you could always go to the library and look up all the old newspapers on those disk things. That might lead you somewhere. In the meantime, the best rule 'round here is to not trust anybody—not a damn soul. Ya hear me?"

"I know."

"Not even that cute little nurse, the doctor, nobody. If what you're thinkin' is true, we're talkin' some real serious shit here, and won't be nobody to stop your heart from beating if they start thinkin' you're sniffin' 'round too much. You're gonna see the free world again soon, Doc. None of us are worth risking that."

* * * * *

The day after the execution, all was quiet in the infirmary.

When Dr. Fletcher went out for a smoke break, Phil walked over to Jenny. "What happened last night? You're both so quiet, like you were the ones who were executed."

"It was bad, Phil," she whispered, then darted her pretty eyes around, as if she feared the doctor would return at any minute. "It took over ten minutes for him to flat-line. He didn't suffer and went right to sleep, but it took a double-dose to stop the poor man's heart. Dr. Fletcher said it was because of his size. I suppose that would come into play. It was just bad, and it frightened me."

Phil reached out his hand and touched her arm. "Jenny, this is more than any young woman should have to bear. Just think about it for a while. You've done your time here, done your civic duty. You've already touched a lot of lives. Sometimes you have to think about yourself."

Jenny said nothing and remained silent for the rest of the day.

* * * * *

Two weeks later, another black man flat-lined on the row, and CPR did nothing to save him.

Phil started spending more and more of his evenings in the library, trying to pull up anything he could. Unfortunately, inmate deaths didn't typically warrant articles in the newspapers, so the details were sparse at best. "Damn it," he said to himself, thumbing and scrolling through old documents and articles. "There has to be something here."

Welles began to ask more and more questions, but Phil was hesitant to talk to him about it. The last thing he wanted to do was draw his friend into anything that might be harmful. He knew he would eventually have to tell him something, though, because Welles was becoming angry and distant.

"What in the world you doin' getting involved in such?" Welles asked after Phil finally broke down and explained what he believed to be going on.

"I don't know what I'm thinking. I just know my conscience won't let it go. You've been around here a long time, Welles. Think a little. Have you seen anything...out of the ordinary? Noticed anything among the staff?"

"Ain't none of 'em ordinary to me. Who'd wanna sit around babysitting grown men for a living?"

Phil ignored the remark and pressed, "How long has the warden been here, and where'd he come from? How about the captains? Or even that Dr. Fletcher? He seems pretty racist to me, some of the remarks he makes."

"The warden's been here twelve years, and he ain't never been unfair to me.

The captains have been 'round a long time, too, as they had to work their way up. As for the doc, I figure he's been here four or five years, and that nurse started showin' her pretty little face 'round here 'bout three years ago, I think."

"Hmm. I just can't figure out what they're giving them to cause the heart attacks. If they were depleting their sodium or potassium levels, the men would be sick first, and there is no record of prior illness. Poisons would also cause symptoms over time, and I can't verify that they were injected with anything. Surely someone would have noticed if they were, especially in the autopsies. Besides, they died right in front of the other inmates. I know black men are more susceptible to heart attacks at a younger age, but this is just strange. I need to get into the files while the doctor's at lunch. I can't even trust Jenny, but I need some damn help."

"So I guess you're callin' on your big brother to do something," Welles said, with a serious look on his face. "No promises, but I'll work on it. In the meantime, you gotta lay low with this thing, or you might be lyin' on that cold slab yerself before yer time."

* * * * *

Phil hated to call collect, but it was his only choice at the prison. He was relieved when Charlie answered. "Hey, man," Phil said. "I know you're busy these days, being a family man and all, but is there any way you and Arthur can pay me a visit soon? I need to talk to you."

Charlie's voice immediately went into panic mode. "What's wrong? Have you been hurt again?"

"No, nothing like that. I just don't want to talk about it over the phone."

"We'll get there as soon as we can work it out."

"Thanks. I'd better let you go. This call's on your dime."

Charlie laughed, a bit uneasily. "Well, I know where to find you to make you pay me back."

After the call, Phil walked back to his cell. He felt a little lighter on his feet, a little relieved, knowing his friends could help with some outside digging. He hoped Charlie might even be able to dig up some medical answers that he couldn't find in the prison library. He climbed up into his bunk and tried to block out all thoughts of it for the next two weeks, until his friends could come to visit.

* * * * *

"Sorry we couldn't make it last weekend," Charlie said, sitting across the table, with a look of deep concern etched on his face. "There was just too much going on. What's wrong?"

Phil looked at Charlie, then Arthur, then leaned forward so he could talk softly. He quickly explained, in as much detail as he could, all that had occurred.

"Maybe it's coincidence," Arthur offered, even though he knew Phil's gut feelings usually proved true.

"Maybe," Phil answered, "but more than likely, it's not." He paused to collect his thoughts, then ran his hands over his eyes and face. "I need some help, guys. All prison deaths are public record and can be requested by any citizen, with the exception of a convicted felon or incarcerated inmate. Arthur, I hope you can check that out. I'd also like to know a little more about the warden, this Dr. Fletcher, and the nurse, Jenny. I'm sure there are others, but I can't pinpoint anyone else right now. It has to be someone on the inside, part of the administration, because the inmates wouldn't bother to try to cover it up—not to mention that most wouldn't know how to create a fake heart attack. As you and I know, they prefer more… crude means, and they like to make a statement."

"Yeah, like rats," Charlie said with a huff.

"Jesus, Phil," Arthur answered. "Can't you just serve your damn time? You'll be out soon, the worst is over, and I don't see why it's your problem to—"

Phil held a hand up to stop him. "I just have to know, all right? For all I know, this shit's been going on for years, and it'll continue to happen unless someone puts a stop to it. Criminals or not, the men don't deserve this, and it's bugging the hell outta me that I can't figure it out. You gotta help me, guys," Phil pleaded. "There's only so much I can do from the inside."

"I know a friend who can run some criminal histories for me, but it'll cost me $100 dinner. I'll get my paralegal to pick up the statistics on deaths."

"Do you think they'll contact the prison? I mean, someone there could be in on this too," Phil asked.

"Okay, now you're going overboard," Arthur said. "That's ridiculous. I don't think you need to worry about that."

"Charlie, what could they be using to cause heart failure without any other symptoms? There's no sign of poisoning or injections. They just collapse in front of everyone. They've got no medical histories to speak of, and they're all young, healthy black men."

"Hmm. I don't know. I'll do some research and ask around, but you're right. It doesn't add up. Be careful, Phil. You know all this snooping around could put you in a great deal of danger."

"I know. That's why I called in my reinforcements." Phil laughed.

"God, Phil. Tell me you don't have a new girlfriend named 'Bubba' to look out for you," Arthur joked.

"Not funny, man. Not funny at all."

They tried to keep the rest of the visit light, and the banter seemed to help Phil. He wasn't even aware of how heavily the mystery had been weighing on him, and it felt good to laugh and let it all go for a while with his friends.

"Thanks for getting Mae here, Arthur. You shoulda seen Welles's face. He cried for an hour."

"I'm glad he enjoyed it, because the whole ordeal was a real pain in the ass. Do you know how hard it is to get someone who's never left the farm to fly all the way across the country on an airplane? Jesus Christ. You have no idea how much this attorney is costing you, no freaking idea," he said, trying to sound serious but breaking out into deep laughter. "These past few years have been crazy as hell, haven't they? I feel like Charlie and I have been in prison with you. Thank God it won't be much longer."

Phil wasn't back in his cell for more than fifteen minutes before one of the officers knocked on the cell door and buzzed it open. "We need you bad, Doc," he said, obviously out of breath and concerned. "There's a lady in the visitation room who's… God, she's pregnant and bleeding like a stuck pig. I guess the weekend help took a break, because there's no one in the infirmary."

"I'm right behind you," Phil said.

They ran as fast as they could to get to the Hispanic lady, who was writhing in pain. The guards quickly cleared all the visitors out of the room as her husband frantically screamed in hurried Spanish.

"Get him the hell outta here and back to his cell," one of the guards yelled.

Phil looked up at him in disbelief. "This baby is in distress, and if he's the father, he should be here. If you make him leave, I'll stop right now, and the blood of this baby's death will be on your hands."

They only hesitated for a second before conceding that the father could stay.

"I need some clean towels and gloves, and, for God's sake, call an ambulance!" Phil demanded.

The woman was dilated to ten, and the baby's head was crowning when the problem came into sight: The umbilical cord was wrapped tightly around its tiny neck and getting tighter by the second.

"Scissors! Now!" Phil screamed as he placed his hand next to the baby's neck, loosening the cord as much as he could.

The baby began turning blue, petrifying the guards, but Phil managed to use the scissors to gently cut the cord. He then quickly pulled the baby out of the birth canal. The child's color started coming back immediately, and it screamed and cried from being removed from its warm, cozy environment.

"You've got a beautiful baby girl here," Phil said, smiling as he handed the infant to her mother, who was weeping with joy and relief. He looked around and saw that the parents weren't the only ones with moist eyes.

The ambulance arrived and began making preparations to load up the mother and child, but the officers granted the father a few moments with them first. The inmate smiled proudly as he held his new daughter, then gently laid her back on her mother's bosom and watched as the ambulance whisked them away. When they were out of sight, he turned to Phil and held out his hand. "*Gracias, Doctor.*

Muchas gracias."

"*De nada.* You're welcome," Phil answered, then went to wash up so he could go back to read to Welles.

CHAPTER 16

Phil continued scanning the old newspapers night after night, to no avail. Growing weary of what seemed to be a fruitless quest, the thought occurred to him to look up Lara's hometown and the man she married. He found the local paper on the database, dating all the way back to when Lara married Jeb and had Lilly. There was plenty of news coverage for the scandalous pair, as they committed several robberies. Every time, though, Lara came out smelling like a rose. *That guy is serving her time just like I am,* Phil thought, almost feeling sorry for him.

He scrolled through a few more years before it hit him, the answer to the burglaries and his wife's evil undertakings: "Armored Truck Heist Goes Unsolved. In the early morning hours, an armored truck loaded with over $8 million was high jacked off Old Quarry Road. No descriptions were given of the suspects, except that there appeared to be a female and male voice. Both wore black ski masks and were armed with semiautomatic weapons. The guards were uninjured but were tied up and carried into the wooded area along the roadside. A reward of $10,000 is being offered at this time for any information leading to the arrest and conviction of the persons involved in this case…"

That greedy bitch. Why'd she need me if she had all that money? He read the article again, then reached over and turned off the computer. It was in the past, after all, and Lara was six feet under. He had no choice but to move on and leave her in the cold ground, where she belonged.

* * * * *

It was four weeks before Charlie and Arthur returned, although they had sent several cryptic, vague letters to him, written in code so no one would know what they were talking about.

Phil was relieved to be called out for his visit and anxious to hear if they'd discovered anything of substance, anything that might answer his questions and save lives.

"Pulled up some background checks and did some digging about the people you asked about," Arthur started before they'd even said their proper hellos. "The warden checks out and is apparently pretty well respected around here. It's hard to land a position like his, supervising one of the worst prisons in the country, unless you're on the ball. This Dr. Fletcher took over the infirmary a little over five years ago. He had a thriving private practice before, but he shut it down to work here. Go figure. His medical license is up to date, and I found nothing unusual, no outstanding malpractice suits or anything. The nurse, Jenny, comes from a wealthy family in Kentucky, wealthy enough to put a horse in the Kentucky Derby. She seems legit to me, though she's gotta be a little crazy to want to work in a place like this. Honestly, that's the only thing I found that's even remotely out of the ordinary."

"No, the doctor's pretty odd too," Phil said. "I mean, who would leave a private practice to come to this hellhole? That doesn't make any sense."

"He's right," Charlie agreed. "For most doctors, having a private practice is a dream gig."

"Maybe he's just got a big heart like that nurse. Who the hell knows?"

"But he doesn't," Phil answered. "That's the thing. He's a racist and a bigot, and he performs the executions, for Christ's sake. Who, in his right mind, would choose that over the comfort of a private practice?"

"Can't answer that one, but I did pull up the stats you asked for. Seems natural deaths are on the rise here and have been for about three years now, since right around the time your girl started working here."

"She's not my girl, but go ahead."

"Well, this comes through the grapevine, so don't quote me on it, but the autopsies performed on inmates are half-assed. It's just too expensive, and nobody really gives a damn."

"No shit," Phil said. "I bet they don't even take any toxicology screenings."

"That costs money, and that's the bottom line, especially with expendable people."

Phil looked down at the table and put his chin in his right hand, his mind deep in thought. "What do you think, Charlie?"

"I've been asking around too. Like you said, without any IV or injection marks, I'm at a loss. If it was poison, there'd be other symptoms. Maybe we're just chasing our tails on this one."

"Out of those stats, Arthur," Phil continued, squinting with concentration, "how many were black youths?"

"I don't remember exactly, but I'm sure it was around 90 percent."

"I need those names so I can look in their medical files."

"What are you talking about, Phil? You get caught digging around in confidential files, and they'll keep you in here till the cows come home."

"Can you get them to me?" Phil asked, ignoring the warning.

"And just how would I do that?" Arthur asked, knowing all too well that it would be a losing battle to argue with Phil.

"Let me think," Phil said, scrunching up his brow. "You and Charlie write me every day. In your letters, you can mention the deceased as if they are mutual friends. Use their first name, but later in the letter, put the last name, spelled backward. They read our mail, but they'll never figure that out. They're not smart enough, and they don't have the time to go solving riddles. They're too busy looking for drugs smuggled in under postage stamps. It wouldn't take long to check two files a day. I am always alone at lunch."

"God, Phil," Charlie said, shaking his head. "I don't like this, not one bit. Wasn't killing Lara enough excitement for you?"

Everyone sat silently for a moment, equally stunned and stung by the harsh remark, and Phil diverted his eyes away from the two men in front of him.

"God, man. I'm sorry, Phil," Charlie said, his face flushed. "I didn't mean it. It's just… Look, for all these years, I've been worrying myself sick over you. So has Janet. And now this? Think about us. We want our friend back, and I don't see why you have to go sticking your nose in where you're likely to get it chopped off."

Phil wasn't angry, for he knew Charlie meant well. "You're a doctor, Charlie," he said, "and if you were in here, seeing all this, you'd do the same thing. We're destined to save lives, took an oath to, not to stand by and watch them being taken before their time."

Charlie reached over and took Phil's hand in his own. "I know. Just be careful. You've been through so much. It isn't worth it to lose it all now."

CHAPTER 17

Phil explained the results of his friends' visit to Welles, and the two put their heads together. A friend in the kitchen had given Welles a lock-picking kit, and Welles explained in detail exactly how it worked. They managed to fit it inside of an ink pen.

"For goodness sake, be careful. This is dangerous stuff, and I ain't lyin' to ya," Welles said.

"I know. I'll be fine."

It took four days for the first letters to come, and Phil was thrilled to decipher them. The next morning, he carried their names in his memory, along with his new pen. It was Drew's day for dialysis, so he filled him in on the latest of his investigation.

As soon as Dr. Fletcher and Jenny left for lunch, Phil picked his way into the filing cabinet and pulled the two files of the deceased men. He was glad they had medical records for every inmate, even if they only contained the results of their initial physicals.

"Damon Parkin," he whispered to himself, realizing that the man perfectly fit the profile. The intake picture was of a young black man, a little on the heavy side but healthy. He had no medical history and had paid no visits to the infirmary. "Jackson McDaniel," he said next. He opened the file quickly, knowing he'd spent too much time on the other file. It was the same scenario.

He wrote the dates of death on the inside of his arm and carefully shut the file. He then crammed half his sandwich in his mouth, just so he could honestly say he'd been eating lunch. He was almost finished with his apple when Jenny and Dr. Fletcher walked in.

Phil continued with the routine every day, and he and Welles notated the dates in the margins of the pages of their books. All of the cases appeared similar, though there was no real pattern to the dates. Clearly, they were dealing with some sort of serial killer, preying on the men behind bars, with some sick motive they didn't yet understand.

"You know, FBI profilers always say that serial killers are typically white males," Phil told Welles one night.

"I didn't know that, as I don't keep up with such, but I guess outta all yer suspects, that only leaves the doc."

"Yeah, but there's Jenny too."

"Um, in case ya ain't noticed, she's not a male. I'da thunk they woulda taught you the diff'rence in that there fancy medical school, Doc," Welles teased with a smile.

Phil laughed. "Well, it's highly improbable that it's her, but I guess it's a possibility. I really like her. She's always kind and gentle and seems sweet enough, but I've been burned before. I guess this place has made me more jaded, or maybe what I went through before I came in here. I refuse to trust anybody, except you and my few friends on the outside."

"Gonna hafta get over that if'n we're gonna run a business together. You won't be able to keep customers that way."

Phil laughed and opened a book. "You're right, Welles…again."

* * * * *

The following day was probably one of the worst Phil spent at San Quentin. It was Drew's day for dialysis, and he came in looking pale and nervous. "What's up?" Phil asked. "You aren't getting any sleep on the row? Do I need to contact somebody in command?" He laughed to himself, but Drew didn't share the humor with him.

"Got my papers yesterday."

"Papers? What do you mean?"

"My date ta walk the walk. Two weeks from today, I'm a dead man."

Phil was speechless. He knew what a horrible thing Drew had done, and it was no secret that the man had reserved himself a seat on death row by his crime, but Phil had grown to like him, and he wasn't prepared for the awful truth. Drew had three beautiful children that he would never see again, and he wouldn't be back for dialysis either. For a moment, Phil's mind refused to let him comprehend it.

"Hey, don't take it so hard, man. You're not the dead man walking."

Still, Phil's mouth refused to allow him to reply, despite his most sincere efforts to say something.

"I'm not dead yet, damn it. You can still talk to me. If dialysis is gonna be like this for two weeks, then to hell with it."

"I-I'm sorry," Phil stammered. "It's just… Hell, I'm not ready for you to go."

"And you think I am? It's not our call, buddy. Like I told ya before, I did the crime, killed my grandmama over $20, and now it's time to pay that back, with a whole lotta interest. It's not like we didn't know it was coming."

"Yeah, I know," was all Phil could mutter.

"Listen, I need to talk to you seriously, Doc," Drew said in a tone that denoted graveness.

"Go on."

"My old lady has a husband now, and it just ain't right to ask her to come be with me when I… Well hell, when I bite the bullet, so to speak. I sure as hell don't want the children here. My friends have long since moved on with their lives and are either serving their own time or have just forgotten the likes of me." Drew paused, looking embarrassed, bordering on ashamed. "I guess what I'm saying, man, is that you're the closest thing I got to a friend now. I'm wonderin' if you'd be willin' to be there for me when I…when I gasp that last sweet breath of air. I know it's askin' a lot, Doc, but I don't wanna go to my death alone. It just ain't right for nobody to go that way, no matter what they done." He looked down at the sheet that covered his legs and twisted it with his fingers.

Phil stood and walked around the small infirmary like an expectant father pacing in the waiting room. "Drew, I-I don't know what to say," he answered, struggling. "I'm flattered. I truly am. You're my friend, too, but I just don't think they'll let me in there. I'm an inmate myself." Phil hid his sigh of relief while, in his mind, he patted himself on the back for finding a handy excuse to get him out of it.

"That don't matter none. I already wrote a note to the warden, and he checked with Dr. Fletcher. 'Cause you work in the infirmary, they got no problem with you bein' there. Course, it don't hurt that I ain't got nobody else. I guess the bastards do feel a little sorry for me after all."

Phil sat back down on the stool beside the bed and placed his hand on top of Drew's. He was ashamed when he instantly jerked it back, but the thought of touching a breathing dead man didn't set too well with him. Phil slowly raised his hand and patted Drew's a couple times, then stood again. "I'll be there, my friend. I know you'd do the same for me."

The answer seemed to take a great deal of stress off Drew, because his color instantly returned, and his weak smile shone through a little more.

That day, Phil couldn't bear to go thumbing through the files of dead men. He already had one to deal with, a friend whose death he'd have to helplessly watch.

CHAPTER 18

The following two weeks were hell for Phil as he waited on the inevitable execution of his friend. As Drew's doomsday neared, he found himself praying for a reprieve. Out in the real world, it wouldn't have been his style to want to stop the execution of a coldblooded killer, especially one who'd stabbed his own grandmother for a hit of crack, but he saw things differently now. *Maybe Drew does deserve to die,* he pondered, *but his children have done no wrong.* There was just something about a healthy man going off to his death that seemed wrong somehow. Phil had already seen so many senseless deaths since he had stepped foot inside San Quentin.

In college, one of Phil's friends was killed in a car wreck, and that had bothered him for a long time, but this was different. There was something grotesque and macabre about knowing the exact minute of one's death. He lay awake almost every night the week before the execution, and even when sleep did finally take him, it was short-lived; he often woke up to vomit.

Welles got up each time to wet a washcloth, just as his mother had done when he was a small child. He never said anything to Phil because he knew that nothing could make things any easier, no matter how many years one spent in that place. "Time don't heal all wounds after all," he said, and wiser words could not have been spoken.

When Drew was escorted in for his last day of dialysis, his face and body reflected his sleepless nights and years of regret. He lay on the gurney and went through the motions, as he had for years, lying still and allowing the bad toxins to be taken from his body, just so he'd be healthy enough to be killed. Jenny spent the entire morning crying, and Dr. Fletcher sent her home a while before the execution.

Phil sat beside his friend, praying for the right words: *A baseball score, the high price of gasoline, just any-damn-thing!*

"My kids will spend the day with me today. It'll be bittersweet, but at least I'll have the opportunity to tell 'em what I need to. Not many people get that chance. I guess, in some fucked-up way, that makes my death special. I won't leave this world regretting things that weren't said. A lotta people have to carry stuff to their graves."

Phil felt his head nod but he hadn't consciously put forth any effort for it to do so. "Well," he started, swallowing past a thick lump in his throat, "I've spent the past few years reading from the Good Book every night, thanks to Welles. At least you know you'll be going to a better place, a place where you can look down on your children every minute of every day, and there won't be any bars, none at all." Phil felt awkward and hypocritical preaching to Drew at that moment, and he wished Welles was around; illiterate as he was, he would know just which scriptures to quote and just what words to say to encourage the condemned.

"Don't think I'll make it through those pearly gates, Doc," Drew said. "I lost that chance when I took a life."

"You've paid your price in here, Drew. All these years on the row and dying for your crime? I think the Man Upstairs will consider your debt settled, and He knows how remorseful you are. They say he's quite...forgiving."

"I wish I knew just how forgiving He is," Drew answered, forcing a laugh. "It'd be nice to know whether I'm gonna be playin' a harp or roastin' like a marshmallow."

Once his dialysis was done, Drew thanked them both and left the infirmary for the last time.

The office was silent, and for a few moments, it seemed like even Dr. Fletcher might shed a tear. It didn't happen though, and he instead turned to busy himself with some paperwork. He hadn't noticed yet that his files were being examined, and Phil wondered just how long he could pull it off. Apparently, the silence was too deafening, because the doctor broke it to let Phil go early for the day.

Phil walked slowly, almost methodically back to his cell, wishing, as Drew was, that the day would never end.

CHAPTER 19

It was after 10:00 p.m. when they came for Phil and led him to the cramped cell that held his friend. All family visits were over, and the ministers and clergy were taking a break before the onset of the execution itself. Two guards sat outside the cell, monitoring every movement the condemned man made, making sure he did not do anything that might put his life in jeopardy before they could kill him themselves.

"What's up, man?" Phil asked as he squeezed through the small opening they made for him.

"Just hanging out. What about you?" Drew answered. He grinned, but his face was drawn and swollen from the tears of earlier goodbyes, and his hands were shaking ever so slightly.

"How'd your visits go?"

"All right. I think I've come to terms with it now. A reprieve would kinda fuck me up, ya know? It's like… I've been dreading this for so long, but I'm almost relieved that it's gonna be over. Weird, huh?"

"Not really. You aren't exactly leaving the Taj Mahal, you know? I understand. I'm sure you already know it'll be painless, right?"

"Yeah. They told me I'll just sorta drift off into Fairy Land and float up to Heaven," he said, smiling, his eyes reflecting a hint of humor.

"Last meal walking!" one of the guards yelled as he opened the cell door. "Just as requested—two Big Macs, two large fries, a medium Coke, a chocolate shake, and a hot apple pie. Hope you got an appetite, Isaacs."

Phil gave the rude guard a disapproving glare for the callous remark, then reached for the two large bags and passed them over to Drew. "Pretty big decision you had to make, right up there with whether the tattoo on your biceps should be a naked lady with pink nipples or an 'I love Mom' heart."

"Pretty good analogy there, Doc, but it ain't quite the same. I thought about a lot of things—steak, lobster, shrimp, and all them fancy things I never could afford out there in the streets—but the bottom line is, a man misses them Golden Arches more than anything else. They may be ashamed to admit it, may wanna seem a little classier, but hell, I ain't got no pride left. I wanted what I wanted."

"More power to ya, my man. Enjoy."

Drew offered one of the burgers to Phil, but he refused it. Even if he had felt like eating, which he didn't, he couldn't take part in a man's last meal. Somehow, it just wouldn't be right. Phil was surprised to see that Drew ate almost every bite, and he appeared to enjoy it, letting out a healthy belch when the last fry hit his stomach. *He really must have come to terms with all this,* Phil thought, *because I'd be damned if I could eat anything.*

"Fifteen minutes, Sawyer," one of the guards said coldly, "and then the clergy will come in. You'll have to watch from behind the glass, like everyone else." Then, with a quick and flawless military pivot on the ball of his foot, he stomped off.

"Once a prick, always a prick," Drew said with an unconvincing laugh.

"At least you're getting out of this place," Phil said, regretting the words the instant they forced their way out of his mouth.

Drew sat silently for a few minutes, lost in his own thoughts, and Phil wasn't comfortable interrupting them, so he said nothing. A few seconds later, Drew asked, "Do you really think I'll get to Heaven, Doc?"

"The Good Book says if you accept Christ as your Savior and open your heart to Him, you will."

"I believe in Him. I really do. Also, I'm sorry for all I done. It's just… I don't know that I'm quite…deservin'."

"Do you know Christ died on the cross so we can all be forgiven for *all* our sins?"

"That's the Easter story, ain't it?"

"Yeah…and I hear it's true—a lot truer than some bunny laying painted, chocolate-covered eggs."

Drew smiled briefly, then shifted his body on the small cot and hung his head. One lone tear escaped his eye and fell to the concrete floor. "I couldn't blame God if He chooses to send me down there. I really couldn't. I'd just like a chance to see my grandmother, to tell her how sorry I am." He looked at Phil, then continued, "Look, man, I'm only tellin' you all this 'cause anybody else would think I'm just bullshittin'. I-I just keep seeing that old purse and my shaking hand going into it. I was like a damn hungry animal, and I took every dime she had left. She was just tryin' to protect me and what was hers, and I left her there like that. I didn't even look back, Doc." Drew's voice was calm, but his tears were flowing like rivers and hitting the floor like raindrops. "I'm no different from those other guys on the row, no different at all. Hell, why should I expect those guards to be anything but arrogant? They probably eat Sunday dinners with their grandmas, and I killed mine."

"Hey, let's not waste these last few minutes beating yourself up. You've had years to do that. As far as the guards and the rest of the world… Well, they may not have killed anyone, or maybe they have, but we've all sinned. Heaven would be a pretty empty place if they only accepted the perfect. You know, when I was a kid, I pictured Heaven like Willie Wonka's Chocolate Factory." Phil laughed at himself. "The rivers were made of chocolate, and the leaves on the trees were candy. If that's what it's like, don't eat it all before I get there. Of course, you can knock yourself out with the licorice. It tastes like shit, even in Heaven."

Drew laughed at that, then looked up. "You've been a real friend, Doc. In this crazy place, I learned to trust ya, and I've always felt like I could talk to you. I guess that's 'cause you don't belong here. This place hasn't turned you into an animal."

"Well, the fat lady hasn't sung yet, Drew."

"If it hasn't broken you down by now, it never will. If the good Lord sees fit, I'll be looking down on ya, keeping up with you. I expect great things from you."

"Don't look for too many great things. I just want to live a normal life and appreciate every day I'm given."

"You will do plenty of great things, Doc. Trust me on that. Take a dyin' man's word on it."

"Times up," said the hostile guard, reappearing out of the blue. Beside him stood a minister, holding a black Bible and harboring deep pity in his eyes. The guard put the key in the lock and motioned for Phil to come out.

Drew stood, and the two embraced as if they'd known each other their whole lives.

"I'll be right outside, Drew," Phil said. "Just look for me. I'll be there until the end."

"I know you will, Doc, I know you will."

The minister walked in after Phil stepped out.

Dr. Fletcher motioned Phil over. "Are you taking it okay, Sawyer?" he asked in his usual monotone voice that never gave away any inclination of emotion.

"Yeah. It's tough, but it has to be done."

"That's my boy," he answered. He then walked over to the vials that would enter the IV that would end Drew's life.

"Tell me a little about these," Phil asked, trying to set his mind on anything other than the execution.

"The first two are sodium pentothal," Dr. Fletcher said. "It will put him to sleep. We follow that with a vial of saline, then Pavulon to shut down the respiratory system, another saline, and last but not least, potassium chloride to stop the ol' ticker."

Phil looked at him with a disgust he could no longer hide. Fletcher spoke of it so robotically, as if he was just performing some magic trick at a circus: *"Just do this and this, and ta-da! One dead man, and we all go home."*

The look on Phil's face wasn't lost on the doctor. "He won't feel a thing. You may hear a loud gasp or a snort, maybe even a grunt, but by then he'll be fast asleep. Don't worry," He tried to assure Phil.

Phil stood at the glass and watched as Drew Isaacs walked into the execution chamber, flanked by four massive guards. His face was expressionless until he saw Phil and managed a weak, tender smile. They strapped him down, then tilted the gurney forward so the media could witness his last words.

Phil's heart sank as he watched a tired, very sad Jenny walk over to put in the IV that would transport the poisons to his body. Her small hands shook ever so slightly, and her eyes were red from crying. She didn't say anything to Drew, and he only smiled at her and nodded. Once she managed to get the line in, she mumbled something very softly to him under her breath, words no one else could hear, and Drew just shook his head and winked at her.

When Jenny walked out, Phil whispered for her, and she responded with tremendous relief to see him.

"Thank God," she said. "Oh, I'm so glad to see you," she said, making no attempt to hide the fact that she was conversing with him. It was all too emotional for anyone to bear, and she no longer cared about protocol. "Did you get to talk to him?"

"Yeah, we had a few minutes. He's gonna be okay. He's come to terms with it."

The warden entered, along with the minister, and the curtains were opened for the media to witness the event. Drew requested a prayer but declined any last words; Phil figured they had long since been said in his cell. They leveled the gurney out again, reclining him, and he rested his head on the pillow and turned ever so slightly so he could see Phil.

"There could never be any other feeling in the world like this," Phil said to Jenny as the two stood side by side. The tears stung his eyes, but he didn't bother to wipe them away. When he saw Drew succumbing to the grogginess, he placed his hand on the glass.

Drew could barely lift his, but he was able to make an attempt to reach his friend's. Then his hand fell by his side, and in one gasp. he was gone, flat-lined out of the world.

"Please, Lord," Phil said, his face looking upward, "let him see his grandmother so he can tell her how sorry he is. Even if You can only keep him up there long enough for that, please let the man apologize."

Jenny walked up and handed Phil an envelope. "This is from Drew. He didn't want me to give it to you till all this was over," she said, smiling sadly at him. "He thought a lot of you," she said softly. "You made his last days better."

Phil didn't answer and just took the envelope, but he waited to open it until he got back to his cell, as he didn't want anyone else to see it. He pulled the note out and read: "Dear Phil, This is probably the most difficult letter I have written in a long time. I want to thank you for being my friend. I never really appreciated friendship till I met you. I guess I never knew what friendship was. I gave away all my belongings to the guys on the row. Didn't have much to give, just a small radio and things like that. But I want to give you something that meant the most to me. I guess it won't mean a whole lot to you, but I held it close to my heart every day. Maybe when you look at it, you'll remember me. Your friend, Drew."

Phil fumbled around with the envelope a bit, his hands still shaking, and found a worn photograph inside, a picture of Drew Isaacs's three beautiful children. "Yes, Drew Isaacs, I will always, always remember you," he said, his voice faltering.

CHAPTER 20

The next morning, Phil lay in his bunk, too depressed to give a damn about going to the infirmary. He had gotten little sleep the night before, and he felt like he was nursing a tequila hangover.

"Better get up," Welles said, his voice filled with sympathy. "If ya lay there ponderin' it fer too long, you'll only feel worse about it. Layin' outta work ain't gonna change a thing. The man ain't coming back, Doc. I'm sorry for ya and all, but he's gone on to another place, a better one at that, if ya ask me."

"You're right, Welles," Phil said, sitting up in bed. His head was throbbing, and he felt like crying all over again. He took a wet washcloth from his cellmate, and the coolness made him feel a little more alive. Phil swung his feet over the side of his bed and jumped down. "It's not a good day to miss breakfast either," he said, then quickly brushed his teeth and dressed. As he did, a sudden, horrifying, crazy thought came to him. "Welles, it's the potassium chloride!" Phil said. "That's what's doing it."

"Do you 'spect me to know what you're talking bout? Do I look like I just stepped outta that fancy medical school?"

Phil began shaking, his mind racing with the possibilities. "That's what stops the heart during an execution, potassium chloride. It'd be easy for Dr. Fletcher to remove some before an execution and replace it with saline solution. Maybe that's why it takes some of the men two doses to flat-line. I'll be damned."

"C'mon, Doc. Surely somebody'd see him if he was up ta no good like that."

"Who wouldn't trust a doctor, for goodness sake? Everyone relies on them to save lives. Nobody would suspect him."

"He can't be the only one who's around the stuff. Maybe it's one of them guards. Don't none of 'em like us."

"That's possible, but someone would eventually get suspicious of guards hanging around the medications. Besides, they're never left alone with it. There's strict protocol, even for those who transport it. If it was anyone else and the doc's not in on it, he would have gotten suspicious by now."

"Reckon you got a point."

"We need to compare the dates of the heart attacks to those of past executions. Those chemicals are delivered a few days prior. They don't just keep them in the prison at all times." "You could find the execution dates in the newspapers. They always print those."

"You gotta help me remember them, Welles. I'll start looking this afternoon, after work, and tonight we'll compare them to the dates we have on the murders."

"Even if this is the truth, Doc, who's gonna listen to us? In their eyes, we're just a couple nonsense-talkin' convicts."

"I don't know, but we'll figure that out later."

Welles shook his head and waved his white washcloth in surrender. "You're killin' me, Doc. Really."

Before they could say anything more, the door buzzed for breakfast, and they followed the crowd to the chow hall.

CHAPTER 21

"Morning, Jenny," Phil said as he entered the infirmary.

"Good morning," she answered. "How are you?"

"I'll be okay."

"Time helps a lot, if that's any consolation," she answered.

"I'm sure it will. Is Dr. Fletcher in yet?"

"No. He usually takes mornings off after executions. He'll be in around noon."

"He's a very private man, isn't he?" Phil asked, hoping he didn't sound too nosy or desperate.

"Yes. His wife was killed before he came to work here. He had his own practice but left their town and their home to make a new life. It must've really hurt him, because he never speaks of it. From the way it sounds, he doesn't have much of a life outside work."

"Poor guy. I guess that explains why he isn't very open with things," Phil answered and ended the conversation there. *It makes sense,* he reasoned. *His wife is murdered, so he comes here to make everyone pay for what happened to her.* "Quiet morning," he said, trying to change the subject. "Hope it stays that way." Phil didn't want to seem suspicious, although that appeared to be the last thing on Jenny's mind.

"Me too," Jenny answered. "There isn't usually much violence after an execution. It seems to kinda sober everyone up for a couple days. After that, it's business as usual."

Phil forced a laugh and smiled at her. "When the doctor gets in, do you think I could spend my lunch break in the library? I told one of the guys in my block that I'd look a few things up for him, sort of a jailhouse lawyer kind of thing."

"I don't see why not. Just double-check with Dr. Fletcher."

The morning was uneventful, and the doctor didn't have a problem with Phil being out of the office for an hour. Phil rushed to the computers and looked up the local paper from the town Arthur had told him the doctor's private practice had been in. He surfed the year before Dr. Fletcher came to San Quentin, and just as his hour was almost up, he hit the jackpot. As it turned out, Dr. Fletcher's wife had been brutally raped and murdered in their home during an apparent break-in. The neighbors claimed they saw a young black male fleeing the home just before her body was discovered, and the killer had never been found.

Damn, Phil thought. *That's it. He's making every black man pay, under the justification of avenging his wife's death. What a sick son-of-a-bitch.*

He quickly shut the computer down and hurried back to the infirmary, praying his face would not reveal the devastation he felt. He had to call Arthur, had to see him and Charlie before anything else happened, before anyone else died.

Welles met him in the library after their work duties were complete. Whenever anyone walked by, Phil pretended to be teaching Welles to read the newspaper. With the exception of one death, every other had occurred within two weeks of an execution. However, they were only studying the ones they were aware of.

Welles nudged Phil hard in his ribs.

"Ouch," Phil spat. "What's the matter with you?"

"Let's get outta here. I ain't feelin' right. We can talk in the cell, but it's getting too crowded in here." Welles's forehead was beaded with perspiration, and his hands were visibly shaking.

"Take it easy, man," Phil said. "We'll go." He shut the computer down, and they strolled gingerly out of the library.

When they got back to the cell, Welles asked Phil for a soda, for the first time in all the years they'd lived together. "I'm scared, man," he said. "I didn't believe you at first, but now? Somethin' ain't right. You was right all along."

"I'm sorry I got you involved," Phil said.

"No, it ain't that. It's just that folks notice when your patterns change. We ain't never gone to that library together, and everybody knows I can't read. We gotta be careful."

"You're right. I won't go back there. My friends can research for me on the outside, now that we've got enough for them to believe us. I'll call them tonight, and maybe they can visit this weekend. Let's not talk about it anymore until then."

"Okay by me," Welles answered, the relief obvious in his voice. "Can we read Du Bois tonight?" he said quietly, as if he was almost afraid to ask.

"You bet, brother," Phil answered. "Du Bois it is."

* * * * *

Arthur and Charlie didn't hide their surprise or their unwillingness to get involved.

"Do you know what this means?" Arthur asked. "We'll have to call in the big dogs, the FBI, have to exhume bodies, for Christ's sake. But how? We don't have a shred of hard evidence. All we've got is an inmate's gut feeling that the prison doctor is seeking revenge on the entire black race. All that aside, do I need to remind you that you're that inmate, locked in here just like all those potential young black victims? Who's watching your back?"

Charlie sat silently for a moment, then interjected, "Potassium chloride has to be injected for it to work properly. You said yourself they all had their heart attacks in plain view of everyone, and no one appeared to be carrying an IV around with them."

"Damn it, Charlie," Phil said, exasperated. "There has to be another way."

"Even if it was injected intramuscularly, it would leave some kind of mark."

"What if they hid it? Drug addicts do it all the time, under their fingernails, between their toes—"

"But you said they weren't drug addicts," Charlie retorted. "And who'd let a doctor inject him in a place like that? It doesn't make sense."

"Suppose he told them he was trying to help them get high, or maybe he promised steroids. They were all in great shape, clearly weightlifters."

"Then where were the syringes? Did they inject themselves at the dinner table and eat the syringe before falling over dead with a heart attack?"

"Shit, Charlie," Phil answered, rubbing his hands coarsely through his hair. "Help me out here. Quit playing the damn devil's advocate."

"Listen," Arthur said, "let's just think for a minute. Even if this is all true, we don't have much solid evidence to stand on. I hate like hell to say it, but if another black man dies of a heart attack in the next few weeks, we can take it up with the State Bureau of Investigation. They'll haul the body in for a full autopsy, and I can get the State Police to pressure them for a toxicology screen. In the meantime, I'll get my poor, overworked, underpaid paralegal to pull all the newspaper clippings you're talking about and match them to all the deaths we got from the Department of Corrections. We'll do what we can. For the moment, though, you'd do best to just forget about it. You've almost served your sentence, Phil Sawyer. Just ride it out."

Phil smiled a tired, lingering smile. "Thanks, guys, but just promise me you'll at least look into it."

"Will do," they both answered.

"Oh, I almost forgot," Phil said, pulling a folded sheet of paper from his back pocket. "This is a copy of an article I found in a Norfolk, Nebraska newspaper. You might find it interesting. It pretty much explains the break-ins at my house and yours, Charlie."

The two men looked it over, then raised their heads up in shock.

"That money's still out there somewhere," Charlie said. "That key is the answer."

"Yeah," Phil answered, "but what does it go to?"

"Who knows? Maybe Arthur's paralegal is getting some leads on that as we speak."

"Jesus," Arthur answered. "She's not a machine. I need a whole damn army to solve the problems you two have. You might be the one with the teenage daughter, Charlie, but I get stuck with all the damn drama from you two!"

Charlie and Phil laughed, but Arthur didn't even crack a smile.

"What I don't understand," Phil continued, "is why she needed my money. She would have had more on her own."

"That's pretty simple," Arthur answered. "You can't just start spending millions of dollars without someone getting suspicious. She was smarter than we gave her credit for. Going on a shopping spree is how most robbers get caught. They start spending money like it's water, buying expensive houses and cars, drawing attention to themselves like crazy. Lara married a rich doctor on purpose, as a cover. She probably planned to spend your money for a while, then divorce you. She would have gotten a decent settlement and alimony, maybe even the house, and no one would have questioned the extravagant spending."

"Am I the dumbest son-of-a-bitch on the planet or what?" Phil asked, rolling his eyes in desperation.

"You're not the first nor the last to make a mistake about a beautiful woman. The question is, though, where is the money?"

"And," Charlie asked, "who is trying to find the key? Her husband, that Jeb, is locked up for more years than we can count."

"I'm not sure who's after it," Phil answered, "but Arthur, have your paralegal get on that, will you?"

They all three laughed that time, a good, hearty, sincere laugh that caused everyone in the visitation room to turn around and stare.

"Meh, screw 'em. Screw 'em all," Phil said, chuckling.

CHAPTER 22

Two weeks and two days later, a young black man died of heart failure on the chow hall floor, right in the middle of lunchtime. Dr. Fletcher called for Phil to go with him, and as soon as Phil got there, he knew his suspicions were right. The young man was dead, his eyes still open in that gruesome stare of death. Phil reached over gently and closed them, then prayed they would stay that way.

While Dr. Fletcher was talking to the officers, Phil took every opportunity to look for an injection mark. He saw none, neither in the man's muscular arms or his healthy, bulging veins. When he looked up, he saw Dr. Fletcher watching him, with an odd expression on his face.

"No use trying to comfort him now, Sawyer," he said. "He's already dead. His mama can cry over him and pat his hands."

For a moment, Phil feared he might lose it and attack the good doctor. It took all his strength, but he managed to hold it together. He walked back to the infirmary and didn't speak a word the rest of the day. Jenny had taken off early, and it was easy enough to ignore Dr. Fletcher

"What's the matter, Sawyer?" Dr. Fletcher said, just as Phil was stepping out the door to leave for the day. "You got a big heart for these niggers, don't you?"

"No, sir," Phil answered. "I don't. I just hate to see any young man die before he's had a chance to live."

"Didn't seem to mind strangling the life out of that pretty wife of yours."

"Guess you're right, sir," Phil answered, trying to step closer to the door.

"This infirmary is my domain," the doctor said in a voice that sent chills up Phil's spine, "and you'll remember that from now on. The warden sent you here, but I can send you back to that laundry quicker than you can spit, understand?"

"Yes, sir," Phil answered humbly. "Yes, I understand."

"Get the hell out of here. Also, remember that nigger friend of yours. He can go back to where he came from too."

"Yes, sir. I'll remember that."

Phil's body was shaking so badly when he got back to the cell that he was almost in convulsions. Welles wasn't in the cell, and that worried the hell out of him. He stepped out and walked down to the floor below, where the other men were watching television. He scanned the area and still didn't see Welles, and panic consumed him.

"What's up, Doc?" Blaze asked, then laughed at his own childish joke.

"It's Welles," Phil answered. "Have you seen him?"

"Nope, not lately. Chill out, man. You look pale as shit."

"It's nothing. I just thought he might like to read before chow."

"No," Blaze answered, his facial expression changing almost to one of kindness. "You're really worried, aren't you?"

"Yes, I am. He's always back in the cell before me."

"Hold up a minute," Blaze answered and walked off. When he returned, he said, "My man in the kitchen said he finished his detail a long time ago. The doc came by to send him on some errands."

Phil felt his legs give beneath him, and he would have collapsed to the concrete if Blaze's strong arm didn't reach out to steady him.

"Hey man, pull yourself together. Did somebody give you something? Did you smoke a rock or somethin'?"

"No, man," Phil answered. "I just haven't eaten today."

Without another word to Blaze, he passed the guards and explained that he was urgently needed in the infirmary. They never bothered to question him anymore, because he had proven his worth to them. He ran down the halls so fast that his lungs began to burn, and he didn't slow down until he reached the infirmary.

Dr. Fletcher was sitting at his desk, wearing an evil smile on his face, when Phil ran through the door.

"Where is he? Where's Welles?" Phil asked, ignoring the tears that were running down his face, neck, and shirt.

"My, my, Mr. Sawyer." The doctor smirked. "Are you all right? Do calm down."

"Where the hell is he?"

"He's just stocking some shelves for me. His detail finishes early, and I had to make a trip to the Bureau today. For some reason, the State Police requested an extended toxicology screening on our heart failure patient. I can't figure that one out, as they've never asked such a pointless thing before. But anyway, I needed some extra help."

"Point taken," Phil answered. "Just leave him alone. I'll go back to the laundry in the morning."

"Oh no, Mr. Sawyer. That would be much too unfair for you and far too much of a liability for me. I'll keep you around. Just remember that your friend is old, and his health isn't that great. Let's try to keep him healthy, shall we?"

"I read you loud and clear, Dr. Fletcher," Phil answered. "You'll never have a problem with me."

"I'm sure I won't. Oh, and should you decide to make some collect calls tonight… Well, let's just say that a little birdie will tell me. Chirp, chirp, chirp," he mocked making a quacking gesture with his fingers and thumb.

"Wouldn't do that, sir."

"Good day, Mr. Sawyer."

"And Welles?"

"Mr. Manning," Dr. Fletcher said, "you are free to go. I appreciate the extra help."

CHAPTER 23

"**D**on't talk about it in the cell," Phil whispered to Welles as he held him tightly in his arms. "God forgive me. The last thing I wanted to do was bring you into this mess, but you kept asking, and—"

"We had to do it together, both of us," Welles whispered back. "We gotta make some good outta the bad we done. We're gonna get him, Doc. Just you wait and see."

"No, we're not going to get him. Let's just lie low. We'll only whisper about this and not very often. I can't use the phone for backup, because he's got someone watching me. Damn it. I'm scared, Welles. I really am."

"Tried to tell ya what ya was getting into, but you wouldn't listen ta me."

"I know, I know."

The buzzer went off for chow, but not before Phil scribbled a note on a small sheet of paper, folded it, and tucked it in his sleeve.

Chow was almost an out-of-body experience for Phil. The noise was excessive, as always, but he just floated through everything, as if his spirit was somewhere else altogether.

Blaze sat across from him, wearing the same look of concern as earlier.

"What ya lookin' at?" Phil asked loudly, offering Blaze a small hit of a wink as he looked down at his dessert.

"Jus' that chocolate cake on your tray," Blaze said, instantly playing along.

"Well, you just go on and take the son-of-a-bitch, 'cause I can't handle somebody staring at my shit while I'm trying to eat."

Blaze reached over and snatched the cake, being careful to hide the piece of paper that was underneath it. Phil was impressed and thankful, and he prayed Blaze would be able to follow through. The guards only looked over briefly and turned their attention elsewhere when they were sure it wasn't going to cause a fight.

"So," Welles whispered, "what did the note say?"

"It's Arthur's phone number, and I told him to use my name to call collect. He'll tell Arthur that we're in grave danger and that the jig is up."

"Goodness, Doc. I hope he flushes that note, or else we're both dead."

"I know, but it's our only chance. Eventually, he'd do away with us anyway."

* * * * *

For the following six weeks, Phil heard nothing from Charlie or Arthur, nor did he attempt to contact them. Blaze had given him a nod to let him know he had accomplished his task, and he knew that whatever was going on was in his best interest. He did exactly as he was told and spoke to no one in the infirmary, not even Jenny, except for a morning greeting. Dr. Fletcher seemed pleased, meaning that nothing had shown up in the autopsy. That threw Phil off a bit, as he knew something should have sent up a red flag.

One Sunday, Phil was called out for visitation and was thrilled to find not only Charlie but also Janet. He hugged her until he hurt. "God, I'm so glad to see you, Janet. I have missed you so much."

She cried openly and could only nod in agreement. It took several minutes for her to pull herself together. "I-I've missed you so much too," she finally answered. "If you only knew how much. We've been praying for your safety, but when I look at this place… Jesus, Phil. I'm so glad you're still alive."

"Now, Janet, I'm fine. Your prayers have helped me make it through all this."

Charlie placed his hand on the table to get Phil's attention. "I brought Janet to throw everyone off. We don't know what we're dealing with here, but you were right about this guy, except for one thing. He's not using potassium chloride. It woulda shown up in the autopsy. It's gotta be something else, something digestible that causes a quick death. I've got everyone working on it, but we haven't figured it out yet." He smiled broadly, then laughed loudly, as though they were having a family reunion, and Phil and Janet followed suit.

"Who is 'everyone'?"

"The State Police, FBI, and so on. Everyone is lying low, till we can figure out what he's using and get you the hell out of there. The warden has been told to halt all future executions until this matter is resolved."

Phil smiled broadly and laughed as he put his arm around Janet. "Can the warden be trusted?" he asked under his breath.

"I'm sure of it. He's been extremely helpful, and this all seems to have caught him off guard. He wanted to pull you out of the infirmary and transfer you to another institution, but the State Police think that might blow everything. Just keep following your routine. Don't call us from the cellblock, and don't write. You'll occasionally get a letter from us, but you won't be able to decipher anything. That's the idea. Just know that we're working like hell for you on the outside." With that he laughed loudly and took Janet's arm.

They both stood, and Phil followed their cue.

"Good to see you, buddy," Charlie said. "Take care."

Janet hugged him and fought off the tears that would fall from her eyes all the way back to Los Angeles. "I love you," she whispered.

"I love you too," Phil answered. "Kiss that beautiful daughter of yours, and tell her she has the most wonderful mother in the world."

CHAPTER 24

Monday morning started as usual, with the exception of Dr. Fletcher being a little late to work. He looked weak and tired and told Jenny that he felt as though he was coming down with something. At first Phil thought it was all part of the game he was playing, until he saw him run to the bathroom to vomit several times.

"Looks like I'm going to have to call it a day, Jenny," the doctor finally said, not even bothering to say a word to Phil. "I ate out last night and haven't felt right since. Damn Japanese. They musta forgot to wash the food before they cooked it."

As soon as the doctor waddled out of the infirmary, Phil heard a sigh of relief coming from Jenny. "You okay?" he asked.

"Sure. I'm just glad to see him go, that's all. It's enough to see him here at work, but he's been bothering me at home too."

"What?" Phil asked, not sure he'd heard her right.

"Yeah, it's nothing."

It's now or never, Phil thought as he looked at the innocent girl in front of him. *I have to trust a woman sometime.* "Tell me about it, Jenny," he said, trying not to alarm her. "I know I've been acting strange lately, but something's been going on, something very serious. I need to know everything you can tell me about Dr. Fletcher."

She looked at him long and hard, and for a moment, Phil regretted that he'd spoken a word. "You see it, too, don't you?" she finally asked. "Too many people are dying, and they're all black and young."

Phil put his face in his hands and heaved a sigh of relief. "Yes, Jenny. I-I just didn't know if I could trust you."

"I would never hurt anyone, Phil. I'm here to help people, not harm them."

He pulled her close. "We still have to be careful. For all we know, he's got this place bugged. He already threatened Welles and me. He's a dangerous man."

"Why hasn't he been caught?" she whispered.

"I don't know, but I've got people working on it on the outside. At first, I thought he was killing them with potassium chloride, but the autopsy didn't reflect that. None of the patients have been injected with anything, nor have they been seen at the infirmary."

"I wish I could help. I just can't think what he could possibly be—"

"Why has he been seeing you outside of work?"

"Oh it's nothing, at least nothing sexual. It's his horses. I come from a family of horse lovers, and his have been having health problems since I've known him. He loves them very much and seems to tend to them well. I've been over to see his stables and his mares. They're beautiful."

"So what does he want from you? You're not a veterinarian."

"He just needed some medicine for them. My family has a stockpile, because we have private vets."

"What kind of medication?" Phil asked.

"Anectine, a muscle relaxant. It immobilizes the animal so he can clean wounds and things like that."

"Is that the same thing as succinylcholine chloride?"

"I'm not sure. Maybe."

"Well, that chemical is used as an anesthetic, to facilitate tracheal intubations."

"Anectine basically does the same thing."

"Oh my God. That's it," Phil said. "It's white and odorless, a very soluble powder that quickly dissolves in water. An overdose would easily yield decreased respiratory reserve and put someone into cardiac arrest. It'd also never show up on a regular tox' screen, especially at a prison." As Phil put it all together, he could feel his own heart beating violently, as if it might beat right out of his chest. "Listen very carefully, Jenny. There has to be at least one other person involved. Right now, it looks like it's someone in the kitchen, but we can't be sure. You've gotta contact the warden right away. Call him from the phone over there. I don't want you walking around the prison or even going to your car."

"Are you sure, Mr. Sawyer? Are you sure we aren't just…overreacting?"

"Yes, I'm sure. Now call," he whispered sternly.

She picked up the phone and dialed the extension, her hands trembling all the while. "Yes, this is Nurse Jenny, down in the infirmary. Dr. Fletcher is gone for the day, and I need to check with the warden before I dispense medication."

"Very good," Phil mouthed to her.

She waited patiently and shrugged her shoulders at Phil as she held the phone.

Phil didn't have time to feel the nightstick before it struck him across the back of the head. His body slumped to the floor, and he immediately fell into unconsciousness. Before Jenny could scream, she, too, was knocked into darkness.

The warden's secretary heard the bodies hit the ground and simply said, "I'm sorry. The warden is not available at this time. I'll have him return your call." With that, she smiled, laid the receiver back in its cradle, and continued to file her nails.

CHAPTER 25

An hour later, Welles showed up at the infirmary to deliver Phil's lunch. The door was shut tightly and locked, and there was a sign taped to it, but Welles had no idea what it said. He felt the surge of panic as it climbed his body, and he held tight to the lunch cart, struggling to stand. His mind was whirling, and he wished desperately that he could just read the sign. *Maybe that would put my ol' mind at ease.* When another inmate walked by with a mop, Welles knew it wasn't a time to be proud. "'Scuse me, sir," he said. "Could you tell me what this sign says?"

"Uh… 'Infirmary is closed for the day. Staff in training.'"

"Th-Thanks, man," Welles managed to say. *Sweet Jesus*, he thought to himself. *They've got Doc…and maybe that pretty nurse too.*

He was afraid and didn't know who he could turn to for help. He was sure the warden was involved, and that only made matters worse. He pushed the tray back to the kitchen, talked one of the other inmates into delivering the rest of his meals for him, then got permission to go to the laundry. That was easy enough, because all the officers knew he was a good man who didn't pose any security risk.

Welles made a quick stop by his cell and dug, quickly and furiously, through Phil's locker, until he found two letters, each with a different return address. He knew they were from Charlie and Arthur, and he prayed that someone could help him find their numbers in the phonebook.

He tucked them in the back pocket of his jeans and tried to walk nonchalantly to the laundry. It only took a moment for him to find Blaze, and he confronted him quickly.

"What's up, Pops?" Blaze asked, noticing the look of panic he was wearing.

"I-I need your help…bad and fast," he stammered. "Th-they got doc, and the infirmary's all locked up. He's gone, man. They jus' took 'im."

"Calm down," Blaze said, trying to follow what the old man was saying. "What can I do to help you?"

"Can't read," Welles said, "but I need to get the numbers from these names and addresses on these letters. Somebody's gotta let 'em know so they can help."

"I get a break in fifteen minutes," Blaze said. "Meet me at the payphones at the end of the hall. Sounds like y'all are in some shit, and it looks like I'm about to be in it too. Don't tell anybody else about this, Pops. It could mean our asses."

Welles nodded and paced the hall for the next fifteen minutes, sweating profusely.

Blaze glanced behind himself as he rounded the corner. "Quick," he said. "Gimme those letters. This place'll get crowded real quick." He thumbed through the worn, tattered phonebooks that had been there since he arrived and swiftly wrote down two numbers beside two names. "This Charlie Evans is a home address, so you probably won't reach him now. The other, Arthur Morris, has his law office listed. Try him first." With that, Blaze turned and walked away, as though the transaction had never taken place.

Pops stood holding the folded envelope, praying someone would listen. His hand wobbled as he picked up the receiver. It had been a long time since he'd used a phone. He knew enough to dial 0 for the operator, so he could call collect.

A young woman answered the phone, and when she heard the name on the other end, she asked the operator to hold for permission to accept the call.

Arthur picked it up immediately. "Yes, we accept charges. Welles, what is it?"

"It's Doc. They done took 'im, and that nurse, too, I think. The infirmary is locked up, and I can't find him anywhere. He woulda told me if he was changin' plans. We're like that, like brothers. Don't none of us do nothin' without the other knowin'."

"Oh my God," Arthur said. "Tell your boss in the kitchen that you don't feel well, and then go back to your cell. That's the safest place to be. I'll do all I can. Watch your back, Mr. Manning, and thanks for calling."

With that, the phone went dead, and Welles did just as he was instructed to do. He felt so helpless just sitting on his bunk, but he knew the problem was much bigger than he was, and he had to trust in the Lord to see him and his friend through.

* * * * *

Arthur was on the phone immediately with the FBI and every other agency he could think of. "Damn it, we should have never trusted that warden. He pushed too hard to get him out of there. We should have seen through it," he told the FBI agent assigned to the case.

"Calm down," Agent Barnette answered. "We've got cars headed to the warden's and the doctor's residences, and several agents are en route to the prison to question the secretary and other admin staff."

Arthur put his hand over the receiver and yelled for his secretary to get him and Charlie the quickest flights out to San Francisco. "I'll be there as soon as I can," he told the agent.

CHAPTER 26

Phil lifted his pounding head and attempted to open his eyes. His vision was blurry, and it took a few minutes for him to realize that he was in a barn, or at least somewhere with hay and the smell of wet, dank animals. He tried to sit up but felt the handcuffs tightening with every move he made.

"Mr. Sawyer?" a weak voice whispered. "Is that you?"

"Jenny?"

"Yes. What's going on? I feel...drugged."

"I'm not sure," Phil whispered back, "but let's not let them know we've come to. Do you know where we are?"

"I'm not sure, but I think it's Dr. Fletcher's stable. What do you think they're going to do with us?"

"I don't know, but you can bet your bottom dollar the warden is in on this too. Otherwise, we...or rather, I wouldn't be outside the prison. This may be larger than we thought."

"What's going to happen?" Jenny whispered, her voice cracking as she struggled not to cry. "They can't let us live. We know too much."

"That's right," a loud voice boomed. "The two of you just couldn't stay out of things, could you?" the warden said. "Dr. Fletcher told me that if he left you two together long enough, you'd put it together and try to get help. He was right."

"But he was sick," Phil said, feeling foolish for falling for the trick. "I heard him puking. Even a third-grader trying to get out of school couldn't fake it that well."

"Ever heard of ipecac?" Dr. Fletcher snidely asked as he walked up. "A few good gags and chunks, and you fell for it, hook, line, and sinker."

"But why? Why are you doing all this? You're a doctor, for God's sake," Phil spat.

"Don't give me that condescending bullshit, Sawyer. It's not like you haven't taken a life before. At least I just kill niggers."

"You sicken me," Phil said, his head throbbing so hard he had to roll over to vomit. "You're allegedly an educated man. You should be above prejudice."

"Oh, just cut the shit," Dr. Fletcher answered. "I can't take this anymore. One of them raped and killed my wife, did that to her without a shred of remorse. They just got away with it because our system is so fucked up. Do you hear me!?" he screamed. "It's so fucked up that killers go free just because their ancestors were slaves to the white man. Have you ever met one worth a shit? They're draining our country with their welfare checks, and drug dealings. I'm only making a dent, but by God, the world can only be better off."

"Where do you fit into this, Warden?" Phil asked, laying his head back on the hay, in the hopes of easing some of the pain.

"His wife was my sister. I've been working in the prison system for twenty-five years, and I've seen them all come and go, only to come back in shackles again. They never learn. The way I figure it, we're saving the taxpayers some money and some families some grief."

"What about *their* families? Those men didn't kill your wife, Doctor," Jenny said, crying softly.

"Don't even try the sweet-little-nurse routine, Jenny. You only worked in the prison to ease your own conscience after being born with a silver spoon in your mouth. Don't think for a minute that any of those men gave a shit about what you did for them. They would've raped and killed you in a second if they'd have had half a chance."

"So," Phil continued, "how do you plan on justifying killing us? How will you explain my absence from the prison? Isn't it about time for headcount? Surely someone will miss me during rounds. I'd like to think at least one person who works there has a shred of ethics or morals."

"Surely, Dr. Sawyer, you don't think we got away with murder for years without having any sense," the warden answered. "It's all been calculated very well. Your little girlfriend here tried to aid in your escape, and in the confusion and hunt, you were both killed. What a pity, especially when you were so close to moving on with your life. You've always had a thing for choosing the wrong women, haven't you, Doctor?"

A brawny guard showed up just as the warden was finishing his explanation. "Get up," he demanded in a husky voice. "Both of you, now! We'll give you five minutes to run, and then it's every man for himself," he added with a sleazy grin.

"Shit. How many different movies do I have to live through before I get to Heaven?" Phil said sarcastically to himself.

"Please," Jenny said, "this isn't necessary..."

"Don't, Jenny," Phil said. "Don't give them the pleasure of hearing you plead for your life. We'll make it out of this."

The guard laughed arrogantly, and the warden and Dr. Fletcher walked confidently out of the stable.

The guard allowed them to be cuffed in front as opposed to behind, then looked at his watch and pointed toward the door. It was late afternoon but not anywhere close to sundown. The odds were against them, and Phil knew it, but he refused to give up hope, for Jenny's sake and his own.

"Five minutes. Go!" the guard announced.

* * * * *

Still groggy from the sedative, their legs wobbled as they made a valiant attempt to run.

"You know the area, Jenny," Phil said. "Where's the closest road?"

She was crying softly, trying to get her bearings.

"Listen, Jenny," Phil said, a little bit harsher than he intended his tone to be, "you've gotta pull yourself together. Stop, look around, and try to remember how you drove in here when you came to visit."

"It's pretty far out. Our best bet would be to hide in the woods until dark."

"That's not an option. I guarantee that they'll have the dogs out soon to track us. We've got to find a road."

She pointed north and began to walk wearily in that direction.

"This isn't gonna work," Phil finally conceded. "We're too weak, and we'll never make it. I guess you're right. Our only hope is to hide out till the guard leaves the stable to look for us, and then we can go back and hide there. Our scent is already there, so the dogs should lead them down the trail we're on now, if they call them in."

"We can't stay there long," Jenny whined. "They'll backtrack and find us eventually."

"All we can do is hide and pray that somebody gets suspicious and comes to look for us. Now get down and cover up with leaves and debris."

Jenny did as she was told.

"Don't move Jenny," Phil murmured quietly through his teeth. "Don't make a sound."

They waited a few minutes, just over five, knowing that the guard would have finally taken off to look for them.

"Quick," Phil said, pulling Jenny to her feet. "Let's get back there. Hold your head down and try not to make any noise."

They reached the safety of the stable and hid under some of the hay. Their bodies were close together, and Phil could smell Jenny's sweet but panicked breath. He reached for her hand and held it gently. They couldn't see each other, but the warmth of one another's bodies made them both feel better.

"It's gonna be okay," Phil said, as assuring as he could.

She squeezed his hand softly, and a few minutes later, he was thankful to hear the rhythmic breathing of her sleep. The sedatives were strong, and he hoped that would keep her from having to face their dire predicament.

It seemed as though hours passed, and Phil spent every minute praying. He prayed for Welles, too, for God only knew what they would do to him. He prayed for Jenny and for himself, but most of all, he prayed for justice.

He wasn't sure, but for a brief moment he thought he could hear the faint whirring of helicopter blades. He strained to listen, and as time passed, the noise became louder and clearer. He squeezed Jenny's hand, stirring her from her deep, drug-induced slumber. "Jenny? Jenny," he whispered, "I hear choppers."

"Wh-What?" she asked, still a little dazed and confused. "What does that mean?"

"I'm not sure. It's either the Department of Corrections or the FBI. More than likely, it's the feds, because the DOC wouldn't suspect that we'd escape to the doctor's farm."

"Oh, please, please let them save us."

"Shh," Phil shushed. "Let's not talk anymore. We'll just have to see what happens."

Like frightened rabbits with a fox on the prowl, they waited until Phil thought his heart would explode. Finally, they heard the chopper land, followed by the sound of feet, hitting the ground and running.

"FBI!" the agents yelled. "Come out peacefully, and no one gets hurt."

Searchlights combed the area, back and forth, and from the sound of it, more choppers were coming, with plenty of armed agents to handle the situation.

"Let's go," Jenny whispered. "Surely we're safe now."

"No, not yet," Phil said. "It could be a trick. If it's not, it's still not a good idea to surprise them. When they get in the stable, we'll call to them from under here. Last thing we need is to startle a bunch of agents with happy trigger fingers."

Footsteps pounded all around the outside of the stable, then made their way inside.

"FBI! Come out, with your hands up," a group shouted sternly.

Phil held his breath and finally answered, "We're over here. I'm an inmate from San Quentin, Phil Sawyer, and I'm with Nurse Jenny Day. We were brought here against our will."

"Come out slowly, with your hands raised," one man said. "We're here to help."

Phil and Jenny moved in slow, deliberate motions, until they had brushed most of the hay to one side. They stood, still a little unstable, and raised their hands as high as the cuffs would allow. Phil was so relieved to see the black outfits with "FBI" stamped on them that he almost broke down.

Out of the group ran Charlie and Arthur, and they embraced him with a love he never knew existed.

"You're becoming more trouble than you're worth," Arthur joked. "God, we were sure we'd lost you."

"How did you even know I was missing?"

"Welles. Poor ol' guy is out of his mind with worry right now. They transferred him to a local hospital for observation. He's safe, so don't worry."

"Hell," Charlie said, "you smell worse out of prison than you did inside. I hope that's no indication—"

"No, it's not," Phil answered with a smirk. "Forgive me. This is Jenny Day.

Jenny, these are my two best friends, Charlie Evans and Arthur Morris."

She smiled and said hello, her face still stained with tears from the events of the day.

The FBI removed their handcuffs and handed them both a warm cup of coffee.

"Hello. I'm Agent Barnette. I'm in charge of this case. Looks like you two have had a busy day. Unfortunately, the other parties involved have left the premises, but we're searching for them now. We'll need any information we can from the two of you, but with the bad guys still at large, our best bet is to get you to a safe house and interview you there. We don't know how far reaching this thing is, so we'll keep you there for a few days."

"Welles?" Phil asked, looking at Arthur.

"They'll transport him there as soon as he's released from the hospital. He isn't safe back at the prison either. Not only is he black, but they may just try to kill him to get back at you."

"I'll have some clothes brought to the house," Agent Barnette said. "No offense, but you two stink like hell. Just give your sizes to the officer over there, and we'll load you in the chopper."

CHAPTER 27

They landed in a wooded area and were met by an SUV that carried them to the safe house. It was a log cabin with a large porch, and it looked more than a little inviting to Phil. There were several agents inside, and, as promised, the clothes were already there, along with toiletries.

"Jeez, we must really stink," Phil said to Jenny.

"Yes, you do," Arthur answered. "Hurry and shower so they can talk to the two of you."

The shower was roomy, such a far cry different from the prison stalls, and Phil wanted to stay in it for hours. He let the water get so hot that it felt as if it would set his skin on fire. He lathered with the soap again and again, until someone finally knocked on the door.

"We've got three fugitives we need to find as soon as possible, Mr. Sawyer."

"I'll be right out."

He dressed in slacks and a polo shirt, both of which fit him far better than the State-issued clothes he'd worn for so long, then went into the kitchen. He sat at the big table, where the agents had set up shop. Jenny was already there, looking worn and pitiful. Apparently, it was a bigger crime syndicate than they realized at first, because the FBI had already arrested over forty guards, and all their mugshots were spread out on the table.

"You're lucky to be alive, Mr. Sawyer. I don't think you know how lucky."

Phil swallowed hard. He told them all he knew and explained his theory about the murders.

"Warrants for exhumations on all black men who reportedly died of heart failure in the last eight years are being processed as we speak," Agent Barnette said. "We expect to arrest several others before this is over. Right now, you, Ms. Day, and Mr. Manning will be held here. Dr. Fletcher, the warden, and the officer who was with them at the time of your abduction are still on the run. The chances of you being safe at San Quentin are nil."

"No shit." Phil laughed. "My chances have never been good there."

The remark, no matter how true, didn't get a laugh out of the agent. He continued in a professional, monotone voice, "It is against policy for any inmate to receive alcoholic beverages, but in lieu of what you've been through and what you have done in the name of justice, we can make an exception. You will find a variety of beverages in the bar and refrigerator. Your meals will be prepared for you, and you will have access to television. There is not a phone here, so if you should need to make contact with your family or anyone else, Ms. Day, you may use an agent's cell phone. I am sure they would like to know you are safe."

"Yes, please," Jenny answered.

The agent motioned to one of the men standing by, and Jenny followed him outside to make her call.

"We've got a great deal to do," the agent said, "but you need some rest, Mr. Sawyer. We'll have some food prepared soon. Why don't you and your friends retire in the den, with a glass of wine?"

"Sounds good to me, but make that a scotch," Phil said, then stood and followed Arthur and Charlie into the other room.

They opened a new bottle and toasted to life and friendship, and Arthur leaned over to speak quietly to Phil. "I don't want to get your hopes up, because we never know what could happen to screw things up, but the plan as it stands now is that you and Welles will be released as soon as the fugitives are found. The State is getting enough bad publicity with this thing. They don't need your deaths on their hands."

"You're kidding, right?"

"Nope. You were both short-timers anyway, and you pose no risk to society. That's obvious, or else you wouldn't have put your life on the line for this."

"Hot damn. Welles will be so thrilled."

"Listen, about him. Phil, he's been through a lot, and his heart isn't in great condition. They weren't real optimistic about his EKG at the hospital."

"Oh, he'll be okay. A few weeks in Maine will be just what the doctor ordered."

Jenny returned and allowed Charlie to pour her a large glass of merlot. "My family was frantic," she said. "They still are, to say the least. They can't believe any of this any more than I can."

"It's pretty crazy, huh?" Phil said.

"Yes it is, Mr. Sawyer, but you're a good man, and without you, this might have gone on for years to come."

"Isn't it about time you started using 'Phil' now, Jenny? After all, we almost left this Earth together today. We should both be on a first-name basis."

She smiled a weak smile and nodded. "You're right. 'Phil' it is."

They had an excellent meal. Phil ate more than he should have and drank a little more as well, but he didn't care.

After they ate, Jenny and Phil sat alone in the den with their drinks.

"I'm sorry about your dream, Jenny," Phil said, "and don't take to heart what Dr. Fletcher said. Those men did appreciate you. I know, because I was one of them. You did a good thing, but now I hope you'll move on with your life."

"I can't even think about the future now. My head is whirling."

Phil leaned over and kissed her forehead so lightly that she may not have even felt it. When he looked up, he saw Welles, his face looking ten years older. Phil ran to him like a son would to his father. They embraced, and both cried until there weren't any more tears to cry.

"Thank God you're okay," Welles said. "I was so scared."

"I wouldn't be here if you hadn't thought to call Arthur and Charlie. That was quick thinking."

"Blaze helped me. Turns out, he's a pretty good feller."

"Yep," Phil said. "You just never know about people. Let me show you around a little bit," Phil said and took Welles on a tour of the house. "We each have our own bedroom, double-beds with mattresses as thick as a house. Real clothes, too, and a shower with scalding-hot water."

"That shower sounds pretty nice ta me," Welles said, "and then I'm gonna call it a night. It's after midnight."

"Goodnight, brother," Phil said. "I love you."

"Love ya, too, little brother," Welles said as tears formed in his eyes again.

CHAPTER 28

It took four days to find Dr. Fletcher and the warden, but they did eventually track them down. Jenny, Welles, and Phil were watching television when the footage came on of them being led into the courthouse.

"I can't believe there are monsters like that out there," Phil said.

"Look at 'em," Welles said. "Ain't got a lick of remorse, not none of 'em."

"I'm just glad it's over," Jenny said. "There will always be more where they came from, but at least we got them."

"We sure did," Phil said, holding his hand up to high-five Welles.

Arthur came in with two agents beside him and sat down with the group. "Got some news you two men might like to hear," he said, his teeth sparkling like snowcapped mountains.

"Good news is always welcome," Phil said. "Shoot."

"Seems the State of California has seen fit to let you two criminals back out into the world again. First thing tomorrow morning, you'll be free men, with plane tickets to wherever you choose to go."

Welles smiled his big, toothless smile and patted Phil's leg. "Manning and Sawyer's Bait and Tackle! I gotta get back to Georgia to help Mae out a little, but you can take them blueprints, go boat-shoppin', and start construction."

"You're damn right I can," Phil said. "I just have one stop first. I want to spend a few days with my friends in L.A. They never gave up on me, not during any of this. Do you think my attorney will have an extra bedroom for an old friend?"

"You bet your ass he does." Arthur laughed. "You bet your ass."

The night was one of celebration; the agents even cooked t-bone steaks and fried shrimp.

Welles took a small sip of wine but decided he didn't want to upset the Lord Who had been so generous to him. "Can I talk to ya by yourself a minute, Doc?" he asked.

"Sure. What's up?"

"I just got a little something for ya."

Phil walked into Welles's room, and the old man reached under his pillow and pulled out the worn Bible.

"I want you to have this."

"Oh, Welles, I can't possibly accept a gift that nice. It belongs in your family."

"You *are* my family, my brother, and it'd mean somethin' to me if you'd take it. It's done me well through the years, and it seen me through to freedom. I'll be fine now. You're still young, and you got a lotta things to figure out. Just 'member to read those scriptures that are all worn out, 'cause them's the most important. Keep it close to ya and stay out of trouble till I can get out to Maine to straighten you out."

Phil felt his throat stinging. "Thank you, Welles. I've never received a finer gift, and I will treasure it always."

"Look inside," Welles said, swelling with pride. "Nurse Jenny wrote it out for me. I told her what to say, but I signed my name myself."

Phil opened the Bible carefully and read the note: "To the only brother I've ever known and my best friend. I love you." Then his name was scrawled like a child's across the bottom. Phil embraced him, then walked out of the room with his heart full of emotion.

Jenny and Phil rocked on the porch after Welles went to sleep.

"You looking for a job?" Phil said.

"Why? Are you going to open a clinic or something?"

"No," Phil said. "That part of my life is over. How do you feel about selling night crawlers though?"

She laughed. "Might not be so bad. Don't be surprised if I show up one day."

"I sincerely hope you will," Phil said. "I really do."

* * * * *

The morning sun came early, and it looked bright and promising, like freedom.

Phil dressed quickly and inhaled deeply, taking in the scent of the hearty breakfast that was being prepared in the kitchen. He tapped lightly on Welles's door, then walked in quietly. "Rise and shine, sleepyhead. Today is our big day." Welles was still in bed, so Phil sat beside him. "We got a big bird to catch today, you know," he said.

Welles didn't respond at all.

Phil tugged at his shoulders, but he already knew it was too late. Just like that, in the middle of the night, the old man's heart had stopped. Welles was simply gone. "Oh sweet Jesus! No! Please no!" Phil screamed, crying so hard that he almost forgot to breathe. He pulled Welles's limp, lifeless body up to his own and rocked him back and forth. "Damn it. I need you. How can I have Manning and Sawyer without Manning? You're my future, my friend, my brother. Don't do this to me, Pops! Wake up!"

By then, the agents still remaining at the safe house had heard the commotion and burst into the room, with Jenny right behind them.

She walked over and checked for a pulse. With tears in her eyes, she looked at Phil. "He's gone, Phil. Let him go. We both know that he is in a better place now."

"I don't give a shit about that. I need him, want him here with me. We had dreams, dreams outside that godforsaken place where he spent most of his life. Welles? Please, brother. Please wake up. I won't know what to do without you."

With Welles still cradled in his arms, Phil turned to the agents and screamed, "He was my friend. I never woulda made it in prison without him. He was the kindest, wisest man I've ever known. We were going to move to Main, far away from this place, with all its rotten memories and horrible nightmares. We were going to open a business, watch the whales swim by. We were going to drink cocoa during the Maine winters, and I was going to buy him his first heavy coat so he could walk in the snow. We were going to catch lobsters the size of small dogs and eat 'em until we felt like we could explode. Damn it, Welles. Please come back," Phil said, sobbing.

There were tears rolling down the faces of the agents as they slowly pried Phil's arms from around Welles's body.

"I'm sorry, man," one said. "I really am, but if he was as good a man as you say he was, that means he's looking down on you right now, and he wouldn't want you to carry on like this."

"You're probably right," Phil answered, "and I know he's wearing a star in his crown."

CHAPTER 29

A s Arthur's new Jaguar pulled away from the airport, Phil heaved his first true sigh of relief. It was over, finally, after months and years of fear, torture, and change. It was all over, and he'd survived the nightmare.

The ride to Arthur's house wasn't a long one, but Phil relished every moment of it: the soft music on the radio, the air-conditioning blowing on his warm face, and those beautiful palms. "God, I missed those trees," he said, more to himself than to Arthur. He felt dizzy as he watched the cars whizzing by on the freeway, but he watched them all just the same.

As they pulled into the driveway, he noticed a large banner that read, "Welcome Home Phil! We Missed You." He looked at it, then looked away. "You've been such a good friend, Arthur. I wish I knew how to thank you."

"There's no need. I'm just glad we can put all this behind us now and move on with our lives. It hasn't been easy for any of us."

"Please tell me there's not a crowd in there right now," Phil said softly. "I could really use some rest, some peace and quiet."

"No crowd yet. We're going to grill some steaks and salmon tonight with Janet and Charlie tonight, though, if that's okay."

"Sounds great."

Phil's stomach held a slowly growing knot of the unknown as he stepped out of the car. Freedom was a new thing to him, something he'd long forgotten. Just opening a door without being buzzed out and being allowed to step on carpet instead of concrete, to feel the handle of a fridge and reach in for a cold bear: It was almost too much for him.

Arthur noticed his shaking hands, and he took the beer from him for a moment. "Have a seat in the den. I'll pour this in a mug and get some snacks. Maybe some food in your belly will help a little."

"Maybe you're right," Phil answered.

He made his way slowly into the den. It looked very much the same, and the couch was as comfortable as he remembered it. He slipped his shoes off and put his feet lazily on the coffee table, then laid his head back on the soft leather. His eyes were shut, but he was far from asleep. He heard Arthur walk in and set a couple bowls of snacks on the table.

Phil reached for his beer. "Damn, this is just so strange," he said. "I wish I could describe it."

"I can't begin to understand what you've been through," Arthur countered.

"I knew it would be different when I got out. That comes as no surprise. I guess I just didn't realize how content I became in that hellish place."

"You were there quite a while, Phil. It happens. Just be grateful you made it out and still have enough life left to carry on."

"It finally hit me when I sat down on this sofa. I don't have a home, no place to go back to, no job, no life...nothing."

"It'll come, brother. It will all come in time. Hell, it's your first day as a free man. Let's get drunk and celebrate new beginnings. Forget yesterday. Let's just celebrate today."

Phil raised his chilled mug high in the air. "Cheers...to new beginnings and freedom. May it always taste as sweet as it does today."

"Here, here!"

Three beers later, Phil got up and went for a nap in the guest bedroom. It felt so good to stretch his legs all the way to the end of the bed and feel the coolness of the satin sheets as he pulled them up to his face. It was like floating on a cloud, and he never wanted it to end. He slept long and hard, and when Arthur finally woke him, it was after 6 o'clock.

* * * * *

"Hate to wake ya, man, but I thought you might like a shower before everyone gets here."

"Damn, that felt good," Phil answered groggily. "And yes, I need a shower." He sat up in bed quickly.

As if reading his thoughts, Arthur said, "Your clothes are in the closet. We brought them over when the house sold. Hell, with all these extra bedrooms and closets, there's plenty of space for your things. You may be a little thinner, but everything should fit okay for now. Believe it or not, your wardrobe still hasn't gone out of style. I guess I couldn't say the same if you were a chick."

"I'm speechless, man," Phil answered. "I mean, I really, really am. You did kind of sock it to me on those attorney fees," he said, laughing, "but you've just been so damn good to me. I can't believe you kept my clothes here all these years."

"Yep, even your underwear and socks." Arthur laughed. "But don't worry. Storage fees will be itemized on your next bill. Now go on and get in the shower. Our guests will be arriving within the hour."

"Oh, I almost forgot," Arthur said. "I gave Lara's key to the FBI, and they found the money stashed in a locker at the Norfolk Airport."

"Justice served, huh?" Phil said. "At least the bitch never got a chance to spend it!"

"You're right, but that's all over now," Arthur said. "There are still a few unanswered questions though."

"What do you mean?" Phil asked. "I don't understand."

"Well, I'm not so sure any of it is related to the break-in at your house. A few witnesses in the neighborhood saw a nurse and a doctor lurking around your house more than once."

"That's strange. I can't imagine what they'd want or who they were. I never made any friends at the hospital, as you know."

"Well, we figure maybe somebody was trying to plant some more evidence somewhere."

"Hell," Phil answered, "they had me dead to rights. I admitted to killing her."

"Who knows?" Arthur countered. "Anyway, the break-in at Charlie's house was different, definitely not the same M.O. They stole a few things, like jewelry, a VCR, like a typical robbery, but there is something else. There's a reward of $75,000 headed your way soon."

"I don't care for any blood money. Tell them to keep it."

"They can't do that. It has to go somewhere. What about Welles's sister?"

"I'm sure she wouldn't want it either, if she understood where it came from. I wouldn't do her like that. I couldn't even lie to her about it."

"Well, then pick a charity, brother, because they've got to sign a check."

Phil could really do nothing but laugh. After all he'd been through, now he was struggling to get rid of $75,000 because he was afraid it was cursed. "Wait," he finally said, his mind quickly jumping to another thought. "I know exactly where I want it to go."

"Dare I ask?" Arthur said, looking at him apprehensively.

"Drew Isaacs," Phil said, allowing his mind to drift back for a moment. "A guy they executed while I was there. He had three small children." He reached in his billfold and pulled out their picture.

Arthur looked at it with little interest, then focused his attention back on Phil.

"I want all that money, every dime, to go to his kids and their mother. Tell her there was a life insurance policy or something. They'll need the money, and they don't have to know the circumstances. Besides, it will give the children something to be proud of their father for."

"Damn, you're a sucker for happy endings, aren't you?" Arthur laughed. "And before you ask, yes, I will take care of it. Jeez, this must be what it's like to have children." With that, Arthur walked out and shut the door behind him, leaving Phil sitting there by himself.

Almost in tears, Phil thought of Jenny and her reasons for working at the prison. He wondered what his first day out of there would have been like if he hadn't had any friends or anyone to turn to. He had been through enough to know how grateful he should be, and he would never take anything or anyone for granted again.

He dressed in a pair of jeans and a thin, long-sleeved shirt. Although it was warm, he wasn't ready for Janet to see his scars yet. He was thankful that his face had healed nicely; that was the most important thing. He slid his feet into a pair of loafers and walked out into the den. When he heard voices in the kitchen, he made his way there.

Arthur was marinating steaks, and a tall, thin, very beautiful black woman was standing beside him, making a salad. She turned toward Phil when she heard him walk in, and her face broke into one of the loveliest smiles Phil had ever seen. "You must be Phil Sawyer," she said in a voice as smooth as silk. "Boy, have I heard a lot about you."

"Well, most of it was probably true," Phil laughed.

She walked over and gave him a light hug and a peck on the cheek. "I'm Dee. It's very nice to meet you."

"The pleasure's all mine," Phil answered.

"I'm having wine," she said, "but what can I get you to drink?"

"Scotch on the rocks please," he said. "Can I do anything, Arthur?"

"Not a thing. This is your night."

Phil accepted the drink from Dee and sat down at the table. "So, Arthur tells me you're an attorney, too, Dee."

"Yes, and yes, being in a relationship with another one is a challenge, to say the least," she said as she laughed and winked at Arthur. "He's a workaholic, you know, and you should hear how our spats go. He's always trying to pull out Exhibit A before I do," she said, pointing playfully at Arthur.

"No shit." Phil laughed. "It's hard to teach an old dog new tricks, but I can tell ya that you're the only one who's ever been able to take his mind off work, even if it isn't for long. There must be something special there."

Dee smiled an honest, sincere smile at the two of them. "Well, he's a pretty special guy."

Phil instantly liked her. She was beautiful, intelligent, and down-to-Earth. He was also relieved that her beauty was not all she had going for her, at least relieved for his friend's sake.

When everything was ready to go on the grill, the doorbell rang. In walked Charlie, Janet, and, to everyone's pleasant surprise, Lilly. It was an awkward moment, and Phil felt his heart racing; he was a little unsure how to handle it.

"Evening, everyone," Charlie said. "Phil, I want you to meet our Lilly. She insisted on coming tonight to meet her old man's best friend. Hope you don't mind, Arthur, but you always cook way too much anyway, so I figured there'd be enough for an extra plate."

"No problem," Arthur answered as he kissed Janet and Lilly.

Phil hugged Janet and Charlie, but before he even had a chance to react, Lilly was in his arms. She was a tall, lithe girl, almost taller than both of her parents. Her long blonde hair flowed like an ocean of silk, and he felt its softness against his cheek.

"It is nice to meet you," she whispered in his ear before she stepped back. "You are my parents' best friend, so I want to get to know you. I hope I don't make you feel uncomfortable, but if I do, I'll understand. You didn't hurt my mother, you know. She's standing right here, and without you, I'd still be back at that home, without a real family. I want to thank you," she said, then hugged him again.

Phil was speechless for a moment before he said, "No, Lilly, I could never feel uncomfortable around you. In fact, I've heard so much about you that I feel as if we're already friends. You're a very kind young lady, a special girl, and I see now why your parents love you so much. Hey, get with me later, and I'll tell you some stories about your dad in his college days. He was no angel, you know."

"Hey now," Charlie interjected. "Those stories have long since been sealed in the archives. No fair telling my kid. Besides, you might have a kid of your own someday, and payback can be hell. Remember the road trip to Ft. Lauderdale?"

"Now, now," Janet scolded. "You boys play nice. Let's act civilized." She laughed, and her heart soared at the happy reunion. "Phil," she asked, "can you believe Arthur snagged such a great catch?"

"No way," Phil said with a laugh of his own. "I think we should fill her in on a few stories as well, right, Charlie?"

"Give that man another drink. Maybe that'll shut him up," Arthur said sternly, before a grin crossed his face. "Damn, this feels so good, doesn't it? The whole gang, all together again."

Their happy banter was interrupted by the ring of the doorbell.

"Who could that be?" Phil asked. "I hope no one has changed their mind and has come back to get me."

"Hardly," Charlie said.

Dee opened the door, and Jenny walked in, dressed in a peach linen pantsuit with matching sandals. Her hair was out of its ponytail and flowed fully down over her shoulders. She had actually applied a light layer of makeup and lipstick that matched her suit perfectly. She looked lovely, so lovely and different that it rendered Phil speechless.

"Welcome to my humble abode," Arthur said. "We're glad you could make it."

"Thank you," Jenny answered, looking a bit uneasy. "Phil, I hope you don't mind that I came. I was afraid it might bring back too many bad memories. Maybe I shouldn't—"

"Stop," Phil said as he walked over to hug her. "I'm just so surprised, that's all, but in a good way. You look so…well, beautiful. I just can't believe you came all this way."

"It's not like I have a job to get back to," she said, smiling weakly.

"Well?" Janet interrupted. "Isn't anyone going to introduce us to this wonderful woman we've heard so much about?"

"I'm sorry," Phil said, his voice changing instantly to a tone of contentment. "This is Jenny Day. Jenny, these are my friends."

He introduced her to each person, and everyone hugged her and made her feel at home. They could tell instantly she was different. Unlike Lara, she was real, a genuinely good person, and they openly accepted her into their clan.

There was no mention of the past few years as they all enjoyed the meal and each other's company. The night ended with four different homemade desserts, and everyone's bellies were full as they made their way out the door. There were hugs and kisses exchanged, this time without tears; Phil was a free man now, so all the goodbyes were only temporary.

As Phil walked Jenny to her rental car, Arthur walked over. "Jenny, why don't you stay? I have plenty of room, so you're more than welcome. I'm sure you and Phil have much more to catch up on anyway."

"Oh, that's very kind of you," Jenny answered with a smile, "but I already booked my flight. It leaves tomorrow afternoon."

"Well," Arthur said, taking her lightly by the elbow, "I won't hear of it, especially on my friend's special night."

She didn't resist this time but walked with him back into the house.

"I'm glad you decided to stay," Dee whispered to her. "I'm sure Phil will be much more comfortable."

Jenny gave her a light hug and accepted another glass of wine from Arthur.

"You guys make yourselves at home in the den," Arthur said. "I have a case tomorrow, so I've got some work to catch up on." He kissed Dee, then disappeared up the stairs.

They sat down, and Phil looked at Jenny for several seconds before he spoke. "It's so strange, us being here. It is almost unimaginable that the past few years even happened."

"I know exactly what you mean."

"What about your family? What are your plans now?"

"They're relieved, to say the least, that I won't be returning to San Quentin. The I-told-you-so's are a little hard to swallow right now, but I'll get past that. I'm not sure what I'm going to do though. I think I'll take a little hiatus for a while and get my head straight."

"That's a smart thing to do. You've been through so much."

"What about you, Mr. Phil Sawyer? What's on your agenda?" she asked.

"I'm flying down for Welles's funeral in a couple days. That's going to be tough. Then I'll fly back here and collect my belongings and head east. I still want to go to Maine, but I'm not sure exactly where yet. I'm thinking of flying into Portland, then driving until I find the perfect spot to spend the rest of my life."

"That's kind of unpredictable, isn't it?"

"Unpredictable but safe. I've visited that area before, and it's all I really want now. It's beautiful, but life moves slow there. That's the pace I want to set for myself. None of us knows what life really holds. I just know I don't want the rest of mine to be like the first part."

"I can respect that," Jenny said, sounding a bit lonely. "I thought I had my life figured out. I was happy, content, but now? Who knows?"

"You'll find that all again," Phil said sincerely. "You have special things to offer. Your destiny is out there. San Quentin was part of it, a stepping stone. Without you, things would still be going as they were, and God only knows how many more men would have died at the hands of Dr. Fletcher."

"Maybe you're right. Time tends to tell a lot of things." She looked into his eyes and smiled warmly. "You're such a good man, Phil. I am grateful to have met you."

"The pleasure was mine," Phil answered, then leaned over and kissed her fully on her small mouth.

It had been so long since he had felt the affection of a woman, and it felt nice. She smelled so good—not of expensive perfume, like Lara, but of fresh, clean soap and flowers. Her skin and hair were soft, and her mouth responded to his in just the right way. He tried to hide the arousal growing in his pants. He didn't want to seem like an animal to her, like someone who just wanted to feed his lustful need for sex. "I'm sorry," he said, pulling away. "I don't want to make you uncomfortable or take advantage of you. You're just so beautiful, and you feel so good in my arms. I just—"

Jenny leaned forward and kissed him again, allowing her tongue to roam around in his mouth until he felt he would explode. "Can I spend the night with you, Dr. Sawyer?" she asked shyly.

He stood up, completely unable to hide the growing bulge in his pants, and led her to the bedroom. He unbuttoned her linen shirt and hung it in the closet, then slowly unhooked her bra to reveal full, firm breasts, much larger than he expected to see. She gasped as he leaned down to kiss her nipples, then her neck, then her mouth again. She finished undressing while Phil did the same, and they crawled into the smoothness of the silk sheets. Phil wanted to take her then, so bad that his groin ached, but she was too special for that. He ran his fingers up and down her body, his breathing growing heavier by the minute. Finally, Jenny couldn't take it anymore, and she crawled on top of him. She felt so light that he wasn't even sure her weight was on him. She slowly slipped him inside of her, and they made beautiful love together until the sun came up the next morning. It was only then that Jenny fell fast asleep.

* * * * *

Phil got up and started coffee just as Arthur descended the stairs. "Up early, aren't you?" Phil asked.

"Yeah. I gotta head to the office to finish up some of this work before the trial this morning. I'll give you a call later," he said, grabbing a cup of black coffee as he raced out the door.

Phil sipped his steaming brew and walked slowly back to the bedroom. Jenny was still asleep, and she looked like an angel lying there, so innocent, with her hair flowing across the pillow. He pulled the covers up around her neck and went into the den, so as not to wake her.

He plopped down heavily on the sofa and stretched his legs out, crossing his feet on the coffee table. His mind raced with all the possibilities his new freedom might afford him, but his thoughts always went back to Welles. It was hard to believe he would be attending the man's funeral. Phil felt lost without him, really and truly lost.

He showered, dressed, and took a walk around the house and down the street. It felt so wonderful to be free, yet it was frightening at the same time. He was ready to move on, to leave that place, to start anew.

Jenny was up and dressed when he returned from his walk, looking fresh and youthful with just a couple hours of sleep under her belt. He kissed her lightly and held her in his arms for what seemed like an hour.

CHAPTER 30

Jenny stayed in Los Angeles to take the flight to Georgia with Phil. He didn't bother trying to change her mind, because he really wanted her to be with him and was sure Welles's funeral would be much easier to handle with her by his side. They caught the red-eye to Atlanta, then transferred to a commuter plane that would fly them into Macon. From there, they would take a two-hour drive to Mae's house for the funeral. They rented a car, and Jenny drove since Phil's license had expired long ago; he envied her position behind the wheel.

The directions Mae gave him were excellent, so they arrived a little sooner than expected. As they pulled into the dirt driveway, they saw the small, weather-beaten house where Welles had lived before he had to call San Quentin home. It was just as Phil had imagined it. Large oaks formed a canopy over the place, and rickety rocking chairs lined the leaning front porch. As they got out of the car, he took in the fresh smell of earth and day-old rain. It was all Welles had described, and he longed for his friend to greet him at the front door with that toothless grin.

Instead, it was Mae who opened the creaky screen and ran out to meet them. She hugged Phil so tight that it physically hurt, and they cried in each other's arms. She had opted to wear her fancy pink dress and hat for the occasion, the same one she used to make the church ladies jealous. "I ain't never met ya," she said, smiling through her tears, "but I know and love you just the same. You gave my brother hope for a future. You was his friend, and he loved you so much. I got on this pink dress 'cause it was what I wore when I visited him. He loved it. I know it ain't exactly proper for a black funeral, but I'm thinkin' he'd want me to wear it for his goin'-home." She paused for a minute to look down at her outfit, then ran her worn hands down the fabric to smooth it, as if trying to look her best for Welles. "He told me you was behind getting me out yonder." she said, causing more tears to spill out of her brown eyes. "'Cause o' y'all, I had a chance to see my brother just once more 'fore he left this world. He was all I had, so I just gots ta thank you."

"No need to thank me." Phil smiled kindly. "He did so much for me. It was just a little something I could do for him."

"He had nothin', Dr. Sawyer. He couldn't have given you anything."

"That's where you're wrong Mae," Phil answered. "That's where you're wrong."

"Please come in the house," she said, motioning to them both. "We got food galore."

Jenny and Phil walked into the old but neatly kept house. There were two elderly women whom she introduced as aunts and a man in his fifties, their new minister.

"Reverend Herron didn't know my brother. Our preacher long since left us for Heaven, so I'm glad you agreed to say a few words on my brother's behalf," Mae said, smiling appreciatively.

There was indeed a kitchen full of food, and she insisted that they eat again, in spite of their stop at a diner on the way in. Just as they were finishing up their plates, the hearse pulled around to the house.

"The funeral people's here," Mae announced. Tears welled in her eyes again as she turned to Phil. "He'll be buried up on the hill, with the rest of our kin. The funeral home agreed to open the casket for a few minutes for you to view his body. We'll give y'all about five minutes before we ride up there."

Phil looked down at Jenny, and she smiled faintly and motioned for him to go ahead. He stepped outside and found the hearse driver on the passenger side, holding the door open. The driver simply nodded as Phil climbed in, and then they drove the 100 yards to the burial site. Four other men drove in front of them in an old red pickup.

When they reached the top of the hill, all five of the men pulled the casket from the back of the hearse and placed it over the gravesite.

The older gentleman gently opened the plain coffin and patted Phil on the shoulder. "We'll leave ya be for a minute, mister, so you can say whatever ya wanna say."

"Thank you," Phil managed before he walked over to look at his friend.

Welles would have been proud of the new dark blue suit Mae had picked out for him. He would have said that she'd gone to too much trouble and that it wasn't fitting for him, but he would have been proud just the same. His old, worn hands, one of the first things Phil had noticed about him, were folded across his midsection. He looked as though he was just asleep, just as he had looked so many nights in that bottom bunk, in their tiny cell.

A knot rose in Phil's throat, and he tried to clear it, but it refused to go away. He wiped away a lone tear that had reached his jawline, then spoke quietly, "I miss you so much already, buddy. I-I guess I never figured this into our plan, you leaving me this soon. I know that's selfish of me, and in my heart, I know you were ready to go. You lived your life and accepted all that came along with it."

He pulled out a cloth handkerchief and wiped his face dry of tears, but they only began to cascade again, coming in rivers this time. "I know it sounds crazy, but if I had it to do all over again, I'd go right back to San Quentin. It taught me so much about life. You taught me so much about life. Without that place, without you, I'm afraid I'd still be in the fast lane, that I'd die never really knowing what it's like to live. I know you're watching over me, Pops. I can feel it. I can feel it when the sun shines just right on my face or when the wind blows light enough for me to enjoy the fragrance of a flower in bloom. I know, Welles Manning, that you'll be my guardian angel my whole life, just as you have been since the very day I met you. I also know that our dream, Manning and Sawyer Bait and Tackle, will be a huge success. I promise I won't let that dream die." Phil's voice then broke into a sob he could no longer hold back.

As he hung his head, he could hear the gravel crunching under an old station wagon as the others came to join him.

The few people attending the service gathered around as the funeral director slowly and methodically closed the casket. Mae gasped softly, then sobbed quietly as she caught the last glimpse of her brother on Earth.

The minister began with a prayer and spoke to the family about the good life Welles would now have. His role was to comfort them, as he had never even met Welles. He shifted from one foot to the other as he struggled to make sense of it all. Sweat beaded on his forehead as he looked at Phil with a hopeful glance.

Phil nodded and stepped forward, with Welles's Bible in his hand. He swallowed hard before starting, "Welles Manning and I met at a most unusual place for a friendship to start, one of the most infamous prisons in the United States. It was an unlikely friendship from the start, to say the least." He laughed as his eyes reflected the memory of their first meeting. "He wasn't very happy to see me that first day, and he wasn't hesitant to say so. I respected that. He was a proud man. Even in prison, he worked twelve hours a day, then cleaned other inmates' work boots on the side to make some extra money. He made it clear from the beginning that he wouldn't take handouts. I did convince him one day to share a soda with me, in celebration of two of my friends coming to visit." Phil looked over at Mae. "He told me about the day the two of you walked into town and shared the cola. He laughed as he remembered that you two drank it in little sips in order to make it last the whole walk home."

Mae smiled and nodded in remembrance.

"He loved you so much, just as he did the rest of his family and this land. We talked about it many times, and he described it so vividly that I knew exactly what it would look like, even before I ever came here. This is where he wanted his body to rest when he left this world." Phil smiled, and his eyes glazed over with a faraway look.

"Someone said to me earlier that Welles had nothing to give me. I want to explain why that couldn't be farther from the truth. He gave me things money could never buy. I know, because I spent my entire life working to make money. That money bought expensive clothes, a mansion in a ritzy section of town, and a car that cost more than most people will pay for a home. I know what money can buy, but Welles Manning knew about the things it can't." He paused again to pull himself together as he ran his fingers through his hair. "Welles taught me the meaning of friendship, true friendship that withstands some of the greatest trials than any of us can imagine. He taught me about the love of a family and the meaning of one's roots. He taught me about the love of Christ and the need to make time for Him in my life. He taught me so many important things, including the little ones, like taking time to read a book or learn a poem, respecting the things that can't be changed, and changing those that can."

Phil looked around at everyone and smiled a faint, heartbroken smile. "There is so much I could say about this good man, but all of you knew him. We will never meet another Welles Manning, no matter how hard we look. He was my friend, my brother, and as we bury the last of my family today, I bury a piece of me with him, for my own life will never really be complete without him. I love you, my brother," Phil said, with deep emotion.

He then opened the old Bible and slowly and gently flipped through its frail pages. "This Bible belonged to Welles's father, then his mother, and he gave it to me before he died. I offered it back to Mae, but she has insisted that I keep it. Never before, nor never again, will a gift have greater meaning to me." He turned to Psalms 16, a passage he had read to Welles many times, and he read the words off the page, though he could have just as easily recited them from memory: "'I have set the Lord always before me. Because He is my right hand, I will not be shaken. Therefore, my heart is glad and my tongue rejoices; my body also will rest secure, because You will not abandon me to the grave, nor will You let Your Holy One see decay. You have made known to me the path of life; You will fill me with joy in Your presence, with eternal pleasures at Your right hand."

Phil closed the Bible, as his hands shook profusely, and the picture of Drew's children floated to the ground. "I will pray every day for my friends that got no second chances," he said, as he reached for the photograph and put it back in the Bible. He then reached to touch the coffin in one last gesture of farewell and walked slowly back to the house.

The rest of the funeral party met him shortly when they drove back down.

He hugged Mae and reached for Jenny's hand. "We'll be leaving now, Mae," he said. "I am very sorry about your brother."

"I know you are," she answered kindly. "Before you go, I have somethin' I think you will want. It was mailed to me with my brother's belongings." She walked down the narrow hallway and turned into the last room on the right. She returned with the rolled-up drawing of the bait shop. "He did a nice job on this," she said as she handed it to Phil. "He was very proud of it. You made his last days, his last years, a whole lot better for him. You gave 'im hope and purpose, and I gotta thank you for that."

Phil embraced her once more. Then, without saying goodbye, he walked to the car with Jenny.

CHAPTER 31

The plane touched down quite abruptly in Los Angeles an hour later than scheduled, but that was not a problem for Phil. He had a lot on his mind anyway, and it gave him more time to think about what lay ahead. Jenny had taken another flight from Atlanta into San Francisco, and they agreed to phone each other when she was settled in.

He hailed a cab and rode to Arthur's house, then let himself in with the key that was left for him under the mat. He opened the closet that held his things and took a short inventory. He was much thinner, as Arthur had noticed, and the clothes reminded him of Lara and days past. He decided to take a trip to the mall to buy a few things to get him by and a couple suitcases to carry him through his first few days in Maine. That would alleviate shipping out any of his things, none of which were of any sentimental value anyway.

He also had to talk to his parole officer, and they agreed to give him a couple weeks to get settled before he had to commit to an address. It was really only a minor inconvenience, compared to all he had been through already. Renewing his driver's license was another task, and he would need Arthur for that. Then, of course, it would have to be changed immediately over to a Maine address. None of it was really a problem though. Phil Sawyer was a free man, and it felt better than he had ever dared to imagine it would. He was no longer uneasy about starting a new life. In fact, he war rather optimistic about his future.

He grabbed a soda out of the fridge, made a sandwich, then phoned Arthur at the office to let him know he would be shopping most of the afternoon. "Let me take you and Dee to dinner tonight," Phil suggested. "I'd love to sit in a restaurant, somewhere expensive and dark."

"Sounds great to me. I'll double-check with her. Call me when you get back. Sorry I'm not there to take you myself."

"No problem. I'm a big boy. I'll buzz you when I get back here."

Phil washed the dish that had held his sandwich and thumbed through the Yellow Pages to find the number to call a cab. The car arrived within thirty minutes. Arthur had already arranged for Phil's credit cards to be reinstated, so he was glad he didn't have to make a stop at the bank. After all, it had only been eight years, and some of the same employees were bound to still work there. He wasn't ready to run into anyone who knew him before.

"Where to, mister?" asked the older cabbie, who was wearing a silly checkered hat.

"To the nearest mall," Phil said. "No preference really."

"You got it," the man answered, then turned his radio to fifties music.

They rode in silence, with the exception of the outdated but lively tunes. Phil's mind spun as they passed shops, drugstores, and supermarkets. It was as if he had stepped into some alien world or another era. For so long, he'd seen nothing but the dark walls of the prison. He enjoyed the ride and was almost disappointed when they arrived at the mall.

He paid the fare and gave the driver a hefty tip, for which the old man thanked him over and over again. Phil felt a surge of panic as the cab pulled away, leaving him alone in front of the mall, as if he was a small child who couldn't find his mother. He walked to the nearest door and opened it slowly, only to find himself feeling rather ridiculous. *This isn't San Quentin,* he told *himself, and nobody's hiding behind the damn door to attack me.*

He forced a weak smile onto his face for his own benefit as he walked in. It was bright, and vibrant, with people bustling about. He was surprised that no one even noticed his presence; they were all going about their own business, too wrapped up in their shopping and purchases to pay him any mind. He felt somewhat like an outcast, but he realized no one would know him, and there was no reason for him to stand out. After all, he wasn't wearing a sign that alerted everyone that he was a convicted felon, a murderer.

He decided to just walk around for a few minutes to admire the scenery. Plants and flowers bloomed inside just as beautifully as they did outside. Bright red sale signs hung on almost every door and window, each store trying to outdo its neighbor. Children in strollers laughed, and retired people walked briskly, getting their daily exercise.

He stopped at Baskin Robbins for an ice cream cone and realized that choosing from the thirty-one flavors was the first decision he had really had to make for himself in years. It took almost ten minutes for him to settle on a single scoop of butter pecan. He sat down on a nearby bench, letting the ice cream melt in his mouth before he swallowed the cold, creamy goodness. Ice cream hadn't been on the menu for the past eight years, and it was even better than he remembered. He thought of Welles and Mae again, of him slowly sharing their cherished Coca-Cola on the walk home, and he smiled; this time, he didn't feel the need to cry, because it was a good memory and one he would always cherish.

He walked into a men's store and was somewhat embarrassed that he didn't even know his pants size. Of course the salesperson, who worked on commission, was more than happy to assist him. Phil welcomed the help and ended up with far more clothing than he intended to buy, so much that he wondered how he could walk out with all of it. He bought four pairs of jeans, eight shirts, and four more outfits that were a little less casual. He also bought a pair of loafers, a pair of Reeboks, and two pair of canvas boat shoes; they seemed so appropriate for Maine that he simply couldn't resist. He didn't worry about the basic necessities, like socks and underwear, because his old ones would do for the time being. With all his purchases, they were more than happy to call a cab and assist him with his bags.

He returned to Arthur's house later than expected, and Arthur was already there.

"I was about to call out the search party, but I see what took you so long now," Arthur said, looking down at all the boxes and bags. "I guess you didn't need my help after all."

"I enjoyed it," Phil said. "It was just so strange, walking around and being able to go anywhere I wanted. I didn't realize it would be this awkward."

Arthur laughed an appropriate laugh for the situation. "I talked to Dee, and she's available for dinner. I made reservations at a small, intimate restaurant about forty-five minutes away. I know you don't want to run into anybody."

"You don't know how true that is."

* * * * *

Dinner was delicious, and Phil felt the most comfortable he had since being released. They shared two bottles of expensive merlot and dined on steak and lobster.

"You won't be paying this much for lobster anymore," Arthur said. "They say it's practically free in Maine. You'll be able to get it for a song there."

"I hope so. I don't think I'll ever get enough of it," Phil said with a grin.

"Oh, you can always get too much of a good thing." Arthur laughed, but then his face turned serious. "Where are you going from here, Phil? I mean, do you think you're really ready to venture out as far as Maine?"

Phil had to laugh. "I'm not a child. I know it will be a greater challenge than I'm expecting, but I can't wait to take off from L.A., knowing I'll never look back. I need to erase this place from my memory."

"I hope that doesn't include us," Arthur answered, his voice stern.

"Are you kidding me?" Phil retorted. "That will never happen, not in this lifetime. You'll just have to come visit me, that's all."

"Are you really going to build a bait shop?" Arthur asked. "I mean, really, man, I just can't see it. What in the hell do you know about bait? Have you ever even been fishing?"

"Oh ye of little faith," Phil answered. "You might be surprised. I want a little cabin, a used car, and lots of books and magazines. I want to take long walks in the morning and stand outside and catch snowflakes on my tongue."

"Tell me you're not losing it. You don't have to completely change your lifestyle, you know. It sounds to me like you're trying too hard to leave your life behind."

"No," Phil answered sincerely, "I'm not losing it. I've had eight years to contemplate this. Believe me, that's a hell of a long time."

"I think it sounds romantic," Dee interjected. "Maybe one day, our lives will be that comfortable."

"Yeah," Arthur said, rolling his eyes playfully. "We'll be eighty by then, but it'll happen."

They all laughed, and the mood changed to a far less serious one.

"There are a few packed boxes in the hall closet for you," Arthur said, "just a few things from the house." He noticed the horror in Phil's eyes and smiled mildly. "Nothing that'll remind you of your life with her," he said quickly. Phil was still showing signs of apprehension when Arthur finally said, "Look, man, you can trash it when you get there if you want, but every man has a past, things he wants to remember and things he wants to forget. I hate to break it to you, my friend, but no matter how far you run or how drastically you change your life, you will always be Phillip Sawyer."

Phil dotted the cloth burgundy napkin across his mouth and looked up. "You're right," he answered soberly. "Thanks for packing whatever it is, and I'll definitely give it an honest chance of staying onboard."

"Good," Arthur said. "I think you may find some things packed away that you've forgotten about, things you might still want."

NEW BEGINNINGS
Solomon Cove

CHAPTER 1

The whole gang showed up at the airport to see Phil off. He felt guilty for leaving after all they'd done for him, but at the same time, he felt a sense of adventure and renewal. He hugged them all, and they promised to visit him as soon as he was settled. He didn't look back as he walked down the corridor that led to the plane; he couldn't bear to see their sad faces. He felt that familiar knot growing in his throat but was determined to fight it. Enough tears had been shed for a lifetime, and he was through with crying.

He smiled broadly as the plane ascended. "Thank you, Lord, for this moment," he said to himself. He had never thought it would happen, but now he was off into the wild blue yonder, flying away to his new life, his new beginnings, leaving the old one entirely behind.

He ordered a bloody Mary and sat back with the paper. His flight was nonstop into Portland, and he was glad about that, because he wasn't sure he could handle all the chaos of changing planes, since it had been so long since he'd done any major traveling, and airports were quite a bit different now. He read the paper from front to back, ate his lunch, drank another bloody Mary, and slept the remainder of the trip.

When the plane began to descend, waking him from his sleep, his stomach knotted again. He was thrilled yet filled with apprehension, wondering if he had done the right thing.

After stepping off the plane, he was overcome with the same feeling he'd felt the first day he arrived at Harvard: intimidated, excited, and unsure. He walked to the first rental car counter he could find to order a small compact. He was glad to be behind the wheel, yet another taste of freedom. His luggage filled both the trunk and back seat, and he considered exchanging it for a larger vehicle but ultimately decided against it. Phil was far too anxious to be on his way, even though he had no idea where he was going.

He followed the coast, up through Kennebunkport, where he stopped in the square to eat at an outdoor delicatessen. He ate his Reuben sandwich slowly as he looked around at the crowd. The differences between the townspeople and the tourists were obvious, and he smiled to himself as he watched them.

Back in his car, he drove for another couple hours, enjoying every bit of the scenery. It was as beautiful as he remembered, and he knew Welles would have been in awe.

Finally, he saw a small sign that read, "Welcome to Solomon Cove," and he decided to stop at a quaint bed-and-breakfast situated on a point. It overlooked a small lighthouse on a miniature island, and it would be perfect for the night.

An older, kind-faced woman showed him to his room. She made sure everything was perfect and even turned back the bed for him, then smoothed it and fluffed the feather pillows. "I hope you find everything to your liking," she said, in soft, smooth voice. "If not, please let me know. We don't have phones in the rooms, but you'll find one downstairs. Dinner is in an hour, and breakfast is at 8:30. Thank you for staying with us."

"Thank you," Phil answered, sitting down his small bag that contained only his shaving kit, a pair of jeans, and a polo shirt, everything he'd need for one night.

He was glad to have a private bath. He undressed and took a long, hot shower. It felt great. He shaved, dressed, and lay back on the bed. It had been a long day, and it only took a moment for him to fall fast asleep.

A short while later, there was a light knock on the door. "Mr. Sawyer?" a soft voice said from the other side.

He walked over to the door and opened it, looking quite groggy. "Yes?"

"Excuse me, but I didn't want you to miss dinner. You're half an hour late."

"Thank you very much," he answered. "I'll just wash my face and be right down. I apologize. The bed was so comfortable that I just fell asleep."

She smiled at him, her eyes twinkling, then walked away.

The dining room was small and cozy, with a fire blazing in the rock fireplace. There were only a few people remaining, finishing up their meal.

Phil sat down by himself at one of the smaller tables and was immediately served a plate. "Wow," he said, smiling, "what excellent service."

"Thank you," said the young server, probably in her teens. "My grandmother would be happy to hear that. Now, what can I bring you to drink?"

"Do you serve Chablis?"

"Yes we do," she answered. "I'll be right back."

Phil looked down at his plate, surprised that it didn't contain a seafood dish. Rather, it was a home-cooked plate of goodness, all of which melted in his mouth, right down to the big, fluffy biscuits.

The older woman walked by. "I love to see a grown man clean his plate," she said. "It makes me feel I've done my job well."

"Yes, ma'am, you sure did. It's been a long time since I've had such a nice meal."

"Well, I'll be back with some dessert and coffee," she said, obviously pleased with her new boarder. "How do you take your coffee?"

"Black please…and thank you."

She returned with a large slice of apple pie *à la mode* along with his cup of steaming coffee.

"Things just keep getting better for me," he said with a laugh.

She smiled at him kindly, studying his face. He was quite a handsome man, probably early forties and very gracious. She wondered where he was from and where he was going. He obviously wasn't traveling with anyone. She didn't dare ask, for she felt it would be rude to inquire, and she'd never been one to intrude on anyone else's business. "Will you be leaving us in the morning, Mr. Sawyer?" she questioned.

"You know," Phil answered, "I just may stay one more night."

"Good!" she said cheerfully. "I'll see to it that your room is in order. My name is Ruthanna Moore, should you need me."

"Thank you, Ms. Moore."

"Please call me 'Ruthanna'."

* * * * *

The morning sun shone through the windows, emitting a warm, gentle light. Phil lay in bed, listening to the sounds of Maine: blowing foghorns and water splashing loudly against the rocks. He could have lain in bed all day, but he wanted to have a look at the town. A little sightseeing would be just what the doctor ordered.

He looked at his watch and realized he only had about thirty minutes before breakfast. He sat up in the bed, then stood slowly, stretching his long arms almost to the ceiling. He pushed the lace curtains back and looked out at the stunning view. When he was finally able to pull himself away from the peaceful, breathtaking panorama, he went into the bathroom and took a nice, warm shower. It was much quicker than the one the night before, but it felt good just the same.

He walked down to the dining room and was surprised to see so many people. The bed-and-breakfast was so peaceful and quiet that he had no idea so many lodgers were staying there. Breakfast was buffet style, with everything one could think of, from fruit to eggs, bacon, and ham. He overate, just as he had at dinner.

Ruthanna came around to speak to everyone, and she patted him on the shoulder as she passed. He watched her make her rounds, admiring how kind she was. It was the perfect career for her to own a place like this. She made him feel at home, something he had never really felt before. As he finished up, she walked back by him, and he held up his hand as he swallowed the last of the coffee.

"Yes, Mr. Sawyer? How can I help you?"

"I was just thinking of doing a little sightseeing. Can you point me in the right direction?"

She laughed softly and placed her thin hand over her mouth. "Goodness, we don't have much to show folks around here. We're a small place. I just have regular customers who come here to get away from it all for a couple days."

"Apparently, it's the place to be," Phil said, motioning around the filled room with his hand. "I'm just trying to get away too," he said. "I just thought I'd have a look around."

"Most of the town rolls up the sidewalks in the winter, but we have a good three months left of our on season. Let's see," she said, her hand gripping her chin firmly. "You know, Portland isn't that far away. It is always a fun day trip. The lighthouse and the outlet shopping are nice."

"Well," Phil answered, not wanting to hurt her feelings, "I'd really just like to look around this place, something not too busy."

"Hmm. Well, you might be disappointed, but just follow the road around the bluff. You can see the whole town in about ten minutes."

"Thank you," Phil said sincerely. "I'll see you tonight for dinner."

"Shall I make you a sandwich for the trip? We do provide lunch as well."

"Oh, no, ma'am," he said, patting his very full belly. "I think this breakfast will hold me over for quite a while."

She smiled, and Phil could sense in her glance that she wondered where he was from. *Maybe I'll tell her a little about me sometime, if I decide to stay a while,* he mused.

CHAPTER 2

He climbed into the small car, cognizant of the fact that it was still over-loaded with his belongings. They would have to remain there until he settled down; it was easy enough to take an outfit out for each day.

As he took the road into town, he slowed several times to enjoy the resplendent view. It was breathtaking, amazing, and he wanted to soak in all he could. The water rumbled over the rocks, turned into foam, then retreated back to its original place, until pushed forward again.

As he wound his way down the road, a small town came into view, something like a small village. Somehow, Phil instantly knew it was home. He just hoped the townspeople were as inviting as the town.

He passed a small patch of little shops and decided to pull over and park. Although there were a couple more months before the cold would set in, it was still a little brisk. He pulled out a thin jacket and slipped it over his head. He stood there, just looking down at the town, still able to listen to the gentle sounds of the water.

He walked into a few shops and browsed around, looking at the few souvenirs: sweatshirts, t-shirts, and even an oversized stuffed lobster, which he immediately purchased to send to Lilly, such a kind, mature young lady.

As he walked through the town, he noticed what appeared to be an old general store and hardware store, all wrapped into one. He was surprised by the wide variety of things they carried, and they even offered a vast array of expensive cigars. He chose several for Arthur and looked around until he had seen almost everything. He was sure he'd make several more trips to that particular shop if he ended up settling in Solomon Cove.

The owner was an overweight man, with a thin, white, rather unkempt beard. Phil figured him to be in his early sixties. What little hair he still had was in the same condition as his beard. "Not from around here, are you?" he asked.

"No, sir," Phil answered. "I'm just out on a relaxation trip, far away from the fast-paced city life."

"Well, you've come to the right place," he said, extending his hand. "Name's Jacob, Jacob Dorough. Nice to have you visiting us."

"Thank you, Mr. Dorough," Phil answered, allowing his hand to meet Jacob's. "I'm Phil Sawyer. Fine place you have here."

"Thank you kindly, but I go by 'Jacob'. Not many people go by last names around here. We like to keep it simple."

"'Jacob' it is then," Phil said with a smile. "I'll just pay for these cigars and be on my way."

Jacob wrapped them carefully and placed them in a thin wooden box. "Hope you enjoy them."

"Actually, I'm sending them to a friend, but I'm sure he'll be happy to get them."

After leaving the general store, he walked along the wharf, watching the lobster boats come in with their traps overflowing. Small, older boats advertised day trips to see the whales. Signs painted on the sides guaranteed, "See a whale or your money back!" Phil smiled to himself. The cost was only $10, so he couldn't imagine anyone asking for their money, but he was sure it happened occasionally.

The men on the boats looked just like the fishermen he'd seen on television: large, healthy, seafaring brutes, with beards and yellow raingear. He watched them with fascination as they heaved their catches of the day up onto the dock. The lobsters clawed over one another, in an attempt to escape their fate. Apparently, Phil had gawked a little too long, because several of the men looked up with casual interest but quickly returned to their work, so he moved on down the strip.

The docks had seen better days, but they looked sturdy just the same. He walked down the small pier. The boats were decrepit as well, but he knew the fishermen would find a way to make them last a few more years.

An older fisherman slowed to lift a hand in his direction, and Phil waved back. The man leaned backward, using his hand to support his back. "It's been a long day," he said. "Not from around here, are you?"

"No, sir," Phil answered, wondering how everyone could pick out a newcomer so quickly. "Just taking a break from the fast pace of the city life."

"Wouldn't know much about that," the fisherman said, sounding quite exhausted. "I've never known anything but this life, and I wouldn't change it if the opportunity presented itself."

"I can certainly understand that," Phil answered, giving him a smile. "This is the most beautiful place I've ever seen."

"Reckon I'm biased," the man said. "Closest thing to Heaven I'll ever see here on Earth." He paused to wipe his face with a cool rag after dipping it into his cooler and wringing it out. "Not sure which is worse, the hot or the cold, but we have to deal with them both just the same."

"Well, in Los Angeles, we don't see any snow. The heat comes and goes, but it never gets below seventy degrees."

"It's not right to have Christmas without snow. Just can't see it myself."

Phil laughed slightly, then thought of his Christmases past. Lara always hired decorators to create the perfect tree, which he never had a hand in choosing. Garland hung from every banister and mantel, with glowing white lights and red velvet ribbons. All the gifts were wrapped perfectly by Neiman Marcus, so the whole place looked like a department store window.

On Christmas morning, the presents were opened slowly and neatly, revealing the same things year after year: overpriced ties for him, along with the latest colognes and Bostonian shoes, his favorite. Lara always preferred diamonds, as many as Phil would allow. She always told him she'd mailed her family's gifts, but now he knew she had most likely purchased her own to cover her ass when she didn't receive anything from them. He smiled lightly again, glad he was finally able to let go of the past and all those years of tormenting himself over her. As he pondered it, thinking back on those days of materialism, he realized just how senseless it all was.

"I guess you are right about having a white Christmas," he said with a laugh. "I can't say I have ever had the privilege, except a couple I spent in Boston."

"Never had the privilege, you say?" he said. "Then you oughtta slow down your pace for a while. A man shouldn't die without ever having cut his own Christmas tree in the snow. There's nothing like it."

Phil agreed. "Nice to make your acquaintance," he said as he turned to walk away.

"Yeah, you, too, young man. Say, if you really want to experience the slow life while you're here, I'm in need of a first mate. Actually, you'd be my only mate." He laughed heartily. "My other wanted to swap places with you, headed off to some fancy college in New York, to learn to be a lawyer or some such thing. Go figure. Anyway, I could use the help for a few days, till I find someone permanent. Think about it. I'll be here in the morning, at 4:30."

"Are you serious?" Phil asked, as excited as a young kid getting his first paper route. "I think that may be just what I need. I have to tell you that I don't have any experience. I can't even remember the last time I went fishing."

"That's not important," he answered. "Can you follow directions and work hard?"

"Sure can," Phil said, feeling a bit foolish for even considering it.

"See you in the morning then," the fisherman said, then gave Phil a salute.

"I don't even know your name. Mine's Phil, Phil Sawyer."

"Nice to meet you, mate. I'm Captain Bill, but 'Captain' will be fine."

"See you in the morning then, Captain."

"Four thirty, or the boat leaves without you. Pays $40 a day to begin with. After that, good workers make a little more. You won't be here that long, so I guess you'll just get paid to see the other side of the tracks. Bring your own big breakfast and lunch. I'll supply the drinks."

Phil smiled and walked away, feeling the best he had in years. He could not help but find the whole situation amusing. It was definitely a pay cut, but he couldn't think of anything more prudent at the time. He knew Arthur, Charlie, and Jenny would find it a real hoot when he told them about it. It was then that he realized he hadn't even called them, so he made a mental note to do so when he got back to the bed-and-breakfast.

He sauntered into town as he felt a growl in his stomach. He didn't realize how far he had walked, but he was out of breath by the time he reached the corner of town. It had been a while since he'd gotten any real exercise, as he'd never taken advantage of the weights in the prison, and he limited his jogs around the track at San Quentin because the yard was just too dangerous. He preferred to avoid that, even at the risk of becoming too lethargic. As a doctor, he knew the importance of exercise, but he also knew the importance of his life. He shook his head quickly, as if there was a fly bothering him, and surprisingly, the gesture helped to wipe away the memories.

The first restaurant and what appeared to be the only one was called the Corner Café, and he quickly walked inside. It was a casual but clean place, not very large, though it was full of customers. A handwritten "Seat Yourself" sign was taped to the cashier's post, so Phil looked around for a small table. He spotted one close to the back and slid into the small booth.

"Looks like you wore yourself out," said a polite waitress. Her hairstyle had clearly gone out in the seventies, teased and slathered with hairspray, but she had the voice of someone who was probably quite enjoyable to be around.

"Yes," Phil answered. "I wasn't aware of how out of shape I am."

"I don't think any of us get much exercise, but what the hell?" she said with a healthy laugh. She patted her slightly overweight belly and laughed again, then handed him a greasy menu and continued, "The daily special is a small sirloin, and I mean small, with corn on the cob and fries. You're welcome to look at the menu if you'd like something different."

"I think I'll just go with the special," Phil answered. "I have a thing for small sirloins."

They shared a good laugh, and then she was gone.

Phil looked around and began to feel the same odd sensation he'd felt in the L.A. mall, as if he expected everyone to stare at him, to know he had murdered his wife. He didn't realize that the people who were looking at him were just wondering who the handsome stranger was.

CHAPTER 3

There was actually much more of the small town to look over, but he knew he should get back to the bed-and-breakfast. He had to make a few calls, especially to his parole officer.

He spotted a small drugstore and walked in. As he did, the small bell on the door made much more noise than he thought it was capable of.

"Hello there," a bright, friendly voice said.

Phil looked around and didn't see anyone.

"Oops. Sorry about that," a woman said, bouncing up from below the counter. "I was putting away some pharmaceutical supplies and just figured you were someone from town. They're used to it."

Phil was startled for a minute and took a few steps back, still not accustomed to such perky service and quick movements, which would have been something to fear in prison.

"Oh, sweetheart," she laughed, "I really didn't mean to surprise you. Trust me, I'm perfectly harmless, though my husband might tell ya different. I tried wallpapering once and… Oh! I'm sorry. I can just go on and on. Anyway, how can I help you?"

Phil smiled, beginning to feel comfortable again. He studied the lady, who was probably in her fifties. She was short and thin, but her small frame didn't seem to hold her back. Energy just seemed to pour out of her, and he was sure that she was always like that. "I'm looking for a long-distance calling card," he said. "I don't have a cell phone, so…"

"Well, we don't get many requests for those, but I do have a few." She then led him to a display of cards and stood beside him like a little dwarf until he made his decision.

"This should do," Phil said, pulling his wallet from his back pocket. "You have a beautiful town here."

"Well, we're awfully proud of it," she answered, as if she'd just won a blue ribbon for her apple pie. "Bet you're here to get away from the congestion of the city, huh?"

"You guessed it," he answered.

"My name is Babette, but everyone calls me 'Babs'," she said, gearing herself up for a long talk. "My husband Vern and I own this shop, have for almost thirty years. His father had it before him. Died young, he did, leaving us with this place when we were first married. Didn't know a damn thing about running a business, but we've done the best we can do."

"Well, it's nice to meet you, Ms…"

"Wakefield, but please call me 'Babs'."

"Okay, Babs. Thank you for the calling card. I'm sure I'll be back in before I go."

"Sounds wonderful, dear. I didn't catch your name."

"I'm sorry. It's Phil, Phil Sawyer."

"Have a good afternoon, Phil," she chirped gleefully as he walked out the door.

Phil shook his head slightly, grinning all the way to his car.

* * * * *

The ten-minute ride back to the bed-and-breakfast seemed quicker this time.

Ruthanna was seated in a wingback chair, with her thin legs crossed and a roll of yarn that was soon to be an afghan. "Hello," she said, obviously happy to see him again. "So? How do you like our quaint little town?"

"It's wonderful, absolutely charming. Believe it or not, I still have more to see. I just needed to get back to make a few calls."

The room was empty of guests, and she patted her small hand on the sofa. "Please come sit a while. For someone trying to relax, you're certainly on the go. I guess old habits die hard," she said, her voice soft, not much above a whisper. "We do have quite an extensive library here, if you're interested. I find that sitting with a good book in one of the swings by the water can be the best therapy on Earth, no matter what ails you."

"I imagine you're right," Phil answered. "Maybe tomorrow I'll give it a try."

They sat quietly for a while as she knitted, and then she began to talk again. "I lived the fast life when I was younger. My sister and I were born in Chicago, and that was all I ever knew. My husband was from Maine, but during those years, jobs were hard to find. He ended up in Chicago and found a manual labor job that he worked till the day he died. Many people disapproved, often voicing their cruel opinion that I was unequally yoked or some such nonsense. It never bothered me, because he was a kind, hardworking man. I have always loved books and education, and he loved working and eating. Boy, did he like to eat! He also loved his church." Her eyes started to mist, and she paused for a moment before continuing. "Saddest part is that we were never able to have children."

"But your granddaughter…" Phil said.

"She's actually my late sister's granddaughter, but she's been kind enough to adopt me."

"How did you end up here?"

"My husband's sister died two weeks after he did, and she willed the place to both of us. She loved this place. I thought it only right that I take over for her and my husband. Maine never left his heart, even after years of living in Chicago."

"What about your granddaughter's mother?" Phil asked, instantly wishing he hadn't probed. "I'm sorry," he quickly added. "It's certainly none of my business."

She reached over to pat his knee. "It is quite all right. Really. She got caught up in drugs in the sixties and never got away from the spell it cast over her. Poor thing died at thirty. Laurel lived with her father until I came to the bed-and-breakfast, and he was more than happy to give her to me. I don't think she's seen him since. She was only three years old then. My, how time flies. She'll start college next year."

"I'm sorry to hear about your husband. It must be lonely without him," Phil said kindly. "You do a lovely job with this place though. I've never stayed in a bed-and-breakfast before, but now I don't want to stay in a hotel every again. They're so impersonal, but this place feels…like home."

"And where is real home for you, dear?"

Phil expected the question, and there was no time better than the present to tell her the truth; it wouldn't ever get easier. "Well," he started hesitantly, "with my family gone, I am just not sure. I think that's what I'm really searching for. I did my undergraduate studies at Georgetown University and completed medical school at Harvard. I did my internship and followed the best offers I could get through the years."

"So," she said, allowing the thin lines of her lips to curl into a smile, "you're a doctor? I knew there was more to you than meets the eye. Do tell me more, dear."

"Ms…er, I mean, Ruthanna, it's really a sad, tragic story that brought me here, and I don't want to frighten you with it. It's still quite raw, very difficult to talk about. Actually, only a handful of people know much about me and my…past." He turned his face in an effort to shadow his tears. "My last job was at Cedar Sinai Hospital, in Los Angeles. I was an orthopedic surgeon there."

"Very impressive," she said. "Maybe one day, you'll feel like talking to some-one about it. If it turns out to be me…well, I'm quite a good listener, and I never throw stones. Passing judgment is the good Lord's job, not mine."

"Thank you very much," Phil said, finally regaining a little of his composure. "Right now, I am just enjoying feeling comfortable."

"I am happy to hear that. Follow me," she whispered, wearing a sneaky look on her face. She took his large hand in her own and led him to the kitchen, where she pulled a large blueberry cobbler out of the oven and placed it on the stovetop to cool. "This is for dinner, but I say we break tradition and eat dessert first. I've got some vanilla ice cream in the freezer."

Phil laughed at her childlike behavior. "You won't get an argument out of me," he said, then closed his eyes and breathed in the aroma of the warm, sweet, baked delight.

"I always laugh when I hear that saying, 'Life is short. Eat dessert first.' Sometimes we tend to take life too seriously. I hate to see you in pain. We all have skeletons, Phil, even the best of us, but there's one thing I pride myself in. I am good at judging a person's character. I've not been wrong yet, and I've got a good feeling about you. Stay here as long as you wish, Mr. Sawyer, and remember that I've always got an open ear."

The two sat together and enjoyed the delicious blueberry cobbler and several laughs about Ruthanna's first days at the bed-and-breakfast.

When they finished, Phil carried their plates to the large sink and rinsed them off. "I really enjoyed this, Ruthanna," he said, with deep sincerity. "Duty calls now, though, and I've got phone calls to make. I bought a calling card in town."

She laughed softly. "Then you met Babs Wakefield."

"Yes, ma'am, I sure did. She's an energetic one, but she certainly made me feel right at home."

"She loves anyone who'll listen to her. Those shopkeepers get lonely throughout the day."

"Yeah, I suppose we all do sometimes," Phil said, then walked into the other room to use the phone.

He took a deep breath and picked up the receiver. He pulled the number of his parole officer out of his wallet and felt a deep, growing panic as he listened to the first few rings.

"Officer Nevin. How can I help you?"

"Um, yes, Officer Nevin? This is Phil Sawyer."

"Phil Sawyer. Good. I've been anticipating your call. Have you found a place to settle as of yet?"

"Actually, I'm sure I have, but I'm staying at a bed-and-breakfast until I can obtain a permanent residence."

"I see," the officer answered, sounding a bit displeased. "You're fortunate, Mr. Sawyer, that the State allowed you to move across the country within a couple weeks of your release. It is in your best interest to accrue a residence, to make things as permanent as they can be for now."

"Yes, I understand, and I'll continue to work toward that. I need to know what I should do in the meantime. Is there someone here I should report to?"

"Where in Maine are you?"

"A small town called Solomon Cove, north of Portland."

"I have to warn you, Mr. Sawyer, that small towns don't take kindly to new people, especially those who've served time in San Quentin."

"I understand, and that's a grave concern for me."

"Extremely small towns don't have parole officers. You'll most likely have to report to the sheriff himself. I will contact him in the next couple days and fax your information over to him. I need a number where I can reach you."

Phil spouted out the numbers, anxious to get off the phone. The conversation ended abruptly, and he felt a wave of exhaustion wash over him. He didn't really have the energy to call Arthur, Charlie, or even Jenny, so he climbed the small spiral staircase to his room and took a long nap. He woke just in time for dinner, grateful that he had, even though his stomach was still quite full of ice cream and blueberry cobbler.

CHAPTER 4

After dinner, Phil made three phone calls, the first to Jenny. She was elated to hear from him, and they talked for over an hour. She had decided to take a break before seeking another nursing position and was even thinking of changing professions.

"Don't do that," Phil said. "When you find your calling, it's where you're destined to be."

"Maybe you're right," she answered. "Just too many bad memories, I guess. By the way, where are you?"

"In a small town in Maine, a place called Solomon Cove. You'd love it, Jenny. Right now, I'm staying at this adorable little bed-and-breakfast, till I can find my own place. It's heaven on Earth here."

"Wow. You sound pretty confident that you found where you want to be. Are you sure you want to make it permanent?"

"That all depends on how the sheriff reacts to me being here. Small towns are…well, you know. Hey, since you're taking a break, why don't you fly out and visit? I can make a reservation for you here. Like I said, you'd love it. I can have you a ticket by tomorrow."

"I didn't think you'd ever ask," she said, laughing. "What about next week?"

"Great. I'll call you in a couple days to make the final arrangements. And, Jenny, I miss you."

"Same here," she answered. "I look forward to hearing from you."

After he hung up with Jenny, Phil placed calls to Arthur and Charlie and shared the same exciting news about Solomon Cove. He deliberately left out his new job, for fear that they would think he'd gone totally insane. Nevertheless, it felt very good to hear their voices.

After his phone calls, he walked out and sat on the swing, just as Ruthanna had suggested. It was dark, but the outdoor floodlights made it possible for him to make his way down by the water. He listened to the soothing sounds of the tide beating against the rocks. For the first time in a long while, Phil's mind melted into peacefulness.

He wasn't sure how long he sat there, but he finally found the energy to drag himself back inside. He planned to be at the dock no later than 4 o'clock in the morning, so he quickly showered and set his alarm for 3:00.

* * * * *

The blaring of the alarm came early, and Phil dressed in his most casual clothing, knowing it would be ruined by the end of the day, at least wet and smelling wretched.

Ruthanna had packed him a breakfast and lunch for the day, but not before telling him he was nuts. He walked quietly to the kitchen and reached into the large refrigerator to retrieve his meals and smiled as he read a note pinned to one of the bags: "Be careful...and for God's sake, don't make this a permanent arrangement. Ruthanna."

Captain Bill was already loading the boat when Phil got there. "I admire a man who's prompt," he said but offered no other conversation.

"I thought you would," Phil answered, climbing aboard the old vessel.

"Tomorrow, you'll need to bring your own cooler. You can squeeze your food in mine today," the captain said, motioning toward a brown cooler that was as dirty on the inside as the outside, making Phil grateful that his food was in a bag. "Orange is our color," he said with a grunt. "We empty the traps with the orange buoys. We've been having trouble with divers robbing our catches. Gonna catch 'em one day soon, and when we do, there'll be hell to pay. The only day I take off is Sunday. Can't leave the lobsters in the cages too long, or they get to fightin', outta hunger, I guess. Anyway, when they do that, they tend to tear each other's claws off. Those are called culls. They only fetch a third of the price, and I can't afford that. Lobster sells cheap enough as it is here." He then started the antiquated boat and gave it a few minutes to sputter and smoke before he pulled away from the dock without another word.

Phil held on tightly to the low windshield, taking in the sunrise as it climbed over the water. It wasn't long before they located the first of the orange buoys, and Phil was surprised at the heavy weight the traps carried; it made him wonder how the captain had managed all those years.

"Just pull up the trap and empty the lobsters into this large cooler filled with water, then cover it with this screen. Smaller ones have to be thrown back. They're called shorts, and it's illegal to keep them. Wouldn't bring a damn thing at the dock anyway. The flounder eat them almost as soon as they hit the water. Easy game for 'em, I guess."

Phil had only dumped his first load and was already feeling pressure on his biceps. Captain Bill drove the boat around for another two hours, and the two alternated in pulling up the traps. He finally turned the sputtering boat off so they could eat breakfast. He handed Phil a cup of hot, steamy coffee he poured from a large thermos, and they sat in silence as they ate. As soon as they were finished they headed out again, and it wasn't until six hours later that he turned off the boat again for lunch.

"Got some Gatorade in the cooler, along with water or soda. Take your pick. It's easy to get dehydrated out here in the sun."

Phil picked up a bottle of water and drank it as if he'd spent days in the desert. Captain Bill snickered. "Not too used to manual labor, are ya?"

"No," Phil answered, "can't say I am."

"If ya think today was hard, just wait till tomorrow. Your body's gonna ache like you never dreamt, mate. In fact, I don't expect you'll even show up again," he said, a challenge Phil intended to meet.

It was after 7 o'clock before their day was done, and the large cooler was filled with some of the largest lobsters Phil had ever seen.

"It's been a good day," the captain said, showing little or no emotion. "You did well, mate. No complaints here." He then handed Phil $40 from his tethered wallet.

"No thanks, Captain," Phil said. "It was worth the experience."

"Take the money, or else don't come back," the captain said sternly. "I don't let my help work for free. It isn't right. I demand that you take it."

Phil finally gave in and took the money, realizing that it was quite insulting for him not to. He folded the two twenties and put them in his front pocket. "I'll see you in the morning, Captain," he said, wondering how in the hell he would make it.

"We'll see about that, mate. We'll see." The captain then laughed, deep and emotionless.

"How have you managed to do this for all these years?" Phil asked.

"Gotta make a living," he answered. "Plus, it's all I know. It's in my blood now."

Phil literally staggered back to his car, feeling as if he'd just finished the Ironman Triathlon. On the way back to the bed-and-breakfast, he stopped by the hardware store to pick up a cooler.

"Hey there," Jacob said. "I figured you'd be long gone."

"Me too," Phil said. "I just enjoy this place so much. Say, do you have any coolers? Just a small one will do."

"I've actually got quite a few to choose from. Don't know how small of one you need. The fishermen like to buy them." He walked to the back of the store, with Phil teetering slowly behind him, and picked up a little red cooler. "This is the smallest I carry," he said. "Will it do?"

"It's perfect," Phil answered. "What do I owe you?"

"Twelve dollars."

Phil reached in his front pocket and pulled out a twenty to pay him. "Thanks a lot, Jacob. I'm sure I'll be back."

"Look forward to seeing you," the shopkeeper answered as he handed Phil his change. "Thanks for the business."

Phil knew where his last stop would be, and that was to visit Babs at the drugstore, for some much-needed Ben Gay. Babs was as talkative as usual, and while he was kind, he made his purchase and hurried out as quickly as he could.

When he walked back into the bed-and-breakfast, Ruthanna couldn't do anything but laugh. "You don't look so good," she said, patting him on the back. "I kept your dinner in the oven," she said, motioning him into the kitchen.

He ate like a horse and went straight to the shower. It was quite a long one, and then he lathered himself with Ben Gay until he couldn't stand the fumes anymore. He allowed it to dry, then crawled into the bed without any clothes on. He set the alarm, determined to meet the challenge of another day on the water.

A couple hours later, Phil he heard a light tapping at the door. "Yeah?" he said.

"It's me," Ruthanna whispered.

He wrapped a towel around his naked body and opened the door to poke his head out, as he didn't want her to see his scars.

"I washed your clothes," she said. "I didn't mean to invade your privacy, but I got them when you were in the shower. There's no need to ruin another set."

Phil was truly moved by her kindness, and as he reached for the neatly folded clothes, he realized they smelled of sunshine. "You are something else," he said.

"I smell Ben Gay," she answered, sniffing the air. "Get your beauty sleep, hon'." She smiled. "You're crazy, but I won't say anything else about it. I'm not sure what you're trying to prove, but more power to you."

Phil grinned, thanked her again for the clean clothes, and shut the door lightly, then climbed back into bed.

* * * * *

When the alarm went off, far too early again, he sighed deeply. His whole body ached with a pain he had never felt before. He debated whether or not to just stay in bed and call it quits, but his pride wouldn't allow him to give up, so he was back at the dock at 4 o'clock sharp, with his food packed neatly in his new red cooler.

The captain laughed. "I really didn't expect to see you again, mate, but I'm proud of you for showin' up."

The same routine was repeated all over again, though they took an even better catch than the day before.

"Can't complain, mate," the captain said. "Matter fact, I'm a little surprised."

"You aren't the only one," Phil answered, his muscles aching, taking another $40 from the captain and feeling guilty for it all over again.

* * * * *

Before long, Phil realized he would have to turn the rental car in soon and buy one of his own; in fact, he could have already bought a decent used one for what he was paying for the rental. That would be his next step.

He called Jenny that night and made arrangements for her to fly in on Sunday, his day off, and he planned to ask the captain for a couple days off to spend with her. He knew it wouldn't make Captain Bill happy, and he was right about that.

"Being a shipmate is a commitment, but I understand your predicament. Take the days off, and let your muscles rest. You'll be a better man for it anyway."

Phil also made arrangements with Ruthanna for a room for Jenny at the bed-and-breakfast.

"Tell me more about yourself," she said softly as he ate his dinner, almost afraid to delve into his business.

"You wouldn't believe it if I did," Phil said. He wanted desperately to talk to someone, but he wasn't sure he should open up about the horrible path that had led him there.

"I saw your scars," she said. "I know you were trying to hide them."

It was then that Phil decided if there was anyone he could trust, it was the sweet old innkeeper. "It's really quite a story, and I'm not sure if you're ready to hear it or if you have the time."

"Oh, dear," she said, wearing a compassionate look on her face. "I have all the time in the world."

"I'm afraid if I tell you, you'll no longer want me to stay here."

"I'm sure it isn't that awful," she assured him. "Like I said, I don't throw stones."

After a deep sigh of resignation, Phil rattled off his story, not leaving out any of it. He spoke of his work, Lara, and Welles and their plans for the bait shop. He told her about his years at San Quentin, and even the nasty bit about how he got his scars.

She listened, captivated by his story, not once stopping him to ask questions. Her eyes brimmed with tears several times, but she controlled them before they rolled down her kind, wrinkled face.

"I'm most concerned about my parole at this point. The sheriff will have to approve it, and in a small town like this, the story's destined to get out. It's difficult for people to accept someone with a murder conviction."

"You poor, dear man," she said, reflecting no judgment whatsoever in her quivering voice. "It may be hard at first, but once people get to know the real you, they'll accept your situation. It just takes time."

The ringing of the phone disrupted their conversation, and she hurried over to answer it. After a short pause, she turned to look at him. "It's for you, Phil. I'll just step in the other room, give you your privacy."

"Hello?" Phil answered, wondering who was calling at such a late hour.

"Phil, this is Officer Nevin. I thought you might like to know the status of your parole."

Phil held his breath, waiting on the news. "Yes, Officer Nevin. I am prepared for the worst."

"Quite the pessimist, aren't you?"

"Well," Phil said bluntly, "I haven't exactly had the best eight years."

"I can't say I disagree with you there. In any case, I faxed the sheriff a great deal of information concerning your case. He was very understanding, even prepared to keep the information to himself, unless, of course, any problems arise."

"What!? You've got to be kidding me," Phil said, trying to control his elation.

"He wants to meet with you at 9:00 sharp, tomorrow. I suggest you get there on time."

"Don't worry about that," Phil said. "I'll be there with bells on."

"Report back to me as soon as you've talked to him."

"Yes, sir, I will…and thank you, Officer Nevin. Now I can start looking for a residence, find a real home."

"I suggest you do that as soon as possible, and, for God's sake, use an out-of-town bank. Money like yours will draw too much attention in a little burg like that. You may want to open a checking there, with a fairly small amount of money in it, just to keep it clean."

"Will do," Phil answered. He hung up and, eager to tell Ruthanna the good news, hurried into the kitchen, where she was waiting on him. He walked over and hugged her as tight as her small frame could handle. "That was my parole officer. Your sheriff has agreed to keep this whole thing under wraps, unless I cause any problems, which I don't intend to do. Now I can start looking for a permanent residence."

"God bless Sheriff Murphy," she said. "I'll make sure to call him myself tomorrow."

"Thank you," Phil said. "I'm meeting with him at 9:00 in the morning. Wish me luck."

"All will go well, Phil."

"I hate to leave Captain Bill with all that work."

For the first time during the conversation, she laughed, and then she laughed some more. "Phil Sawyer, you were not meant to be a fisherman," she said. "You need to accept that."

"I know," he said, laughing along with her. "I just like to keep my word when I commit to something," he said, rekindling so many fond memories of Welles and all the lessons he'd learned from the man.

CHAPTER 5

The sunrise seemed to come earlier than usual. When Phil pulled up to the dock at 4:00, the captain was already loading the boat, and he looked up at him as though he knew something was wrong.

"Sorry, Captain," Phil said, with regret in his voice, "but I won't be able to work today. I have some…outside commitments, something I can't get out of."

The captain looked at him suspiciously. "I understand, mate. Thanks for getting up at 4:00 to let me know. Shall I expect you tomorrow?"

"Sure. I'll be here, right on time."

Without another word, the captain turned and continued his work.

Phil took that as his dismissal and drove back to the bed-and-breakfast, with plans to meet the sheriff at 9:00 and then go on a quest for a new car, just something reliable.

Nine o'clock came much quicker than he anticipated. He dressed in his finest, wishing he would have bought at least one suit. The sheriff's office was right in the middle of town, an appropriate place for the Police Department. Phil heaved a deep sigh and said a silent prayer, something he never would have done if he and Welles had never crossed paths.

He opened the door and found everyone staring at him like he was some kind of ghost. He instantly felt out of place, like some kind of freak show, and he wondered if the sheriff had failed to keep his word and had already told them all about his situation. He soon realized that wasn't the case; they just wondered who the outsider was.

They clearly noticed his discomfort, because the two deputies looked away.

"Can I help you?" asked a young woman who was sitting at the front counter.

"I am here to meet with Sheriff Murphy. My name is Phil Sawyer."

"Just a moment please," she said. She then picked up an old, out-of-date phone and pressed a white button on the side. "Sheriff, there's a Phil Sawyer here to see you." She placed the phone back in its cradle, pointed, and said, "Just follow that hallway. His office is the third door on the left. It is marked clearly, so you can't miss it."

"Thank you," Phil answered, then he walked away.

"Wonder who the stranger is," Officer Evan Isaacs said.

"I don't know," Rachel answered, shrugging, "but he sure is a handsome one."

"Uh-oh. Should I tell Hank about this?"

"No, Evan," Rachel said, "but it's every woman's right to look."

*****

Phil knocked lightly on the door, hoping against hope that the sheriff would be away on a coffee break, but he had no such luck.

"Come in, Mr. Sawyer."

Phil opened the door apprehensively. As he reached his hand out to meet the sheriff's, his mouth was so dry that he found it hard to talk. "I'd like to thank you for arranging to meet with me so quickly and for agreeing to keep this serious matter under your hat."

"It wasn't a hard decision to make. I've received many letters of recommendation, from attorneys to the FBI, the DEA, a well-respected doctor, and a parole officer. That's a first."

"I have to say I am quite shocked," Phil answered, feeling a little more at ease. "I can't believe that many people spoke up for me."

"This is a small town, Mr. Sawyer," the sheriff said. "The townsfolk will want to know what brought you here. Very few newcomers choose to settle down here, but I do understand why you'd want to. Most of the people in Solomon Cove grew up here. I'd suggest that when they ask, which they will, you just tell them you've saved enough money to retire early to get away from your fast-paced life."

"You are very kind, Sheriff," Phil answered. "I didn't expect this sort of reception."

"Just play it cool, don't give me or my deputies have any problems, and things will work out."

"You have my word," Phil answered, already liking and respecting the man.

"Well, good day, Mr. Sawyer. I look forward to seeing you in town."

"Thank you very much. I'm looking for a place to live, small and inconspicuous, of course. Do you have any suggestions?"

"As a matter of fact, I do," he answered. "Take a right out of here, and you'll come upon the only realtor in town. Believe me, she'll be thrilled to see you. Business is slow, if not nonexistent around here." He laughed a little and stood to open the door.

*****

As much as he loved staying at the bed-and-breakfast, Phil knew he couldn't stay there forever. He was anxious to get to the realtor, so he walked quickly down the sidewalk. He opened the door and called out to see if anyone was in.

"Hello?" a woman's voice said from the back. "I'll be right with you." She was shocked to see a newcomer and such a handsome one at that. "Good morning. My name is Heather Thomas," she said. Her light, quiet voice didn't at all match her body, which was rather chubby. "How can I help you today?"

"Well," Phil said, searching for the right words to explain his presence in Solomon Cove, "actually, I'm looking for a small house, something like a cottage."

"When did you arrive in our little town Mr…"

"Sawyer, Phil Sawyer," he said. "I've lived in Los Angeles for several years, working like a maniac. I decided I need a break from the mad pace and picked the most beautiful spot I could find. I want to do some reading, a little writing, and enjoy a lot of relaxation."

"I can't say I disagree with any of that," she said, smiling, obviously happy at the thought of some rare business. "I have some rather large houses. Are you adamant about a small one?"

"Actually, yes," Phil answered. "I had a large one in L.A., and I just want something warm and cozy for now, though I might want to upgrade later."

"We don't have a high turnover rate here. Most people live here all their lives."

"Yes, I've noticed that," Phil said, smiling. "It's one thing that makes the place so endearing."

"Can we start looking tomorrow, around 9:00 in the morning?"

"Actually, I'm afraid I've already got other commitments to tend to," he answered, not wanting to upset the captain again. "Can you meet with me on Monday?"

"I always make time for someone who is seriously looking to buy. Same time, at 9:00 a.m.?"

"Sounds great. A friend of mine is flying in, so she can help me decide."

"Good. I'll see you then," Heather said, then bid him farewell.

* * * * *

As Phil was heading back to the bed-and-breakfast, he came upon a small, makeshift produce stand. He couldn't resist the urge to stop to look over the merchandise. He was immediately drawn to the birdhouses that the old man was making while he waited for someone to come along to purchase some fruits and vegetables. They were made of birch, and his mind drifted to Frost's poem of the same name:

I'd like to go climbing a birch tree,
toward Heaven, till the tree could bear no more,
but dipped its top and set me down again.
That would be good, both going and coming back.
One could do worse than being a swinger of birches.

His mind must have taken him away far more than he realized, because the man had a strange look on his face.

"I'm sorry," Phil said. "I was just admiring your birdhouses."

"Don't get many requests for 'em, but I still like making them just the same. Gives me something to do in my old age," he answered.

"Well," Phil said, smiling brightly, "I find them intriguing. How much would four cost?"

"Four? Are you serious?" the old man asked, not quite knowing what to say.

"Yes, sir, absolutely. A friend of mine in Los Angeles loves gardening. She'd be thrilled to have a couple, and I'm looking for a small cottage myself. They're perfect."

"I don't even know what to charge for the old things," he said, smiling and swelling with pride.

"How does $50 sound?"

"Sounds pretty generous to me," the man answered.

"Not too generous," Phil said. "They're absolutely beautiful." He looked over the produce, too, and decided on a small basket of blueberries and peaches. He handed the man $54 and excitedly put his purchases in the trunk, knowing that Janet would be delighted to receive such wonderful things in the mail.

It was almost closing time at the little post office, but the clerk was happy to help him before she locked up.

"I have two birdhouses, and I don't quite know how to mail them," he said with a laugh.

The young lady looked them over. "I think I've got a couple perfect boxes in the back. Hold on." She then pulled out two brown paper bags, they kind grocery stores always used before they went to plastic. In a swift minute, she had the birdhouses boxed, wrapped, and weighed. "Just put the address on them, and we'll send them off."

Phil smiled and wrote the address on the box with a Sharpie, amazed at the service and the speed in which she worked. "Thank you very much," he said as he left, thinking back to the horrendously long lines in L.A. post offices and the people who always seemed aggravated to have to work there. For once, going to the post office had actually been a pleasant experience.

He pulled into the bed-and-breakfast just in time for lunch: warm, open-faced roast beef sandwiches, drenched in gravy and accompanied by homemade French fries. "Just what the doctor called for," he told Ruthanna. "I've accomplished so much today," he said, smiling excitedly as he told her about it all.

"You look like a youngster filled with the joy of childhood." She laughed lightly. "It makes me feel warm inside to see that."

"I will really miss you and this place when I find a house," he said sincerely.

"Oh, Mr. Sawyer," she said, blushing, which only made the lines on her beautiful face more prominent, "even after you move out, I'm sure that won't be the last we'll see of one another, unless you don't find our friendship as pleasant as I do."

"Indeed I do," he said, smiling. "Indeed I do."

CHAPTER 6

Early Friday morning, Phil arrived at the dock.

As usual, Captain Bill was packing up the boat. "Hey there, mate," he said, actually sounding as if he was beginning to enjoy Phil's company.

"Good to be back, Captain," Phil answered as he placed the small red cooler in its place.

Nothing more was said until they stopped for breakfast. The day off had taken its toll on Phil, and he could feel his muscles aching again.

"Lobsters are strange creatures, you know," Captain Bill said, leaning back in his seat and looking as though he was preparing for a long talk. "They fight each other like hell, sometimes losing both their claws. Ain't the smartest things floating around out there. They can grow them back, but it stunts the rest of their growth in the meantime."

"Really? I had no idea," Phil said, genuinely interested in what they were catching.

"Bet ya didn't know they shed their old shell, pretty much like snakes do. If it takes 'em too long to shed it, they suffocate. It usually takes forty-eight hours for 'em to grow a new shell," he explained, swelling with confidence as he shared his great lobster knowledge with his rookie mate. "Yep," he continued. "The females carry 'bout 100,000 eggs a year, but the damn cannibals feed on each other. Only about 1 percent of 'em live. Guess we're lucky to catch as many as we do."

"With those odds, I'd say we are," Phil answered.

Without another word, the captain rose and started the engine. Breakfast was over, and so was the lesson of the day.

They worked two hours later than usual, and Phil surmised that it was because of his absence the day before. He knew the captain had missed his extra muscle, especially when he pulled $45 out of his pocket and handed it over.

"What's this?" Phil questioned. "I haven't gotten a raise already, have I?"

"No raise, mate," the captain said bluntly. "That there's overtime pay for today."

Phil pocketed it without question, knowing he would be forced to take it in the end anyway.

They worked like hell on Saturday, too, and Phil was glad when he got back to the bed-and-breakfast and into the hot shower. He dressed to go down to eat the warm dinner waiting in the oven for him.

Ruthanna walked in and looked him over as if she was putting him through a military inspection. "When are you going to stop this craziness, Mr. Sawyer?"

she said sarcastically.

"What are you talking about?" Phil teased.

"You know exactly what I mean," she answered in a huff. "That boat is going to kill you. You've proved your point, so just let it go."

"I will soon," he promised. "Besides, I have a few days off next week with Jenny."

"Do tell me more about her," Ruthanna said as she sat down with a cup of hot tea.

"You'll love her," he answered. "In fact, I'm sure the feeling will be mutual. She reminds me of you in so many ways. She's kind and gentle and cares so much about people and their feelings. I hate to think about her working in that prison. All those horrible memories have to haunt her, just as they do me. Her calling is definitely nursing, and I'm sure she has no real desire to let it go, as I've been able to let go of being a doctor. We have different goals in life now, but that's okay."

"Do you love her?" Ruthanna asked, shocking Phil for the first time.

"I've never thought about it," he answered, wondering why he hadn't. "I don't think I've ever really experienced love. Besides, I can't let that happen with Jenny. I don't want to hold her back. This is where I wanna be, the life I want to live now."

"*Now* is the keyword there, Phil," she said, smiling knowingly. "One day, you may decide you want to return to another life, another part of this vast world we all live in. She sounds like a good catch, one you shouldn't push away. Maybe she needs a break, too, so give her one. She's a grown woman and has the right to make up her own mind, just as you do." She smiled, her eyes twinkling.

"Okay, Ms. Cupid." Phil laughed. "You can reevaluate the situation after you meet her."

"Trust me, I will," she said, and he knew she wasn't kidding.

* * * * *

Phil stood at the airport gate with a dozen red roses wrapped in green foil and tied with a bright red bow. He would be hard to miss, especially with that wide, cheesy smile on his face. Jenny was one of the last to disembark from the plane, but she was worth waiting for; she looked just like the angel he remembered, and her bright smile challenged his as they embraced.

"God, it's so good to see you." Phil smiled, placing a hand on each side of her face.

"You're a sight for sore eyes yourself." She laughed. "So tell me, does this state have any restaurants? I'm starving."

"They sure do," he answered, "but you have to promise not to each much. Ruthanna is cooking a special meal tonight."

Kim Carter

"Oh." She smiled. "So you're already on a first-name basis, huh?"

"Weird you should ask," Phil said. "It's strange. Everyone in this little utopia goes by first names. You won't hear 'Doctor,' 'Nurse,' 'Officer,' 'Reverend,' 'Mr.,' or 'Mrs.' around here."

"Sounds awfully good to me," she said.

They drove all the way through Portland, even though Jenny complained the entire time of hunger pangs.

"If you can just survive a few more minutes, we'll be at the really great restaurants, the places with checkered floors and jukeboxes."

"Oh, lovely." She laughed. "I've never been one to decline a meal at a dive."

A small restaurant came into view, with picnic tables sitting outside it. "Perfect!" Phil, pointing at it as he pulled the overloaded car into a small parking spot. "Have a seat," he said. "If it's okay with you, I'll order for us."

"It sounds like you're an old hat at this, so I guess I can trust you," she answered, brushing her hair to one side.

He ordered two fried scallop and shrimp baskets with fries and large sodas. They were hot and greasy on the bottom, so he hurriedly walked back to the table.

"You call this eating light?" Jenny asked. "How am I supposed to have room left for a special dinner?"

"I have faith in you," Phil said with a laugh.

Jenny studied his face. For the first time since she'd met him, she saw life there. She saw his hopes and dreams coming into view and fruition. She didn't mention the change, knowing Phil would only laugh at her, but it was undeniable.

"These have to be the largest shrimp and scallops I've ever seen," she said, eating them in a hurry to stave off the growls in her stomach. "This will definitely put a few pounds on me."

"I don't think anyone will notice," Phil said. "Besides, Ruthanna will be happy to see that you like to eat. It's sort of her thing."

"Ruthanna this, Ruthanna that. Gee, should I be jealous?"

"Well, she has won my heart, I must say," he answered, "but it's nothing for you to worry about."

He carried their two paper baskets and dumped them into the nearest trashcan. They were saturated in grease, but it was an excellent meal and a good introduction to Maine.

"I can't wait for you to see the coast," Phil said, his eyes dancing with excitement.

They drove slowly as the road wound around the water and rocks. Jenny didn't say a word; she appeared mesmerized by the presence of such beauty.

"Well? Did I exaggerate about this place or what?"

"No," she answered, keeping her eyes on the water. "Not at all. It's like…a postcard."

"And then some," Phil said.

They then rode in silence, right through Solomon Cove.

When they pulled up to the bed-and-breakfast, Jenny finally spoke. "This place is perfect for you," she whispered, so quietly that Phil wasn't even sure she'd said it. "It's so perfect that I'm afraid it'll take you away from me."

"Stop." Phil laughed, although a bit nervously. "There'll be none of that. This is a place of peace, and we can't ruin it by fearing things that'll never happen."

He reached for her small hand and led her up the front steps.

Inside the bed-and-breakfast, Ruthanna was sitting in her chair, knitting and trying to pretend she wasn't anxious to meet Phil's special lady friend.

"Well," Phil said dramatically, "here she is, Jenny in the flesh. She actually showed."

"Hush, Phil," Jenny said playfully, extending her hand to Ruthanna. "I've heard so many wonderful things about you."

"And I about you, dear. It's hard to believe there are two perfect women in the world." She chuckled and gave Phil a wink, her seal of approval. "You must take a walk along the rocks and enjoy your time here," Ruthanna said, looking sternly at Phil. "Your friend here has a strange longing to keep busy, all under the façade of taking it easy. Go figure."

"It was my understanding that he has been taking it easy," Jenny said.

Ruthanna laughed. "If you only knew the half of it, sweetheart."

"Now, now," Phil said, panicking at the thought of Ruthanna telling about the wharf, "I'm sure you ladies can find something far more interesting to talk about than little ol' me." He then reached for Jenny's elbow. "C'mon. There's something you've gotta see."

He led her outside, down to the rocks. They walked for a long time in silence, stopping to look at the starfish that clung unsteadily to the boulders, hanging on for dear life against the powerful crashing waves. They admired the colorful flowers that made their way through the rocks to flourish in the afternoon sun.

He smiled at her and stood. "Ruthanna will kill me if we didn't spend some time in the swing up near her place. Come on."

They walked slowly, taking in all the beautiful sounds of the nature around them. By the time they reached the swing, they were both ready to sit down for a bit.

"Guess what we have to do tomorrow," Phil said, wearing a coy smile.

"Dare I ask?"

"House-hunting. There's only one realtor in town, and she's determined to sell me something elaborate. If she only knew where I came from! Anyway, it should be interesting."

"Sounds like fun to me."

"Well, at least we'll see more of the countryside. For now, let's get inside and get you settled into your room. Dinner is in an hour."

"You've gotta be kidding, right?"

"Nope," Phil said, "and don't you dare embarrass me by not eating. Ruthanna will take it personally."

"Jeez, no pressure there." Jenny laughed. "I'm anxious to see my room though."

Inside, Ruthanna handed her a key and smiled broadly as she watched the two go upstairs. Phil deserved some happiness, and she was glad to see him get it.

Jenny's room was delightful, and Ruthanna had clearly gone well out of her way for her. Fresh flowers in a crystal vase offered a pleasant scent, a fruit basket sat on the nightstand, and wine was chilling in a bucket, with two glasses beside it.

"Damn," Phil said. "Even I didn't get this kind of royal treatment."

"This is just splendid," Jenny said. "I've stayed in some pretty fancy resorts and suites, but I've never seen anything like this. It's like…well, like the home I've always envisioned."

"Me too, only not quite this large. I want something quaint and cozy, something isolated and comfortable."

"I can see that. Phil, we really all thought you were crazy, running off to this place, but now that I'm here, seeing it for myself… Well, it's clearly healthy, and it's a perfect fit for you."

"Thank you, dear. Now, can we have a glass of wine before I freshen up for dinner?"

"I suppose I'm willing to share," she said, smirking.

They drank slowly, until Phil took her glass and placed it gently on the nightstand. He reached for her face, rubbing her hair at the same time. "Do you even know how much I missed you? Do you have any idea?"

"Well, if it was as much as I missed you, it must have been quite a lot."

He lightly grazed his lips against hers as he held her close to him. It felt so right to hold her, and he didn't want her to ever leave. He knew it was a foolish fantasy, but Phil relished the thought of having both Jenny and Solomon Cove.

CHAPTER 7

After a hefty breakfast, the two jumped into the rental car to hurry to Heather's office by 9:00.

She was waiting at the door and locked it behind her without even inviting them in. "We can take my car," she said, hopping into the driver seat and cranking up.

Phil and Jenny looked at each other and climbed into her car, with the feeling that she had a full day planned for them.

On the way to wherever they were going, Heather handed Phil several snapshots of houses on the cliffs.

"These are all beautiful," he said, but they're just too much house. I am a single man, and while I've got no immediate plans to leave, I may not stay here for a very long time. I'm looking for something smaller, maybe a fixer-upper, something somewhat…secluded."

"I see," she answered abruptly, not even attempting to mask her disgust. "In that case, I suppose we have some options, but I'm not sure you'll be interested in them. Believe me when I say they are all in need of serious repair. The most secluded is out on Carter's Lake, about ten minutes outside of town. It's the only house on the lake, and frankly. I've always found it quite spooky."

Phil and Jenny covered their mouths to hide their laughter, and Phil said, "Well, it sounds like it's worth a look to me. Let's give it a try."

"Okay, but don't say I didn't warn you."

"I'm not that kind of man, Heather," Phil answered, letting his laugh loose this time.

Heather did not reciprocate and just drove on, with a serious look on her face.

It did take about ten minutes to get there, and it was on the opposite side of town from the bed-and-breakfast. The old mailbox leaned so far to the left that Phil couldn't believe it was still standing.

"This is the driveway," Heather said, sounding a little friendlier now.

It was about a mile long, a nice drive in its own right, and Phil looked around at all the trees, foliage, and wildflowers. Before the house came into view, he saw the lake, so tranquil that it looked almost like a mirage. They were almost to the water before the tiny cottage came into view, and when it did, he instantly knew it was the home he wanted. It was desperately in need of repair, just as Heather had warned, but he fell in love with it nonetheless. He practically leapt from the car, even before Heather applied the brakes.

The place appeared to have been deserted for quite some time, but the stone walkway that led to the porch intrigued him. It was made from old logs and had a sagging tin roof. The front porch offered a view of the lake; it was so close that one could almost reach out and touch it.

"This is it," Phil said, with a thrill in his voice that Jenny hadn't ever heard. "This is the one I want."

Heather looked at him as though he'd lost his mind. "You can't be serious, Mr. Sawyer," she said, completely shocked. "This old place has been vacant for ages. In fact, the town's been trying to have it torn down. What makes you think you could repair it? It ought to be condemned."

The remark made Phil think of Drew Isaacs, and he only wanted the place more; he wanted to give it a second chance. "I want to see inside," he said, reaching for the doorknob. He was pleased to find it unlocked.

The wooden floors were rough, almost full of splinters, but the place was much larger on the inside than it appeared from the outside. The den was rather sizable, and the small kitchen was connected to it without any petition or wall. There was an old wood-burning stove and heater, and a large stone fireplace stood in the middle of the den. Phil imagined how great the pitter-patter of the rain would sound on the tin roof, a lullaby in its own right, and that only confirmed that it was the home for him.

"How much is she?" he asked, knowing money was no object.

"Well, it's uh…$15,000," Heather said, thumbing through her paperwork. "Believe me, that's no deal. As a matter of fact, you'd be getting screwed if you paid that. Are you sure you wouldn't like to consider—"

"I'll have a certified check for you tomorrow," Phil said, cutting her off as he walked through the rest of the cottage. There was only one bathroom, and it needed an update. The cottage had only two bedrooms, but he only needed one. Already, he was envisioning the possibilities.

"Phil," Jenny said, with a twinge of doubt in her voice, "are you sure you aren't making a hasty decision? After all, it will take a fortune to make this place livable."

"Like I said, Heather," Phil said, ignoring Jenny's comment, "I'll have your check tomorrow."

The realtor looked at him again like he was crazy, but she wasn't one to turn down a sale and quickly agreed to the deal. "Well, it seems your mind is made up. I'll see you tomorrow with the deed."

They rode back to town in silence, with Phil's mind racing with the possibilities for the old house. It was obvious that Heather was disappointed, but he wasn't concerned about that. He remembered the $800,000 home he'd left behind, and he was thrilled to death with the old fixer-upper.

* * * * *

Back at the bed-and-breakfast, Jenny shook her head at him, clearly appalled. "I can't believe you're serious, Phil. I mean, really! A shack like that? What are you doing? I just simply cannot believe it."

"Life is full of changes, Jenny, and I'm in need of one. I am ecstatic about the place, and no one can take that from me."

She rolled her eyes and faked a laugh. "You continue to bewilder me."

"Hey, we've gotta go car-shopping now," Phil said. "I've spent enough on this rental car to buy a used one. Do you mind riding out of town to the nearest dealership?"

"Will you take no for an answer?"

"Of course not."

She laughed. "I'm here to spend time with you, Phil. Where you go, I go. It doesn't matter, as long as we're together."

They let Ruthanna know where they were going, and he placed his boxes in her toolshed so they could drop off the rental car. They had to bypass the coast to get to Portland, where he looked at cars. He chose a used SUV, something he knew would be necessary to get back to his cabin. It was reasonable, so he signed a check from his out-of-town account and bought the vehicle right off the lot, much to the delight of the salesman.

"Perfect," he told Jenny as he sat in the driver seat and leaned back. "Just perfect."

She smiled and got in the rental car to follow him so they could drop it off. "You really are nuts," she said as she climbed into the SUV, "but I love seeing you happy."

"That's the attitude I was looking for," he answered. "Hey, before we go back to the bed-and-breakfast, there's someone I'd like you to meet."

"You've already made friends?" Jenny joked. "Boy, this is your kind of place."

They walked down to the wharf just as Captain Bill was just coming in with his catch of the day. "Hello there, mate," he said in a tired, weak voice.

"Right back at ya, Captain," Phil answered. "I just wanted you to meet my girl, Jenny."

"Pleasure," Captain Bill answered. He then turned to Phil. "Looks like you're off the hook for a while," he said. "I got a new mate starting tomorrow, coming in from Bangor. He's got a lot of experience, but he tends to take his drinking a little too far. I can deal with that, so long as he does his job. I'd like to know I can call on ya, though, should he need a break."

"No problem," Phil answered, happy to pass up his job.

"Hope to see around, mate. You did one helluva job."

"Thanks for the experience. I don't regret any of it. I just bought an old house on Carter's Lake, so that'll keep me busy for a while, so I'm glad you found some help."

"I know the place you're talkin' about, and you're right. It'll keep you busy for a helluva long time. Hell, if you thought lobstering was tough, you're in for a surprise. Maybe I'll stop by on one of my days off."

"I'd like that," Phil answered, hoping he meant it.

As they got back to the car, Jenny looked at him in total shock. "Please don't tell me you've been working for that man."

"I told you I wanted the whole experience," he said. "Besides, I made $40 a day."

"What!? Okay, that's it. Phil Sawyer, I am convinced you have totally lost it. You are certifiably insane."

"And what's so bad about a little insanity?"

"Jesus. If you're happy, so am I," she finally said, laughing at him and shaking her head again.

By the time they got back to the bed-and-breakfast, it was dinnertime, Ruthanna scolded Phil with her eyes for being gone so long, but he just smiled sweetly, forcing her to forgive him.

Laurel immediately brought their plates and smiled at them both. "Here ya go," she said. "Enjoy."

"I know you hate to leave this place," Jenny said. "It is so beautiful."

"So you didn't like my new home?"

"Let's just say I hope you finish it before Arthur or Charlie come to town, or else they'll have you committed."

CHAPTER 8

There wasn't much to the closing of the house. The certified check changed hands quickly, as well as the deed. Phil immediately drove to his new home, with renovations racing through his mind. He knew he would have to get a canoe or a kayak to enjoy the lake, but that would come later.

As he looked at the sagging front porch before him, he immediately thought of the old man making the birch birdhouses. He thought birch banisters and new birch columns would really give the porch a lift, literally and otherwise. Without any further thought on the matter, he went straight to the fruit stand and approached the man, who was still whittling away on the birdhouses.

"Ah, you're back," the old man said.

"Yes, sir," Phil answered. "I have a proposition for you."

"What kind of proposition would that be?" he asked suspiciously.

"First of all, my name is Phil Sawyer," he said, extending his hand.

"I'm Joseph Gibson," he said. "Now that we've been properly introduced, what are we talking about here?"

"I just bought the old place on Carter's Lake," Phil announced, then waited for the usual sigh.

"You're in for some work then, son," Joseph said. "But I don't see how I can possibly help ya."

"I know the place needs some major repairs. I love your birdhouses, and you clearly have a knack for working with wood. I need to replace the columns to hold up the front porch, as well as add some banisters. I'd pay you well."

"I'm too old to help you hold up columns," he said, "but I sure can make 'em, and I can put banisters in for ya too. When do you need it done?"

"As soon as possible," Phil answered, heaving a sigh of relief. "She looks like she might fall at any moment."

That made Joseph laugh openly. "I'm still committed to my stand here, ya know. I can work on your place in the evenings, as soon as you get me some measurements. The banisters won't be a problem. Shouldn't take more than a couple weeks, but you better get electricity out there soon as you can. That might take longer than you think. Start with that, 'cause they'll have to come from the city."

Phil was so relieved that he couldn't hide it. "Great! I'll be back in a day or so with those measurements," he said.

"Look forward to seeing you again, Phil."

When a customer pulled up and got out to look over the produce, Phil took that as his cue to leave.

Electricity was a must, and since he had no idea how to go about arranging it, he stopped by the sheriff's office next. The sheriff got a good laugh about the old house being back in use again.

"We haven't put electricity in a place for so long I really don't know what to say. We'll call in the nearest electrical company. They should be able to get you phone service out there too. Don't get impatient though. I can't give you a timeline, but I'll get on it. I thought you'd at least pick something in town."

"I just like the solitude," Phil said. "Besides, a low profile will be good for me."

"I s'pose so," the sheriff said. "How are things going for you?"

"Very well. I'm in love with this town and its people. I just hope they don't find out too much about me."

"Even my deputies don't know. Just don't make it too obvious."

"I don't plan on it. I'll be patient with the electricity. Candles will be fine for now, along with some camping lanterns."

"Brave man. I just hope the place doesn't fall down on you. It's pretty wobbly."

Phil laughed and walked out of the Police Department and straight over to the hardware store. "Hello there, Jacob."

"I already heard about the house. I guess you'll be giving me a great deal of business."

"I'm sure I will. Right now, I don't have any electricity, so I'm looking for some lanterns and a large supplies of candles."

"I can help with…that," Jacob said, sounding a little nervous.

"Are you all right?" Phil asked as he watched him walk erratically down the aisles.

"Yeah. Just some bad indigestion, I guess." Sweating profusely, Jacob rubbed his hand across his forehead.

"Hey, take a seat," Phil ordered. "Does your chest hurt, by chance?" "

"Just a little, sorta in the middle."

"How about your left arm?"

"Feels kinda odd, come to think of it."

"Stay seated. I'll be right back." Phil hurried over to the door and yelled for the sheriff, who was standing outside on a smoke break. "We need some medical attention over here right away," he said. "I think Jacob may be having a heart attack."

"I'll call the medical examiner. Our doctor is basically just on call."

"You've gotta be shitting me," Phil screamed. When he heard Jacob fall out of the chair and onto the floor, he hurried over and felt for a pulse. He found only a faint one, but it was racing, and Jacob's lips and hands were already turning a slight blue. "This man is about to go into full cardiac arrest! He needs medevacced out of here right away. Call for an air flight."

"I'm not sure how to do that," the sheriff answered, his voice shaking with fear.

"Well figure it out damn it!" Phil screamed when he lost track of Jacob's pulse.

The sheriff made a mad dash to the office, blurted out orders for a helicopter from the nearest city, and demanded that the medical examiner get his ass over as soon as possible.

When he returned, Phil was performing CPR on Jacob, working so hard at it that his own sweat was dripping down onto Jacob's face. "We've got to get to a cardiac care unit now," Phil said. "Half the deaths occur three to four hours after the symptoms begin, and I'm not sure how long he has felt this way."

By this time, he had a full audience.

"Get these people back now, Sheriff. We need our space. I'm not sure how long I can keep this up, but it's keeping the blood flowing to his brain."

The medical examiner arrived within minutes.

"We've got a myocardium," Phil told him between breaths and chest compressions. "I need some help. I'm exhausted. Let's work as a team. You continue with the compressions, and I'll do mouth-to-mouth for a while."

Dr. Chambers did as Phil said, without questioning his orders.

"Hold on." Phil said, stopping briefly to check for a pulse. "It's weak, but it's there. Let's just say a prayer and hope that helicopter can find a place to land."

Dr. Chambers looked at him in shock, wondering who he was and how he knew so much. He was too stunned to say anything but continued doing as Phil told him.

The chopper landed within minutes, even though it seemed as if it had taken an eternity for it to get there. The deputies carried Jacob to the gurney, and he was whisked away before anyone even realized what had happened.

Silence reigned as everyone looked at Phil.

"I just had a few CPR and first aid classes in college, and I'm glad I did," he fibbed. "I'd recommend it for everyone in town, especially if you've only got an on-call doctor."

Everyone left slowly, still in a state of confusion and grief.

Dr. Chambers looked at him with both bewilderment and suspicion. "I call bullshit," he finally said. "How do you know all that?" he asked.

"Like I said, that training in college is a life-saver...literally. In all my years, I've never put it to use, but now I'm glad I took it, and—"

"No way," Dr. Chambers snapped. "There's much more to it than that. You don't learn about myocardium in first aid classes, nor would you know that most deaths occur within three or four hours. I don't know of any CPR classes so in depth."

Phil looked at the sheriff, hoping for some help, but the sheriff was speechless.

He, too, was stunned and still shaking.

"Fine. I had a couple years of pre-med, but I don't like to talk about it."

The answer didn't seem to satisfy the doctor, but he didn't press the issue. "I'm Dr. Rusty Chambers," he said, lightening up a little. "It is nice to make your acquaintance."

"Phil Sawyer, and it's nice to meet you too. You're the medical examiner here in town?"

"Yep. Can't say I get much business, but that's a positive thing, seeing as though it's such a small town. We appreciate you helping out. Maybe one day you'll come by and visit our facility. It's not a very happy place, but it's as close to a doctor's office as we have in town. Our doctor is on call for things like colds and ear infections, but he's getting up in years, and we can't afford another one with our tax issues."

"I'd love to visit your facility sometime," Phil said, already knowing that it would be the wrong move, one that might inadvertently throw him back into a life he no longer wanted or expose a past he did not wish to share.

"You're welcome anytime."

Phil followed the sheriff into his office and sat down in a chair across from his desk. "I'm sorry about that," he said, waiting to be scolded. "I'm a doctor. I couldn't let him just lie there and die."

The sheriff was still not himself; his face was as pale as a ghost. "It doesn't matter," he said, openly trembling. "What truly matters is that you saved a life. I'm not sure how we'll explain it, but we'll worry about that later."

"I think I'll go back to my cottage for a little while. It'll take my mind off things and help me decide what problem needs to be tackled first."

The sheriff didn't offer a reply and just nodded his acknowledgment.

* * * * *

As he drove down the long gravel drive, Phil tried to clear his mind of the events of the day. He felt a bit of relief when his peaceful little cottage came into view. He was also thankful it wasn't cold out; he had a couple months before he would have to worry about that.

Jenny was there, sweeping the old floor, as if it would somehow make a difference. She smiled as Phil entered the little place, but the smile faded from her face when she noticed that something was wrong with him.

Phil explained it as well as he could, taking brief pauses as he told the tale. "There will be a great number of questions now. I may be exiled from this place."

"Oh, don't be silly. I am sure you're the hero of the day, and people will move forward from here. Just enjoy your fifteen minutes of fame. Things will die down soon."

"You're leaving tomorrow, aren't you?"

250 / G Street Chronicles

"Yeah…and I'll miss you so much."

Phil wanted to ask her to stay, but he just couldn't expect her to live in such an environment. She had such potential, and he wouldn't dare interfere with that. "Maybe you can come back after the renovations," he said, laughing. "It might take a few years though. You could always stay at the bed-and-breakfast. Ruthanna would like that very much."

"So would I. I know I said you're nuts, but I kind of envy you."

"How could you possibly envy me?"

"Because you've made a decision about your life, where you want to spend it and what you really want to do. Mine is still in limbo, and it'll probably remain that way for quite sometime."

"Well," Phil answered, trying to sound aloof, "if things get rough out there, you can always join me in this paradise."

He expected a different response than he got: Rather than laughing, she looked at him seriously and asked, "Do you mean that, Phil? I can't think of anywhere I'd rather be right now than here with you, in this old shack, with the most beautiful view in the world. I bet there are more fish in that lake than we could eat in a lifetime."

"I can't hold you to that," he said, with all the sincerity he could muster. "My dear, sweet Jenny," he said, rubbing her hair and then brushing it back from her face, "I could never take your life away from you, expect to live in some godforsaken place like this. You have so many options, so many possibilities."

"Well, Phil Sawyer, don't you think I'm old enough to make that decision? I've saved some money through the years, and I know this town needs a nurse. I could always call the doctor for prescriptions."

"Well, why don't you fly back to San Francisco and think about it, then make a decision? You can do it with a clearer mind there."

"Maybe you're right. I'll call the bed-and-breakfast in a few days, but don't expect a different answer. If nothing else, I can be getting my business in order."

"Just don't make a snap decision, one you'll regret or resent me for later. I love you too much for that."

CHAPTER 9

The next few days were filled with work on the cottage. Phil found a big renovation company in Portland, and they were willing to refurbish the floors, update the bathroom, and even help with the birch columns. It was obvious that they didn't know what they were getting into, other than all the money they'd make in the process. When they came out to do an estimate, they literally laughed.

"You can't be serious," the foreman said, looking at the cottage with a smirk on his face. "The first thing I'd do would be tear this old shack down and start over. Believe me when I say it'd save you a whole helluva lotta money, not to mention a helluva lot of headaches."

"I know that it may sound insane," Phil answered, "but there is something about this place, something that makes me want to save it."

The man shook his head and walked inside. He wanted to tell Phil again that he was crazy, but he knew it would mean a great deal of income for his business, so he just let it go. He walked through the house slowly, taking notes and making measurements.

"There are several things I'd like to salvage," Phil said. "I want to keep the wood-burning stove and heater, though I also want to install central heating and air. The stone fireplace is perfect, but the mantel is in such need of repair that it'll have to be replaced. Is there anyway to repair the floor without tearing it out?"

"Where there's a will and a checkbook, there's a way, mister, but to be honest, this is going to cost you more money than this disaster is worth. You'll need an extraordinary amount of insulation just to survive the winds and snow."

"Do you have an estimate in mind?"

"I'll have to go back and look over the plans, but we're looking at a minimum of $60,000."

"I'm not surprised," Phil said. "I'm willing to pay it, if you are sure your men can handle the job. How long will it take?"

"If you're willing to pay as we go, we can get started right away. My guess is at least three months."

"Can you start with the central heat and air? Winter will be arriving soon."

"We can do that as soon as you get electricity down here. Otherwise, we'll start in the bathroom. The plumbing won't be ready for a while, but we can also work on the floors."

"When can you get underway?"

"I can have a crew out here at the beginning of next week. I wouldn't plan on staying here while the work is in progress though. It'll be a mess, and you won't be able to walk on the floors."

"No problem," Phil said, excited at the prospect of at least starting the project. "I'll come down every day to check on the progress."

"Is there a number where I can reach you? I'm sure I'll have more than a few questions."

Phil recited Ruthanna's number by heart. "I'll be there most of the time," he said.

"I'm looking forward to working with you, Mr. Sawyer."

"Same here."

Phil watched as Zack Henry drove off in his lumber truck, and he hoped the renovation would go as planned.

* * * * *

He walked back into the bed-and-breakfast, wearing a look of satisfaction on his face.

"Don't tell me you're that happy about that little shack on the water," Ruthanna said, then immediately placed her hand over her mouth. "Sorry! I know I should be kind."

"Okay, okay. You may have your mouth covered, but your eyes are giving away your laughter. I know you think it's crazy, but I don't care."

"I'm sorry. I really am," she said, smiling at him. "It just seems ridiculous, that's all. On another note, you'll be pleased to know you saved Jacob Dorough's life. He needed triple-bypass surgery, but he made it through."

"I'm glad to hear it."

"It sure made Dr. Chambers suspicious. It won't be long before he figures something out. You might talk to the sheriff and consider paying the doctor a visit."

"I don't know, Ruthanna. If it gets out to one person, it'll snowball till the whole town knows. Before you know it, I'll be the talk of the town…and, more than likely, exiled."

"Don't be silly. I just think you should talk to Sheriff Murphy about it. Dr. Chambers can be trusted, and I'm sure he could use some of your advice on a few things."

"You know I can't practice medicine, Ruthanna," Phil said.

"You won't be. You'll just be sharing some…educated guesses."

"Maybe I'll talk to the sheriff. We'll see. The contractors will be working on the cottage for quite some time, but it should be fairly livable soon. The floors will be the first thing they do, and when they finish that, maybe I can finally get all my junk out of your shed."

"Don't worry about that, dear. You take all the time you need."

CHAPTER 10

Later the following afternoon, Phil decided to check on Captain Bill and his new mate. He hoped everything was going well and that he wouldn't have to return to the lobster business. He found the captain unloading the last of his catch. "How's it going, Captain?" Phil asked, looking at the tired, sweaty man.

"Hell," the captain answered, "my new mate doesn't hold a candle to you. He's older, and he comes in reeking of booze, but he's better than nothing, I suppose. Don't know a damn thing about working lobster boats though. I called his supposed last employer, and he said he ain't never heard of him. Wasn't a surprise to me. These people come and go, real hand-to-mouth types, you know."

Phil helped him heave the last of his catch up and grabbed his old, filthy brown cooler for him as well.

The captain patted him on the back, a little harder than Phil appreciated, but he knew it was a sentiment of respect. "Take care of yourself, mate," the captain said, grinning, "and don't kill yourself fixing up that piece of shit."

"Hey!" Phil said playfully. "A man's home is his castle."

"Or his shit hole," the captain jabbed.

After his trip to the dock, Phil stopped by the police station to talk to the sheriff, but he was out on an errand. "Have him give me call if he gets a chance," he said to Rachel, then gave her the number at the bed-and-breakfast. "It's nothing important. I just want to talk to him."

"Sure thing, Mr. Sawyer."

"Please call me 'Phil.' You're making me feel old."

"I certainly didn't mean to," Rachel said, blushing. "Oh, I almost forgot. I have a message for you. The electric company will be down at your place next Monday. That's pretty quick service around here, but it'll take them a while, since you're so far out and all."

"That's great news. Thanks," Phil said, feeling a little lighter on his feet, knowing that things were moving even faster than he hoped. "Have a nice afternoon."

"You too."

* * * * *

Back at the bed-and-breakfast, he was surprised to swing open the kitchen door and find Sheriff Murphy sitting on a stool, with a piece of pound cake and large glass of milk in front of him.

"Hello there," Phil said. "I was just looking for you down at your office. How are you doing today?"

"Pretty good. And you?"

"All right, I guess. Ruthanna approached me today about Dr. Chambers. He didn't seem to buy my story about the first aid class."

"That's why I'm here," the sheriff answered. "He's been asking a lot of questions. Like I told you before, I'm a man of my word. I assured you that I'd keep this secret between the two of us, but Ruthanna is right. It's tough to pull one over on Rusty. He's a good man, Phil, and he could probably use your help every now and then."

"It would be nice, but I can't practice medicine."

"I'm not asking you to, nor would Dr. Chambers. I just think you could trust him with an explanation, that's all."

"Well, to be honest with you, after all I've been through, trust isn't exactly in my vocabulary."

"I respect that, but if you decide to confront him with anything, I'll be happy to tag along."

"If you don't mind," Phil said, feeling his palms growing sweaty, "I'd like you to tell him. You know about as much about me as I do."

"If that's the way you want it, I'll talk to him tomorrow. I think it'll be for the best."

"Have you heard from Jacob Dorough?"

"As a matter of fact, I have. That's another reason why I stopped by. He's doing great, pulled through the surgery like a champ. Now he's bitching about all the business he is losing. He's a tough old coot." Sheriff Murphy laughed. "I'm sure you will be on his hero's list when he gets back home. They're thinking he'll be discharged next week."

"Who'll take care of him? Does he have a wife?"

"He'll probably stay here, so Ruthanna can play nursemaid."

The remark made her roll her eyes, but Phil could tell she would be more than concerned if he went anywhere else.

"As for a wife…" The sheriff laughed again. "Well, have you seen the old guy? He's not much to look at."

"Elias Murphy!" Ruthanna admonished, slapping his hand. "What a cruel thing to say."

"I'm sorry," he said, taking Ruthanna's scolding like a small child. "Excuse me, Phil," the sheriff continued. "He's never married. His folks handed the business down to him, and it's kept him busy through the years."

"He seems like a good guy," Phil said. "I'll sure give him enough business when he gets back. It should more than make up for his losses."

"I've gotta give you a heads-up, Phil," the sheriff said. "You're the laughing-stock of this town now." Elias closed his eyes, expecting another slap on the hand from Ruthanna.

"That's not funny," she said, fighting to hold back her smile. "If that old shed is where he chooses to invest a fortune, the man has a right to."

Phil laughed. "Don't tell me you're one of the doubters now too," he said. "I am anxious for all of you to eat crow when all is said and done."

"I hope we have to, dear. I really do."

CHAPTER 11

P hil awoke to a dark sky and the sound of hard, beating rain, the kind of storm that promised to stay all day. It was just what he needed, a respite from his work at the house and a chance to talk to his friends back in Los Angeles.

He tried Charlie's house, hoping to talk to Janet. Summer was nearing its end, and he wasn't sure if she had started back to school. To his delight, she was there and awfully glad to hear from him. He had so much to tell her, and she soaked up every word. She laughed when he told her about the old house, but she was proud he had found something to do with his time and someplace to call his own. He talked until he could talk no more, then finally realized he'd left little time for her to get a word in edgewise. "What's going on with you folks?" he finally asked.

Janet also had a great deal to talk about, especially Lilly. She had gone to cheerleading camp for two weeks and had come back exhausted. "She's quite involved in many things at school," she said, "growing into a young woman faster every day." She sighed deeply. "I'm so glad to hear from you, Phil," she said, her voice cracking. "We miss you so much, but we knew you'd call when you were ready to."

"I've missed you all too," Phil answered, feeling guilty for not calling sooner. He really had no excuse, and he silently scolded himself. "I should have called long before now. When the house is finished, in about three months, I want you all to visit. It is so beautiful here. It would be a great vacation. In fact, maybe we could all spend the holidays together," he said, becoming more excited by the minute. "Maybe we could have a white Christmas, for the first time in a while."

"You know, Phil," Janet said, "I can't commit without the consent of the rest of the family, but I can't think of anything more exciting!"

"Don't go getting my hopes up," Phil said. "I'm very serious about this. I mean it."

"So do I."

"Great," Phil said, thinking of Captain Bill, the cold weather, cutting down his first tree, buying ornaments, and the whole shebang. "Now, how is my boy?" he asked, changing the subject. "Is he working too hard?"

"Well, as always, he sees the whole community as his family, but that's one of the reasons I love him. He's been home more than usual, to see Lilly, but since she's a teenager, she's rarely home herself."

"I can understand that." Phil laughed, remembering his own teen years. "Tell Charlie I called. I'll try to catch him tonight. I love you all."

"We love you, too, Phil. Take care."

For a moment, he just listened to the buzz of the dial tone, realizing for the first time in weeks how much he had missed them.

He caught Arthur at the office, and he received the same happy reception from him. He also posed the question to him about Christmas, and it didn't take Arthur long to ponder it.

"I need a getaway," he said, "and Dee's parents will be out of the country. I'll have to talk to her, but as for now, count us in."

"Great," Phil answered.

"You sound better than you have in years," Arthur said. "It must be that unpolluted air."

"Yes, it must be," Phil said.

He could hear the receptionist over the intercom and told Arthur he would talk with him later. He gave him the number to the bed-and-breakfast again, and Arthur promised to contact him as soon as he had talked to Dee.

CHAPTER 12

The following afternoon, Phil received a phone call from Dr. Chambers. "I heard all about you from the sheriff," he said. "I can't say I'm surprised. I won't judge you for it, so don't be concerned about that. He brought your file over, and it sounds to me like you got screwed. Anyway, I can always use your expertise."

"Well," Phil said, "I'm not going to be much help on the forensics side. As long as I practiced, I still get the creeps with dead people."

"It really never gets easier. You just... Well, I won't say you become immune to it. You just learn to deal with it. It's the profession I chose. I guess it's a little weird, but somebody has to do it."

"I'm not judging you, Dr. Chambers. It is a vital part of medicine."

"Call me 'Rusty.' I'm getting older, and 'Dr. Chambers' makes me feel like I have one foot in the grave and the other on a banana peel. Know what I mean?"

Phil could only laugh. "I sure do."

"That's not the only reason I called," Rusty said bluntly. "I hate to start asking for assistance so quickly, but I sure as hell could use some. Do you think you could come down?"

"Well, the contractors are just working on the floor at the cottage, so it's off limits to me at the moment. I can spare the time. I'll see you in a few minutes."

"Thanks a lot," Rusty said, with little feeling or gratefulness in his voice.

* * * * *

Phil walked in the door of the facility, thinking about how cold it looked on the outside. It looked nothing like the other buildings in town and seemed as if it would have fit in better in the ghettos of New York. It was small, and the outer part was made of painted white cinderblock. He opened the door slowly, already wishing he hadn't volunteered to show up. He was surprised to be greeted by a beautiful receptionist who wore a friendly smile, despite the type of work she faced on a daily basis.

"Good morning," she said. "You must be Phil Sawyer. I am Alex Murphy, Elias's wife."

"Oh," Phil said. "The sheriff is a good man. It is nice to make your acquaintance."

"Same here." She smiled. "Dr. Chambers is expecting you. He's the second door on the left."

Phil entered slowly, afraid of what he would find. Luckily, he only saw a crisp white sheet covering the body.

"Good afternoon," Rusty said, his face devoid of emotion. "Found a fisherman floating on the water this afternoon, his boat still empty nearby. I figure he was only dead a few hours, but it looks like a homicide. Strong, blunt trauma to the head." He then pulled the sheet back.

Phil felt a wave of both shock and nausea come over him. "Captain Bill?" he said, almost in a whisper. "My God. I worked for him for a few days, just to get the feel of the place, you know? The real Maine scene? I visited him just two days ago. Damn."

"Well, I'd say that puts you in a bad position," the doctor said, "especially with you being on parole. It seems you were the last person to see him, and very few people knew much about him."

"Come to think of it, neither did I. He was just…the captain. He knew a helluva lot about lobstering, and he needed help. Beyond that, I don't know anything about the man. I never even asked his full name. You can't possibly think that I had anything to do with this. I'd never… Look, Doctor, my situation was different, not some random killing. Besides, I have an airtight alibi for the entire day, and you said he's only been dead for a few hours."

"The water in the harbor can keep a body as cool as a freezer in the morgue, but no, I don't think you had anything to do with it. I'm just afraid others might think so."

Phil heaved a sigh of relief. "Well, it's good to know you have faith in me. He did have a new helper," Phil said. "The captain said he was old, a boozer from Bangor. Bill complained that the man knew so little about the work that he checked out his last employer. The shipping yard knew nothing of the man, but Captain Bill kept him onboard anyway, because he needed a hand. Maybe someone at the wharf saw him and can identify him."

"Highly unlikely down there. Nobody gives a damn about anything but making the next buck and catching that next lobster. The two run hand in hand, I suppose."

"When will the deputies pull the boat out of the water and start investigating her?"

"When it comes to murder investigation, we just don't have the resources the police in the big cities do. We have to put a call in to Portland, Augusta, or the Maine Bureau of Investigation. More than likely, it'll be Portland. It's the closest, and the Maine Bureau isn't that interested in the death of an old, worn-out fisherman, no matter the cause."

Phil hid his shock and disbelief as well as he could and decided against his usual ranting of expletives, knowing it would be a waste of time.

"I know what you're thinking," Rusty said. "That's why any help from you is appreciated. When they arrive, the more I know, the better it makes this town look."

And you too, Phil thought. *Way to look out for your own damn reputation, Doc.*

Rusty turned abruptly back to business. He turned the sheet down with the perfection of someone folding the flag at a military funeral. He finally stopped when he got almost to the feet.

"He looks almost alive," Phil said. "He hasn't lost any color, except that redness on his cheeks from working too hard."

"Like I said, the cold water and Maine's cool temperatures tend to act like preservatives."

Phil looked on as Rusty carefully cut away the old t-shirt from Captain Bill's lifeless body. He stared at the large, white, oversized belly that had taken in too much food and beer through the years. The long incision on his stomach looked as though it had been cut and sewn hastily, not at all the careful job Phil would have done, as he was always mindful of scars. Then again, he had to remember that his patients were left alive. He supposed it didn't really matter on a dead man.

"I haven't found anything but the blunt trauma to the head. Check this out," Rusty said as he struggled to turn the body over onto its side.

Phil stood there, frozen, unable to offer any help.

"Put on some gloves, Phil. Jeez, it hasn't been that long, has it? Just pretend like it's someone who's hurt and has come to you for help. Hell, my receptionist handles this better than you."

The insult hit Phil's ego hard, which was probably the intent. He snapped on a pair of latex gloves, taking time to stretch them until he heard them pop against his forearm. It brought back memories in such a rush that he had to step back and reposition himself.

"Must feel strange, huh?" Rusty asked.

"Yeah. I'll be fine in a minute."

The two looked at the head and both agreed that it was a depressed fracture.

"Actually, there are numerous fractures here," Rusty said. "They must have surprised him from behind. None of the wounds are bad enough to be the direct cause of death on their own, but they were enough to put him out long enough to drown. His lungs were filled with water."

"I agree with you there. A strong person could have killed him with one blow, maybe two. Regardless, they would have had to catch him off guard. He wasn't a stupid man, by any stretch of the imagination."

"An older person could hit him hard enough to shock him. Another blow would render him unconscious. All he had to do was heave the captain overboard, and voila! He'd drown without ever coming to."

Phil shook his head. "I still can't believe this," he said.

"Well, thanks for your input, Phil," Rusty said. "I know you had nothing to do with this. Let's just hope someone saw that old man with Bill, or we'll have a great deal of explaining to do."

"I fully understand that. I can see the headlines already, 'Killer Plays House in Small Town and Starts Fresh Killing Spree.'"

Rusty didn't laugh or even change his expression. "Listen, I need you to meet Eric Riley, with *The Solomon Cove Gazette*. He also writes for *The New York Times* occasionally. That was his job before he moved here and married his girlfriend at the time. Anyway, he's one hell of an investigative reporter. He investigates and solves more murders than all the homicide divisions in New York combined, and he works right out of Solomon Cove."

"Sounds impressive," Phil answered, wearing a nervous look on his face. "Hell, should we just make a public announcement to the town?"

"Phil, we have a bit of a…little clique here when it comes to solving crime. The sheriff, Eric, and I all work on deaths around here. Eric's a good man and an extremely intelligent one."

"I apologize," Phil said. "I'm just… Well I finally found my paradise, and I don't want it to slip through my fingers."

"That won't happen. All I can give you is my word, but believe me, it won't happen."

"We have to establish some reasonable time of death," Phil said. "As I said, I don't know very much about forensics. In fact, I steered as far away from it in college as I could. I do know that the environment here doesn't help any. He was alive and well when I left him two days ago, and the old man had already left. He couldn't have possibly gone out in the storm yesterday. It was too strong, and the lightning would have made it impossible. That leaves today. I know it's virtually impossible to determine the exact time of death, but have you examined his body for any food particles? That could give us something."

"Yeah, I tried that. He must have had some breakfast, because I found a few remains of what seemed to be sausage and eggs, nothing that looked like lunch."

"Well, if there were some remains of breakfast, that gives us between two to four hours, depending on the amount he ate. Looking at that gut and the large incision, I'd say he ate a heavy breakfast. That leaves us with more of a four-hour window. My next question is, how did the killer get back to the wharf if the boat was found out in the water?"

"Good question, and the answer might lead us to someone who saw him at the wharf."

"I wouldn't bank on it. That'd be too obvious. And, what would be the motive? The old captain couldn't have had shit but the old boat, and they left that. He was blunt and forthright but not enough to piss anyone off to the point of homicide. It had to be planned."

"I'll set you up with Eric Riley. The two of you can go over and look at his cottage. Maybe you'll find something there that will help." Rusty gave him the directions to *The Gazette* office, which was right in the middle of town, along with everything else. "I'll give him a call to let him know you're coming."

Phil had no idea what he was getting himself into, but he went along with it just the same.

* * * * *

It only took five minutes to pull into a parking space right in front of the office.

An unattractive woman greeted him when he walked through the door. She had an irritating, nasally voice and was filing her nails nonchalantly and thumbing through the latest issue of *Vogue*. She buzzed for Eric and he came out to meet him.

"Come on back," he said, greeting Phil with the same unimpressionable look as the coroner.

"I'm Phil Sawyer," Phil said. "Nice to meet you.

"Same here," Eric said without extending his hand or even looking up. "Listen, I know all about you, so don't feel like you have anything to hide from me. We're shorthanded, so any help we can get from a man as intelligent as yourself is greatly appreciated."

Phil didn't respond. Instead, he just looked around at the articles pinned to the walls and others that were strewn out on the floor.

"I know I don't look very organized," Eric said, "but I know where everything is. If someone were to come in and move one thing, I wouldn't know where to find shit."

Phil laughed.

Eric returned the chuckle, thawing out a bit. "Rusty said we really don't have anything to go on. The Portland PD will come in today to pull in the boat, but I don't expect them to find much. They'll spend a couple hours and be on their way. If it doesn't make the evening news, they're not interested."

"Got ya."

"I understand you were the last to see him."

"Yeah, about three nights ago. He seemed fine. He had found new help, an old wino. The guy didn't seem to know much, but he was an extra set of hands, better than nothing. Bill didn't mention his name, but he said the man claimed he came from Bangor."

"Well, we may never find out who the old guy was, unless we find some fingerprints. He doesn't sound very bright, so maybe we'll get lucky. For now, let's head over to Bill's place."

Phil felt like he was invading someone's turf and expressed that to Eric.

"I don't think we're going to find much without going in there," Eric said.

"He's dead. He'll never know the difference."

"Gee, that makes me feel better." Phil laughed, a fake one that was obvious despite his attempt to mask it.

The ride took about twenty minutes, and that surprised Phil; he expected the captain to live closer to the wharf. The place was small and unkempt, and that was as he expected it. Parked in the lawn were several old lawnmowers, along with two rusty cars, none of which appeared to be functional.

"Nice place, huh?"

"Well," Phil answered, "it's kind of what I expected."

They entered the house; it wasn't at all strange for a door to be left unlocked in Solomon Cove. The place was littered with beer cans, dirty dishes, and an overflowing trashcan, and it smelled of cigarette smoke and old beer.

"Well," Eric said, "not exactly neat and clean, but it definitely hasn't been ransacked. They weren't looking for anything here."

"Strange," Phil said. "They didn't come here, and they didn't want the boat. What the hell did they kill him for? That early in the day, his catch wouldn't have been that valuable."

"Had to be a diver," Eric answered. "There is no other answer. He swam up to the boat, and the captain felt sorry for him and pulled him aboard."

"But he hated divers, resented them. He said they robbed him of the catches in his traps. He never would have pulled one onboard."

"Maybe it was a pretty lady, somebody who seemed helpless enough that he'd let her onboard."

"Possible, but you're forgetting about the old man."

"Like I said, no one on the wharf would have noticed him. He could have been in and out in no time."

"But there's something else," Phil said, "The boat was still floating on the water."

"Damn. You're right. I guess that blows our theory out the window."

"Not necessarily. Maybe another body just hasn't turned up yet. Maybe the old man was in on it. Then again," Phil said, "I don't have any idea what the motive would be."

"Hell, I'm beginning to feel like the Portland PD. It was just an old captain."

"I know you don't really feel that way," Phil said. "You've solved more crimes than I've done surgeries, according to Rusty. You won't allow yourself to give up on this one."

"Damn Rusty." Eric laughed. "Can't keep his mouth shut for anything."

They looked around some more, until they found a tattered address book with two names scrawled in a childlike hand: "Belle" and "Beatrice."

"Let's start with the first one," Eric said and dialed the number. "Is this Belle?" he asked in a calm voice when a woman picked up the phone.

"Yes. May I help you?"

Eric could tell by the sound of her voice that she was elderly and fragile. "Do you know a gentleman by the name of Captain Bill?" he asked.

"I sure do. He's my brother," she said, with panic rising in her voice. "Why? Is there something wrong?

"Unfortunately, he has been in an accident, ma'am. I recommend that you try to get here to visit him."

"Oh my goodness," she said, her panic growing by the minute. "I'll fly out as soon as possible. I live in Michigan, and our sister, Beatrice, is in Arkansas. I'll contact her, and we'll get there as quick as we can. What hospital is he in?"

"It is quite hard to find and not on the map. I recommend that you drive to Solomon Cove and drop by the sheriff's office. He'll take you to see your brother, ma'am."

"Thank you, dear. We will hurry. Tell Billy we'll be there."

"Why didn't you just tell her?" Phil asked when Eric hung up the phone, thinking it cruel to lead the woman on.

"For God's sake. She's an old woman. She never would have made it here before having a heart attack."

"I suppose you're right. Anyway, where do we go from here?"

"We let Portland do their thing. That's all we can do for now. Don't get your hopes up. They're a bunch of uppity assholes who don't give a rat's ass about the people here."

"I just feel like someone is trying to make it look like I did it."

"Don't get paranoid on me. We've got too much to do. Besides, no one knows about your situation but the people who don't doubt you. Just ease up and help me with this case."

CHAPTER 13

Officer Nevin laid his head back in the old, squeaky chair and glanced at the growing stack of parole folders that seemed to multiply before his very eyes. His desk was so outdated that he had to use a couple phonebooks to keep it level. The budget would not allow sufficient staff, much less new office furniture.

His case files numbered well over 100, a number that no one person could substantiate, not even if they half-assed it. He had earned his master's in social work fifteen years earlier, and his work had caused more arguments with his wife than he could count. Every day, he promised that he would be home early, but it never seemed to happen. He had warrants to send over to the courts for those who'd failed to report to him, and he received new files for new cases every day. On and on it went, a never-ending cycle. He was amazed that his colleagues could just walk out of the door at 5 o'clock without worrying about their jobs until the next day. It had never been his work ethic to do so, but when he found himself still sitting there at 9:00 p.m., he wanted to give himself a firm kick in the ass.

Reluctantly, he called home. "Hey, babe," he tentatively said to his aggravated wife when she picked up.

"Hey," she answered flatly, offering him no more conversation than that.

"I'm sure you've already eaten by now, but I was wondering if you'd like to meet me at Brewsters for a beer, maybe an appetizer."

"I'm a little tired."

"Listen, it's a celebration."

"For what? You making it home before 10:00?"

"No, smartass." He laughed, even though it really wasn't funny. "Today is a new day for me, or at least a new night."

"And what, may I ask, are you talking about?"

"I've decided that you're right. This place is a dump. I'm underpaid, overworked, overqualified, and I miss spending time with my wife. Tomorrow, I'm going to start faxing *résumés*. How does that sound?"

"Sounds like Brewsters to me. I'll have a couple beers, maybe even dinner all over again." She laughed a laugh he hadn't heard in far too long, and he pictured the corners of her mouth turning up in a broad smile.

"I'll meet you there in thirty minutes."

"See you there…and hey…"

"What?"

"I love you."

"I love you too."

He hung up the phone, feeling an elation that had been a long time coming. He wondered why it had taken so long for him to come to that conclusion. The writing had been on the walls for years. He lifted his head and stretched his back that always seemed sore from leaning over the files. He took the extra time to separate the new from the old and stacked them neatly. Then he reached down for his briefcase.

A brief stir in the room caused him to look up.

"Hello. Officer Nevin," Someone said.

"Hello," he answered, startled for a moment. "How did you get in here? The building was locked hours ago."

"I have…connections."

"Listen, if it's a file you want, you can have it. I have a few dollars in my wallet and two major credit cards, and—"

"I don't want any of those things, Officer."

"Then what do you want?" he asked, feeling the perspiration beading on his forehead and upper lip.

"I want you to revoke Phil Sawyer's parole. You know, the wealthy doctor who took out his wife."

"I'm very familiar with him, but I no longer have any jurisdiction over his case, absolutely none at all."

"What do you mean, you have no jurisdiction?"

"He moved, and his case is now being overseen by another parole officer in another state. Only they have the power to—"

"Officer Nevin," the intruder interrupted, "perhaps you do not understand the gravity of this situation. You have two days to put him back in prison, or you and your family will pay for it."

"Believe me, if I thought there was any way I could, I would. I damn well would, because I don't need trouble like this, but no parole officer on the other side of the country is going to listen to me. They'll just turn me in for violating my oath." He felt the heat of the tears rolling down his cheeks as his mind scrambled for something that might satisfy the visitor long enough to get himself out of the building and both he and his wife out of the country. "I can make a trip tomorrow to see what I can do. Maybe a little bribe is in order, and I can—"

"You are so full of shit. You're talking out of your ass now, just so you can walk out that door and report this. It is too late now, Officer Nevin. You are expendable. Goodnight."

He didn't even hear the last word before the bullet struck him low on the forehead, almost right between his eyes. His body didn't even move. Blood splattered across the back wall and up to the ceiling, and Officer Nevin, dead, still sat eerily upright in his chair, as if he was conducting a meeting.

CHAPTER 14

The house was coming along great; in fact, it was almost finished. The floors turned out just the way Phil had pictured them, and he was quite pleased. They maintained the old look, yet he felt comfortable walking across them barefoot. The fireplace was perfect, left rustic, just as he had requested, but his favorites were the banisters and the columns. Joseph had outdone himself, and the old whittler knew it and proudly showed his work off to anyone who'd pay attention. The plumbers and tile workers had shown up to refurbish the bathrooms and the kitchen, and the new appliances would be delivered the very next day.

"Mornin', Mr. Sawyer," the foreman said. "I have a suggestion for you."

"Go ahead."

"That roof is in pretty bad shape, and we're not sure what's under that tin. While we're out here, you might consider having it redone. That would involve replacing the plywood and the tin, but it should hold you for a few years."

"What the hell," Phil answered. "We've come this far, so go ahead and fix 'er up."

The foreman laughed and shook his head. "I have to say that the place looks a whole lot better than I ever thought it would. Wouldn't mind having her myself, but I'd never put so much money in such a small place."

"Sometimes you just have to live on the edge." Phil laughed, more proud of his house every day. When he heard an odd noise, it took him a minute to realize it was the first phone call he was receiving in his new home. He made a run for it and caught it just in time, before his old friend hung up.

"Hello there," Janet said. "Sounds like you're a little out of breath."

"I am. I was outside, and yours is the first call I've received on this phone."

"Wow. Does that mean I win a prize?"

"You certainly do, ma'am—a big hug the next time I see you."

"Sounds great. Hey, I just called to see if that invitation for Christmas is still open."

"You've gotta be kidding. Of course it is. Please tell me you'll make the pilgrimage to my humble abode."

"Yes, Phil Sawyer, we will, and we're delighted to do so."

Phil was so thrilled that it took him a couple seconds to react. "We'll have a great time, just like always."

"Can I bring anything?"

"Not a thing, but you may have to cook the turkey."

"I'm banking on it. Anyway, I'll call later for more details. Oh yeah, Arthur and Dee are planning to come too. Just don't tell them I told you."

"My lips are sealed. And, Janet, I love you."

"You, too, dear. I look forward to seeing you."

For several minutes, Phil just stood there like some kind of weirdo, smiling to himself. *Maybe things are coming together after all. Just maybe they are.*

After such a wonderful phone call, he was in such a good mood he decided to go to the bed-and-breakfast to plead for Ruthanna's help in furnishing his new place. He found her in the kitchen, making strawberry shortcake, which only lightened his mood further.

"Hello there," she said, smiling. "If it isn't my favorite boy. What brings you my way?"

"Do I have to have a reason?" he asked, hugging her. "I still live here, you know."

She smirked at him. "I'd never know it. I rarely get a glimpse of you these days."

"Well, I'm here for a favor."

"Of course you are. What is it?"

"Could you come to Portland with me to look for furniture for the cottage? I just realized I'm going to have to sleep on the floor if I don't go shopping."

Ruthanna smiled at the thought. "You're just now realizing that? For heaven's sake, Phil!"

"Okay, maybe I waited until the last minute, but I could use some help. I don't even have silverware."

"Good Lord," Ruthanna said, rolling her eyes. "How old are you now, about eight?"

"Funny. Real funny."

"Tomorrow might be a good day for me," she said. "Believe it or not, I have my weekly helper coming. You just happen to have caught me at a good time."

Phil leaned over and kissed her on her cheek. "I love you, Mrs. Moore."

"Well, you might as well call me 'Mom,' because I have to tend to you like a child."

"Anyway," Phil said, changing the subject, "I'm also here to pick up my boxes and take them down to the house. I thought you might like to ride down and see how things are coming along. It's been a while since you stopped by the place."

She reached for her old, tattered cardigan and nodded her head in agreement. "I've been wondering if you were ever gonna ask me, young man," she said. "It is about time."

Ruthanna stood by patiently as Phil loaded the boxes, some heavier than he remembered. It was strange that he still hadn't opened them, but he frankly had no desire to do so. It only took a few minutes, and he held her by her arm and elbow to help her into the SUV.

"I'll never understand why people like to drive these big old gas-guzzlers," she said. "You don't even have a family to drive around. By the way, that better happen soon, or I'm going to prearrange a marriage."

"My God, Ruthanna," Phil said. "Do you really think I'm ready for that?"

"Time is running out," she said, sternly enough to make him laugh. "How is Jenny anyway?"

"Fine. I talked to her a couple nights ago. Oh, and I forgot to tell you the good news. My friends are coming in from L.A. to celebrate Christmas. I need to reserve a couple rooms. My place is just too small."

"That's wonderful!" she said as a broad smile crossed her face. "Does that include Jenny?"

"Yes, Mother, it does. She's going to spend Christmas with her family and come here a couple days later. We can all celebrate the New Year's together."

They rode along, both satisfied that things were looking better. It wasn't long before they turned onto the dirt driveway.

"The first thing we're buying is a proper mailbox," Ruthanna said. "That thing is ridiculous, hanging there like that, just daring someone to push it to its long-awaited death."

"Yeah, it is pretty bad, but I'm not getting mail here yet anyway."

The cottage came into view, and Phil's body rippled with goosebumps of pride. The workers were busy roofing the place, and Phil was so glad he'd taken care of everything. He helped Ruthanna out of the SUV, and together they walked down the stone pathway that led inside.

She stood with her mouth open, obviously impressed by the improvements. "I can't believe it, Phil," she said, astonished. "It's absolutely charming, absolutely… perfect."

"Just as I told you." He chuckled. "All I need is some silverware and a mail-box, and life will be good."

While Ruthanna looked around the place, Phil unloaded his boxes and stashed them in the spare bedroom, very proud of himself for the first time in a long time.

CHAPTER 15

When they returned to the bed-and-breakfast, they saw an unfamiliar car parked out front.

"Are you expecting anybody?"

"Oh, that's Jacob Dorough's niece. She's staying for a while to take care of him. He's going home today. I've never met her, but it's awfully nice of her to come and stay with her uncle."

"That is nice. Doesn't she have a job though? How can she put her life on hold for him?"

"She divorced a few months ago and wanted to get out of town for a while. She'll be here for about three weeks."

They walked through the front door and found Jacob downstairs, with his bags packed and sitting beside him. "I couldn't leave without at least thanking the two of you."

"Oh, Jacob," Ruthanna said, placing her hand on his, "you never have to thank me. You're my friend. One day, the shoe may be on the other foot."

"A thank-you is in order," he answered stubbornly.

They heard footsteps coming down the stairs, and they both looked up. The man's niece was younger than Phil expected, probably in her early thirties. She had a small bag in her hand. "Hi there," she said. "I'm here to take my uncle off your hands. You must be the woman I've heard so much about. He sure thinks a lot of you."

"Well, the feeling is mutual. He's a fine man, and I'm sure he's grateful to have you here."

Phil studied her for a minute. She wasn't really pretty, but she was cute, with a friendly demeanor and wide, sincere smile. Her hair was cut short, almost in a bob, and was natural blonde. She was short but thin and dainty. When she turned to look at him, he was almost embarrassed, as he knew she'd caught him staring. "Hi there," he said, smiling lightly. "I'm Phil Sawyer."

"Oh my," she chirped. "You're the man who saved Uncle Jacob's life. I owe you dearly." She walked over, stood up on her tiptoes, and hugged him.

"Like Ruthanna said, there isn't any need for thanks. I figured he must be worth saving, since he has the only hardware store in town."

That made Jacob laugh. He stood slowly and reached down for his bags.

"Gimme a break," Phil said. "I think I can manage those bags for you."

"Don't need any help," he said, with aggravation in his voice.

"I'm sure you don't," Phil said, looking over to his niece and rolling his eyes.

She covered her mouth, trying to hold in a giggle.

"You've got your hands full with this grouchy old man," Phil said. "I'm sorry, but I haven't even asked your name."

"My goodness," she said. "I forgot to give it to you. It's Louisa."

"Nice to make your acquaintance, Louisa. I'm sure I'll see you around before you leave."

"Sounds great."

Phil and Ruthanna helped them load the few bags of luggage into the car then waved as the two headed off to Jacob's cottage.

"I saw that look, Phil Sawyer. I didn't fall off the cabbage truck yesterday."

"I have no idea what you're talking about. I just thought it kind of her to be here."

"Oh? Is that all?"

"Yes. Besides, I don't know a thing about her. She could be a serial killer, for all we know."

"I refuse to give that a response."

Phil laughed and walked to his room. "I hope lunch is soon. I'm starving."

CHAPTER 16

Phil was up with the chickens, dressed and ready to leave for Portland. For once, he actually beat Ruthanna to the punch.

Thirty minutes later, she finally came down, dressed and inhaling the coffee he had already brewed. "The stores don't open before daybreak, dear," she said.

"It's the little boy in me."

"So I see. Do you suppose we can eat breakfast first?"

"Let's get some on the road. Besides, you should let someone else do the cooking for a change."

"You won't get any argument out of me," she said.

They both enjoyed their coffee and headed toward the big city.

"How does this café look to you?" Phil asked.

"It looks fine."

Phil was surprised to see how much Ruthanna ate, but it pleased him, just as it pleased her when he cleaned his plate.

It was after 9:00 when they pulled into a furniture store with a pretty promising display in the showroom window.

Ruthanna laughed as she watched the owners unlocking the doors for the day. "I bet they haven't had a customer this early in years, especially one who actually intends to buy."

Phil didn't answer, for he was far too excited, like a kid on Christmas morning. As soon as they walked in, he immediately spotted what he wanted, a red and white checkered sofa that felt like sitting on a cloud. It was overstuffed and comfortable, just right for the cottage. Around it were two matching red chairs, along with two end tables and a coffee table. "I'll take all of this," he said, watching as the salesman's face turned into shock.

"Phil," Ruthanna asked, "are you sure you don't want to look around a little?"

"Positive," he answered.

"We need to look at the beds and mattresses as well."

The salesman walked them quickly to that section, afraid that his brief rush of good luck would run out.

This time, Phil and Ruthanna took their time, looking up and down the aisles. In the end, Phil chose two beds, both rustic. The mattresses took the longest amount of time. Ruthanna and he lay on almost all of them, laughing until their sides ached.

"Um, excuse me," Ruthanna said, tapping him on the shoulder, "aren't you forgetting something?"

"My God," Phil said. "What else is there?"

"Let's see. Maybe a table and chairs?"

Phil laughed. "Perhaps you are right."

They settled on yet another piece fit for a bachelor, a rustic table with matching chairs. He paid for everything with his credit card and made arrangements with the very happy salesman for all the items to be delivered the next day.

"What great luck," Phil said. "If only they knew what they were getting themselves into, bringing all that stuff up that driveway!"

"Well," Ruthanna said, "you've got that big gas hog. Let's see how much we can get into it. You still have hundreds of things to buy."

"Hundreds? My vehicle isn't *that* big."

"Well, we'll fill it to capacity," she said firmly, trying to wake him up to the needs of a household. "Other people have been taking care of you for far too long."

Phil licked his index finger and held it up. "Strike one, for the lady in the front seat."

She didn't respond to the comment but led him toward the bath and linen store. As soon as they walked in, she immediately took charge. She grabbed a cart for herself and pushed one in his direction.

"Jeez. Do you think I'm made out of money?"

"As a matter of fact, I do, but even if you're not, you can still afford towels and sheets. Now, you picked out the furniture, and that's about all a man is capable of."

"I'll give you that."

"Good. Now leave this up to me," she said as she put a dozen fluffy white towels in her cart, almost filling it. She then added at least a dozen dishtowels, along with hot pads. "With the weather getting colder," she said, "you'll need flannel sheets." She picked out two sets of dark plaid and two down comforters. When the carts were both stuffed full and overflowing, she pointed to the front of the store. "Come on," she said. "They'll be happy to hold this for us, and we'll get two more carts."

"Is all this necessary?"

"Let's see," she said, with sarcasm and seriousness dripping from her voice. "Are you planning to sleep on a bare mattress? Do you intend to drip dry when you get out of the shower? How are you going to wash or dry your dishes and wipe off your counters and—"

"I get your point. I just didn't realize—"

"I know, I know," she said. "You're lucky to have me."

"I've never doubted that for a minute," he answered, leaning to kiss her on the cheek.

A shower curtain and liner filled the fresh carts, along with a bath mat, extra pairs of sheets, and a few matching candles, both for decorations and in case of any power outages. When they checked out, they had to have help hauling it all out to the SUV.

"I hope I have enough money left to buy you lunch," Phil laughed.

"You better. I'm starving again…and stressed."

They looked for a diner and found one right away.

Phil was surprised to see Ruthanna order a bacon cheeseburger, a large order of French fries, and a chocolate shake. "I have to say I'm shocked," he said.

"It's rare that I eat things like this," she said, smiling. "I usually just eat at my place." She took a bite of the juicy burger and closed her eyes, relishing every moment of it. "Mmm, mmm, mmm. I forgot how good this can be. Today, I'm not worried about my cholesterol. It's not worth it. Life is too short." She also ordered dessert, making Phil feel as though he had made her day.

"Do you feel up to shopping anymore?" he asked.

"Are you kidding? Shopping is always great, especially on someone else's money…and a full stomach!"

They stopped to buy pots and pans, silverware, red dishes, glasses, various kitchen utensils, a wine rack, mixing bowls, and numerous other knickknacks, and Phil somehow made room for all of it in the SUV. He laughed as they made their way down the street. "I can't believe we fit all that in here," he said. "If there is anything else, we'll just have to make another trip."

"You'll see what else you need as you go along," she said.

"I know you're exhausted," Phil said, "but I have one more stop."

"Yes, I'm tired," she admitted, "but I'm here for the duration."

Phil stopped by a quaint little boutique, and they both walked in.

"Christmas shopping for Jenny already?" Ruthanna asked with a laugh. "You *do* care about her."

"Actually, it's for…another woman in my life."

"Do you care to share something with me?"

"No. Damn, you're nosy."

She rolled her eyes and laughed. "Watch your language, Phil Sawyer."

"I apologize. Please forgive me."

A young woman met them at the door, looking snooty and ready to make a sale. "And what may I help you with today?"

"This is my mother," Phil said, "and I'd like you to help her pick out a new wardrobe—dresses, shoes, accessories, and the whole nine. Money is no object. Just make her happy."

"Oh, Phil, I can't possibly—"

"You can, and you will," he answered sternly. He then turned to the woman and reiterated his order. "She'll need several different outfits, the whole shebang. I'll be back in about an hour, and I expect her to be treated like a queen while I'm gone."

"That will not be a problem," the saleswoman answered.

After leaving a stunned Ruthanna at the boutique, Phil walked into an L.L Bean store and purchased another pair of boots, one more suitable for Maine. Along with that, he bought a heavy coat, some long johns, several thick sweaters, and a few shirts. He took his purchases back to the car, then stopped for a chocolate ice cream cone, of which he enjoyed every bite. When he figured he'd been gone long enough, he wandered back to the boutique.

The young lady had indeed listened to his plea, for several boxes and garment bags, filled with the latest styles, were sitting on the counter.

"My, my. Won't you be the belle of the ball?" Phil asked.

Ruthanna looked guilty. "I just feel awkward accepting all this."

"Listen, you've been my savior for a long time. It makes me happy to do this. Please don't deny me that."

She nodded, still looking as though she feared she'd spent his whole inheritance.

He pulled out his card and handed it to the clerk, and they walked down the street to the full car.

"You shouldn't have spent so much."

"Ruthanna, my wife spent thousands of dollars on one dress. I think I can afford it."

"You are such a dear, dear man in my life," she said, then began to cry.

"I'll put you out if you start that."

"Really? You obviously don't know who you're dealing with."

They laughed for a while, then discussed more necessities.

"You can buy dishwashing detergent and so forth at the grocery store. Do you need my assistance for that?"

"No offense, but there are a few things I can actually handle on my own."

The ride home was a quick one, and Ruthanna insisted that she go to his cottage to help him unload. Phil's excitement only escalated as they carried everything inside.

"I'll take the towels and sheets back to the bed-and-breakfast and wash them for you."

They put the comforter in his bedroom, then walked into the guestroom. Phil and Ruthanna gasped when they saw the contents of his boxes, his old possessions, strewn everywhere. Phil was shocked, then saddened as he looked at the shattered frames of photographs of Charlie and him at a frat party and graduation.

"What the hell?"

"We have to call Elias right away," Ruthanna said. "I don't know what's going on here, but we need answers."

"They're long gone, Ruthanna."

"I'll make the call myself."

While she talked to the sheriff, Phil tried to pick up the remnants of his past, a bit shocked by some of the things Arthur had saved for him.

It only took Elias a few minutes to get there, along with one of the deputies. He looked around for a while as the deputy dusted for prints. Phil didn't expect they would find any other than the workers', his own, and Ruthanna's.

"I don't know what's going on here, but we intend to get to the bottom of it," the sheriff promised.

Phil could only nod, wondering who broke into his place and why.

CHAPTER 17

A ll the appliances and furniture had been delivered, and the cottage was finally complete, but it wasn't all that exciting for Phil anymore. Whoever had trespassed there had really broken his spirit.

He decided to go into town to take his mind off things and to pick up his sheets and towels from Ruthanna, the official sign that he was leaving the bed-and-breakfast for good. He decided to make that stop last.

As he walked toward the grocery store, he noticed an "Open" sign on Jacob's hardware store.

Please tell me he isn't up and running the place already, he thought. When he walked in to scold him, he found Louisa there, stocking the shelves for her uncle. "Hey there," Phil said, shocked to see her. "And what brings you to the store?"

"Hi, Phil," she answered, with that cute smile that Phil remembered from the bed-and-breakfast. "My uncle couldn't stand this place to be closed for another day, so I decided to ease his mind a little." She could tell Phil was looking at her in a state of confusion. "Don't worry, I'm closing to take him lunch. He can call me if he needs me."

"Oh, I'm sure he's in good hands."

"So that look is wondering how I can run this place, huh?"

"I'm sorry. If I can help in any way…"

"I've helped Uncle Jacob lots of times over the summer. Heck, I can probably run this place better than he can."

Phil laughed, embarrassed that his look had given his doubts away. "I'm sure you're quite capable."

She smiled at him, a grin that almost melted him.

"Would you like to go to the café with me? We can get a to-go plate for your uncle."

She blushed for a moment, then accepted his offer.

"Great," he said, as he watched her turn the sign over to "Closed."

They walked the block and a half to the diner and found that conversation was very easy between them, which surprised both of them. They ordered and talked until their food arrived. Phil told her he had moved to Solomon Cove to get away from the city, and she told him about her divorce and how much she loved the place too.

"So you're only here for three weeks?"

"That depends on how long my uncle needs me. I think it'll be a while before he goes back to work. He's happy I opened his store back up."

"He's a good man, one of the first people I met here. I'm glad you can ease his mind a bit. What do you think he'd like for lunch?"

"He won't like it, no matter what I take to him, but I think I had better order him some meat and a couple vegetables, hold the bread."

"So, that's how you stay so small? Eating all the right things."

"I have to admit that I exercise quite a bit as well. It helps to clear my mind."

"I can understand that."

They argued over the bill until Phil convinced her to allow him to pay for it.

"This is quite a treat, not having to prepare lunch."

"I enjoyed the company. I'll be by a great deal in the next few days. I just had a cottage remodeled, and I'm not sure how many things I will need."

"We look forward to the business."

Louisa walked back to the hardware store, and Phil headed to the grocery, where he singlehandedly purchased fruit, enough meat for a few meals, dishwasher and laundry detergent, cheese, and two bottles of the finest merlot.

He drove back to the bed-and-breakfast to get his laundry, but he had to leave in a hurry because he had groceries in the car. He was pleased to see Ruthanna in one of her new dresses and told her how great she looked in it.

He pulled up to the cottage, happy to have a fridge to put his groceries in. He made both of the beds, ignoring the mess of the break-in. He washed the dishes, silverware, and utensils in his dishwasher, then sat down to read. He had a few more hours of light but quickly realized one thing he'd forgotten to buy any lamps or light bulbs. "Damn. What was I thinking?" he mumbled to himself.

Frustrated, he climbed got back in his SUV and made another trip into town. He was happy to see Louisa again. "Believe it or not," he said, "I don't have any lights. Setting up house is more than I bargained for."

She laughed and helped him find the light bulbs, then showed him the small array of lamps that the store carried. "They're not very attractive, not exactly designer, but I guess they'll do in a pinch," she said.

"I can order some others from a catalog. What color is your furniture? You do have furniture, don't you?"

"Yes, I have furniture," he said sarcastically. "I did remember that."

"What color?"

"Red and white plaid."

"I'll see what I can do."

"Thanks a lot. See you around."

"See ya."

He left feeling giddy, just like a schoolboy.

* * * * *

Back at his place, he called Barnes and Noble and ordered some more books, then had a glass of wine. He decided to call Heather Thomas to invite her over for cheese and wine and, of course, to rub her face in the fact that the cottage had turned out to be a jewel. She said she had plans for the night but agreed to stop by. It was worth its weight in gold to see her face as she entered the house.

"I have to give you some credit, Mr. Sawyer. The impossible has happened."

"Just what I needed to hear."

"You invited me here to show me you could do it, huh?"

"Basically, yes," he said, laughing along with the realtor.

"Mission accomplished."

After she left, he grabbed the unopened bottle of merlot and some cheese, with plans to pay Jacob a visit. He wanted to see him, but he also had an ulterior motive. If Louisa hadn't figured it out by now, she didn't have both oars in the water.

She answered the door and asked him in with a wide grin on her face. "Hi again," she said.

"I just wanted to check on Jacob. How's he doing?"

"He's great, just a little antsy to get back to the store."

"Of course." Phil could smell the fresh scent of Pine-Sol and noticed that everything was spotless. He walked into the den and found Jacob watching a football game, holding the remote control in his right hand. "Looks like you've been busy keeping house, Mr. Dorough. Don't put too much on yourself."

He laughed wholeheartedly. "You must be kidding. It's that little princess in there. I haven't cleaned this place in years. Hell, I didn't even have a vacuum in this place till she brought one in the other day."

"Well, count your blessings."

"What brings you out this way?"

"Didn't realize a friend needs a reason, but I came by to check on you."

"You know you don't need no reason. What you got in that bag?"

"Red wine. A glass a day is good for the heart, though I can't say the same for the cheese and crackers I brought. Mind if I share a glass with you?"

"Hell, you brought it. The least I can do is to share it with you."

Phil laughed and got up to find Louisa in the kitchen. "Thought you might like to join us for a glass of wine. Do you have an opener and three glasses?"

"I'll look."

He went back into the den to visit Jacob, who seemed to be recovering well.

"I'm ready to go back to work," he whined, like a child.

"I figured as much," Phil answered, "but in the meantime, it seems to be in good hands."

"Yeah. I just miss the old place. Gives a man purpose, you know?"

Louisa entered with a tray of three small drinking glasses and a corkscrew. "This is the best I could find. My uncle isn't much on fancy stemware."

"Oh, I forgot to ask," Phil said. "Do you have a plate? I also brought cheese and crackers."

"Certainly."

They sat around the fireplace and talked for far longer than Phil intended.

"I'm sorry to keep you up past your bedtime, Jacob, but I enjoyed my visit."

"Me too, buddy. Come anytime."

* * * * *

Back at his own place again, Phil called Jenny. He was eager to talk to her, but he also felt guilty. It was a good time to call, since she was three hours behind him, and they had a nice conversation. He enjoyed telling her about his shopping spree and that he was now living in his cottage, a place she could send letters to. She seemed equally excited to hear from him. He told her about the Christmas gang, and she was happy, both for herself and for Phil.

"Have you found a new job?"

"Not yet. I figure I'll wait till the first of the year. My parents send checks every day, even though I'd been stashing enough money away for a while. They are so grateful for me to be away from that… Well, you know."

"Yeah, I understand. Can I still expect you to ring in the New Year with us?"

"Of course I'll be there. I'm sorry I can't be there at Christmas, but I'll try to make it up to you."

"Oh, I think I can come up with some way for you to do that," he said, "but it might put both of us on the naughty list."

They talked for over an hour before Phil hung up. He wondered if there was still anything between the two of them. He didn't want it to be over, but he wasn't ready for a permanent commitment. Besides, he couldn't picture her in Maine. In spite of what she said, the place just didn't fit her personality or her dreams, and he wasn't sure he was willing to give up one of his loves for another.

CHAPTER 18

The next afternoon, Phil received a frantic call from Rusty. "Shit, Phil," he said. "I need you right away. The doctor is out of town, and as usual, a terrible thing has happened."

"What is it?" Phil asked, afraid to hear the answer.

"Remember Joseph Gibson, the birch banister man?"

"Of course. Why? What's going on?"

"Well, he opened his mailbox this morning and found a timber rattlesnake. The nasty sucker bit him twice before he could get away. We haven't had those in Maine in years, and the closest place they're native to is Massachusetts. As a matter of fact, it's been years since Maine has seen any snakes at all."

"What are you saying?"

"I'm saying that somebody had to bring that thing here."

"Jesus. How is he?"

"Not good at all. His neighbor brought him in. He's swollen like crazy, his pulse is dropping, and he is getting delirious."

"I'll be right there."

Phil drove way too fast, but he got there intact, and that was all that mattered.

Rusty had Joseph up on one of the autopsy tables, smart enough to know to treat him for shock. "Should we suck out the venom or what?" he asked.

"Only if we have to. That's a thing of the past."

He tied a loose tourniquet above the bites and told ambulance drivers to rush to meet the Portland Hospital ambulance right away. He then told Rusty to call the hospital to make arrangements for a place to meet. He and Rusty followed the ambulance, praying out loud all the way there. The hospital staff was ready for him, prepared to treat him immediately.

Joseph was not a young man, and Phil was scared to death that he wouldn't make it. The two men sat silently for six hours, hoping the long wait was a good sign.

Finally, the doctor came out to talk to them. "He's gonna make it, but he's still a very sick man."

"Can we see him?" Phil asked.

"You can go in, but we've sedated him, and he won't know you're there."

"I don't care. I want to see him."

The two walked into Joseph's room, and Phil reached for his hand. Joseph was sweaty and so bloated that he didn't even look like himself. Phil looked over at Rusty, and neither could say a word; both were still in shock that something so crazy could happen in their little corner of the world.

"I'm getting a hotel room near here until he comes around. You take my car, and I'll take a cab back," Phil said.

"I'll stick around a little while."

Phil wrung his hands, paced for a while, then sat back down.

"Shit, can you just calm down?" Rusty said. "You're driving me nuts."

"Listen, Rusty, I'm afraid this whole thing is my fault."

"What do you mean? Do you collect snakes or something? You didn't put that damn rattler in his mailbox, Phil."

"Hell no I didn't, but…"

"But what? What are you talking about?"

"It's happening to everyone I know. Think about it. First Captain Bill, then my cottage was ransacked, then Joseph. Is this shit normal for Solomon Cove?"

"Well, not really."

"Exactly. Someone even killed my parole officer in Los Angeles. I don't know what to do."

Sheriff Murphy walked in at the end of the conversation, and Phil reiterated, a little louder and more animated.

"Phil," Elias answered, "I'm sorry, man, but I'm starting to believe you now. When we get Joseph out of this hospital, we're all going to sit down and try to figure out what, in God's name, is going on here. Something or someone is trying to screw things up for you."

"Oh my God," Phil cried out, as if in pain. "Ruthanna! What if they go after her?"

"We'll put a watch on her, night and day. She won't be in any danger. As for the rest of your acquaintances, we'll just have to be on the lookout."

CHAPTER 19

It took over a week for Joseph to come out of his coma and for the swelling to start going down. He was still in quite a bit of pain but was starting to look like himself again. "What are you doing here, Phil?" he asked. "You've got a lotta work to be doing to that cottage of yours."

"It's finished. I couldn't leave here without you."

"How long will I be here?" he asked, looking down at the hospital bracelet dangling from his arm.

"They might let you out tomorrow," Phil said, smiling down at the old man who'd suffered through such needless pain.

"What happened with that rattler? Ain't seen one of them around since I was a kid."

"We're not sure, but believe me, I'll make sure someone gets to the bottom of this."

"I know you will, Phil. I know I can count on you."

"Listen, I'm sorry about your wife. I didn't know you were a widower."

"Good woman, she was. I miss her a lot."

"Well, with my cottage finished and all... Look, I've got a spare bedroom, just waiting on you to recuperate in. You need somebody to look after you."

"I can't impose like that. Besides, I've got a business to run."

"Your business will wait. Without your health, you won't have a business at all. I could really use the company, and it's so peaceful out there. You'd enjoy sitting on that front porch of mine, looking out over the lake. Some nice man made me a really cool porch out of birch."

"I guess I can't turn down an offer like that," Joseph said, smiling. "It might be like a vacation, not being home and all."

"Just get some rest. I'm right down the street, at a hotel. The nurse can get me on the phone anytime. I'll see you in the morning, hopefully to take you home."

Joseph had already started to fall asleep, but Phil saw the half-smile creep across his face.

* * * * *

The following day, Phil and Joseph caught a cab and took a ride back to Solomon Cove. Joseph was still uncomfortable, and although he didn't complain, he was in a great deal of pain. The hospital had filled his pain medication, so they had one less stop to make.

"I'll go over and get you some clothes in a little while," Phil said. "I have a washer and dryer to wash what you have on. I'm sure you want a real shower. I have a robe you can wear while your clothes are washing. It shouldn't take long."

"Wow. I'm not used to the royal treatment."

"Well, don't get too used to it." Phil smiled.

When the cab pulled over the hill, Joseph spotted Deputy Evans outside the cabin. "What's he doin' here?" he questioned.

"Just looking out for the place," Phil answered, "but don't worry. I'll explain it all later."

Joseph looked apprehensive as Phil helped him out of the car. "Place don't look bad," he said as he walked in.

Phil helped him to the couch and saw the relief in his eyes; the man was clearly glad to be out of the cab, with its fake leather seats and that bumpy ride.

"Just sit a while. I'm gonna talk to the deputy," Phil said, trying to sound casual.

Evans met him halfway, waiting patiently at the beginning of the rock walkway.

"What's up?" Phil asked.

"The sheriff just wanted me to keep an eye on the place while you were gone. Some crazy shit is going on."

"You aren't kidding. I appreciate it. I've got Joseph Gibson inside. He'll be staying with me for a while, until he recuperates. I feel very uneasy sending him back home."

"I understand that. Let me know when you leave the house, and one of us will come down to watch the place and pay him a visit if need be."

"I really appreciate that."

"Oh yeah. The sheriff told me to give you this," Deputy Evans said, then handed Phil a revolver. "He also said something about it being just between the two of you. And here." The deputy also handed over a box of bullets.

Phil stood strangely still, unable to reach for either of them.

The deputy looked at him like he was crazy. "What's the matter? Haven't you ever shot a weapon before?"

"It's just...been a very long time."

"If you need a refresher, just let me know."

"I'll do that," Phil said, reaching for the gun and ammo, slowly and carefully. "Thanks," he managed to choke out.

When he walked back inside, he tried to conceal the box and the gun. Fortunately, Joseph was so tired that he didn't notice.

"Let me help you get in the shower so you can go to sleep," Phil said.

"Ain't never needed help to get in no shower. Makes me feel—"

"You haven't ever been bitten by a rattler either. Let me help you."

It didn't take any more convincing. It was a struggle to keep Joseph standing in the shower. He was exhausted and didn't want anything to eat, so Phil helped him into bed quickly, so he wouldn't see the ransacked boxes.

"I have to say," Joseph said wearily, "you did a helluva job on the old place. She looks good." And with that, he fell fast asleep.

Phil washed his friend's clothes and had them ready long before Joseph woke up. He hated to call the deputy back so soon, but he needed to get some more clothes from Joseph's house, as well as some more groceries.

The deputy didn't seem to mind and quickly pulled back down the drive.

"I'll try to get back soon," Phil said. "I just need to run a few errands. I appreciate all you guys are doing for me." With that, he cranked up the SUV and headed straight for Joseph's place.

The key was cool in his hand, and the gun was uncomfortable, tucked in his waistband as he entered the house. He hoped he wouldn't ever have to use it; he wasn't even sure he could if the moment presented itself. He was shocked to see how neat and clean Joseph kept his place, as he expected it to be more like Captain Bill's. It wasn't hard to find Joseph's underwear and t-shirts, and all of his shirts and pants were hung in an orderly fashion in the small closet. He didn't want to take too much, as he didn't want to make Joseph feel as though he was going to be there for the long haul, so he only took a few outfits.

He passed the hardware store and just threw up a hand to Louisa, not wanting to make his crush too obvious. The grocery store wasn't crowded, making it a whole lot easier for him to browse. He knew he'd need extra food and healthier choices to feed his friend. When his cart was overflowing, he made his way to the cash register.

"Got yourself a load there," the cashier said, smiling.

"I just haven't really bought groceries since I got here. I have to stock up." He then kindly helped her bag them and made his way to the car.

Louisa came out of the store to meet him this time. "I heard you have a housemate. That's very kind of you."

"Yeah, that makes two of us," he said with a laugh. "Maybe we can get them together and go out for a nice dinner sometime."

"You don't know how good that sounds," she said, looking tired. "I ordered a couple lamps for you. They should be in soon."

"Great. I'll be in touch. I've got a ton of groceries in the car, so I'd better get home. Nice to see you again."

"You too."

Phil unloaded the groceries and peeked in to check on Joseph. He was still in a sound sleep, snoring quietly.

He made himself a sandwich, along with chips and a soda, then sat down and put his sock feet up on the new coffee table. It felt good. In fact, it felt just right.

CHAPTER 20

The next morning, Phil met with Eric Riley and Elias. They all put their heads together but still couldn't come up with anything feasible.

"I don't understand. I don't really know who would want to hurt me. I talked to my friend, who's also my attorney, and he said the guards and warden are still incarcerated. In spite of the break-ins, nothing's been stolen. I don't even know the motive. I only know it all leads back to me."

"Why do you think it would all lead back to you?" Eric asked. "You killed your wife, justifiably so from what I know, but she didn't have any family, and neither do you."

Phil glanced over and saw that all the newspaper clippings about his trial were pinned to Eric's bulletin board.

"We're the only ones in town who are aware of your situation," Elias assured Phil yet again, "unless someone has gotten hold of an old newspaper from Los Angeles. How likely is that around here?"

"At this point," Phil answered, "nothing would surprise me."

They spent the next couple hours going over any possibilities.

"Wait! I forgot," Phil said, feeling foolish. "Someone trashed my house, my wife's car and mine, even before the house was sold. There wasn't anything to look for, unless Lara had something to hide. If she did, I certainly don't have it with me. The only people seen around the house were a nurse and doctor. I didn't socially interact with anyone at work, and unless Lara lied about a couple shopping excursions, neither did she."

"So?" Sheriff Murphy asked. "You don't have any idea what they were looking for, do you?"

"No," Phil answered, looking exhausted and confused. "I just know that's it's turning me into a crazy man."

* * * * *

The next couple weeks were uneventful, and Phil was glad for that, even though he was constantly on guard. He phoned Jenny to ask her to Thanksgiving dinner, but she already had family commitments, and he fully understood. He was envious that she had such close family ties, as that was something he'd always wished for.

"I love you," she said to end their conversation.

Feeling guilty, Phil parroted, "I love you too." He wished his feelings for her would come back, and he hoped they would if he saw her again.

He was enjoying Joseph's company, and the feeling seemed to be mutual. They sat on the porch with coffee every morning and a glass of wine every night. The moon illuminated the water, making it look like glass, absent of any ripples except in the wake of the stones Phil occasionally skipped across the water.

Two days before, Thanksgiving, Ruthanna called with an invitation to dinner, an invitation Phil couldn't possibly turn down.

"After Thanksgiving," Joseph said, "I'll be ready to go home. I'm well, all better. I just stayed around because I enjoy your company, but all good things must end, my friend."

Phil fully understood, for there was no place like home. He understood even more when he pulled into the bed-and-breakfast, the only real home he'd ever had, the one place where he knew someone loved him dearly.

Ruthanna met them at the door, wearing one of her new dresses and a long strand of pearls.

"You look lovely, Mrs. Moore," Joseph said.

"Well, I had a little help from a dear friend." She winked at Phil.

"I smell some delicious things. I just have to put my nose to the test."

"We're having a little bit of everything," she said.

The bed-and-breakfast was empty of any boarders, as it was a slow time of year, with the weather being so cold and it being a holiday.

Phil was happy to see a few of his friends there, including Jacob, Louisa, Rusty, and, of course, Laurel. She looked so much older than eighteen, especially in a beautiful beige dress. Phil knew she would definitely break some hearts when she went away to college.

"It's nice to see everyone," Phil said, smiling at each of them. "What is Thanksgiving if you can't spend it among friends?"

Everyone agreed, and Louisa handed both Joseph and him a cup of eggnog.

"Watch out," Ruthanna said. "That has a little punch to it."

"Oh." Phil laughed. "So in other words, you spiked our drinks?"

"Call it whatever you want, dear, but I need you and Laurel to help me in the kitchen. Everyone else can take a seat at the tables."

Louisa followed, ready to lend a hand as well. She floated around the kitchen as if she knew where everything was.

"So you spend some time in the kitchen, huh?" Phil asked.

"I sort of have to if I'm going to eat."

They all laughed as they filled each plate with turkey and dressing, yams, green beans, creamed corn, and macaroni and cheese. There were also baskets of cornbread and biscuits for each table.

"I guess we can carry two plates each," Ruthanna said, obviously proud to have everyone there.

They marched out like soldiers and placed a full plate in front of each person.

The tables had already been set to perfection, and Ruthanna walked around until all the candles were lit. Each held two bottles of wine, open and chilling, chardonnay and merlot. The room was filled with laughter and loud conversation, and that warmed Phil's heart. For a moment, he forgot about all the problems that had surfaced here, and he truly had much to be thankful for.

Strawberry and blueberry cheesecake and coffee followed the meal, and everyone ate every last bite, till they thought they would burst. Phil and Laurel cleared the dishes, and Louisa washed them. Ruthanna was delighted to mingle with her guests.

When the last of the dishes was done, everyone kissed their hostess, loosened their belts, and headed home. Phil let her know how much it all meant to him, and she believed every word.

He dropped Joseph off at home, and he could tell the man was happy to see it. He was well enough that he didn't need any help to get up the old stairs. He opened the door and, with a sigh of relief, invited Phil in.

"No thank you," Phil answered. "I think I'll go home, watch some football, and take a long nap. I may never eat again," he said, patting his stomach.

"That'll pass. Believe me." Joseph reached over to hug Phil, then changed his mind. Instead, he placed both hands on his shoulders and squeezed hard. "I'll never forget your kindness," he said.

"Just be careful when opening your mailbox from now on. Tap it first, and leave it alone if anything rattles."

"Ain't as dumb as I look, pal. I won't let the same thing happen twice."

"Well, the deputies will ride by the place on occasion. Take care of yourself, and don't stay out in that cold too much."

"I'm older and wiser than you, young man. Let me give out the advice."

"Point taken." Phil laughed and walked down the rickety steps, back to his SUV.

CHAPTER 21

Thanksgiving came and went so quickly that Christmas was right around the corner before they knew it. He thought about asking Ruthanna to go Christmas shopping with him, then decided against it, as it was something he wanted to do by himself, if only to prove that he could.

After much thought, he did invite Louisa to go. He knew she'd appreciate a respite away from her babysitting duties, and the store could afford to close for one day. She was thrilled with the aspect of a trip into town and met him at the car with a thermos of hot cocoa and two bagels, swiped generously with strawberry creamed cheese.

"What a treat," he said. "Not only breakfast, but great company too."

"I really want to thank you for asking me. God only knows how much I need this. Besides, I'm not even sure if my uncle has any Christmas decorations. I can really use a little Christmas spirit this year."

"I know what you mean," Phil answered.

Their first stop was, of course, L.L. Bean, which had become one of Phil's favorite places to shop. He was sure everyone on his list would appreciate a thick, classy sweater. He picked out different colors for Charlie and Arthur, and Christmas sweaters for Dee, Janet, and Lilly. He hoped everyone was still the same size, but he bought them a little big anyway, just in case. He also bought matching gloves for each and had them all wrapped in colorful paper, since he was sure he'd be no good at that part. He bought Godiva chocolates for the ladies, along with a different perfume for each of them, scents he hoped they would like. He chose two nice ties for Arthur and two casual shirts for Charlie. For Janet, he also purchased a gardening set, including thick rubber gloves, and he finished off with gift certificates to the Gap. He figured that would be enough to fill the bottom of the tree.

He stood back and watched as Louisa browsed the store, making a few decisions of her own. He looked on with deep feeling as she folded the shirts and sweaters after holding them up, trying to decide on the right sizes and colors. His feelings for her were different than those he had for Jenny. Even though Jenny was a kind, caring person, and even though they'd been through hell together, she would never fit into this place. She was a talented nurse, and he cared very much for her, but the feelings were simply not the same as what he felt for Louisa, even after knowing her for such a short time. His mind drifted back to the times he'd watched her at the hardware store, picking out nuts, bolts, and cement nails for customers. He smiled, not realizing that she was standing right beside him as he reminisced about her.

"My, my. Don't we have a lot of friends?" she said, looking at his many packages.

"Didn't I tell you my friends are coming for Christmas?"

"No," she said, "but what a great holiday that will make for you."

"They're coming from L.A., so they're in for a surprise. I'd love for you to meet them, and I know they'll adore you."

"Just coming to Maine from such a different environment might be all the surprise they can handle."

Phil let it go, knowing he could talk about it later. For the time being, he just wanted to focus on her and enjoy being with her on their Christmas shopping excursion.

Louisa bought several purchases of her own before they left for another store.

Phil had two people left to buy for, Jenny and Ruthanna left, and they would be the toughest of all. He decided it would be inappropriate for him to shop for Jenny while he was out with Louisa, but he bought Ruthanna a pretty gold necklace and a bracelet to match. The jeweler said it was one of a kind, and while Phil doubted that sales pitch, it was certainly unique and something he was sure she would appreciate.

By then, they'd made several trips to the SUV, and he was just pulling out when Louisa reminded him that they needed to shop for decorations. He drove until they found a variety store. He picked up four sets of colored lights, two boxes of red ornaments, two boxes of green, and even some candy canes. Then he spotted them, the gleam of silver icicles. While a lot of people thought they were tacky and Lara had certainly never allowed such a thing in their home, they had always intrigued him. He bought three boxes, at fifty cents each. He carried his last packages of loot to the car.

Louisa stepped out of another shop two doors down and walked out at almost the exact same time as he did. Her bags were full, and he would have reached for them if he'd had an extra set of hands. He was so proud of himself that he sang along with the radio all the way home. They were already playing Christmas music, even before December 1st. Louisa joined in, and they didn't stop crooning carols until he dropped her off at the house.

"I hope Jacob isn't too mad," Phil laughed. "Just tell him you'll work extra hard tomorrow."

CHAPTER 22

Phil couldn't decide if he wanted to cut his own tree or if he should wait for everyone to get there to help him pick one out. He was sure it would be a first for them, just as it would be for him, so he ultimately decided to wait.

When he got home, he realized he needed to clean up the spare bedroom. He was picking up the ransacked pieces of his life when the doorbell rang, giving him one more excuse to procrastinate on the project.

There, on the doorstep, was Louisa, fumbling with two large boxes.

"Let me help you with that," Phil said, grabbing them from her. "Please come in."

"Thanks. This is a lovely place."

"Thank you. I like it. It's rustic but homey. I know it's small, but it's perfect for just me."

They both stood quietly for a moment, until Phil realized how awkward it was.

"God, I don't know where my manners have gone. Please sit down."

She smiled and took a seat.

"So…what have we got here?" he asked, pointing to the boxes on the table.

"Your lamp order finally came in. I think you'll be pleased. They match perfectly." Louisa then helped him urge the lamps out of their boxes and the taped Styrofoam. It wasn't long before they made their exit, and Phil was not disappointed.

"You're right. They are perfect."

Both of them were the same color red as the furniture, as if someone had actually been in his house. They had an hourglass shape, with white shades.

Louisa placed them on the end tables and stood back to admire them. "Okay, it's up to you to find the light bulbs," she said.

He went into the pantry to fetch the light bulbs, then quickly installed them in the lamps and turned them on. "They're so cool," he said, smiling. "I think it tops off the decorating. I don't want to go overboard, being a bachelor and all."

"It's nice, really." Louisa grinned. "The view is splendid."

"How about a glass of wine? We can sit out on the porch and enjoy it better from there."

"I have time for a small glass," she answered, "but I just closed the store, and my uncle will be looking for me."

"You might want to give him a quick call. My place is off the beaten path, and he might worry."

She made her phone call, then met him on the porch. He handed her a glass of wine, and they talked about all the lovely foliage around them. A few colorful leaves still clung to the limbs, refusing to give in to winter. The conversation went on for over an hour before either one of them even noticed.

"Oh my goodness," Louisa said. "I shoulda been home a half-hour ago."

"Well, I've enjoyed the company," Phil said. "Come by anytime." As he stood, something dawned on him. "Wait a second," he said, stepping inside. "I almost forgot to pay you for the lamps. How much were they?"

"Believe it or not," she said, "they are a gift from my uncle."

"I can't possibly accept that."

"Listen, don't deny him this," she said sternly. "It's his way of thanking you for saving his life. You men aren't too good at that, so he just sent the lamps over instead."

"I'm pretty sure I won't argue my way out of it, so please just tell him how much I love them."

She laughed, then looked up at him from her short, small frame. "I'll tell him. He'll be thrilled."

* * * * *

Phil refused to put off the guest bedroom anymore. He picked up the biggest shards of glass, then swept as much as he could. He looked at the picture of him and Charlie, with their arms over one another's shoulders, grinning like drunken fools at a frat party. He let his mind drift back to that day and many others. Lara had messed up a good portion of his life, but that didn't mean he hadn't enjoyed a great one before her.

Among the photographs were some of his parents, both of whom died the year he entered college. Rushes of memories floated back, although not many good ones. His parents were not exactly loving or affectionate, but they weren't abusive either. With all his heart, he wished he could conjure up one fond memory of their time together. They never had a Christmas tree or stockings, and the Easter Bunny and Tooth Fairy never visited their house. He was, however, always clothed and well fed. He thought maybe their neglect, the fact that they basically ignored him, had caused him to delve into books, which wasn't necessarily a bad thing. He placed those photos in the bottom of the box. He was sure he would never look at them again, but he would have felt like a traitor for throwing them out.

He came across pictures of Janet and Charlie's wedding, in which he served as the best man. Their smiles were huge, understandably so, for it was a good day. He put those photos aside to share with Lilly, and he would choose one to frame and put on the mantel. He found his high school and college yearbooks, which he stowed in the box with his parents' photos. He found his college ring under the bed and had to lie on his stomach to reach it. It was too big now, as he was much smaller than he had been in years.

There were two mementos in particular that sent him into an emotional swirl. The first was his worn-out, oversized, favorite sweatshirt from Harvard. He took a moment to feel its softness, almost like a baby's blanket. Lara detested when he wore it, but now he quickly put in on over his t-shirt, and he loved the feel of it. His medical diploma was still intact in its frame. He picked it up carefully, as if it was a Faberge egg. It reminded him of hard work, dedication, sleepless nights, and good times. He ran his finger across the frame, as if to make sure it was real. He decided to hang it above the mantel as well, for it was something to be proud of, something he'd worked hard to earn, and he would tell the truth to anyone who questioned it.

His trip down Memory Lane gave him an idea: He would call the school store at Harvard in the morning. It would be great for Charlie, Arthur, and him to sport new sweatshirts, and he knew that would make the alumni memories roll over the holidays.

CHAPTER 23

The rain and wind were blowing so hard against the windshield that it was difficult for Alex to even see where she was going. It reminded her of the tornado in *The Wizard of Oz*. Elias was already at work and had called to discourage her from heading out in the weather, but she knew stacks of files were waiting on her desk; she was tasked with revamping the latest filing system, and it was a big job. They had finally gotten a computer, so she intended to start a program that would hold the same information the hard copies held.

She pulled up to the building, as close to the door as she could, and looked around for Rusty's car. He wasn't there yet, and she couldn't wait for him. It was the first time she had ever beaten him to work. She felt guilty for a minute and wondered if he had had an accident. She rummaged through her back seat, looking for her umbrella, knowing it was more trouble than it would prove to be worth, since the storm was fierce and she only had to walk a few steps. Nevertheless, she found it and opened it as she stepped out of the car, only to have the wind blow it almost out of her hands. The only thing that remained dry was her hair. Her clothes stuck to her body like glue, and she left a trail of water as her shoes squeaked across the tile.

"Damn," she said out loud as she grabbed a couple of towels in her office. "Now I'll be cold all day." She started the coffee and plopped down in her seat.

Deputy Sam Ware answered the phone when she called the Police Department. "Good morning, Sam," she said, "Great weather out there, huh?"

"Yeah. Makes me wanna go for a nice walk," he joked, with no humor in his tone. In spite of his monotone voice, he had a great personality, and Alex really liked him.

"Can I please speak to that husband of mine?"

"One minute, ma'am."

She smiled in spite of herself as she pictured him walking slowly back to Elias's office.

"Well? I take it you made it," he said as he picked up the phone.

"Of course."

"You're such a stubborn woman. Do you know you could have—" he started.

"I thought that was one of the reasons you love me, because I'm… independent."

"Independent and having a car accident are not quite the same, dear, but I'm glad to hear you made it in one piece."

"Listen," she said, whispering in the phone, "I beat Rusty to work this morning. Won't he be pissed when he finds out I can brew coffee too?"

Elias didn't like it, but he knew that Rusty, in his old age, was probably not even going to bother to come in because of the nasty weather. "I don't like you being there alone. Make sure you lock the doors behind you."

"Done, Captain." She laughed. "I'll talk to you later."

"Call me when Rusty gets there."

"Ten-four."

Time flew, so fast Alex didn't even realize how much had passed. Even if Rusty decided not to come in, she was sure he would have called. Her concern grew, enough to make her call Elias.

Sam answered the phone again, probably remaining at the station to stay out of the storm.

"I hate to bother you again, but can I speak to my husband?"

"Not a problem, ma'am," he said slowly. "I'll get him now."

Elias answered the phone quickly. "What's wrong, Alex? Is everything okay over there?"

"Yeah. I'm just concerned about Rusty. He still hasn't made it in yet, and he didn't even call."

"Don't worry yet. I'll send Sam over to his place. Maybe he had a small accident. Fender-benders aren't uncommon, Mrs. Murphy, on a day like this."

"Point taken," she answered.

After two long hours, Elias appeared at the door. "Couldn't find him anywhere."

The pit of Alex's stomach began to churn. "I think I'm gonna be sick," she said. "Something is wrong. This isn't like him, not at all."

"Don't worry," Elias said. "We'll get to the bottom of it. Let me make a couple calls."

His first call was to Eric Riley, and his second was to Phil Sawyer, and they both arrived at the medical examiner's office as quickly as they could, within fifteen minutes. He explained the situation to them both.

"What did I tell you?" Phil asked, his face going ashen. "What the hell did I tell you? He's dead. I just know it," his said, his voice growing loud, like someone at a college football game.

"Phil, please," Elias said calmly. "My wife is already a wreck."

"I'm sorry," he said, feeling as though it was the final straw.

"We have to remain calm," Eric said. "There's gotta be an explanation for all this, and we aren't gonna solve it if we can't think clearly."

"Think clearly?" Phil asked. "How can I do that, knowing this is my damn fault?"

"Phil, you've gotta pull it together," Elias interjected. "His car could be in a ravine somewhere. I've got all my deputies on it. It is only a matter of time before we solve the problem."

"I sure as hell hope so. The weight of this guilt is getting too heavy for me."

"Could he be around the office?" Eric questioned. "He often stayed late. Maybe he had a heart attack."

"That's a thought," Elias said, "but where is his car?"

"Hmm. Don't know," Eric said, "but it's worth a look."

The autopsy room was closed, as usual, and Elias was the first to open it. He gagged when he saw blood all over the floor, so much that it was in coagulated pools. He stepped out to vomit on the floor. "Go tell Alex to go straight home," he said to Sam as he wiped the drool off his chin with his long-sleeved shirt. "Tell her to lock all the doors and to get out her .22."

Sam did exactly as he was told and refused to answer any of Alex's panicked questions.

"Jesus! What happened to him?"

Phil couldn't believe it, but he didn't yet feel the urge to vomit; he was too concerned about what had happened to his friend, who was lying on the floor, covered with a bloody sheet. "Sam, I need your help to turn him over for me."

Sam did as he was asked, closing his eyes periodically.

There was a stab wound just below the shoulder and one to the back of his leg. His hands were bound with thick, rough rope, so tight it had left bruises and abrasions.

"Those would have been painful but not enough to kill him. It would have definitely been enough to double him over. Let's turn him back over. These wounds didn't kill him, even if he was left all night to bleed."

They slowly rolled him over, afraid of what they would find, which was exactly what Phil expected: the Y incision, used in autopsies. Again Elias stepped in the hallway to puke, then returned to the room.

"This isn't what any of us wants to hear," Phil said, "but he was alive when this autopsy began."

"What in the hell do you mean?" Elias asked, afraid to hear the answer.

"When an autopsy is performed on someone who's already dead… Well, since the heart isn't pumping, there's no blood. These wounds are bleeding, a lot."

"So what you're telling us is that he was alive when the motherfucker did this to him?" Elias said. "He suffered through all this torturous shit?"

"Unfortunately, yes, though once the scalpel began its job, he wouldn't have lasted long. The blood loss would have been quick. Most likely, he passed out from that or the pain."

They all stood silently, turning their heads away from the body. It was too much for any of them to fathom.

Elias broke the silence. "We need help, really, really bad. Sam, call the Maine

Bureau of Investigation. They'll jump on this."

"We can't disturb the crime scene," Phil said, "but I have to put a clean sheet on top of this bloody one. The man deserves some respect."

Elias began to cry like a baby, leaving Phil at a loss for words. He felt uncomfortable reaching over to hold him, so he patted him on the back.

"I wish there was something I could say, man. I really do. This has to be a tragic event for you. I only knew him for a short time, but I grew to respect him. He was a good man."

"You're damn right he was," Elias said, "and although I don't believe you're doing this shit, Phil, you are somehow responsible for this. Somebody's following you, and I sure as hell wish they wouldn't have followed you here. You stopped in the wrong town, my friend," he said, his voice oozing with sarcasm and hatred. "Maybe it's time for you to move on down the line."

"You're right," Phil said. "You're absolutely right. I'll leave two days after Christmas. I just need some time to get my shit together, and then I'll be on my way."

CHAPTER 24

With Christmas just four days away, Phil decided he couldn't change his plans; it wouldn't be fair to his friends. He had to act as if nothing was wrong. He decided to go ahead and cut down a tree, because he wouldn't have time to waste on it once they got there. He preferred to spend time visiting with them, especially since it would probably be his last. After that, he would be on the run. He refused to report to his parole officer any longer, just a fugitive from justice. He wouldn't be able to be tracked with a new name, at least until the police caught up with him.

He found a beautiful fir tree, then realized he had forgotten a stand for it, so he fashioned one out of lumber scraps left over from his remodel. He knew the tree would dry up soon, but it would last for a few days. He spent the next day purchasing eight bottles of wine and six twelve-packs of imported beer. He drank himself into oblivion for the next three days.

Ruthanna had someone drop her off for a visit, and she looked at him with worry. The deputies had explained everything to her, but instead of drinking, she had spent three sleepless nights doing nothing but crying. She hugged him hard. "You're a mess," she scolded. "You can't drink any of it away, so you might as well stop trying."

"It helps to be numb. I just have to pull myself together before my friends arrive, and then I'll be on my way."

"Elias didn't mean what he said. It's not like him to be that cruel. It was just... in the heat of the moment."

"I can't blame him, Ruthanna. It's my fault, this whole horrible tragedy...or rather, tragedies. It is time for me to move on. This was the perfect little town, and I've turned it into the killing fields, a damn bloodbath."

"I love you, Phil," she said, tears cascading down her face. "I love you like a son."

"I love you too," Phil said, too drunk to cry anymore. "I'll never forget you, as long as I live. You're the only real mother I've really ever known."

"Phil, I can't take this pain anymore." With that, she walked out and got into the car that was waiting on her, and they were off.

Phil grabbed another beer from the fridge.

* * * * *

On Christmas morning, he lit the tree and stood back, proud of what he had done. He decided to wash away the memories and enjoy his friends for two days. It was only fair to them. He knew he had to make a trip to the grocery store, so he dragged himself there, nursing a hangover that wouldn't seem to go away.

He bought a ham and turkey, along with several other things. The cashier didn't look his way and just spat his total at him in a spiteful voice. He was hurt, but he had only two more days to worry about it. He had already decided he would leave the cabin to Joseph, someone he knew would enjoy and appreciate it.

In about three hours, the crowd would begin arriving. He put on a Christmas CD and tried desperately to get into the mood. He opened a beer, thinking a little hair of the dog that had bitten him might help his hangover. It did, along with four Tylenol capsules.

Babs stopped by, wearing a sad look on her face, to deliver a basket of home-made cookies and brownies. She didn't say much of anything, other than to wish him happy holidays.

Realizing he hadn't eaten in days, Phil mindlessly ate two cookies and a brownie.

It wasn't long before he heard two cabs pull up, and he rushed out to meet everyone. He forgot about everything that had happened when he hugged them all. They all seemed just as happy to see him. They looked out at the lake and the front of the cabin and were all quite envious.

"You were right about the place," Janet said. "I'm so happy for you."

Phil smiled and nodded at her. *If she only knew.* "Come in, come in," he said, excited to lead the way.

They knew they would be spending the night at the bed-and-breakfast, but other than that, they would spend their days with him. Lilly had grown into a beautiful woman, much taller than he expected. They all looked great, and Dee didn't waste any time in showing off her engagement ring.

"We wanted to wait and see your face when you found out," she giggled.

"Wow! What a rock." Phil laughed. "I think I may have paid for that."

That remark, no matter how true, got a laugh out of Arthur.

Janet looked at the tree, then back at Phil. "Somehow I knew that if you decorated a tree, it would have those gaudy red and green balls. I think that's a man thing."

This time, they all laughed.

"The only hope of salvaging it is to string popcorn and cranberries. Thank goodness I thought of you and brought some along."

Charlie chuckled. "Remember that night we popped all the corn for Janet's class? You don't have those worries now. Now you're just living the good life."

"What can I say, my man?" Phil smiled. "Some of us just have it like that. How'd you get all these tree decorations here Janet?"

"Actually, via carryon. It stunk up the whole plane with the popcorn, but sometimes you just have to do what you have to do."

Phil shared a genuine smile of happiness filled with sadness.

It took over two hours for them to complete their job, and they were all exhausted, even with the help of the beer and wine. The tree looked like something out of a magazine, one Phil had only dreamt of. Even with the so-called tacky red and green ornaments, he was proud of it.

"Let's open gifts," he said, excited to hand out the things he'd bought.

"Sounds good to me," Lilly answered.

"You two kids," Arthur laughed.

"You know you want to open yours too," Phil said.

They gathered around the tree and let Lilly pass out the gifts. The mound seemed to grow by the minute.

"My goodness," Janet said. "This is the biggest Christmas we've ever had."

They all loved the things Phil had picked out for them, especially the sweaters. The ladies immediately put theirs on, making Phil feel like a success.

Lilly had made potholders for everyone, and since she had a part-time job, she also bought everyone a special ornament.

"Lilly, if you only knew how much I needed these potholders," Phil said, "and obviously, according to some people, I needed the beautiful ornament as well."

Janet and Charlie had brought so many gifts that Phil wondered how they had gotten them on the plane, and Arthur and Dee weren't any different.

"I suppose we should get busy on Christmas dinner," Phil said. "I already started the turkey and ham in the oven."

"So that's what we smell," Dee said. "Maybe you're learning to take care of yourself after all, but you'd better leave the real cooking to us."

Phil rolled his eyes. "Fine. The men and I will sit on the front porch with our beer and make a bonfire for later. Isn't it s'mores you Girl Scouts like?"

"There's nothing better," Janet said.

The guys grabbed a couple beers each and headed to the front porch.

"I have to say," Arthur said, "this is a beautiful place. The lake is so serene. I could sit here forever."

"This is what you need," Phil said. "Get away from all that stress and live the easy life."

"Like he's gonna do that," Charlie said, laughing. "You're preaching to the choir on that one."

"Let's walk down and make a fire. I've got the wood ready to go. There are a lot of things I need to tell you guys."

The bonfire burned hard enough to keep them warm, especially with their new gloves.

"Is there a problem, Phil?" Charlie asked. "I don't see any problems here."

Phil told them about everything, from the great reception of the sheriff to all the crazy things that had followed. In spite of the friends, food, and liquor, he quickly found himself in that deep hole of depression again.

"Why don't I go get another round of beer?" Charlie said, getting up slowly. He returned quickly, trying to keep his expression away from the girls.

"The sheriff also said I have to move on down the road."

"Oh, Phil," Arthur said, with deep sadness. "I wish we could come up with someone who has a vendetta against you, a strong enough vendetta to kill."

"I've racked my brain enough for all of us. None of it makes any sense."

They heard the crunch of gravel as Louisa made her way down the driveway. "Merry Christmas!" she said happily as she exited the vehicle. She was carrying a big basket filled with steaming homemade breads and desserts. "I thought you might enjoy these."

"We sure will. Let me introduce you to my friends. This is Arthur and Charlie, my two best friends. Guys, this is Louisa. She's running the hardware store in town, until her uncle gets well enough to take over again."

"It's my pleasure," she said, smiling brightly.

"Now, you must come in to meet everyone else." He walked her in and carried the basket for her. "Ladies, this is a good friend of mine, Louisa." He introduced all of them, then passed the basket to Janet.

"Oh my goodness," she said, "an honest-to-goodness cook. It is great to meet you. Won't you stay for dinner?"

"It sounds wonderful, but I have a sick uncle to take care of, and we've got a small ham cooking, with all the trimmings. Thank you for asking anyway."

"You're welcome. It was nice to meet you."

"Same here. Have a good holiday."

Phil walked her to the car and looked sad as she drove off.

The men never acknowledged her, as they were far too deep in thought. It wasn't long before the dinner bell rang, and they were glad to be distracted.

"That was an awfully cute young lady who brought the bread," Janet said.

"Janet," Charlie said, "leave well enough alone. She's still playing cupid. I've given up on changing it."

"She's a very nice young lady," Phil answered. "She is very smart as well, perfect for this place. I don't think I've ever seen a woman run a hardware store so well and be so cute at the same time." He quickly changed the subject, letting them all know that the conversation about Louisa was over.

Hot apple pie, sent over from Ruthanna, along with the other homemade goodies, made an excellent dessert. The men unbuttoned the tops of their pants, and everyone left the dishes for later. They all ended up at the fire, sitting on the cut logs as makeshift stools. The full moon illuminated the area, making it almost as bright as daylight.

Again the crunch of gravel was heard, this time surprising Phil. "I wasn't expecting anyone," he said, looking up at the rental car.

Out jumped Jenny, and she immediately ran over to the fire and showered everyone with hugs and kisses.

Phil felt the pit of his stomach churn. She was really the last person he wanted to see. Unfortunately, everyone except Jenny noticed it.

"How did you manage this one?" Phil asked. "I thought you had family commitments."

"I just couldn't miss Christmas with you all." she smiled, and that made Phil feel even guiltier. "I didn't think it would be fair for everyone to be here and for me to miss out on the party."

"You're right," Janet agreed. "It is only fair."

Phil pulled up another log for her, and she sat down.

They roasted marshmallows and were in the middle of making s'mores when the gravel crunched again.

"My goodness." Phil laughed. "I can't think of anyone else."

It was an old truck that looked like Joseph Gibson's, and Phil immediately felt bad that he hadn't thought to invite him to dinner. He assumed Ruthanna had done that.

They were all surprised to see a young girl and old man get out of the truck. The man was holding a large shotgun, and the girl held a .45 pistol.

"What the...?" Phil started, but they quickly cut him off.

"Listen," the girl said, "we ain't here to hurt nobody. We just want what's ours."

"What are you talking about?" Phil answered, fear building in his heart. He prayed they wouldn't hurt Lilly.

"I recognize you two," Janet said, not allowing them enough time to speak. Her mind was racing as she fumbled with her thoughts. "I remember now. You were at the hotel in Nebraska."

"Pretty bright lady," the girl answered, "but that don't mean nothin' now."

"So you're the ones who trashed my place?"

"Yep. Like I said, we want what's rightfully ours," the old man said, aiming the shotgun directly at them, poised to shoot any minute.

"I don't understand. Really," Phil said, trying to remain calm.

"The key! The key to the money."

"What key?"

"Oh, now I know," Arthur chimed in.

"Niggers don't know nothing 'bout this," the old man spat.

"I'm afraid I do. It was a key to a locker filled with cash."

"My daddy was married to Laraleen. He took the rap for her when they done that robbery. He's been sitting in that filthy prison for years because of that greedy woman. We just want the money and the key. We oughtta be able to live off it.

My daddy is due that money," she said, screaming and waving her pistol around.

"The FBI has the money," Arthur said calmly. "There is the reward money, $75,000."

"That's a start," she answered, "but we want more."

"I understand that," Arthur answered. "I'm an attorney, and I can get more for you. Just let me get back to L.A., and I'll wire it to you then."

"How do we know you will?"

"I will. I just want my friends to be safe," he said, looking over at the ladies, who had started to cry softly.

"We ain't never done nothin' to hurt him. We just looked for the key is all."

"Why?" Phil said nervously. "Why did you have to kill people to make your point? Why didn't you just come to me? I could have given you a great deal of money."

The two looked at each other in shock.

"We don't know 'nothin about that," the girl said. "Ain't about killin' folks. That's against the Lord's Ten Commandments, and we don't mess with God. We're God-fearin' folks."

For some reason, Phil believed them, and that frightened him more than he had ever been frightened before. "But if not you, then..."

"Look, mister, we just brought the guns to scare ya. We thought Christmas day might make you give the key to us."

"Put the fucking guns down," he heard a deep voice say, a voice he hadn't heard before.

When Phil turned around, he saw Jenny holding a .22 handgun, pointing it at the two of them.

"Thank God," Janet said, heaving. "There is a God in Heaven."

Phil stood up to hug her, but she pushed him away.

"Not so quick, you sorry son-of-a-bitch," she said in that deep, snarling voice. "Sit back down now!"

The young girl and man immediately dropped their weapons and stood straight up, as if to impress her.

"Why?" Phil asked. "Jenny, was it you who killed those people?"

"Somebody had to frame you and get you off the streets. The sheriff was gonna be next."

"But, Jenny, I-I love you," Phil lied, trying to make her change her mind.

"Cut the shit, Phil. I never loved you. You were a means to an end, one more off the street. I just took a little more time with you than the others. I was actually enjoying myself."

"What are you talking about? Have you lost your mind?"

"No. As a nurse, I've seen a few to many acts of violence. Too many innocent people, especially women, die without a cause. When you take a life, you don't deserve a life of your own. It turned my stomach to think of you living in this 'perfect utopia.' That was what you called it, wasn't it?"

"Jenny, please! You don't understand. I—"

"Oh, that's where you're wrong. There are no second chances when it comes to murder, Mr. Sawyer. I intend to be the vigilante who sees to as many of you as I can!"

"But my case is different, and you know it. You disagreed with the warden, remember?"

"You're right, but he wasn't killing murderers. He was just killing blacks. I'm not racist."

"So you just kill murderers who've already paid their debt to society?"

"Ha! You people will never pay your debt to society. Now, as you know, I can't possibly leave any witnesses. Any volunteers to go first?"

"Just kill me. You said you hate to see innocent people die, and they're all innocent, Jenny."

"That doesn't matter now. In fact, I think I'll kill you in front of them."

The young girl reached for her pistol, but before she could grab it, Jenny pulled the trigger, making the girl step away.

"Throw that shotgun over there," she demanded.

The old man did as he was told, leaving the group without any hope.

"I'll kill you two next, but first…" She held the gun to Phil's head. "The world will be a better place without you in it, you murderous bastard."

The shot rang out so loudly that Phil's ears rang. He reached for the blood, amazed that he was still alive. *Maybe it's just a mirage and my body will fall at any moment,* he thought, but somehow, he stayed upright.

Instead, Jenny fell with a thud, thanks to a bullet that went straight through her own head.

They all stood by in shock as they heard a car racing down the driveway. It was Sheriff Murphy, with Sam in the car beside him.

"How did you know?" Phil asked.

"I didn't. I just came by with a basket of fruit, hoping to apologize for the things I said to you. The moon made everything so bright that I didn't miss a thing."

Phil hugged him hard. "You saved my life."

"Don't get mushy on me. You know I don't play nursemaid." The sheriff then turned to Sam. "Call an ambulance and get this bitch out of here. These people are here for the holidays, and a holiday they shall have. I guess a decent Christmas is out of the question, but this little cabin will hold the biggest New Year's Eve party this town has ever seen."

"Does that mean I can stay?" Phil asked.

"Stay? You're taking over Rusty's place. I talked to the medical board, and they agreed to it. You won't have to dispense any prescriptions, and technically, you won't be working with live patients, but it's far more fit for you than lobstering."

"Thanks a lot!" Phil answered. "God, I never thought I'd end up examining dead bodies, but you're probably right. Only thing is, it will have to be part time. I'm opening a new business."

"A new business? And what kind would it be?"

"Manning and Sawyer's Bait and Tackle."

The sheriff looked at him strangely but didn't question it. "You guys get in your cars and follow me to the bed-and-breakfast. Ruthanna is ready to pamper you to death, and believe me when I tell you she'll make you almost forget tonight. I know all this will follow you throughout your lives, but it has finally ended the hell your friend has gone through. We'll have this place cleaned up before you know it. Phil, you can ride with me, and we can talk about your new job."

Phil turned to his friends. "If you guys wanna catch the first plane out, I'd understand—especially you, Lilly. You've seen enough pain for a lifetime."

"We've all been through a lot of pain with you, my friend," Charlie answered, "but to know it's finally over... God, we're so grateful. As for leaving, I think I speak for all of us when I say, who would wanna miss the biggest New Year's Eve party the town of Solomon Cove has ever seen?"

CHAPTER 25

Elias did not let Phil down when it came to New Year's Eve. He hadn't returned to the house since Christmas, nor had the others. That left Elias and Alex to recruit the town to decorate and bring food and drinks.

Two sheriff's cars arrived to take them all to the party. Phil prayed that they would be able to enjoy themselves.

He felt a lump in his throat as they pulled into his driveway. A new mailbox greeted them, covered in balloons. They had to drive through a large paper sign to get to the cottage, with "Welcome to Solomon Cove, Phil!" painted on it.

Phil turned to Sam and smiled. "This is just too much."

"I don't think so. This town can never have too many good people, Mr. Sawyer."

"That's 'Phil,' Sam. You know we don't use last names around here."

Charlie reached from the back seat to squeeze Phil's shoulder. "He's right, you know, Mr. Sawyer. The world is a better place with you in it."

Phil turned to look at Lilly. "I'm so sorry for you, sweetheart. This is a most horrible holiday for you, not at all what I intended it to be."

She smiled that angelic smile and answered, "The holidays are about love for friends and family, and that's what I've experienced here. Thank you for that."

"I am amazed at both your courage and your kindness. I love you, Lilly."

"I love you, too, Phil," she said.

"Enough talking. Let's get out of the car," Sam said.

The other cruiser pulled up behind them, and Dee and Arthur hopped out.

Phil was shocked and more moved than he had ever been in his life. Camping lanterns dotted the small yard and cabin. A bonfire was blazing, and everyone had brought lawn chairs and small benches. It was the largest party Phil had ever seen, even more special than the cocktail parties his wife pranced around at.

It seemed as though everyone in town was there, and they cheered as he walked up. Jacob and Joseph were standing right in front, and Phil was given hugs and kisses from people he hadn't even met yet.

Elias had a keg of beer brought in, and he poured it for Phil and his Los Angeles friends. He now had a growing list of friends, of course, Charlie, Janet, Lilly, Arthur and Dee would always remain his dearest friends, but he now had more to add to his life.

Phil had three beers before going inside and closing his bedroom door behind him. He returned soon after and stood on the large log he used to sit on. "Excuse me! Excuse me, everyone," he yelled.

It took several minutes, but everyone finally fell silent to hear his speech.

"I am speechless when it comes to all my new friends and what you've done here tonight. I have never had a place to call home, not until I came here. I've never had such a dear woman in my life that I would consider her a mother. I never would have dreamt that my life could change so much for the better. I only have one regret about tonight, and that is that one person, the one person I love and respect the most, is not able to be here, at least not in body. I know he is here in soul, looking down on us with a big, toothless smile." Phil looked up and smiled. He knew Welles was looking down on him, and giving him the thumbs-up. "I hope all of you get a chance to meet my dearest friends from Los Angeles. They aren't accustomed to this type of reception."

They all laughed.

"I've never been one for long speeches, but I want to thank you all from the depths of my heart."

Everyone cheered, but Phil held up his hands and encouraged them to fall silent for another moment.

"I don't mean to be so brazen as to ask what I am about to, and contrary to popular opinion, I'm not so bold as to jump into anything without deep thought. I know life is too short for all of us, so I've decided to put my heart on my sleeve tonight." Phil took off his right glove and reached into his pocket. He pulled out a small box and opened it, then held out the large engagement ring for everyone to see. He could hear the oohs and ahs, and he wouldn't hold them at bay any longer. "If it's all right with Jacob Dorough, I'd like to ask Louisa to be my wife, if she'll have me, to share in the rest of my life, to share in this place we both love so much, to—"

He wasn't able to finish bumbling before she was in his arms, kissing his cheeks and then his mouth.

"Well? What's the answer?" someone from the crowd yelled.

"Yes, yes, and yes!" she screamed.

The crowd went wild, and as he turned to his friends, he saw broader smiles than he'd ever seen from them before. He hugged his future bride one more time and then, holding her small hands, led her to them for several rounds of hugs and kisses.

"Looks like you'll be making another trip to Solomon Cove," he said.

"Yes it does," Charlie said gladly. "Yes it does."

"Just one thing," Phil said. "Do you think it's okay to have two best men?"

End

Coming October 2015

SWEET DREAMS, Baby Belle

KIM CARTER

Author of "Deadly Odds" & "No Second Chances"

We'd like to thank you for supporting G Street Chronicles and invite you to join our social networks.
Please be sure to post a review when you're finished reading.

Like us on Facebook
G Street Chronicles
G Street Chronicles CEO Exclusive Readers Group

Follow us on Twitter
@GStreetChronicl

Follow us on Instagram
gstreetentertainment

Email us and we'll add you to our mailing list
fans@gstreetchronicles.com

George Sherman Hudson, CEO
Shawna A., COO

CPSIA information can be obtained at www.ICGtesting.com
Printed in the USA
LVOW11s2148310715

448460LV00001B/9/P